Savage Warrior, White Captive

She heard him enter and purposefully ignored him, her eyes on her hands as she rubbed her feet. She felt his eyes on her and looked up to see him staring down at her. Suddenly the *gohwah* seemed too small for the two of them, and the long night was here.

"Let me do that," Jack said, kneeling and taking her foot in his hands before she could object.

"I don't think . . ."

His hands were large, warm, and gentle. "Stop thinking, Candice. There's no point. What is, is."

He was right. She was here and she had no choice. This man had traded for her, and she belonged to him. She was at his mercy.

"Feel better?" he asked, his voice husky.

She had heard that tone before, and she looked up abruptly. His hand had stilled on her ankle. Her body began a slow throbbing of fear mingled with anticipation. He slid his hand up her calf, its grip tightening possessively.

"You have the most beautiful legs I've ever seen," he murmured.

Her heart was beating erratically. "I . . . I . . ."

His hand moved up her thigh, slowly moving higher and higher. Oh, dear God, she thought, what is he going to do?

QUANTITY SALES

Most Dell books are available at special quantity discounts when purchased in bulk by corporations, organizations, and special-interest groups. Custom imprinting or excerpting can also be done to fit special needs. For details write: Dell Publishing, 666 Fifth Avenue, New York, NY 10103. Attn.: Special Sales Department.

INDIVIDUAL SALES

Are there any Dell books you want but cannot find in your local stores? If so, you can order them directly from us. You can get any Dell book in print. Simply include the book's title, author, and ISBN number if you have it, along with a check or money order (no cash can be accepted) for the full retail price plus $2.00 to cover shipping and handling. Mail to: Dell Readers Service, P.O. Box 5057, Des Plaines, IL 60017.

THE DARKEST HEART

Brenda Joyce

A DELL BOOK

Published by
Dell Publishing
a division of
Bantam Doubleday Dell Publishing Group, Inc.
666 Fifth Avenue
New York, New York 10103

ISBN: 0-440-20472-0

Designed by Jeremiah B. Lighter

Printed in the United States of America
Published simultaneously in Canada

December 1989
10 9 8 7 6 5 4 3 2 1

PART ONE

Scandal

CHAPTER ONE

The New Mexico Territory of the United States—1860

She knew she was dying.

At first the realization had been horrifying. Now she no longer cared. She wanted only relief—relief from the blazing sun as it burned her back and legs through her shirt and pants, relief from the choking dryness of her mouth, from the scorched sand as it burned her palms and belly and cheek.

She knew she was dying. She had seen cattle that had died from heat and dehydration. Their tongues had been grotesquely protruding from their rigid corpses, black and stiff and swollen. Her own tongue felt just as thick. She could no longer swallow, there was no saliva left, and she could taste sand and grit. If only she had water.

The day seemed to get hotter. Impossibly, unbearably hotter. She moaned from the pain—a choked, whimpering sound. She wondered, through the torpid haze, how much longer it would take. She wondered what her brothers and her father would do when they found out.

And she wanted to cry for them, for their grief.

Please forgive me, she moaned silently. I never wanted to hurt you.

She loved them. They were her family. Three big strapping brothers, Luke and Mark and Little John, all close to six feet tall with the blond, blue-eyed Carter good looks. And her father. He would be in a frenzy. He had been in a frenzy since the night she had run away—that she knew without a doubt. Oh, God. To think she had been betrayed like this.

At least they would never find out the truth.

She thought she was becoming delirious. She could see Virgil as if he were really there, with her. But his face wasn't handsome—it was ugly in rage. And she could feel the painful blow as he hit her, hear herself cry out, feel his hands, grabbing her. . . .

All her life she had been gloriously spoiled. Her father had raised her and her three brothers alone. They had come to the Territory ten years earlier, before it was even a part of the United States. Her father had abruptly packed them all up, she and her three brothers, when she was eight years old —and they had moved from their Tennessee farm to Tucson to start over as ranchers. That was exactly one month to the day that their mother had abandoned them all, running off with another man.

And I'm just like her, she thought miserably.

She hadn't meant to do it, hadn't meant to hurt her family. She was used to the adulation she got from the men in her life, whether it was her father and brothers or the towns-people, the cowboys and drifters. She wasn't exactly vain, but it was hard not to know that she was extraordinarily beautiful —especially when everyone kept telling her so. She had seen a miniature of her mother once, who had also been known for her beauty, and Candice knew that she looked a lot like her. Oddly, that pleased her. They both had brilliantly blond hair, long, thick, and wavy, enough to stop a man in his tracks without him seeing any more. Add to that a perfectly heart-shaped face and full, rose-colored lips, a straight, delicate nose and large, almond-shaped eyes . . . Candice had had fifteen marriage proposals last year alone, when she'd been seventeen.

And she had accepted Virgil Kincaid's.

No one had approved.

He was lean and dark and so very handsome. Candice had been letting men steal kisses from her for years—nothing more than a few chaste pecks, unless her suitor was really favored, and then she would allow him to brush her lips with his. She was used to the courting, the cow-eyed looks, and the awkward, endless declarations of undying love. But Virgil Kincaid took her by surprise. He was from Georgia, a planter's second son, he said, and his courtship took her breath away. His words were honey soft and thickly Southern, he was well read, he could quote the finest poetry . . . and his looks weren't cow-eyed but bright and hot. He was no awkward, bumbling teenage cowboy, stumbling over his words and his eagerness, but a handsome, well-bred Southern gentleman, one who knew how to treat a lady.

Her father, approached by Virgil, absolutely forbade the marriage.

The next night they eloped.

They rode hard day and night to make it to Fort Yuma before anyone had time to follow them. It was a wonderful adventure, exciting and romantic. . . .

Until Fort Yuma, where Virgil refused to marry her.

"I don't understand," she cried, her eyes dark with the betrayal.

He grinned. His hands closed over her shoulders, pulling her close. Still dazed, Candice didn't try to draw away. "Candice, I'm not a marrying man."

She stared, bewildered from the magnitude of everything —what she'd done, what they'd done, what he was doing now. "But—I don't understand." She knew she was more than marriageable—she was the most sought-after belle from Arizona City to El Paso.

He raised her chin. "You were made for loving, Candice. And marriage just isn't my game." His grip tightened. "God —I want you. I've never wanted any woman as much as I want you."

It was sinking in. She tore away. "You lied! You promised —you told me you loved me! You said we would get married as soon as we found a preacher. I ran away with you!"

He laughed. "I'm afraid, dear, that you're going to have to learn to play the game according to new rules. Mine."

She backed away. "What are you going to do?"

"Surely, Candice, even you aren't that naive?"

She was afraid. Her back hit the wall of the small room they had just checked into. "God, Virgil—no."

"I'm going to make you my mistress, darling. And I'll make you very happy, I promise."

She choked in shock.

"Candice, don't look so damn innocent. You were made to be a man's mistress, my dear, in beautiful silks and taffeta, diamonds and lace—not some rancher's wrinkled-up wife. Come here."

"You're mad."

"Mad? Maybe. About you. I'm just glad I'm going to be the first."

He reached for her. Candice didn't think. She had never had to hit anyone before, never—not with three strapping brothers to chaperone her. But now her hand shot out and she sent a ringing slap to his face as hard as she could. He immediately backhanded her brutally, sending her spinning to the floor, stunned.

"Get it through your head, Candice. You are no longer Miss Carter, belle of the Southwest. You are my woman, and you do as I say."

She raised herself to her elbows, panting, her ears ringing, her face throbbing. She shook her head once to clear it. Fear spread icy claws deep into her intestines. "No."

He grinned. "Fight me, then."

Her eyes went wide as he threw his jacket casually on the bed and knelt beside her. Candice scrambled to her knees. He yanked her back by her waist. She cried out, writhing. He clamped an arm around her and flipped her onto her back, hard. Candice was terrified, and when she looked into his eyes she saw that he was laughing—he was enjoying himself. With a tremendous effort, she kicked out, one of her feet catching his jaw.

He yelped, releasing her.

Candice crawled frantically toward the door.

"Bitch!" He grabbed her ankles and pulled, hard.

Candice's arms went out from under her, and her chin hit the floor, sending a spasm of pain through her. She was on her stomach, helpless. Virgil wrenched her hands behind her back, hurting her. He prodded her legs apart, and sheer terror and sudden understanding coursed through her. "We can do this any way you want," he said, panting, as he tossed her skirt and petticoat up over her hips.

Horror.

He was going to mount her as a stallion does a mare.

He released her hands, tore down her pantalets, and grabbed the cheeks of her behind. Candice felt something thick and hard rub against her.

With a desperate cry, she twisted onto her side, legs flailing. He reached for her hands to capture them, but lost her balance from her frantic motions. She reached for the gun that was strapped in the holster at his side. He loomed over her again, his face bright with lust, on his knees between her thighs, his member obscenely enlarged and poking the air. Candice's hands closed over the smooth handle of his gun. In one abrupt movement she wrenched it free. His eyes widened. Hers closed—and she fired.

CHAPTER TWO

The rider leaned low over his stallion's neck, urging him on.

Behind him, the United States Cavalry was in hot pursuit.

He glanced over his shoulder. Long sable hair whipped his face. Sweat trickled down from his temple, despite the red cloth headband. It gleamed on his bare, powerful back, thick muscles rippling as he rode the stallion as hard as he could, pumping the beast furiously with his body. The entire column was chasing him, an eighth of a mile behind.

The black's hooves tore into the dirt and dry grass, pounding furiously. The rider guided him with his buckskin-clad legs through a stand of saguaro, then into a dry wash. Ahead loomed a narrow path between two sheer granite cliffs. Without hesitation, the rider hurled the black forward, the animal stumbling once, the width between the rock walls barely enough to accommodate them. Once the rider felt a stabbing of pain as flesh was torn from his thigh, and the stallion screamed, grazed also. They exploded into the sunlight on the other side, once again in a headlong gallop, racing down toward the swollen river below. The troops appeared to be a quarter of a mile behind.

The river was still high from flooding. At any other time, the rider would have waited to decide where to ford. Now he rode his black mercilessly down the riverbank, sweat blurring his vision, his heart pounding almost painfully against the walls of his chest. His left hand was already pulling his gunbelt off and slinging it over his shoulder, then reaching for the rifle, holding it high. The black obeyed his summons and plunged unhesitantly into the raging river. The stallion swam hard against the current before finding solid ground on the other side and bursting forth.

A few minutes later, from a new vantage point on the far side of the riverbank, camouflaged by octillo and agave and saguaro, the rider slowed his mount and slipped off. He kept one hand on his mount's muzzle, speaking softly. His own shoulder, slick with sweat, was pressed into the animal's hot, wet neck. The horse was blowing heavily. He watched the soldiers cantering down to the riverbank. Their horses were scrawny and fatigued, thickly lathered from the chase, and he knew without a doubt that many would die if they tried to ford the river. He listened to the men's indecision, catching bits and pieces of their conversation until they all turned and rode away.

The rider threw back his head and laughed.

The troops, with the aid of a Papago scout, had been tracking Chiricahua Apaches led by Geronimo. They would never catch them now. The rider, although not a part of Geronimo's band, had succeeded in leading the soldiers astray. Even though he hadn't been back to the Territory in three long years, when he had seen the soldiers pursuing the Apaches he hadn't been able to resist interfering. Satisfaction gleamed in his silver eyes.

He led the stallion down to the river where they both drank thirstily. Then he mounted again and rode downstream, looking for a good place to cross. He didn't trust the Papago, who were sworn enemies of the Apache. He would not take the chance that the Indian scout leading the troops back across the river might try to circle around on him. And just thinking about how he had sabotaged their efforts to track down Geronimo's band brought a smile to his sensuous lips.

The stallion shied. Moving with the horse as if he were a part of it, soothing him with a single touch, he searched the saguaro-studded landscape. The rider saw a piece of blue. As the horse took another stride he made out the crumpled form of a youth lying facedown in the dust. . . .

He slipped off the stallion and lifted the youth's head gently. The Stetson fell off, revealing the most incredible cascade of blond hair he had ever seen. She was in bad shape, but he'd seen worse. Ants had just started to get to her, and he brushed a small marching band of the insects from her cheek, then raised the canteen to her parched, split lips.

Her mouth opened, her throat pulsed. "Easy, *ish' tia' nay,*" he murmured. "Not too much." He pulled the canteen away.

Her eyes flew open, and she made a choking protest.

He stared. Navy-blue eyes, tilted up at the corners, big

and almond-shaped and thickly lashed in black. Then they drifted closed. He eased her back down, disturbed. He imagined, if she were cleaned up, that the girl would be a beauty. With eyes like that, a man was in jeopardy of having his entire soul drained away. What was she doing out here alone in the desert, on foot, without supplies, and in a man's clothes?

He picked her up and carried her to his stallion, looking at her more thoroughly now. She was full-breasted, with long legs and slim hips. The kind of body that set up an instant hunger in a man, made his loins tight and full just by looking. He placed her carefully on his mount, then leapt up behind her.

Where was she from, and where was she going?

And—who was she?

They were a two-day ride from Tucson, the closest settlement. To the east and south, along the Santa Cruz River and Pantano Wash, there were a few ranches. Americans had been settling in the area since 1853—since the United States had acquired the strip of land containing Tucson from Mexico.

He set up camp by a trickling wash. She needed care, and that was his first priority. More water, and then an herbal tea that would help to rehydrate her. She was swallowing greedily now, although she didn't open her eyes again. Her skin was dry and chapped like leather, and he found more ants on her right arm. He stripped her quickly and efficiently, tossing her clothes aside, trying to be impersonal about it—and failing.

He hadn't had a woman in a while, and just touching her made his groin tight and heavy.

He bathed her, his hands shaking slightly, to his disgust, and forced more tea down her. He wrapped her in his bedroll —a sheet of buckskin that served as either spare blanket or loincloth. Then he made a small fire, watered and rubbed down and hobbled the stallion, then settled himself down with a tin mug of coffee.

A white man's habit.

He smiled derisively, showing a glimmer of white, even teeth.

And he looked up at the Santa Catalina Mountains, feeling their pull—the pull of the people, the pull of the only home he'd ever known.

He sighed. It had been three long years since he had been back. The decision to leave hadn't been easy—in fact, it had been the most pain-filled decision of his life.

His name was Jack. He didn't know his real last name and wasn't sure where he had been born. He didn't even know much about his real mother, just that she had been a squaw and had died when he was very young—before he had any memories of her. His father was a big, strapping, blond giant of a man, and Jack knew he had gotten most of his physical attributes from him. His earliest memory was standing ankle-deep in a freezing, rushing mountain stream, his hands chapped and numb from the icy cold, the metal pan sticking to his flesh. His father was a miner.

He had never loved his father. He tried to do as he was told, to avoid getting hit. One slap from a man like that was enough to crack a bone. As long as he worked long and hard and occasionally had a few gold flakes to show, his father was pleased. When, upon occasion, his father sat down with a jug of whiskey, the little boy made sure to stay as far away from the cabin as possible. And that was probably what saved him.

He was six or seven, and he was hiding in the woods, afraid of his father, who had been drinking steadily for days. He heard them first—the thundering of horses' hooves. It could only be Indians, because the Mexican troops never strayed far from the Presidio at Tucson. He crept closer to see.

He watched his father drunkenly antagonize the small group, then die defending his home. The little cabin went up in flames. The Indians proceeded to loot everything of value. Very, very afraid, the boy turned and ran.

He didn't know how the leader saw him, but he knew the instant the Indian on the big bay horse came galloping after him. He ran frantically into the trees, weaving through thick stands of juniper and pinyon. He fell, skinning his hands and knees, and dared a look over his shoulder. The Indian, a tall young man with waist-length loose black hair, was leaping off his horse. He was clad only in thigh-high moccasins and a breechcloth, and he carried a knife. The boy got to his feet and started running.

He was grabbed from behind and swung into the air.

"Fucking savage!" Jack shouted, having learned the phrase from his father. "Let me go, damn fucking savage!"

The Indian slung him over his shoulder.

The boy sank his teeth as hard as he could into the man's neck.

The Indian never made a sound. His hand closed over the boy's jaw, fingers digging in painfully, forcing his mouth open. The boy tasted sweat and grease and blood. He was thrown onto the ground, where he lay stunned, nausea and bile welling up within him.

Laughter sounded.

The other Indians had gathered and were openly amused. The boy slowly, warily got to his knees, panting, his mouth ringed with the man's blood. His heart was thudding wildly in his ribs as he met the tall Indian's gaze. It wasn't black with anger, just dark and enigmatic.

Jack turned on his heels and fled. He knew it was hopeless, but he would die before he quit.

More laughter.

He was caught instantly. This time the Indian was careful, holding Jack in front of him in his arms while the boy twisted and spat like a wildcat, trying to claw his adversary's face. The man spoke sharply. Jack didn't have to speak his language to know he was being told to be still. He didn't listen.

He was thrown on the big bay horse, the greased man leaping up behind him. Even as the Indian's body was touching down, the boy was sliding off. He was hauled unceremoniously back up by one ear—and it hurt.

So did the hard, stinging slap to his buttocks when he was flipped abruptly over on the rider's lap. Six smacks, and each hurt worse than the one before—but he wouldn't cry out. He'd gotten worse from his father many times.

The man who had captured him was the son of the chief of a band of Chiricahua Apaches, and his name was Cochise. Out of respect for Jack's fierce bravery, Cochise gave him a name—Niño Salvaje, Wild Boy Child. Mistakenly, the Apache had assumed he was Mexican because so few Americans had drifted this far west.

Jack did not speak either Spanish or Apache, and it was many years before he understood what his name meant—or the great honor it was to be named by a respected, famous warrior whom everyone knew would one day be their next chief. Cochise gave him to a Coyotero Apache couple as a gift. Jack knew he was a captive and a slave. He did not know that the gift of a brave boy child to an Apache couple was a special and great honor—for everyone expected him to one day become a fierce Apache warrior.

And he did.

CHAPTER THREE

Oh, my God.

She squeezed her eyes tightly shut, not daring to breathe, not daring to move.

There was an Indian sitting just a few feet away, across a small fire.

Where was she? What had happened? My God—she couldn't have seen what she thought she had seen. Taking a small breath, Candice opened her eyes the tiniest amount possible and peeked out through her lashes.

She hadn't been hallucinating.

And she wasn't dreaming.

He was still there—looking straight at her.

She quickly closed her eyes again, praying that he hadn't seen her looking at him. He had been staring at her expressionlessly from where he sat just outside the firelight. She had seen enough to know that he was naked from the waist up, his hair shoulder length and kept out of his face with a headband, his legs clad in soft buckskins.

Had he seen that she was awake?

It all came flooding back. She had run away with Kincaid, he had betrayed her, and dear God forgive her, she had murdered him. In self-defense. And then she had fled Yuma on horseback, in terror of being arrested and hanged. A snake had killed her horse, and the last thing she remembered was walking, falling, burning—knowing she was going to die. This Indian must have found her.

She dared to peek again at the man sitting in the shadows of the fire's light. He was no longer gazing so relentlessly at her, but into the flames. He was the largest Indian she had ever seen—Indians were usually thin and of medium or small height. Even though he was sitting in shadows she could see he had broad shoulders and a broad, muscular chest. Something was glinting on that chest—something silver, a necklace. If only it was daylight, if only she could get a better look, she could tell what kind of Indian he was. She prayed he wasn't Apache.

His glance lifted and caught hers.

Candice slammed her lids shut, holding her breath, freezing her body, praying. She heard him move. The tempo of her prayers increased. There was a hiss of flames licking logs, and she started, eyes flashing open, to see him stirring the fire. He turned his head and looked directly at her.

It was too late. She knew he knew that she was awake. Still Candice didn't move. She couldn't. She was frozen in terror.

He was Apache.

He had stood up to tend the fire, stepping closer to her at the same time. She had seen his leggings. Thigh-high but now rolled to the knee and beaded across the instep. The giveaway was the toe tip, and the way it curled up. It was very distinctive. They were Apache moccasins.

Candice started to shake.

It was then, as he approached with a silent tread, his shadow giving him away, that she jerked her head up in horror, no longer feigning sleep. He looked even taller and larger from this perspective, standing over her while she lay prostrate on the ground, the fire behind him now, illuminating his broad, hard outline and face.

With a start, she realized he was a half-breed. His eyes were pale, gray or blue, his features very white and perfectly chiseled—high cheekbones, a straight nose, a strong jaw, and sensual lips. He was very dark, whether tanned from the sun or from an Apache parent, she couldn't tell. He was wearing a large, crude necklace of silver and turquoise. From a row of stones, two silver conches were suspended, and beneath that, two flat, rectangular pieces of silver. She had seen a necklace like that once before. It had belonged to an Apache warrior.

He was also fully armed. He wore a low-slung gunbelt boasting two tied-down Colts. Around his waist was a heavy, studded belt, and from it glinted a dangerous-looking knife. Candice was trembling.

As he squatted down beside her, the full extent of her predicament hit her—she was naked beneath the buckskin blanket. Completely naked—without a single undergarment. A choked sob rose up in her throat. Had he already raped her while she was unconscious? Dear God—and would he do so now?

He met her gaze again, and from the guarded expression

on his face something hard and angry appeared, darkening his features, making his eyes a silvery gray glitter. She shrank back. He gritted and reached out. One large, thick hand caught hanks of her hair, preventing any further movement. She whimpered at his touch.

He cursed in his own language.

She was stiff with fear. He raised her head, his expression becoming more thunderous. She resisted, becoming more rigid. He was holding a tin mug, which he set down as he clamped his arm around her back and pulled her abruptly upright, into the crook of his arm and chest. His bare flesh was warm and hard against her own naked shoulder. And in the process, the blanket drooped, revealing her full, white breasts.

Candice's hands came up to press against his chest, lightly furred with dark hair and as hard as a rock. "No."

His arm tightened. "Be still."

"No."

He looked at her, his eyes smoldering. She cringed. His gaze dropped to her naked breasts. With a growl, or maybe it was an Apache word, he pulled the blanket up, yanked her arm over it, pulled her even harder against his torso, and picked up the mug. "Drink this."

"What?"

"Can you sit up by yourself?"

Not only did he speak English, but except for a soft accent, it was perfect. "I—I think so."

"Good."

He released her so abruptly she sagged backward, catching the blanket just in time. He shoved the mug into her hand, and she realized it was full of a steaming liquid. He walked away.

Relief swept over her.

He had only wanted to give her tea.

CHAPTER FOUR

Candice held the mug and watched the half-breed Apache, making sure that she didn't let go of the blanket. What was he going to do with her? She had to escape.

She had been living in this Territory since she was eight, and she knew everything there was to know about hostile Indians, especially Apaches, who were the worst. They didn't just kill—they raped women and tortured and scalped their victims, including children. Candice shuddered and set the tea aside. A vivid memory assailed her, one she would never forget, no matter how hard she tried. A little boy. Lying dead, flat on his back next to a gutted-out wagon. Two arrows protruded from his small chest. His blue-and-white homespun shirt was covered with blood. His eyes were still open. And—his scalp had been lifted. His skull was raw and red.

Apaches had done that.

She had to escape.

But she also knew that Apaches were the best trackers in the world. If she did succeed in escaping, he would find her easily. Which meant only one thing—she would have to kill him. Her gaze had been glued to his broad, powerful back as he stood facing the fire. Now he turned and she inhaled sharply, stiffening. His glance was piercing, stripping her, and knowing that he actually had done so, and had possibly raped her too, made her feel sick deep inside.

"Why didn't you drink it?"

She started.

He moved, only two steps closer, but it was the coiled, barely contained energy that mesmerized her. He reminded her of a stalking mountain lion, waiting to leap for the kill. Her fingers were white on the blanket.

"Drink the tea."

She reached for the mug, not taking her eyes off him until she felt the smooth metal under her hand, and then, with a gasp, she drew back as she knocked it over and the hot liquid burned her fingers.

He squatted, taking her hand.

She held every muscle so tense she wondered if her body might snap. Her eyes had closed, and when she realized that, she opened them to find him studying her. "It's not burned." He stood, refilled the mug, and brought it to her. "Drink this, it's good for you. You need the liquid."

She obeyed at first because she had no choice, but the moment she swallowed she couldn't get enough of the warm herbal tea. She drained the cup and he refilled it. After she had drunk another cup, she set it aside and lifted her gaze to his. He was standing, staring openly. At her hair.

It had fallen in a riotous mass of curls over one white shoulder. She shoved it back instantly. His eye followed her movement, narrowing. All she could think of was that he had probably never met a woman who had hair like hers—and was already coveting her scalp.

His expression hardened. "I'm getting tired of the way you're looking at me."

She sucked in her breath at the menace in his tone.

"Damn it," he exploded, squatting and grabbing her chin in one callused hand. "I am not going to hurt you!"

No man had ever touched her with such violent anger before—not even Kincaid. He seemed to expect an answer, so she breathed out a barely audible yes. He cursed again, in English, words she'd never heard, and she blushed furiously. He stood, paced away, and then back.

His expression was even darker. "Who are you?" he demanded.

She didn't answer, and he repeated the question angrily. "I'm . . . Candice Carter," she managed.

Recognition flared. "One of the High C Carters?" At her nod, he said, "What are you doing out here alone, on foot?"

Kincaid's death flashed before her mind and she went white. "I—I eloped." When there was no response, she went on, hearing the anxiety in her own breath. "My husband, Virgil Kincaid, was killed. A—a robbery. In Arizona City." She had been looking at the blanket, blood pounding in her ears with the telling of such an astronomical lie. What if there was a bounty out for her capture? What if he turned her over to the authorities? Then her family would find out the truth —that she had killed Kincaid when he had tried to rape her— and she would be ruined forever. They would be unbearably shamed. She darted a glance up at her captor. He was un-moved. Tears came to her eyes. Tears of hopelessness, frustra-tion, and self-pity . . . because of Kincaid, and because of this man standing half clad before her.

"That doesn't explain what you were doing out in the desert, dying." The statement was flat and emphatic.

More tears glimmered. "I was stunned. It was right after the wedding," she whispered. "I—I came back—to our room —and there he was—on the floor." She started to cry. She couldn't help it. She didn't intend it as a strategy to stop the questions that only lies could answer, but it worked as such—for he made an exasperated sound and walked away. When she looked up, blinking, he was lying on the ground, on his back, staring at the stars. She sniffed and wiped her eyes with the back of one hand. Still staring. She was stunned when he closed his eyes and appeared to fall asleep immediately.

She sat very still.

He wasn't going to harm her, at least not now. She breathed a fast prayer of thanks.

What was he going to do with her? She knew of other stories too. Stories of white women who disappeared forever when their menfolk were killed by Indians. One, a woman with unusually lovely light-blue eyes, had been taken captive when her husband and another family were slaughtered by Comanches near El Paso. She had been badly beaten, her hair chopped off, and passed around to all the men. When she turned up ten years later at a trading post, she was barely distinguishable as white. Her skin was tanned to a nut brown, and she was clad in buckskins and calico—a cradleboard and infant on her back, and four half-breed children following close behind. She was a pathetic echo of the woman she had once been, perhaps insane. A sister and her husband took her in, but she was never the same.

Candice would kill herself before letting this Apache take her back to his camp.

The moon was a perfect, pale-champagne crescent. There was no breeze, and the night was perfectly still except for the yelping of a distant coyote. Her captor was sleeping motionlessly. Candice knew she had no choice. She would wait a little longer to make sure he was sound asleep. Meanwhile, her gaze scanned the ground next to her for a rock big enough to kill him with.

She found it, her hand closing over it. It had a jagged edge, enough to do the trick. She felt ill. Killing in cold blood, even if the man was an Apache . . . she didn't know if she could do it. He's a half-breed, an inner voice said. Partly white. Candice thought of the scalped boy, of the captive woman. She picked up the stone.

Not even a branch rustled. The desert's silence was complete. No owls, no scurrying opossums. Candice clutched the blanket more tightly with one hand, the stone in the other. She began crawling toward him.

CHAPTER FIVE

She moved with all the grace of a cow.

A drunken cow.

She could be a mile away and he would still hear her, and if what she was doing wasn't so serious—if she didn't have that deadly stone in her hand—he would be laughing. Instead, he didn't move. His breathing was relaxed and even. His lashes lay thick and dark on his skin.

She was a foot away from his right shoulder, and she paused. Her breathing was loud and shallow. She was afraid. As she should be, he thought grimly. She inched closer, now on her hands and knees. He moved with the speed of a striking snake.

One moment she was poised on all fours, the next she was on her back, landing with a thud, and he was on top of her, pinning her body with his, her wrists ensnared in one of his large, strong hands, their faces inches apart. The stone fell out of her grasp and rolled away.

He stared into her eyes, the color of the desert night, so dark a blue they were almost black, and saw her fear. Even as that registered, he became aware of the feel of her beneath him. So soft. She had managed, miraculously—and he wasn't surprised—to keep the blanket in place. But it was thin and he knew she was naked beneath it—knew every lush curve of her body. His knees were between hers, his groin nestled in hers. Desire uncurled, his body stiffened.

"Doesn't it bother you," he snarled, "that you were about to murder a man who saved your life?"

Her mouth opened, lips trembling, but only a whimper escaped. He cursed, his hold on her wrists tightening, causing another frightened sound. Maybe he was angry at himself too. His manhood was thick, throbbing, the ache heavy and persistent. Too bad Apaches didn't rape. She expected it, he knew—had expected it since she'd awakened, and it was almost in him to fulfill her expectations. Of course he couldn't rape her—it went against every value he had been raised to believe in. "Well?"

"I—I wasn't."

"No?" He cupped her face with his free hand, catching some of her glorious hair. "A liar, are you?"

"Please, I'm sorry."

"So am I." He wanted to kiss her. Instead he raised himself to all fours. "Did you really think you could sneak up on me and kill me?"

She began to cry.

He stood abruptly, wrenching away. Then he twisted back to her. "Do I have to tie you up?"

She sat, clutching the blanket to her breasts. "No, please, don't."

"I sleep with one eye open, one ear listening. It's the Apache way. Lie down, go back to sleep. And don't try anything so foolish again."

She rose and turned to move away, back across the fire. He grabbed a hank of her long hair, stopping her. "No, *inlgashi,*" he said softly. He gestured to where he had been lying on the ground. Her eyes went wide.

He used her hair as a leash, pulling her close then pushing her down. He slipped down behind her, forcing her onto her back and throwing one arm over her waist. She was holding her breath—not that he cared—and he closed his eyes. Sleep, of course, would not come.

He would have to take her back.

He imagined the reception she would receive and almost felt sorry for her. But he cut off his sympathy. There would be a lot of talk about her being rescued by a "breed." He couldn't spend his energy worrying about that—better to worry about his own reception. Of course, he wasn't going to harm her, but that didn't necessarily preclude danger to himself from the bigoted whites. He didn't feel like facing an angry lynch mob.

Carter, however, did have a reputation as an outstandingly fair man. And there had been little trouble between the Carters and the Apaches. Just the usual winter raiding, which was actually for subsistence needs—an occasional, minor fray. Carter seemed to understand that the theft of a few head of cattle every year was not war, but a way of life for the Apache.

He decided he could risk bringing her home.

Home. He was close to his own home, and after three years his feelings were mixed and strong. On the one hand, he thought of seeing his mother again, his brother, his clan. God, it had been so long, and he had missed them.

On the other hand, he had decided to leave three years ago, and going back would only stir up old feelings. He had become used to the path of his life—one he walked alone, torn between the two cultures.

He had left after what was, for him, his last raid as an Apache warrior. He had been twenty-one years of age. A small raiding party of twelve warriors had gone south, looking for cattle to see them through the hard winter months. They had found three steers bearing Pete Kitchen's brand and had slaughtered them on the spot. They were butchering the carcasses when a dozen of Kitchen's hands had ridden up, taking them by surprise. A full-scale battle had ensued.

And he had killed his first white man.

They had been in hand-to-hand combat, and afterward— the man's blood on his hands and face—Jack had gotten sick, retching violently. No one had seen, no one had known. That didn't matter. He knew.

He knew he could not ride with the people who had raised him and war on the people whose blood also ran in his veins. That night he told his wife, Datiye, that he was leaving —and he hadn't been back since.

The first town he had come to was Tucson. He had been called a breed right to his face, and he had pulled his knife furiously on that man—a white—and flipped him, prepared to cut his throat. Usen, the Life Giver, did not preach "love thine enemy" like the white God, and his instinct was to kill. He was alone, in hostile territory. He realized this in time and caution intervened. He released the man.

He had gone to the saloon—a one-room adobe shack with straw on the floor, a few broken stools and tables. An old Spanish woman refused to serve him whiskey until the hard look in his eyes compelled her to change her mind. Later he rode out—and hadn't been back since.

The adjustment had been slow and painful. He had left the Apache, yet the white people shunned him as a half-breed. Jack had always been proud of who he was—one of the fiercest warriors in the Territory—and now his pride became a hard and angry mantle that he wore defiantly in the white man's world.

One day in that first year he was pushed too far. He was referred to as a savage, almost but not quite to his face, and it was one time too many. The man who had defamed him quickly repented—at the feel of Jack's knife against his throat. Moments later the saloon girl he was with asked him his name. With an amused, mocking smile, he had said, "Savage. Jack Savage." And he had been going by that name ever since.

As he drifted he gradually changed a few details of his dress—wearing a Stetson hat, exchanging the buckskin shirt for a cotton one, even trying to wear the white man's boots, as painful as they were. Without the moccasins with their distinctive Apache style, he found he encountered less bigotry and hostility.

He rode the Chisolm Trail, joining the cattle drive. He was a man, with social needs. At first he did not find any camaraderie among the crew. Their ostracism was blatant, as was their fear. Jack knew nothing about punching cows, yet he learned with fierce determination, and quickly. He worked twice as hard as any man there. Shortly after his first week on the drive, as he came in exhausted, covered with dust, slipping off his mount at the edge of the camp, prepared to eat alone, the ramrod came up to him and handed him a mug of coffee. It was a turning point. He had gained the boss's respect, and that of the crew followed. While he hadn't exactly made friends, and nor did he expect to, he was finally accepted.

In Texas he did a brief stint as a scout for the army in their campaign against the Comanche. It was not uncommon for Indians of other tribes to be used as scouts against their traditional enemies. Word of Jack's skill as a tracker spread rapidly. He was working closely with an Irish sergeant named O'Malley. O'Malley's feelings for him changed instantly one day when they encountered a war party and became engaged in vicious combat. Jack fought tirelessly at O'Malley's side, then risked his life to drag a young, wounded soldier to safety, getting shot himself in the thigh in the process. After that, O'Malley became his first real white friend—they shared many evenings together in the local cantina—and Jack's reputation soared throughout the fort and among all the troops.

Although he was living somewhat successfully on the fringes of the white man's world, he was always aware that the respect he gained for his skill and courage and intelligence was always accompanied by uncertainty and fear.

He might have white blood flowing in his veins, but it meant little to anyone except himself. To the world he was an Apache breed. Just like he was to this girl, Candice Carter. He turned his head to look at her.

She had fallen asleep. Her full lips were parted slightly, and a graphic image rose to mind—his mouth on hers, thrusting his tongue into her while he drove himself deep and thick and urgently inside her. His loins stirred again. It had been too long.

But he could never touch her.

They would hang him if he even tried.

CHAPTER SIX

She blinked into bright sunlight. Candice was instantly aware that she was alone—that he was gone. She sat abruptly upright, blanket in hand, her heart thudding with the possibilities.

"Good morning."

She gasped, twisting to see him near a stand of ancient saguaro. Then, noticing where his hands were—fastening the drawstring of his pants—she went red. And looked away. *How am I going to escape?*

"Are you hungry?"

She looked at him again, and to her relief, he was finished with what he had been doing, standing very relaxed not far from her. In the bright desert light, she was struck by many things at once. His hair wasn't black, but a rich, dark sable; in the sun it glinted with warm highlights. His eyes were paler than any she'd ever seen, a silvery gray. His features were even finer by daylight—as if sculpted by an artist. His torso, still bare, was just as carefully sculpted, but with hard sinew, not bone. When he shifted, his wet muscles gleamed and rippled. The buckskin pants were indecently soft. They molded powerful, near-bulging thighs. They also cupped his prominent sex. If he wasn't a half-breed he would be considered a stunning man. Candice glanced away. Her face was warm.

"You have hungry eyes," he said, low. He was stiff, tense—and angry.

"What?"

"Are you as hungry as those eyes of yours?"

"I don't understand." Candice drew back.

"No? Maybe you don't." He stared at her.

"Wait!" She cried. "Where are my clothes?"

For a moment he just looked at her, then he nodded to his right. She followed his glance and saw her things hanging to dry on boulders and two cactus arms. Seeing her lacy pantalets and the sheer chemise made her blush—it was indecent. She didn't want to look at him again, didn't want his unsettling attention, but she had to know. She just had to. "Did—did you . . . ?"

He *had* been looking at her undergarments, as if reading her mind. Now he gazed blankly at her. Her color rose. "Did you?"

"I have no idea what you're asking me."

Her heart picked up its tempo. Everything was bad enough . . . being stripped naked, forced to remain that way, having her intimate clothes hanging out . . . his looking at her as if he could see through the blanket she was wearing, then looking at her clothes as if he could see her in them. But not knowing what she was asking? Was this a poor attempt at a joke? "Did you—while I was unconscious—did you—" she choked. "Did you ravish me?"

His expression went black.

She could barely look at him.

And then she had no choice, because he pounced on her, grabbed her bare shoulders, and snarled into her face. "I think you have one hell of a preoccupation with my raping you."

She blinked. His breath was warm on her face, and her heart was beating thickly.

"Does it excite you, the thought of my raping you while you slept?" He shook her once. "Does it?"

"No," she whimpered.

He tilted her chin up until it touched his. His beard was rough and scratchy. His lips, up close, were beautiful. "Does the thought of a half-breed taking you, driving his shaft into you, deep, hard"—his hand slid into her hair and anchored itself—"does that excite you?"

"No."

He abruptly released her and stood. "When are you going to figure it out?" His tone was disgusted. "This breed isn't going to rape you, and he's not going to scalp you, and he's not going to kill you."

She sat trembling, still feeling his hurtful touch on her bare skin, the tingly warmth of his breath. When she looked up, he was gone.

Stunned, she sat very still, then carefully looked around. He was gone. She choked on a sob—of fear and despair. Then she hugged her arms tightly over her bosom. He had

said he wasn't going to rape or kill or scalp her. That should
have been reassuring. It wasn't.

What ugly things he had said.

Her heart still hadn't slowed its tempo. If he wasn't going to use her or kill her, then what did he have in store for
her? She froze up thinking about her only other possible fate.
Maybe, being a half-breed, he was one of those men who sold
white women to the Indians, into slavery. It really didn't
matter that he himself wasn't going to rape her; what mattered was that if he wasn't going to kill her, it meant he was
going to pass her along—in one way or another. She thought
of the woman who had had four half-breed children. She
would die before bearing a half-breed, or any bastard, for that
matter. She would die before submitting to multiple rape.

A horse snorted.

Candice whirled to see his stallion nosing the dry gama
grass, hobbled with twisted rawhide. She couldn't believe her
luck.

She yanked on her clothes frantically, as fast as she
could, stumbling over her pant legs. She shrugged on the
boots and ran to the black horse, breathless, managing to
restrain herself when his head shot up and his ears went back.
The whites of his eyes showed. He bared his teeth.

"Shhh, shhh, good boy," she crooned softly. The stallion seemed to have the same temperament as his owner. Like
his owner, he was also big, and although Candice was an
expert horsewoman, she felt a shiver of apprehension. She
ignored it. She reached her hand out slowly to stroke the
thick corded neck. The stallion swung his hindquarters away,
moving awkwardly because of the hobble, but then he began
to relax.

"Good boy," she whispered. "Good, good boy."

She grabbed the red saddle blanket and swung it on,
then the forty-pound saddle. The stallion had lost interest in
her, fortunately, and was nibbling on the grass as she cinched
up the girth. She was panting from her efforts, from the
hurrying, from the fear. She threw the reins over his neck,
crooning nonsense softly, and bent and untied the hobble.
She tossed it aside, threw a nervous glance over her shoulder.
Thank God, *he* was nowhere to be seen. She lifted one leg to
put one foot in the stirrup and swing up.

"Don't get on that horse," Jack warned from behind her.

Her foot found the iron, and Candice grabbed the pommel desperately. His hands closed around her waist, and she felt a vast despair. He set her on the ground and she twisted around, furious with frustration, her fists coming up to bang against his chest. He grabbed her hands and stilled them. Behind him, the stallion shifted uneasily.

"Are you a horse thief, too?"

"I wasn't stealing your horse!"

He yanked her hard, pulling her up against him, thigh to thigh, chest to breast. "Oh, I see. You were in the mood for a ride in the park?"

"Let me go!" she choked.

"What kind of woman are you? Last night you were going to bash me over the head with a rock, kill me if you could; today, steal my horse, leave me stranded in the desert. And to think I bothered to save your ungrateful neck." His pale gaze scorched her.

Candice was shaking, desperate yet strangely angry too. "What am I supposed to do? Wait for . . . wait for . . ."

"I've told you I'm not going to hurt you."

"You're going to give me to your Apache friends," she flung.

"What?"

"Like that woman, the one who was captured by Comanches." Her breast heaved.

"I don't know what in hell you're talking about," Jack said.

Calming, she became aware that he still held her wrists in an iron grip, that her back was against the stallion's barrel, that his thighs pressed hers. A shudder swept her, her heart quickened its beat. As if discerning her thoughts, he released her, stepping back a slight distance. "She was a slave," Candice said. When he showed no sign of comprehension, she wondered if he was dim-witted. "They used her, all the men. She had four half-breed babies."

The line of his lips tightened. "I see."

"I'll kill myself before I let them touch me," she whispered, staring into the coldest eyes she had ever seen.

"I wonder if you would, Miss Carter."

She was taken aback.

"What is this fascination of yours?"

Her eyes went wide.

He reached out, rubbed her chin with his knuckles, and she couldn't move. "If I weren't Apache," he said, "I would find out."

She made a sound.

His fist opened, the fingers closing over her jaw. "All Indians are not alike. Has that thought ever occurred to your lily-white mind? Apaches are not Comanches. We revere women and children. We adopt them—absorb them into our tribes. And we never rape."

She stared.

"Not unless invited to, of course," he added.

She found her voice. "You're lying. Everyone knows that's not the truth."

He stiffened, then relaxed with effort. He turned his back to her. "Make a fire while I clean the game."

She didn't know where the courage came from; maybe his words had reassured her. She ran after him, grabbing his sleeve. "Wait! If you're not going to make me a slave, then what are you going to do with me?"

He stopped. "The civilized, white thing to do, of course. I'm taking you to the High C—and if you make that fire we can eat and be on our way."

CHAPTER SEVEN

She rode, he walked.

Apaches could make seventy miles a day on foot if they chose, and Jack was no exception. Of course, that was at a ground-eating dogtrot, not at the pace they were now traveling. For some reason he was not in a rush, although he refused to examine his motivation. He kept one hand on the black's thick neck to keep him calm—the horse wasn't used to other riders. He was very much aware of the woman's gaze on his back all morning.

She had changed. She was no longer in abject terror of him, which was fortunate, because it more than irritated him. Still, the few times he had looked at her (and she had quickly averted her wide eyes) he had seen wariness, mingled with tempered fear. She was ready at the least sign of aggression on his part to take flight. His disgust grew.

They had had one exchange earlier in the morning. Jack had said, "What happened after your husband's murder?"

There was no immediate response, and he had felt her tension, turned to look, saw her pale face under his battered rawhide cowboy hat, which he had given her to wear. There was no mistaking the look on her face. Guilt. And then, abruptly, it was gone. What is she hiding? he wondered.

"I—I was in shock with grief," she answered. "I wasn't thinking right. I hired a horse—and left. I wanted to get home to my family."

He was studying her because she wasn't being honest. "That wasn't the smartest thing to do."

"No."

"What happened to the horse?"

"A rattlesnake."

End of conversation, and that had been four hours ago. Still, he was very much aware—too aware—of the woman in man's clothes on his horse.

The clothes hadn't seemed indecent when she was dying. This morning he had looked at her legs, completely revealed —long and beautiful and strong from riding, the kind of legs to wrap around a man's waist, he thought, while he plunges into her. And it wasn't his fault for thinking that, he reassured himself—not with the way the trousers were divided, molding the plumpness of her buttocks.

He had never seen a woman with a figure like this in pants before. It was the most blatant and suggestive sight he had ever seen—and that included when she had been naked under the buckskin hide.

He almost wanted to ask her if she was tired or needed to stop. He didn't. He had only to think of how she saw him—as a dangerous half-breed—and he grew angry. She wanted to get home? Well, they would just push on. The sooner he got her there the better, anyway, because from the High C he was heading north, into the mountains. Anticipating that part of the trip filled him with a fierce joy.

"Mr. . . . uh, *hmmch.*" She coughed, as if she couldn't speak his name.

He stiffened his back and didn't stop or look at her.

"Mr. uh, Mister . . ." She coughed again. "Savage. Please."

He stopped, taking the reins and looking at her unhelpfully. She was red. "I, ah, could we stop for a few minutes?"

He lifted one brow.

When she saw that he was waiting, she slid off the stallion, and he tried not to look too long and hard and hungrily at her. She kept her shoulders back and straight and her head high, and walked into the shade of some mesquite trees, then beyond. He thought: Be careful. But didn't say anything. He took a sip of water.

She reappeared a few minutes later, long-legged and slim-hipped, the shirt tight over full breasts, and he handed her the canteen. She took a few modest sips and handed it back. "Excuse me," she said, blushing again. "But at this rate it will take us a week to reach Tucson."

"So eager to get home? Or just to leave my company?" he mocked.

"Maybe we could, uh, share the horse?" Her voice tipped precariously upward on the question mark.

He was stunned. There were several reasons why he wasn't riding with her. But—he had to face it, the prime one was his untrustworthy male member, which was stirring too easily and too frequently these days. He could easily imagine what would happen with them riding together—his uncontrollable reaction would probably horrify her. He would rather avoid it at all costs. Still, she had actually suggested it.

"Is this a change of heart?" he asked, eyes smoking. When she didn't answer, his mouth tightened. He lifted her into the saddle, picked up the reins, and trudged on.

A few hours later he saw light glinting a short distance away. They had company. The flashing light was caused by the sun's reflection—either on field glasses or gunmetal. He worried that it might be soldiers from Fort Buchanan. After decoying them the other day and leading them away from the Apache raiding party, he imagined they would be only too glad to nab him, assuming it was the same patrol and they would recognize him. It was an assumption he would go by, because his horse was unforgettable. Not to mention that he was a half-breed. In one lightning movement, he catapulted onto the stallion behind her, catching her when she started in surprise.

"Someone's up ahead past those saguaro," he said quietly. She stiffened in his arms. He knew she was worried about any number of things—more Apache, Pima, Papago, outlaws, banditos from south of the border. He almost reassured her. Instead he urged the stallion into a lope and angled discreetly around toward the spot where he was sure they were.

"What are we doing?" she whispered.

"Checking to see who it is."

"Why don't we just circle around them?"

"Because they may have seen us too."

Candice was not reassured. She was worried, yes, but not enough so to take her mind off the more imminent problem—how to ride in front of him without being physically intimate. He had one arm wrapped around her waist, a firm anchor, and it supported the underside of her breasts. That made her very nervous. It was also making her nipples hard and sensitive. Or maybe it was his hard chest against her back, because it was impossible to keep distance between them no matter how rigidly she sat. She shifted her bottom, meaning to get closer to the pommel. The motion only set her higher on rock-hard thighs.

"Just relax," he growled.

She, of course, went stiffer. And her face flamed. She was very aware of his body behind hers, touching hers. She could even smell him—it was a distinctive scent and, if she was honest, not at all unpleasant. In fact, her heart was thudding a bit too quickly and, for some reason, her pants had become tight, making her uncomfortable.

He pulled the stallion up and slid off, pulling her down abruptly, one arm around her. "Be quiet and just do as I do."

She nodded. She knew he didn't trust her, or else he'd leave her alone with the stallion while he went to investigate. And he was right. If she had the opportunity, she would be on his horse and galloping across the desert in one split second. In a semicrouch, his arm holding her clamped to his side, he pulled her toward a thick stand of saguaro and boulders. Then he pushed her into a crevice of rock, growling, "Stay there."

Candice watched him duck away. She could hear male voices and laughter. She hesitated. It was just possible the men were hands from one of her neighbor's ranches, or, please God even better, troops. She followed him.

He was on his stomach, peering down an incline, shielded by thick octillo clusters. Candice got to her hands and knees and scrambled down to join him. She was ten yards away when he whipped onto his back, drawing one Colt so fast she wouldn't have believed it if she didn't see the gun pointing right at her chest. She cried out, freezing.

He lunged up and grabbed her, throwing her down.

She gasped for breath.

He reared up and started firing. Three fast, rapid shots in near succession. Then a long pause, and Candice twisted to stare and saw him taking a long, careful bead even as she heard the galloping beat of a departing rider. He fired. The horse's stride never faltered. Jack straightened to his full height and began scrambling down the slope.

Candice sat up, wiping sweat out of her eyes. She stood cautiously and looked down the slope, then cried out. Three bodies lay sprawled in blood on the ground. Three riderless horses were cantering away. The dead men—and she did not for a minute doubt they were dead—were cowboys clad in thick chaps and range clothes. She cringed at the sight of the cold-blooded murders. Then she heard another shot.

He was standing over an Indian who was staked out Apache style and sheathing his gun. Candice saw the red flower blossoming on the Indian's chest and knew Savage had killed him too, and she felt sick. For a minute she just stood there, fighting nausea, barely aware of how he was standing motionless, his head hanging. Then he straightened, turned slightly, raised his eyes and looked at her. The timing was perfect. Candice was already falling to her knees and retching.

She stayed on her hands and knees for a long time after the heaves had stopped, trembling and numb. She realized she was clawing the dirt, and she sat back on her heels, taking a few deep breaths. That was when she thought she heard a man's moan. She looked up.

Savage was wrapping the Indian in his buckskin bedroll. Candice watched him and was stunned. He folded the blanket over the brave's face and body as if he were bundling up a fragile infant. Then she heard the moan again, and saw one of the prostrate cowboys move his head. She was standing without realizing it.

Jack whistled, a sharp sound, and the black came galloping down the slope. He lifted the corpse and settled it on the saddle, speaking softly as the animal shied uneasily. Candice ran down the slope, falling, skinning her palm and running again. She ran past Jack, who was tying the corpse to the saddle. She stopped and knelt. The man's eyes were open. His face was white and wet with sweat. She saw that he had been gut-shot. She knew enough to know that it was fatal—and that he would take hours and hours to die. She rose. "Mr. Savage! He's alive!"

His back was to her, and he continued to tie the Indian corpse to the saddle, as if he hadn't heard.

"Mr. Savage! He's alive! This man is still alive!"

"Help me," the man gasped, a barely audible whisper.

Candice was frantic. Jack hadn't turned, hadn't even responded or given any sign that he had heard. She ran to him and grabbed his arm. "He's alive! Are you deaf? For God's sake—"

"I know," he said tonelessly, not glancing at her.

She dropped his arm, stunned, and backed away. "He's gut-shot," she croaked.

No response. He patted the stallion.

"Are you just going to let him die like an animal?"

Jack turned to face her. "He is an animal."

Her eyes widened.

"Let's go," he said.

"What kind of man are you?" She gasped. "You're the animal, not that poor dying man—you killed his friends in cold blood . . ."

"Let's go," he said again. Taking the stallion's reins, he started walking away.

"You can't leave him like that!" Candice screamed, running after him and grabbing his arm and hanging on to it, pulling him up short. To her total shock, he threw her off violently, and she fell on her backside onto the ground. He took one stride toward her, and she cringed, half frightened, half furious. He towered over her, his words low and enraged. "The Apache was only a boy," he rasped. "Fourteen winters, that's all. A Child of the Water—a novice in training to be a warrior. His status is sacred, special, protected. He was left behind by the raiding party so he wouldn't be put in danger, because he is unproven and untried. Do you know what they were doing to him?"

Candice didn't say a word.

He knelt. His eyes sparked. "What kind of courage does it take for four grown men to capture an unarmed boy who is all alone, and tie him up and stake him out and carve him up, then watch the ants crawl into his raw flesh?"

She was gasping, unable to breathe.

"There was no skin left on his chest," Jack said. "Even his face was crawling with ants—his eyes, nose, his mouth."

She sucked in her breath, and it sounded like half a sob.

He leaned closer. "That pig will die—slowly. In great pain. Just like the boy was dying."

Her voice was very faint. "It's wrong."

"Vengeance is our way." He stood. His bare chest was rising and falling rapidly.

Candice pushed herself up into a sitting position. "That doesn't make it right."

He turned his back on her and started toward the black.

"Oh, God," she moaned, and got to her feet, her eyes tearing. She brushed the moisture away and stumbled to one of the dead men. More moisture came, blinding her. She was weeping. She took a revolver out of one man's limp hand. It weighed more than any gun she had ever held, and it was cold, so very cold, in her grip. She stumbled toward the dying man. She had to brush at her eyes so she could see.

"Please." The words were so faint, barely audible, with a gurgling quality.

"I'm sorry," she whispered, and raised the gun. Her hands were shaking uncontrollably. He was dying and in great pain—she had to do it. But she couldn't pull the trigger. Her hand fell against her leg and she fought to control tears and to find the strength to put the man out of his pain.

Hard hands grabbed her from behind and sent her stumbling out of the way. She looked up just as the shot rang out. Jack turned to her with a black, murderous expression as he slammed his gun back into its holster. He reached out, pushing her toward the black, sending her stumbling forward. His footsteps, usually soundless, were hard on the ground behind her.

CHAPTER EIGHT

He didn't look at her—he didn't trust himself to.

He was aware of her stumbling behind him, then running doggedly to catch up, but he didn't slow his long, hard strides. The sun was very high now, and blazing in its intensity. It was late September, probably a hundred degrees, and without a cloud in the sky. There was no shade offered by the saguaro that was giving way slowly to juniper and chaparral as they ascended the foothills. He heard her fall. He didn't stop.

He didn't know what was happening to him. She was revolted by him and all his "kind," yet he had been moved enough to give in to her will and show mercy to the dying *pindah*. As he well knew, the man did not deserve mercy. Vengeance was preached by Usen, and he had been reared in it. He had never enjoyed torture, few men did—it was left to the women, as was right. He inflicted torture only in vengeance, which was also right. Even then, it was not something he did lightly or enjoyed. It was something that had to be done, like leaving the man in his agony to be broiled by the sun, craving water, eaten by ants, and bleeding to death inch by slow inch.

But Jack had put him out of his misery.

He wasn't sure if he was furious with himself or her, or both of them.

They covered another mile, the ascent getting rocky, pinyons joining the juniper to offer shade and respite. He heard her fall again and stiffened himself against her. But she didn't cry out, didn't ask him to wait. She got to her feet and continued to stumble after him.

Hours later when the sun was starting to touch the mountain ridges, turning heavy and orange, he stopped. He didn't look at her, and he didn't have to, to know what she was doing. She sank gasping onto the ground. He untied the bundled corpse and removed it from the black, very gently.

The boy had recognized and called him by name, asking Jack to send him into the other world. Jack, of course, could not refuse. For one, it was not the Apache way. And also, the boy had called him Niño Salvaje, and the Apache never called each other by their names unless it was a special or dire occasion. At such a time, the person named could not refuse whatever was asked of him. Jack had been only too glad to obey.

He hadn't recognized the boy.

It was three years since he had last seen his people, but that wasn't why. It was because the boy was unrecognizable.

He had left the People—*nnee*—so he wouldn't have to take part in the killing of the White Eyes. Now he had only just returned, and it was the same vicious cycle. This time the killing had been just, but the lesson was old, weary, and blatant. He was a fool to have returned.

As Jack slowly unrolled the blanket, Candice found herself watching. She was badly out of breath, and her feet hurt terribly—her boots were fashioned for riding, not walking. But she watched as his big, callused hands moved over the dead body. His touch was whisper soft and very gentle, as if he were handling china. She didn't understand how he could handle the dead boy like that after killing so many in cold blood.

She stood. There was a stream nearby, and she was desperately thirsty. He hadn't offered her water, and just as she hadn't asked him to slow his pace, she hadn't asked him for a drink, either. She stumbled to the bank and sank down, tossing the hat aside. She drank unabashedly with her hands, then rinsed her face the best she could. She dried her skin on the edge of her shirt, then turned slightly, too tired to get up, to see what he was doing now. She stared.

He had shed his pants and moccasins, his guns and knife belt, and was wearing only a loincloth and the turquoise and silver necklace. For a moment she couldn't move, or even breathe. He was bending over the corpse, doing something. She watched his body, the powerful thighs, the flat stomach, the bulging biceps in his arms. Then she went very red and looked at her feet. What in God's name was he doing?

She consciously averted her gaze, until she saw his bare feet moving past her silently. She looked up and realized he was carrying the corpse, which was now naked, into the stream.

"What are you doing?" she said.

"He must be washed."

Candice was standing. He was lowering the body, and she saw it and gagged. She averted her head, her heart thumping. How could anybody inflict such torture on another human body? She fought to keep the rising bile down.

She walked hurriedly away, limping a bit. She busied herself with removing her boots and inspecting her blisters, anything to occupy her attention, but found herself compelled to watch. He was bathing every inch of the boy's body, even his hair. After Savage carried the brave back out, he redressed him in the pants, leggings, and elaborately feathered war bonnet that he had been wearing. The boy hadn't been wearing a shirt, and Candice blinked when Jack went to his own saddlebags and pulled a buckskin blouse out and dressed the body in it. She had an inane thought: So he did own a shirt—and then a valid one: Why is he giving it to the boy? She grew even more amazed when he tucked one of his Colts and one of his knives into the boy's belt.

"What are you doing?" she said again.

He didn't look up. "Burying him."

"Why did you give him your shirt and gun and your knife?"

Jack lifted the boy and carried him to a rock outcropping, placing him in a natural crevice. He began to pile rocks over it. "He had no shirt, no weapons," he said simply.

She had heard that this was the way Apaches buried their kin, in natural crevices, but she hadn't believed it. She watched him pile on the stones until the body was no longer visible, the sight making her feel cold and clammy. "I don't understand."

He lifted a large boulder and heaved it on top. When he turned to face her he was sweating freely. "It might be cold."

"What?"

"It's a four-day journey to the afterworld," Jack said, gazing at her. "He had no shirt. He could get cold. And he might encounter spirits—evil ones. He had no weapons." He walked past her.

Candice just stared.

He began collecting firewood. Once he had a blaze going he added green juniper and, from his saddlebags, sprigs of what looked to be sage and thyme. Then he strode to the stream, saying "Come here."

Still stunned by the entire afternoon, it took Candice a moment to respond. She approached cautiously while he stood impatiently, hands on his hips. "Strip."

"What?"

"Strip. Then get in the water and bathe."

Her mouth opened, and she was so affronted and incredulous that for an instant no sound came out. "You have got to be kidding."

"No, I'm not," he said, casually removing his loincloth.

Candice instantly glanced at his groin, at the flaccid member nestled there, and then she went beet red, turning on her heel. He grabbed her and spun her around. "Just get out of your clothes and into the goddamn water."

"What are you going to do?" Her tone was fearful.

He smiled, not with amusement. "I am not going to do what I'm beginning to think you want me to do," he said. "Either you take off those clothes or I will."

Candice looked away and slowly began unbuttoning her blouse. She dared look at him. He was washing the loincloth with sand and water. She hesitated, reluctant to remove her blouse. She darted another look at him—he was now scrubbing his foot, his ankle. "Take it off," he said.

She took it off. "I'm not taking off my underwear," she stated, removing her jeans.

He didn't look up. "Fine."

She waded as quickly as she could into the water and began washing without looking at him. She heard him splash out and started to relax. The water was delicious. She had been dirty. This wasn't so bad, and using the sand as a scrub was an innovative idea. She dunked her head and began to rinse her long hair. Her gaze strayed to the bank.

She tensed, while something hot flamed inside her.

His buttocks were high and hard and tight, a pale bronze color, a stunning contrast to his darkly bronzed back and arms. She quickly looked down, anywhere but at him. Didn't he care that he was standing there nude? And what had he been doing, immersing himself in the smoke from the fire like that?

"Wash your clothes and come here," he called.

Her glance strayed. "What are we doing?"

He didn't turn to face her. The smoke was thick and

fragrant. "The dead carry disease. It's bad to touch them, to be near them. The smoke is purifying."

She washed her clothes and didn't tell him what she thought about such primitive beliefs. Then, clad in her wet underthings, her arms crossed tightly over her breasts, she hesitantly approached—pausing behind him and careful not to look at his nudity. He stepped to the left, she stepped forward. The smoke was awful. She coughed.

"Just relax," he said. "Do as I do."

He bent and picked up the canteen and began dousing the fire. Thick steam rose, blanketing them with its warmth. She could hear his breathing, deeper and louder than normal. He had told her to do as he did. In their precarious state of undress, she didn't want to attract his attention by not obeying. She began imitating his deep, uneven breathing, matching the sound, careful not to look at him. It was a ragged duet. He said, "What in hell are you doing?"

She looked at him without thinking. His jaw was clenched. He was looking at her—specifically, he was looking at her breasts with their hard nipples. Candice instantly covered her chest with her arms—unsuccessfully. "You told me to do what you do."

He exhaled loudly, his eyes moving to her guileless face. Candice reddened and looked down, then quickly away.

Too late—nothing would chase away the image of his thick, swollen shaft impaling the air. So thick, so big. She decided she didn't care about contamination. She ran to her clothes and struggled into them. He didn't say another word.

CHAPTER NINE

At dawn, he awoke.

The world was still gray, with the faintest pink blush in the east. Last night they had moved a half mile downstream and made a camp for the night. Jack got soundlessly to his feet, his gaze instantly searching her out. She lay curled on the other side of the dead fire beneath the buckskin hide. He looked at her for one long moment, then turned and left the camp.

Many images assailed him. How she had looked standing in the steam of the fire clad in her thin, wet undergarments; her expression when she had seen him. He almost smiled. Of course he hadn't meant the erection to happen, as he didn't mean it now, but he needed a woman—and he wanted her.

They were only about thirty hours from the High C, and he couldn't get there too soon. It was the enforced intimacy, he was sure. If she had been just another beautiful white woman he had seen in passing, he would have forgotten her. His body wouldn't be going crazy with impossible, hopeless need.

Of course, there were so few white women in these parts, and even fewer pretty ones, much less a woman like Candice Carter. *Kincaid*, he corrected. Candice Carter Kincaid. He resolved to take care of his needs as soon as possible, and knew he was only kidding himself if he thought some whore's arms were going to erase her image.

He was angry again—a dark, frustrated anger of the heart.

The growl sounded above him.

The instant he heard it he had many thoughts in one split second. The mountain lion was belligerent. He hadn't been aware of it because he was so preoccupied with her. The woman was going to be the death of him.

He pulled his Colt, but too late. From above on the rock, the tawny cat was flying through the air. The force of the contact sent him backward before he could even fire, twenty claws cinching through his skin, the gun falling from his grasp as his hands came up instinctively between them.

It was like the burning of hellfire. They rolled, a mass of human flesh and furred beast. The claws lifted, sank in, contracted—but he did not scream. He knew he could not get the cat off with brute force. His hand closed over his knife. He pulled it from his sheath and plunged it upward with desperation and sheer intent.

For an instant he thought he had failed, then the cat's eyes went wider and its mouth formed a screaming growl of fury. The claws embedded in his flesh stretched and pulled. The big body went rigid, then limp. The animal relaxed and Jack pushed him off, freezing up at the agony of those claws scorching through his flesh as the cat rolled aside. His knife protruded from its heart.

Jack lay very still.

He was panting, sweat streaming down his face, down his body. He had been trained to withstand pain, but the agony was close to unbearable. He needed a few moments to find the strength to move. His heart slowed, his breathing became less rapid. His hands found the dirt beneath him and he levered himself up with difficulty. The pink and gray morning darkened, spinning, and he fought not to pass out. He succeeded.

He looked at the cat, which must have weighed over 150 pounds, and he looked at his knife. He got to his knees, every movement causing shots of searing pain, then pushed himself to his feet. He swayed, panting and fighting more waves of dizziness, then took two steps toward the cat, where he promptly fell to his knees again.

It took a few moments to get enough strength, but he finally reached out and pulled the blade from the tawny chest, automatically wiping it in the dirt and sheathing it. The world was still spinning, and he thought, It's only a few scratches, get up.

He knew he could not take care of himself properly. The girl was only twenty yards away. There was more pain at that thought, a pain of the heart, of the soul. Now she could kill him and ride away. He couldn't trust her. He needed his strength and his wits. He would have to force her to clean his back.

He rested for an eternity that went too fast, then pushed himself to his feet again. He walked carefully, so as not to stagger, one foot in front of the other. The camp wasn't far; there was no question in his own mind of not making it. But he paused once, holding on to a branch of scrub oak, willing strength, not weakness. Then he pulled his Colt, the handle strangely clammy in his hand, the weight of it surprisingly heavy, forcing the nose down. He pushed himself away from the tree. The ground was still spinning, but slowly, manageably.

She was up, stoking the fire. She looked up as he neared, and her face went white. She leapt to her feet.

He stood with the Colt hanging in his hand and wondered if he was swaying or if the ground was moving.

"Oh, my God," she said.

He sank to his knees on the ground. When he looked up she hadn't moved. He could see it all in her mind—her horror, and the leap of knowledge, too. She glanced at the stallion and he knew, with more pain, that he had been right. Given the chance, she would leave him to live or die. He raised the gun. It seemed to waver in front of his eyes, but then, she did too. "Get water. There's—there's whiskey—in my bags."

She didn't move. Not at first, and then she turned and ran for the canteen, grabbing the saddlebags off the ground and hurrying back. She paused abruptly before him. He wanted to close his eyes. Never had they felt so heavy. He realized with a start that the gun was pointing at the ground, and he tried to lift it. She dropped the bags and the canteen, and before he could react, she had taken the gun away.

He looked up. Now. Now she was going to leave. Or kill him first. But wasn't it better this way? She was torturing his soul. "Go," he whispered. "Go. Run. Leave."

Their gazes met. She glanced at his horse. Then her lips pursed together and she turned her back to him, and in that one instant, when he knew she was going, it was unbearable. But she removed her shirt, and her chemise, then replaced her shirt and turned to him. He watched her with new understanding, closing his eyes as she ripped the cotton. When she tenderly touched his shoulder where the skin was unhurt, his eyes flew open. "I have to clean these wounds," she said. "It will hurt. Drink some whiskey, here."

She forced a few swallows down his mouth before he

could object, to tell her, no, use the whiskey on my wounds, don't waste it that way. But he was too tired and in too much pain to speak. Then he gasped as she poured the alcohol over his back, but it was the only sound he made. When she drenched the wounds on his chest, ribs, and legs, he didn't make a sound. Sweat poured from his chin. She washed everything with water, rinsing the dirt, sand, and stones out. The red haze of pain was incessant. He wondered how long he could sit up, and knew it wouldn't be much longer. His world was swaying precariously now.

"Just another minute," she soothed. "Here, let me put the blanket down. There. Now, careful . . ."

She helped him and somehow he was lying down, and it was blessed. Then he became aware of something else—a soft damp cloth moved tenderly over his temple, his cheek, his jaw and chin as she bathed the sweat away. His last conscious thought was: *She didn't leave.*

CHAPTER TEN

When he awoke the sun was high, and he knew he had slept through all of yesterday and half of today. He also knew, as he tensed his muscles expectantly, that he was well on his way to recovery. He was sore, he ached, but from the feel of it everything was scabbing up. He was famished. He pushed himself up into a sitting position, ignoring the twinge of pain, looked around, and froze.

His horse and the girl were gone.

His heartbeat quickened, and his disappointment was too acute to ignore. Then he shrugged it off—she hadn't killed him—in fact, she had stayed until he was well enough to make it on his own.

He heard the horse approaching when it was still out of sight, and he slowly rose to his feet. He looked around, then spied the saddlebags and his gunbelt and knife belt. He retrieved a Colt, moved into the shadows of some boulders, and waited.

Candice Carter trotted into the clearing, two dead squirrels hanging from the pommel of his black.

He stepped out and her gaze shot to him. They stared at each other.

"You're up," she said.

She hadn't left. She was still there. He couldn't believe it. He looked away so she wouldn't see any of the turbulent emotions in his eyes, then moved back to the blanket and slowly sat.

"You shouldn't have gotten up," she said, sliding off the black.

"I'm a lot better," he said, not looking at her.

"You should be, you slept for about thirty hours. You had a fever, but not for long. You were very lucky."

His gaze pinned her. "Why didn't you leave?"

She shifted. "It wouldn't have been right. To leave a hurt man."

"Even a half-breed Apache?" There was a mocking quality to his tone.

She flushed and couldn't meet his gaze. "I owed you," she said, turning away.

He watched her skin and clean the game with determination, her face set, and an aching grew in him. It wasn't physical. Yesterday she had cared for his body with the tenderness of a wife. Now she was cooking his food, the most domestic of acts a woman could perform. It was as if she were his woman, doing these things to take care of him. Yet it was just a shimmering desert illusion. He looked away.

When Candice had the squirrel roasting on a spit, she rose to her feet and looked at him. He met her gaze, then found himself looking at her full breasts, unrestrained by a chemise, bare beneath the cotton shirt. He felt a familiar tightening in his groin, but it was hard to look away. When he raised his eyes back to hers he saw her standing there with a frozen, startled look. Poised for flight, but mesmerized.

He ducked his head. "Could you look at my back? Everything else is healing quickly."

"Yes, of course."

Candice hesitated, wringing her hands briefly. It was one thing to have tended him while he was desperate with pain and half conscious, another to have tended him while he lay sleeping and slightly feverish. Now he looked like a healthy man, except for the slight sheen of perspiration on his brow. She thought of how she had wiped his brow many times last night with the same tenderness she would give to a hurt animal. She had forgotten, really, who and what he was. The question of leaving him had crossed her mind only once, initially, when he had come into the clearing staggering on his feet and covered with blood. It had been an instinctive reaction, the urge to flee while she could. But something had held her back—a natural compassion. It hadn't mattered that he was part Apache and her enemy.

She had never touched an Indian before. That thought hadn't occurred to her since yesterday. After cleansing his wounds, the only times she had touched him was to bathe his face, as his fever had stayed low. The man had the constitution of an ox.

She was afraid to go near him now, much less touch him.

She knew she should have left a few hours ago, when he seemed better and she'd had the chance.

Candice approached slowly, apprehensively, and she saw the look of contempt flash through his eyes. He shifted his back to her and she looked at the broad, hard flesh, crossed in three places with scabbing claw marks that were healing without the least sign of infection. Again, his health amazed her. "Everything is fine," she said.

He shifted back and looked at her. "If you get too close, I might bite."

She reddened, and grew angry too. "That's not fair."

"No? Then stop looking at me as if I'm some kind of half-human animal."

She stiffened. "I haven't . . ."

"I'm a man," he said. Then, crudely: "Surely you remember that?"

She went even redder, thinking about how a few nights before he had stood in the smoke with his penis rigid like a stallion's. She turned her back abruptly, trembling. She very deliberately walked to check on their dinner, trying to get those images out of her mind. It wasn't easy.

They ate in a tense silence, not looking at each other. He fell asleep soon after the meal, while it was still light out. She sat and studied him openly. His lips, almost full and certainly not thin, were parted slightly. Her gaze riveted there. His mouth, his face, so hard in waking, was relaxed and vulnerable in sleep. There was a growth of stubby beard, but it couldn't detract from his evenly sculpted features. He was part Indian, but he was a good-looking man.

Candice blushed at the thought and resolved never to think it again.

She didn't understand him. He was Apache, wasn't he? Yet he hadn't acted like one. He hadn't hurt her, abused her, forced himself on her. Or worse. In fact, other than the few times he had lost his temper, he had even been decent. And when he had been injured, in terrible pain, he had been so stoic . . .

She abruptly tore her gaze away from him and stood. He was well on his way to health. They weren't far from the High C. Now was the time to leave. She had owed him her life, she had paid in full. Of course, she would be stealing his horse.

She wondered if she could be hanged for stealing a half-breed's horse.

The guilt could have been consuming, but she was determined, and she started tacking up the black quickly and quietly. She found herself wishing that there was another way. The stallion was no longer nervous around her; in fact, he turned to nuzzle her, pushing against her side and blowing softly. She patted him and yanked the cinch tight.

She thought about how Savage had stared at her breasts with bright silver eyes.

She looked over her shoulder at him as he lay sleeping. He moved slightly, and she froze, her heart slamming, and for a moment she thought he was awake. But he settled again.

She swung into the saddle and rode off into the approaching night.

CHAPTER ELEVEN

It was twilight the next night when Candice rode through the fortified walls of the High C. The gate, of course, had been closed and barred, but the sentry recognized her and swung the heavy door open. That produced the usual result, and she had gotten only halfway to the low, long adobe house when her family came pouring out, Little John in the lead.

"Good God, Candice," he shouted, whipping her off the horse and into his strong, warm arms. She clung to him, laughing. He whirled her around and passed her to Mark, almost as tall as their younger brother. Then Luke, the oldest, was embracing her wordlessly, before she was swept into her father's arms. By now she was crying.

"Are you all right?" John Carter demanded, peering into her face.

"Yes, yes, Pop, I'm so sorry."

"We'll get into that," he assured her.

"Where in hell is Kincaid?" Mark demanded.

Candice pressed against her father, who still had his arm around her as they started to the house. Luke said, "Easy, boy, give her a chance."

"I think I'll kill Kincaid" was Mark's hot retort.

"Whose horse?" John-John was asking. "Are you alone, for Christ's sake?"

"John-John," his father reproved.

Candice saw the husky form of Maria, who had raised her after her mother had left, and she rushed forward for another embrace. The big Mexican woman was crying. "Candita, how could you? You put us all to hell!"

"I'm so sorry," Candice cried, meaning it.

Inside, Maria ordered her niece Conchita to prepare a bath. "Are you hungry?"

"Starved," Candice replied. Maria left and she turned to face her family, flushing with guilt because now the lies would start.

"Where is Kincaid?" her father asked.

"I'm going to kill him if he touched you before the wedding," Mark said.

Her color went deeper. She looked at Luke, not the tallest and not the shortest but the coolest, then at her father. "Kincaid is dead. There was a robbery. Right after the wedding. I was in shock, and I had to get out of there. I got a horse and left."

They all stared in dumbfounded silence.

"Candice, I'm sorry," her father finally said.

Candice's mouth began to tremble. "Oh, Pop. It was awful," she said, thinking of how Virgil had betrayed her and tried to rape her, and how she'd had to defend herself.

Her father hugged her again. Then he raised her chin sternly. "Where is *there*?" he asked.

She started chewing a nail. "Fort Yuma."

More stares and more silence. Little John broke it. "God, Candice! You left alone—you came alone—all the way —alone!"

She bit her lip. "I'm so sorry."

Even Luke was looking appalled. "I can't believe it," he said. She gave him a pleading look, and he softened and hugged her.

"Well, at least Kincaid got what he deserved," Mark said.

"Mark," John reproved.

"I don't care. He ran off with our sister. She's gonna never live that down. Who'll want to marry her now?"

Candice inhaled sharply. She should have known Mark wouldn't hold back, and it was true—it would be even more true if they knew she'd never married Kincaid, and if they knew about the half-breed. . . .

"Mark, that's raw," Luke said. "I don't think Candice will have too much of a problem. Tim McGraw's asked her three times this year, and Judge Reinhart was about to pop the question before she eloped. It'll be just a matter of time."

Candice gave Luke a grateful look. Her father affirmed what Luke had said, adding, "Besides, there's no rush, and there's mourning to think of." He reached out to hug her. "Honey, it's so good to have you back."

Candice smiled back, relieved.

She tried not to think about stealing Jack Savage's horse. She had a niggling thought. He wouldn't come looking for his horse—would he? She assured herself that he would not. The guilt was too much to bear, so it was easier to put it out of her mind and concentrate on the reunion with her family. After the warmth came the lecturing, which she staunchly braved. And when she finally crumpled into bed, she said a brief prayer of thanks to the Lord, asking for forgiveness for the murder, and the lies and the horse-stealing.

And why, God, was it the last that preyed on her mind and nerves? She had killed a man, but all she could think about was stealing an Apache's horse while he lay sleeping and wounded.

CHAPTER TWELVE

"Candice, get up."

She opened her eyes to see Luke standing in the doorway. "Huh?"

He was grim. "There's a half-breed Apache in the yard and he says you stole his horse."

She sat up, her face paling. "Oh, God." *He had come.*

"Pop wants you downstairs. Now." Luke stalked out of the room.

Candice leapt from the bed, shaking. She felt fear and sought control as she pulled on a chemise and petticoats. Her whole family was there, so he couldn't do anything. She didn't have to know him very well to know he would be furious. And her omission of the truth was about to be exposed. . . .

She shrugged into a skirt and blouse and ran downstairs, barefoot, her hair still loose and uncombed.

He was standing in the yard, facing the verandah, at gunpoint. One of the hired hands had his rifle trained cautiously on his back, and three others ringed him warily. Mark, Little John, Luke, and their father stood facing him. His eyes were blazing, and he was wearing only the loincloth and moccasins, an empty gunbelt and the knife. One of the hired hands had his Colt stuck in his own waistband. The scabs on Savage's chest and knee had opened, and were raw and bleeding slightly.

Their gazes locked.

Candice was shaking, and she could barely breathe.

He smiled, a mere baring of his teeth. "I believe," he said harshly, "you have something that belongs to me."

Candice opened her mouth to speak, but no words came out.

Mark whirled, eyes wide. "This breed was at the gate, demanding to come in. He says you stole his horse."

Candice looked at Mark and then at Jack. His gaze was ice cold and filled with contempt. Yet his face seemed pale beneath the bronze of his tan. "I . . ." She faltered completely. Oh, why had he come!

"I want my horse," Jack said softly, slowly, enunciating every word, his gaze pinning her.

"Do you know this man, Candice?" her father said.

"Yes."

Mark took a step toward her, incredulous and furious all at once. "How in hell do you know him?"

"Is it his horse?" John-John demanded, as angry as Mark.

"Yes." Candice looked back at Jack and flushed with the guilt that resurfaced with full intensity. She quickly faced her father and Luke, the only ones who might show her any sympathy. "Pop, I didn't tell you the whole story."

"I can see that," her father said, but he was cut off by Mark, who was shouting.

"Did he touch you? Did he? Did this red-skinned bastard touch you?"

Candice stepped back, flushing. Thinking many, many thoughts—waking up naked, standing together nude in the smoke, cleansing his body. Mark met her gaze and his own went wider, and then he whirled, drawing his gun in the same motion. Candice cried out, "No, Mark, no, he didn't, I swear it!"

Before she had even finished the sentence, Jack grabbed Mark's arm, hard, and the gun went clattering to the ground. Luke quickly moved between the two men. He said to his younger brother, very softly, "Don't be a hothead."

"If he touched her, I'll kill him!"

Jack laughed, the sound hard and short and mirthless. "I have no interest in her."

It was, of course, a lie, and they both knew it. Candice went crimson, wishing, with all her heart, that he hadn't come.

"What happened, Candice?" her father injected firmly.

Candice took a breath, glad to turn away from Jack. "I bought a horse in Arizona City, but she got bit by a rattlesnake. I walked until I couldn't walk any longer. I had no water, no food. I finally passed out. It had been three, maybe four days. He found me."

Mark made a noise, and even John-John gasped. Everyone, including the hired hands, looked at the half-naked man standing tautly in their midst. Jack smiled again, savagely.

Luke spoke. "You were alone with him, in the middle of the desert?"

Candice flushed again. "He saved my life."

Again, all eyes went from her to Jack.

Candice hurried on into the tense silence. She could feel the male anger, the maelstrom of hostility, the urge for violence. "He saved my life. He didn't touch me. He's part white, he speaks like a white man. There was a mountain lion —he got hurt." She faltered and found herself looking at him, saw the fury in his gaze, and this time she couldn't look away. Her voice went to a whisper. "That's when I stole the horse."

Their gazes locked in another silence, this one endless. Then Candice thought she saw him sway, but the movement was so slight and he was standing so rigidly that she had to have imagined it. John-John said, "He has a helluva nerve, coming here."

"I don't believe her," Mark accused. "She's lying."

"Mark!" her father said.

Candice held her breath. Mark turned his hot, angry eyes on her. "If he didn't touch you, why are you so guilty looking—so red? He's a damn red-skinned breed. You were unconscious when he found you. They don't do any different from animals. You might not even know if—"

"Enough!" John Carter roared.

Luke said, "If he had touched her, little brother, horse or no horse, he wouldn't be foolish enough to come here."

"I didn't touch her," Jack gritted. "At least, not the way you mean. I saved her damned life—and all I got out of it was a stolen horse and a delay in my journey north."

Candice was shaking. She looked everywhere but at Savage.

"Pedro, get his horse," John said. The hand immediately turned to obey. John looked at Jack. "You saved my daughter's life, and for that I thank you."

Jack smiled again. It didn't reach his eyes.

The stallion was led out, saddled. Candice looked at Jack again. He wasn't looking at her, but at the horse. She saw the slick sheen on his oozing chest. Her mind started to work. He had trailed her on foot. He was still hurt. She should have never stolen the horse. She would never forget the look in his eyes—or how close they had all come to violence and maybe murder. Pedro handed him the stallion's reins. He didn't move to get on. His hands on the leathers were white.

"You'd better ride out of here while you can," Luke advised.

Jack met his gaze evenly. His was strangely bright. "My gun."

Luke looked at Red Barlow, who still had his rifle aimed at the man's back. He nodded. "Give him his gun, Red."

Red hesitated. "You sure?"

"Give it to him, Red," John said.

Red hesitated again, then, still training his rifle on Jack, he gingerly removed his gun.

"Wait," John-John said, and moved in between them to take the Colt and quickly empty its chamber. He wheeled and thrust it at Jack. Jack sheathed it and moved stiffly to the stallion's side. His back was bloody. The scabs had opened, and Candice inhaled sharply. He must have heard, because he tensed.

"Pop," Candice said swiftly, "he's hurt. He came all this way on foot. At least—at least he could have something to eat."

Everyone stared at her.

"What in hell's wrong with you?" Mark shouted.

"He did save my life," Candice said, her chin coming up and her heart pounding furiously. She wasn't looking at her brother or anyone other than the man whose bloody back was facing her. How could he have done it? Did the stupid horse mean so much to him? And how—how was he going to get on it and ride?

"You, boy," John Carter said.

Jack was still standing with his back to them, facing the horse. Now he put his foot in the stirrup and swung into the saddle.

"Go around back to the kitchen. Maria will give you something to eat."

The stallion swung sideways and Jack faced the Carter family with scorn blazing in his eyes. Candice blushed, knowing this proud man would never go to the back to take scraps like a dog. She felt a sudden shame for her family—and for herself. His glance settled on her and it burned.

Candice bravely held it, her hand coming up to her mouth. Something seemed to choke her from deep inside. She saw that his face was beaded with sweat. "Please," she heard herself say. "Go around back and get some food and water."

"To hell with your charity," he said in a low voice.

He tore his gaze away and turned the stallion, who was prancing restlessly. As he did so he slumped slightly, from the waist, then pulled erect again. The stallion snorted and shook his head.

"He's hurt," Candice said.

And he fell from the horse with one crashing thud at their feet.

CHAPTER THIRTEEN

Candice moved with a cry, but not fast enough. Luke got to Jack first, bending over and feeling for his pulse. Candice became aware of her father's hand on her arm, restraining her. Luke straightened. "He's got a high fever. Looks like them marks got infected."

"Red, you and Willie take him into the barn," John Carter said.

"Pop!" Mark protested. "Set him on his horse and send him out of here!"

Candice opened her mouth to object, but Luke was already ordering Red to help him move Jack. He bent and lifted the man by his armpits, and Red took his ankles. Candice watched worriedly, blaming herself for everything. As they started across the yard, she took exactly two steps after them before her father grabbed her shoulder. "Where do you think you're going?"

"He . . ." She faltered. "To see what I can do."

"Maria will tend him, just like she tends everyone on this ranch when they get hurt."

Candice flushed. But she met her father's piercing stare and wondered what he was thinking. She soon had no doubt about what Mark and Little John were thinking.

"What do you care about that breed, Candice?" Mark shot. "You seem awful concerned."

Candice tensed and was furious. "How dare you, Mark. How dare you call me a liar and—"

"Do you know what the talk is going to be?" Mark demanded.

Candice inhaled. She had been hoping no one would ever find out about her and Jack Savage. But now it would be spread around Tucson and all the ranches as soon as the first hands rode into town for a few drinks. And it didn't matter that nothing had happened between them—or almost nothing. People would speculate. Talk. Condemn. "I don't care," she said, lifting her head. "Nothing happened. For God's sake, Mark, he is a human being first. And he's very white. I don't need you siding with everyone else."

"I'm sorry, but I don't want you around him," Mark said tensely.

"That's enough," John interrupted. "Mark is right, Candice. Stay away from him while he's here. And you, Mark, keep your opinions to yourself. You too, John-John. Now don't you have some work to do this morning?"

Both young men turned, Mark still angry, Little John a shade less. Candice met her father's gaze. "You have a lot of explaining to do," he said.

"I wanted to avoid all this, I didn't want you to worry."

"Maybe if you'd told the truth from the start, we could have been prepared for this. Mark is right. There will be some talk." He put his hand on her shoulder. "The sooner he's well enough to ride on, the sooner we can get past this."

Candice nodded, knowing he was right, but she couldn't resist one last glance back.

She couldn't sleep.

She wondered if he was all right.

The day had dragged endlessly, and Candice had kept thinking about the hurt man in the second barn. A visit from one of her beaux, the widower Judge Reinhart, did not help the time to pass any easier. And after all the accusations and confusion of the morning, she was afraid to ask after him. When she finally did, Maria barely answered, unusually curt, brushing her off.

She was forgiven, she knew that. Even Mark was acting normally toward her, with teasing affection, except when he would glance out the window toward the barn—and then his face would become grim. Mark was not just the most volatile of her brothers, with John-John following close in his footsteps—he also hated Indians. That had never bothered Candice before, because everyone was afraid, so to some degree they hated the natives of the area. Mark, of course, had stronger personal reasons than most. He had been in love with a pretty Mexican girl from Nogales. She had been killed by Geronimo and his renegades—and not prettily, either. Candice hadn't seen the body, but she had heard that Mark wept when he did. That had been two years ago.

Of course, Candice reflected, this man didn't even belong to Geronimo's band—or did he?

No, he couldn't.

Everyone knew Geronimo had once ridden with Cochise. But a few years ago when Cochise had made an alliance with the whites, Geronimo had left the tribe—taking with him many Chiricahua warriors who wanted to fight. Apaches on the warpath were deadly. These renegades showed no mercy, ever, to women or children, much less men. They were worse than deadly.

Candice knew he couldn't belong to Geronimo, because if he did he would have certainly killed her—after using her brutally.

Trying to sleep was hopeless. She got up and slid on a cotton wrapper. What would one peek hurt? Everyone was asleep. This was all her fault—she had no doubt about that. If she hadn't stolen the horse, he wouldn't have had to come after her, pushing himself while he was still healing, infecting his wounds with sweat and dirt. She took a small lantern with her but didn't light it, stealing through the house in the blackness like a thief.

She hurried across the yard in her bare feet, seeing by the moon and stars. She swung the big barn door open, then knelt to light the lantern. After carefully adjusting the wick, she held it up to see.

She gasped.

He was lying on his back in the straw, without a single comfort. No blanket, no water. He was sweating heavily and shaking. Candice's heart ripped in two. How could Maria do this to him?

She rushed forward and knelt. "Jack." She touched him. He was burning up.

At her touch his eyes flew open and he twisted his head violently. Recognition flared. "Don't touch me," he said hoarsely.

She froze, her hand still on his wet, slick temple, then said, "Nonsense. I'll be right back." She ran out of the barn.

She returned with water, linens, and whiskey. He was waiting for her now, his eyes bright and angry. She knelt beside him and spread a linen sheet alongside him. Then she gave him a coaxing smile. "Let me help you up and onto this sheet. It will be much more comfortable. Come on." She touched his shoulders.

He wrenched violently away. "I told you—don't come near me." His teeth clacked together on the last syllables.

"I'm sorry," she said. "I am sorry."

He closed his eyes and turned his head away.

She hesitated only a moment. Then she dipped a linen strip in the water and proceeded to wipe his face. In the next instant his hand was on her wrist, yanking her chest on top of his, surprisingly strong, hurting her. Her face was inches from his, her eyes wide with surprise and shock.

"I told you, Candice Carter, get the hell away from me. Or don't you understand English?"

He was hurting her, but she deserved it. "I'm not going away. I'm not leaving you like this. Now let me up, Jack." Her voice wasn't calm—it shook slightly. Partly because she was afraid—he was still so strong and so angry, and possibly crazed with fever—and partly because her breasts were crushed on his hard, wet chest and she could feel his heart pounding and smell his male scent. And then his grip went lax.

His head went back and his eyes closed, and she knew he had no more strength. She straightened and proceeded to bathe him with cool, clean water, cleaning the wounds as well on his chest and legs. They were angry looking and oozing yellow pus. When she drenched them with whiskey he jerked upright, eyes wide and startled until he recognized her.

She took advantage and grabbed him around the waist, blushing from the intimate contact. "Turn over, Jack," she coaxed. "Onto your stomach, on the sheet."

To her surprise, his eyes drooped and he obeyed, giving her the chance to get to work on his back. She picked out pieces of straw and dirt. She bathed the wounds with soap and water, then disinfected them with alcohol. As she was wiping his shoulders down with a cool cloth, another lantern flared in the doorway, making her look up, frozen.

Luke stared.

Candice felt resolve stiffen in her. Despite the frantic beat of her heart, she calmly wrang out the cloth.

Luke said quietly, "What's going on here, Candice?"

"What does it look like, Luke?"

He approached with his lazy, relaxed stride. "Not good."

Candice dumped the cloth in the water and glared. "How could you leave him here in the straw, without water or a blanket, Luke? I'd expect it of Mark, who's never gotten over Linda, or even John-John, who is too young to know better—but not of you!"

Luke squatted. "I told Red to see that he had what he needed. I didn't know they just dumped him here."

His blue gaze was steady on her face. "I asked you a question, little sister. What's going on?"

"This is my fault," she told him, relieved to be sharing the guilt. "Luke, he saved my life, and how did I pay him back? By stealing his horse when he was hurt. Now he's even worse, because he came after me on foot when he was too ill to do it. I had to come out and tell him I was sorry. And when I saw him like this . . ."

Luke regarded her. "His fever still high?"

"Yes."

"I won't tell anyone about this, Candice. But you'd better go on back to the house. I'll go get Maria."

"This is her fault too," Candice protested. "It's because he's part Apache. You know how much the Mexicans and Apaches hate each other. We should have known she wouldn't give him any care."

Luke absorbed that, then squatted again. "You can't stay here."

"I won't leave him while he's like this." Her dark blue eyes flashed. "It's not right!"

Luke sighed. "I'll stay, I'll do what you're doing. You go on back to bed."

Candice realized she still didn't want to go, even though she trusted her older brother completely—and even though she was proud of him for offering to help. But she realized she should give in now, so she hugged him tightly. "Thank you, Luke."

He smiled slightly. But his gaze was still probing, questioning.

CHAPTER FOURTEEN

The Henderson womenfolk came to call the next day.

Millie Henderson was one of the town's matriarchs, the rather weathered wife of a local rancher who was taking a beating from the raiding Apache and rustlers from south of the border. Her sister-in-law Elizabeth was Candice's age, fair-skinned, petite, and dark. Candice wasn't close to Elizabeth, even though she was one of the few women her own age in the area. First of all, the Henderson spread was at least half a day's ride from the High C, which made visiting a big event. Candice had also never had a need for women in her life, other than Maria. With three adoring brothers and a doting father and a territory full of women-hungry suitors, she had about all she could handle in the way of company. And finally, Elizabeth was very quiet. They had never had a chance to get to know each other.

So the visit was a surprise.

In a way.

As soon as the two women were settled with lemonade, Candice saw Millie Henderson staring at her hands. And she flushed because she obviously lacked a wedding ring.

"We came to offer our regrets," Millie said. "We hear poor Virgil Kincaid was killed."

"Yes."

"Such a tragedy, and right after your wedding," Millie continued.

Candice wished she wasn't so red. "Yes."

"You're not wearing a ring."

Her color went crimson. "I know you've probably already heard the story, Millie. It fell off, when I almost died in the desert."

"Eloping like that," Millie said. "If Elizabeth ever did that my husband would tan her good."

Candice squirmed. Both women had been staring incessantly. Now Elizabeth spoke. "Is he still here?" Her eyes were wide. Her voice was wispy soft.

Candice's heart started a slow thud. "Who?"

Millie interjected. "Why, the *Indian,* of course."

A silence fell. Candice broke it with a breath. "Oh, you mean the man who saved my life—Jack Savage is the name he goes by. Yes, he is."

Another silence.

"So it's true," Millie said. "You left here with Kincaid and came back with a half-breed Apache."

Candice gripped the arms of her chair. "Not quite—"

"Kincaid not a week in his grave, and you showed up here on the breed's horse."

Candice stood. "If you're here to accuse me of something, then you can just leave."

"Why, Candice Carter," Millie cried, standing also. "Excuse me—Candice Kincaid. It is *Kincaid,* isn't it?"

Candice flushed.

"Dear girl, we didn't come to accuse you, we came to offer our sincere sympathies. My God, to think of what you had to endure, alone with that . . . that . . ." She shuddered.

Candice stood very still.

Elizabeth turned wide, fascinated eyes on her. "Did he . . . did he . . . hurt you?"

"He saved my life," Candice said stiffly. "Now, ladies, if you'll excuse me, I have a terrible headache."

"Of course," Millie said graciously. "But, Candice, you can tell us. I mean, you look remarkably well. But—you must need to share such a horrible experience with other women. Other *white* women."

"There's nothing to share."

Millie put her arm around her. "I don't know how you can be so stoic. If it were me, I'd kill myself."

Candice wrenched free. "You have a sick mind. Sick. He never touched me."

Millie and Elizabeth both turned pitying, disbelieving glances on her.

"If he had touched me, do you think he'd still be alive?" Candice said too shrilly. "Still alive and on this ranch?"

"We thought about that. But John probably doesn't want to make too much over it, for your sake, of course, and we understand. On the other hand, he's probably got the Indian under guard. He'll hang for what he did to you. Has he sent for the major?"

"Nothing happened," Candice said stiffly, striding ahead of them and to the foyer, where she opened the door. "And if you'll excuse me, I have to lie down."

Millie and Elizabeth exchanged knowing glances. "Of course," Millie said. "We certainly understand, don't we, Elizabeth?"

CHAPTER FIFTEEN

Every time Candice thought about Millie's and Elizabeth's insinuations, she felt sick.

It was bad enough eloping and returning without the man she had supposedly married, but to return with a half-breed Apache . . .

She took a breath. The talk would die down. Nothing *had* happened. Not like they meant, anyway. But she was ashamed when she thought of what had happened—and what the reaction would be if anyone knew the whole truth. How had her life come down to this?

She managed to sneak in to see Jack after the Henderson women had left, and was relieved to see him sleeping peacefully, although he still had a fever. Later she cornered Luke as soon as he came in off the range. "How is he?"

"His fever was lower this morning. I'll check on him again now."

"Thank you, Luke."

"The size of your heart is starting to worry me, Candice," he said.

"Luke, if it was his horse in there sick, I'd be sitting with it all day."

Luke just gave her a queer look and left, heading toward the barn. Thank the Lord for her brother's compassionate nature. She bumped into Mark on her way back to the house. He was angry. "I saw the Henderson ladies on the road a while back when I was coming in," he said.

Oh, no, Candice thought.

"Jesus Christ, Candice! They started asking me things, and insinuating things . . ." His face was red. "If they'd been men I would have called them out!"

"Leave it be, Mark," Candice said. "It doesn't matter. They're just two dirty-minded gossips with nothing better to do."

"It doesn't look right, him being here, sick or not. We should turn him over to Major Bradley. There's probably a price on his head. Christ! What if there is?"

"Mark, he saved my life, and we're not turning him over

to any troops," she said, thinking about the three cowboys he had killed in front of her very eyes. In cold blood. Good God —was there a reward out for him, as there was for Geronimo? Her thoughts must have showed, because Mark demanded to know what she was thinking. "Nothing," she lied, turning away, agitated.

Before dinner, Luke took her aside and gave her good news—that Jack's fever had broken and he was sleeping. Candice felt a huge relief, and she gave Luke a grateful smile, which was quite brilliant. He looked at her and frowned thoughtfully. Candice didn't notice. But she did have a frisson of fear when Mark announced to the table that he was riding to Fort Buchanan that night.

"Tonight? What for?" her father asked.

"We got that breed here and we don't know anything about him," Mark said vehemently, not looking at Candice. "I want to know if he's wanted. Just curing him and turning him loose isn't right."

"He saved my life," Candice protested, aghast.

"Son, we owe the man that."

"Pop, Lynch was telling me that the other day the troops were cutting off Geronimo when some brown-haired breed interfered, led them away. If this man is him then he's damn sure wanted for questioning at least. I'm going. It's got to be done; what's going on here isn't right."

Candice was standing, her fork flung on the table. "What you're doing isn't right, Mark, and I'm sick of your interfering. He doesn't ride with Geronimo—I know!" She turned and strode out, angry and upset. She could hear her family arguing about what Mark was going to do—whether they agreed or not. Later, when she was in her room waiting for everyone to fall asleep, she heard him riding out.

She couldn't help but think that there were so few half-breeds with sable-colored hair and gray eyes.

That if such a man had interfered with the army, it had to be he.

Did that mean he was Geronimo's ally?

Geronimo was at war with everyone except Cochise.

She had bitten down all her nails by the time the house was bathed in darkness and everyone except Mark had come to say good night. Then she scrambled out of bed, downstairs, and into the barn, closing the door before she lit the lantern. She held it up.

Jack turned his head toward her and stared, his gray eyes lucid and angry.

He was lying on his back, his hands bound in front of him, his ankles trussed as well.

Candice hurried forward, dropping to her knees. "Who tied you up?"

"Your brother and a few of the men."

Damn Mark, Candice thought, and reached for his wrists. The knots were thick and tight. She felt his gaze on her face and met it. "I need a knife."

"My gear's over there," he said.

She looked behind her and hurried to his saddlebags, the gunbelt and knife belt. The knife slid effortlessly out of the sheath and she knelt beside him again, slicing the bonds in one motion. The instant she had done so he was on her, flipping her beneath him, pinning her with the full weight of his body, one hand coiled in her braid, the other flinging her two hands above her head. She stared, breathless, stunned. His face was so close his breath was hot on her face.

"Do you know the trouble you've caused me?"

"I'm sorry," she cried, meaning it. "You're hurting me."

"Good."

They stared.

His eyes had gold flecks in them, and his lashes were a dark, dark brown and thick and long. He had beautiful eyes, too beautiful for a man, even when so angry, although she could see the anger fading, changing, even as her own body started to relax and throb in awareness. He was hard, but not heavy. His thighs were like steel. He had quite a beard now, and his lips . . . his mouth was parted slightly, sensually curved, the lower lip fuller than the upper. She fixated on that mouth. Warm breath. She was vaguely aware that she might have stopped breathing, that her own mouth was slightly open, wet. Waiting. Something stirred between them, became heavy against her thigh. Her heart picked up a slow, heavy thud.

His head moved slightly, lowering. Candice thought, He's going to kiss me, and a hot thrill flamed through her veins. She closed her eyes, lifted her head. Their lips touched.

It was the softest of testing, the barest of brushing.

Candice opened her mouth wider, dazed, and pressed her hips against his, her thigh up into the fullness of his groin. His mouth opened and came down hard and voraciously on hers. The intensity was bruising, his teeth cut her mouth, his tongue plunged deep inside, taking her by surprise. He lifted his head, her lower lip between his teeth, pulling, then came down again, opening, sucking her lips in, then parting them urgently and thrusting his tongue deep again. And again. She opened her mouth wider to admit him, a shocked heat racing through her when his tongue flicked over hers, circling it, wrestling, trying to entice hers into a response. And then he shifted his weight abruptly, so that his thick, swollen penis settled in her groin intimately. She gasped, arching.

His hands released hers and slid down her back to grab her hips firmly, hard. His devouring mouth moved over her jaw to her neck, biting, teasing, hurting, exciting her. She arched her head back. His mouth slid abruptly down, his hands up, pushing up her breasts, and he buried his face between them.

Candice opened her eyes in shock when he was suddenly gone. He was standing, slicing through the ankle bonds, not even looking at her, moving away to the stall with the black, leading him out. She sat up, clutching her robe to her, panting, on fire. Comprehension came cruelly. She flooded with color. Her hand clamped over her mouth. Oh, God! How could she—how could they—

He was throwing the saddle on the black, already having strapped his guns on. He was moving with the speed of a hurricane. The cinch and then the bridle. Candice rose unsteadily to her feet. He swung his saddlebags on, strapping them efficiently. "You're going to open the gate."

He still hadn't looked at her.

He had kissed her.

She had let him.

"Move," he said, turning to her.

She turned wide navy-blue eyes on him.

He smiled, with no mirth. "I'm not in the mood to be hanged."

She moved then, although tears seemed to lurk at the

back of her eyes. She hurried out into the night without the lantern, and across the yard. She could feel him behind her, and hear the horse.

There was no sentry at night because Apaches rarely attacked at night, and never attacked their fortified spread. The bolt was heavy, and he leaned over her to throw it. She felt the heat of his chest and it made her heart slam. They thrust open the heavy wooden door.

She turned as he swung into the saddle. This time he was looking at her, but she couldn't see much in the shadowy night. She wished she could clearly see his eyes. She hugged herself. He pinned her with his bright gaze for one more instant, then turned and galloped away.

CHAPTER SIXTEEN

He traveled relentlessly through that night and the next day.

He wanted to get as far away from her as possible, as quickly as possible. As if doing so might erase her from his mind.

The anger was not so hard and hot anymore. It was mostly the kiss that had mitigated it. The feel of her beneath him, how she hadn't fought, hadn't been repulsed, how she had arched her soft, hot groin into the thickness of his. She had wanted him. For that one kiss, she had wanted him. But the triumph was tempered with the knowledge of defeat.

Candice Carter was not for him, no matter what.

It didn't matter that her father and her oldest brother's bigotry was tempered somewhat by fairness. Nor did it matter that she had come herself to tend him—taking care of him again. Or even that her brother had, too. What mattered was that he was considered the enemy. Even by her.

When he had awoken to find his horse and her gone, he had been more than furious—he had been acutely disappointed. Maybe it was because for a moment he had dared to hope she could be more than a pampered, frightened white woman. She was a fool not to know that he would go after her—as much to retrieve his horse as to look her in the eye with all the contempt he could muster. He had started out at a ground-eating dogtrot; he could track at night as well as in daylight. And he knew she had only a few hours on him. But he wasn't up to it. His pace had slowed. He'd had to stop. When he'd gotten to the ranch gates only his determination drove him on and kept him rigidly upright. If he'd been in better health he could have scaled the walls silently, maybe even stolen his horse back without anyone knowing. But he wanted more than just the horse. He had to see her. And it had almost been the death of him, both because of the fever and because of the white men who were too eager to kill him for having saved her life.

Then the compassion in her eyes, along with the guilt, had nearly caved him in right there.

But none of it mattered, and he was regaining his strength—and his senses. Kissing her had been the most uncontrolled, impulsive thing he had ever done, and he'd half done it out of anger. But the desire had been too close to the surface, and her response hadn't helped.

If only he could forget it.

The night before he arrived at the camp Jack sent up a signal with torches. The message was simple. He was a friend, carrying bad news, and he was coming.

Shozkay's band was larger than most. Over two dozen *gohwahs* spotted the little canyon that was lush with fall foliage, bright with leaves turning gold, and well watered by a racing creek. Beyond the camp, the fields had been cleared and planted with maize and pumpkin. The harvest had already begun. Several long irrigation ditches ran through the fields. As Jack rode in to the camp, he could smell venison and elk smoking, and hides newly hung, drying in the sun. There was even the spicy-sweet aroma of mescal cakes baking in deep ovens. He inhaled deeply—savoring the wonderful smells.

He was recognized instantly as he rode into the camp. Squaws and braves smiled at him, and he heard a woman running, gossiping already, crying to anyone who would hear that the second son of Machu had returned, looking like a White Eyes. He smiled. To the whites he knew he looked unmistakably Apache.

He slid off the black and saw his brother approaching.

Shozkay was chief, so he did not run, but he walked with long, rapid strides, clad only in thigh-high moccasins and a traditional buckskin breechcloth. His name meant "White Bear." He was as tall as Jack, and as broad of shoulder, but less massive. A headcloth kept his long black hair out of his face, and he wore an elaborate necklace similar to Jack's, except that a row of wolf's teeth made a double strand with the turquoise. There was a broad smile on his face as he embraced Jack. "*Shik'isn.* My brother. Usen has guarded you well."

"*Shik'isn,*" Jack returned the greeting. "The many winters sit well with you." He clasped Shozkay back, and they separated.

"What is this?" Shozkay said, straight-faced, fingering

Jack's rawhide Stetson, which was hanging on the pommel of his saddle.

Jack bit back a smile. "A hat."

"A white man's hat?" Shozkay picked up the hat and put it on his head. He started laughing. Some of the tribe's people who had gathered started laughing too.

Jack tried not to smile, but failed. "You look ridiculous," he said softly.

Shozkay stopped posturing abruptly, eyes wide with mock incredulity. "Me?" He pointed at Jack's chest. "And what is this?"

The laughter died. "I think you know well enough what this is, you wear one yourself."

"The necklace of a warrior," Shozkay said.

Jack said nothing.

"An Apache warrior." Shozkay let the words sink in, then put the hat on Jack's head. They stared at each other. "Does wearing the hat make you white?"

"I am already white," Jack said quietly.

"Then why do you wear the necklace?"

"Because I am also Apache."

"The hat does not go with the necklace," Shozkay said firmly.

"It goes if I say it does," Jack said, hard and grim.

They looked at each other for another beat, then Shozkay grabbed the hat and placed it back on the pommel. "At least while you are here, leave it there." He turned to Savage. "I thought you would never come back," he said intensely, and he threw his arm around him again, giving him a hard, brief hug.

Jack relaxed. "It's been too long," he said softly.

"Three winters too long," Shozkay returned.

"If you mean for me to feel guilty . . ."

"Have you found what you are looking for?"

"No," Jack said, shortly. He adroitly changed the topic. "I have buried a Child of the Water," Jack said soberly.

"Tell me," Shozkay demanded. He listened intently, anger showing only in his midnight-black eyes. "These men must pay," he said at last.

"The fourth man is marked—I shot him in the shoulder —and will be easy to find."

Shozkay nodded.

"How is Mother?"

Shozkay placed a restraining hand upon him. "She has not been well," he said.

Jack stared.

"Father has been calling her."

Jack's startled emotion showed in his silver eyes. Machu, his adoptive father, was dead. If he was calling Jack's mother, it meant only one thing. He quickly turned and left, making his way through the camp deliberately, overwhelmed with what he had just found out. Returning was hard enough.

No one stopped him, although some children who were too young to know him shrieked and pointed. Normally, Jack would have stopped to tease them, winning them over eventually. But now he could only think of what Shozkay had said. She wasn't well. She was dying.

Inside the *gohwah* he could see Nalee's large bulk lying on a bed of hides. The old woman seemed to be sleeping. In her youth, she was said to have been as fast a runner as all the boys, and a beautiful girl. There was still beauty on her face, which was high-cheekboned and aristocratic. Jack sank down next to her, for a moment just looking at her. In sleep, her wrinkles were minimal, and he glimpsed the young girl she had once been. His heart ached unbearably. He loved her.

When he had first seen Nalee, he had been a frightened, wary boy. He didn't speak Spanish, and obviously not Apache, so there was no way he could be told that he was being given to this woman as a special gift. He had stopped fighting his captors very rapidly—there was no point. But he had tried to escape once, only to be caught before he had even left the narrow entrance of the stronghold canyon where the tribe camped.

Nalee gave him food and then sent him with the other children of the tribe, including Shozkay, who regarded him suspiciously. An old man was showing the children animal tracks, then instructing them in tracking the animals to their lairs. Jack found himself tagging along, unable to understand except by perception what they were discussing. When the old man found a new set of tracks and pointed to him, Jack knew it was his turn to trail the squirrel. It was in his mind to refuse stubbornly, but Shozkay gave him a push. Everyone was waiting to see what he would do. He tracked the animal right to its tree with pure determination, and maybe a little luck. The old man clapped him on the shoulder. *"Enju, Niño Salvaje, enju."*

Jack had already learned his name, the one they were calling him, and he had learned a few simple words, including this one, which seemed to mean "well done" or "good." He felt a stirring of pride.

And later that night when Shozkay was talking and pointing at him, relating what had happened that afternoon, he grew hot with being the object of their discussion. But when he looked up, when the man, Machu, smiled, and the woman, Nalee, beamed, he felt more than a stirring—he felt pride. He knew they were pleased with what he had done.

Now Jack took Nalee's hand. Her eyes fluttered open, and she started. He smiled tenderly. She smiled back. "I knew you would come."

"I am here, *shimaa,"* he said, emotion creeping into his voice. She wasn't his natural mother, but she was the only one he had ever known. And as far as he was concerned, she was as much a real mother to him as she was to Shozkay. "Is there anything I can get you?"

"No, *shiye'.* Now I have everything." She reached up to stroke his cheek. "It has been too long." She sighed.

"I'm sorry," he said, meaning it. He saw that she had lost weight. She was still a large woman, but not as large as she had been. He held her hand tighter.

"Now I can go in peace," she said softly. "Machu awaits." She smiled weakly at him. "I am so tired."

"Shimaa, not yet," Jack said, his voice breaking. "Please, don't go. *Shitaa'* has waited this long for you, he can wait a little longer." He felt tears welling up in his eyes.

"I have only been waiting to say good-bye to you." Her eyes were suddenly crystal clear. "How is life with the white man, *shiye'?"*

"Enju," he managed. *Good, it is well.* He would never tell her the truth. That he could walk in both worlds, white and Apache, but not easily. That he did not belong to their world and could not remain in this one.

"Have you chosen a warrior's name for yourself, son?

The time has long passed for you to take a proud, brave name."

"Yes," he murmured, not wanting to tell her.

"Tell me." She smiled.

"Jack Savage." He regarded her steadily and could not miss the disappointment that rose in her eyes.

"A name of the *pindah*."

"Yes."

"First you leave the people to live in their world. Now you choose their name. Are you turning your back on the people, on everything your parents have raised you to be, have given you?"

"No, *shimaa*, no."

Nalee sighed wearily, trying to raise herself up. Jack gently propped her up, a tear spilling onto his cheek. "Don't distress yourself, *shimaa*. It's not important." But of course it was.

"It is important. When my son comes home wearing a white man's name, it is important. You are as much Apache as white, *shiye'*, and you must never forget it—Niño Salvaje."

A command, using his name of childhood. "I could never forget, believe me," he said, very softly.

" 'Jack' was the name your natural father gave you," she mused, stroking his hand. "The great warrior Cochise named you Niño Salvaje. I will know you from today as Salvaje—the Fierce One."

Jack fought the overwhelming urge to cry. Not now, he told himself, it is too soon.

"Soon you will marry?" It was a hopeful question.

"There is no one I want," he replied honestly.

"Then find someone, Salvaje," she said. "You are too fine a man not to have sons."

The mention of finding a woman to bear his children added to his grief in one vivid, painful memory. He could still see Chilahe, his first wife, lying so still and dead, in a pool of all her life's blood, their daughter stillborn. But the way his mother had used his name had turned her wish into another command—one he could not refuse. "Yes, *shimaa*," he said respectfully.

"There is always Datiye. She still wants you. She would remarry you."

Jack nodded, choking up from deep inside.

"But I feel in my heart that you will take a white wife this time. I do not understand. Although white blood fights red blood in your veins, your heart and soul are Apache." She closed her eyes. "One day, *shiye'*, you will have to make a choice."

Jack lifted her hand to his face. Tears rolled freely down his cheeks. And her words echoed. Didn't she know that he had already made his choice?

Nalee had fallen back to sleep. Shozkay came in and the two brothers sat with her for a long time, until the moon had risen well into the sky. No one interrupted, respecting their right to be with their dying mother. Somewhere around midnight she awoke, asking for water. Shozkay raised the bowl to her lips, helping her to drink. "I see Machu," she murmured. "Still as handsome as the day we met."

Jack stroked her hair. "Yes, *shimaa.*"

"He beckons. He is very happy," she said, so softly he could barely hear.

Nalee died an hour later. Her breathing suddenly slowed and stopped. Just before she died, she opened her eyes and smiled at her sons.

Immediately two elders came to bathe and dress her body. The camp echoed with distressed wailing and keening, an eerie, distinctly Apache sound of mourning. Jack stumbled away. With his knife, as was the custom, he chopped his near-shoulder-length hair as short as possible. The tears flowed easily but silently—he couldn't make the noises that wanted to rack his body with grief.

As soon as Nalee was prepared, she and as many of her personal possessions as possible were placed on her favorite horse, and the burial party, consisting of Jack, Shozkay, and two of their male cousins, set out. She was buried in a deep crevice far from the campsite—which would now be moved, because of her death—along with most of her possessions, including a beautiful hunting knife with a turquoise-encrusted handle that Jack had made for her. The grave was filled in, her horse killed, and the rest of her possessions scattered about the gravesite. By the time they had returned to the camp, the sun had been up for several hours.

Jack wandered down to a running creek. The water was

icy cold but he didn't care; his grief had numbed him. He stripped off his buckskins.

He bathed in the creek mindlessly. His sadness would not lessen. Nalee was joining her husband in the afterlife all Apache believed in. Jack believed in it too, but he wanted her back. He stepped out of the creek, then tensed. There was someone in the shadows of the pinyon trees. His gun lay on the ground by the heap of his buckskins. Suddenly, without warning, he darted one hand out and grabbed the intruder.

It was Datiye, and she gasped in pain.

Jack stared at her, still holding her wrist. She had loosened her long, jet-black hair, and the sunlight danced from it. His grip relaxed. Her eyes searched his. She was one of the prettier squaws; she had Apache features—high cheekbones, deep-set eyes, a straight, slightly hooked nose. Her figure was almost perfect, long-legged and slim-hipped, with small but enticing breasts. She was Chilahe's younger sister, and he had married her as was his duty almost a year after his first wife's death.

And he had divorced her when he left his people, so she would be free to remarry—to be cared for by another brave.

Jack released her. "What are you doing here? You could get in big trouble if someone sees you here, watching me bathe."

"I don't care," she said softly. "You are grieving. I have come to take away the grief."

Jack turned away. "You can't take away the grief, woman. No one can." He bent for his clothes. When he straightened, he felt her soft buckskin-clad body against his back, her hands on his shoulders. He quickly turned to face her, removing her hands and pushing her away. "No."

"Please," she breathed. "I waited a whole winter for you to return, and then I married. Now I am a widow. Let me love you. It will make you forget."

"I do not want to forget," Jack snapped. "And the last thing I feel like doing now is making love."

Datiye's mouth trembled. "I helped you to forget once, or have you forgotten? I want to be your woman."

Jack had pulled on his buckskin pants. He buckled the gunbelt with the solitary Colt. "I already have a woman," he told her.

"A white woman?" Her voice quavered with tears.

"Yes." Not that it was true. But this infatuation had gone on long enough. Even before he had married Chilahe, Datiye, who was only a year younger than her sister, had indicated to him that she was open to his attentions. He had not given them. When they were only children—boys and girls being taught together in the ways of the woods by Grandfather—she had always trailed after him in particular, and had begged him to teach her the strange language of the White Eyes. He had. When Chilahe had died, even after mourning, he had not wanted to wed Datiye, but it had been his duty to do so and provide for her family.

Chilahe had been a good wife, a hard worker, and eager to please him in their bed of hides. He had married her in his sixteenth or seventeenth winter, shortly after being given warrior status. Never had he dreamed that the most beautiful girl in the band would want him, but she had. His desire for a wife had been natural—he needed a woman to care for him and share his bed. It was the next logical step for a brave after attaining warrior status and enough possessions to pay the bride price.

So he had cared for Chilahe. Together they had lived and laughed, and learned a hot, adolescent passion. And even though that had been a long time ago, he would never care for another woman again. The reason was simple. He had no room in his life for any woman—Apache or white.

CHAPTER SEVENTEEN

Jack sat under a tree by the creek, alone with his memories. After Datiye had gone, no one approached, knowing his thoughts would be full of his mother. The other Apache were both polite in not wanting to intrude, and afraid—for thinking about the dead could cause her ghost to linger.

Shozkay joined him, his approach so silent that Jack didn't even hear him coming. When they were younger they had had a game: One would hide and the other would have to find him. The object was to escape if you were the prey and to capture if you were the hunter. In either case, only by moving soundlessly and stealthily could one win. Jack had never been able to beat Shozkay—although his brother had assured him that he was as quiet as any Apache. Even back then, Shozkay had exhibited those traits that had eventually made him the band's chief. He was not just brave, he was cunning; not just smart, but fair; and he was the best hunter and tracker, the fastest runner, the most deadly shot with the bow and arrow when he reached manhood. Although Jack could outride him from their youth, and could later outwrestle him, Shozkay was the band's obvious choice to take over leadership when Coyote Fijo wanted to step down.

Jack half smiled. "Once again, my brother, I have lost our childhood game," he said.

Shozkay sank down beside him. "I do not think you would lose anymore, if you were not so buried in grief." He handed him a clay jug filled with *tulapai*, liquor made from corn.

Jack absorbed his brother's compliment. He knew Shozkay never said anything he didn't mean. He guzzled the *tulapai*, then handed the jug back. Shozkay swigged.

"I already miss her," Jack said after a while, careful not to mention her name. It was bad luck to even speak of the dead, much less refer to them by name.

"My heart is heavy too."

They drank in silence. A breeze stirred the pines and grass, and an owl hooted. Both men started, looking at each other quickly. Everyone knew spirits favored returning as owls and coyotes. After a while Jack said, "At least she is with Father."

Shozkay nodded. "Or she will be," he murmured, and the owl hooted again. In broad daylight. There was no doubt who it was. He was starting to feel the effects of the *tulapai*, and he leaned against a rock. "She told me one of her wishes was for you to have sons."

Jack started. Then: "Yes, I know."

"We have many fine squaws."

Jack managed a faint smile. "Twice was enough." A vivid image of Candice Carter assaulted him. And with her image came a poignant yearning.

Shozkay regarded him with an attempt at sobriety. The jug was half empty. "It is not healthy to have no woman—just like it is not healthy to have too many too often."

"True," Jack agreed, nodding thoughtfully now that the alcohol had lessened his grief a bit. As an Apache he had been raised to believe in sexual moderation. With both of his wives he had not been very successful at attempting to avoid excess. He had always, deep inside, believed that the reason for that was his white blood. Now he imagined having a white woman like Candice Carter for a wife. He would never be able to stay out of her bed. He made a sound, not exactly a laugh, with a hard edge to it.

"What is so funny—or so sad?" Shozkay was too perceptive.

Jack didn't want to tell him, but he had been alone for too long with no one to talk to. He pulled a fistful of grass from the ground and clenched it. "I hate the white man's whores."

"The few I have seen were ugly, fat, and dirty," Shozkay agreed.

Jack threw the grass away. Candice was beautiful, slim except for her voluptuous breasts—and clean. His loins tightened with the memory of her.

"So you have not taken a white wife."

Another derisive sound.

"Why not?"

"Why not?" Jack laughed. "A breed like myself?"

"I see," his brother said. "Do not go back to the *pindah*. We are your kind. Stay here."

"I can't," Jack said, guzzling from the jug.

"Your second wife has moon-eyes for you."

"No."

"Then there is someone?"

"No," Jack gritted, then looked his brother in the eye. "Yes. Maybe. Ahh, she is white. You don't understand."

"Tell me."

"There's nothing to tell. To her I am not a man but something less—a half-breed."

"Then make her change her mind," Shozkay said.

Jack looked at him. He drank again. The advice echoed, disturbing him.

"Can one woman defeat Niño Salvaje?"

Jack met his gaze. "Maybe," he said softly, "this one can."

"I don't think so," Shozkay replied.

"How is your wife?" Jack asked, abruptly changing the topic. But he couldn't shake the words: *Then change her mind.*

"Ahh . . ." Shozkay grinned broadly. "Very impossible. I have to beat her twice a day."

Jack laughed with real humor. Shozkay had married one of the most beautiful women he had ever seen. Her name was Luz. She was not from their tribe, but a Chiricahua Apache. Although usually when a warrior married he joined his wife's people, to provide for her family, it was not unheard of for an elder son or a single son to remain in the band of his birth and uproot his wife from her own kin. Shozkay had done just that.

Luz was very tall, just a head shorter than her husband, and willowy. Her face was oval, her hair jet black. She had green eyes. Her grandmother had been a white woman. Although she had initially shown Shozkay that she was interested in him, she had rejected his subsequent advances, and he had courted her furiously for six months before he had dared allow his kin to send gifts to her family for her hand.

Luz had returned the gifts—which was an unequivocal rejection—but Shozkay had persisted, and the next time he had sent gifts, they had not been returned.

They had been married four years. Jack had never seen two people as close. Sometimes the way they looked at each other amused him. Sometimes it gave him a strange, disturbing sensation. He and Chilahe had never shared the depth of emotion that his brother and his wife had. "She is a good woman, Shozkay," he said softly.

"Yes."

Jack smiled. "Maybe you had better beat her three times a day, heh? To make her better."

They both chuckled at the absurdity of it.

Jack had to focus hard to find his bedroll, even though he knew he should have been able to locate it blindfolded, or without the nearly full moon to see by. But that was the problem. He was having trouble with his vision. He chuckled aloud. He and Shozkay had drunk several jugs of *tulapai*. They were both going to think they were dying in the morning, but right now he didn't give a damn.

After a thorough search of the area to the southeast of the camp, which he determined was where he had laid his gear, he finally found the spot.

Shozkay had offered him his *gohwah*. So had Hayilkah, and numerous others, including the dead brave's family. But Jack had refused. There was nothing he liked more than sleeping in the starlight, especially when the air was mountain fresh and slightly cool, like now. He lay on his blanket and fell right into sleep.

He had a wonderful dream. A woman was pressing her bare, soft breasts against his back, kissing his neck, his ear. The whole length of her strained against him, and she pressed the soft heat of her womanhood against his buttocks, her hands stroking the hair on his chest. Her hands roamed lower, light and deft, and Jack was in bliss—an excited bliss. He rolled over to face her, enveloping her in his arms, his mouth seeking hers, finding it. It was so real. It was too real. Jack woke up.

He did have a woman in his arms, and she was naked—as was he. She was silky soft, writhing against him, making soft little noises. Her hair was long and straight, and spilled over his hands as they roamed her back. Her nipples were hard and teased his chest.

Her hips arched up against his and begged him on. Jack's whole body was trembling, on fire. He thrust into her, hard, fast, and when she cried his name he knew it was Datiye.

When he awoke she was gone. She was the second thing he remembered. The first was his mother, and the heaviness in his heart, the awful feeling of loss. Then he recalled that Datiye had come to him in the night. He knew she had deep feelings for him, and he sensed that becoming involved with her again would cause him trouble. Although he did not consider last night a renewal of their relationship, he was sure she did. He grew angry.

Angry at her. For she would never have gotten what she wanted if she hadn't taken advantage of his inebriated state. If he was going to lie with a woman he would have chosen someone else, maybe the slim young widow Barhilye. But not Datiye. And he was angry at himself. Inebriated or not, he should have resisted. He did not want a woman in his life who would make demands on him.

He thought about the three *pindah* he had killed, the ones who had staked out the novice warrior—the young boy. He thought about the fourth man, the one he had marked by shooting him, and he thought of the vengeance that would follow shortly. A war party would probably go out within a few days.

He packed up all his gear, feeling grim.

He heard them before he saw them. He was cinching up the saddle, and he turned slightly to see Datiye standing with Shozkay and Luz. He had just finished when she ran to him. "You're leaving!"

He turned abruptly, his silver eyes hard. "This does not change anything."

"Do not be angry," she said softly. "Last night was beautiful, all I have dreamed of. I wanted you very much."

Jack did not reply.

"I will never marry again," she said seriously. "I am yours now. I will wait for you to return."

Jack's jaw clenched. "No, Datiye. I do not want you to wait for me. You are not my woman."

Her expression didn't change. "You have my heart. What happened last night was only right."

"Last night means nothing!" Jack exploded.

"No." She touched his shoulder, making him turn back to her. "You are very wrong."

He shifted impatiently, looked past her at his brother

and his wife. Datiye gave him one last look before drifting away and disappearing into the trees. Shozkay and Luz came forward. It was hard meeting his brother's expression. "So short a time with us?" Luz asked. "Usen walk with you, Salvaje. Do not stay away so long this time."

He smiled. "Usen walk with you, Luz."

She turned and left.

Jack faced his brother's dark, disturbed gaze. "One day," Shozkay said, "maybe you will explain this to me."

"One day," Jack said, "maybe I could try."

"My heart is too heavy. This time our paths must come together sooner."

"I do not belong here."

"Your place is here."

"As a coward?" Jack said bitterly.

"You are no coward," Shozkay said.

"I cannot ride against my own blood."

"The Apache have many, many enemies. Papago. Pima. Ute. Comanche. Mexican. Spanish. Not just the White Eyes."

"Shall I stay here, then, and ride only when we war on the Pima? And when we cross the path of the blue soldiers—shall I turn to hide in the bush and wait for the battle to finish? And then will you still call me Salvaje—after I have watched Apaches die?"

"Go, then," Shozkay said passionately. "Go back to the *pindah* and stay with them." He strode angrily away.

"Shoz!" Jack started after him, but stopped when his brother disappeared into the forest. His grip on the black's reins was tight. For a long moment he stood beside his mount, looking at nothing but the flat expanse of leather saddle. Finally he swung up.

Would it always be like this? he wondered, new pain fighting the old.

And then he turned and rode away.

CHAPTER EIGHTEEN

He knew he shouldn't stay. But there was no urge to ride on.

Tucson lay before him, a dry, hot town that was nothing more than a collection of flat, square adobe homes, broken-down corrals, and sore-backed mules—all surrounding the thick, crumbling Presidio walls. An American flag floated atop a sentry tower. It had been hoisted there in March of '56, when the last of the Mexican Federales had left.

Jack rode into town clad from head to toe in buckskin, a rawhide, flat-brimmed hat on his head. He was aware of the looks he was getting. He sat straight and tall and did not miss a single thing. As usual, Tucson had more than its share of drifters—miners, vacqueros, Indians, half-breeds, bandits—as well as the gamblers and settlers that passed through, and the occasional soldiers from Fort Buchanan. He kept his eye out for the latter. Interfering with the troops the other day had not been the smartest thing he could have done—but he hadn't been able to resist.

He wondered if she might come into town.

Instantly, he was angry with himself for thinking about her, and he headed into one of the saloons, a single-room adobe shack with straw and dirt littering the floor, the tables rickety, the chairs broken down. The owner was white and sported two heavy revolvers. He stared briefly, then turned away—in his establishment he saw everything. A thin, dark-skinned, half-breed girl served. The patrons were all armed and varied from swarthy types who had obviously drifted north from the border and were up to no good—to sun-burned, teenage soldiers and a couple of cowboys from an outlying spread. Jack took a chair, set it with its back to the wall, and settled down. The thin girl came over.

She looked all of fifteen. She did not register a single emotion when she looked at his Apache leggings. He ordered a whiskey, watched her walk away stiffly—as if she were in pain. One of the cowboys near his chair at a table said the word "Apache," and Jack's ears instantly became attuned.

"You think so?"

"Don't know. Warden said it was Cochise."

"Ah, shit," said the first, a boy of about twenty. "If Cochise stole Warden's boy there's gonna be trouble. But why would he steal the boy?"

"Don't know. It was a raid. They also made off with some oxen. The boy ain't even his—belongs to that Mexican woman he's living with. But Warden says it was Cochise, says he trailed him all the way to the San Pedro River. Last I heard he was up at the fort, begging for troops. But there's none available—least that's what the major told him."

"Damn," said the first. Then: "Well, guess there's no point in worryin' now." He stood. "Got to get the supplies or the boss man will lay into me. You gonna be at the Bastas' barbecue tomorrow?"

The second man grinned. "Wouldn't miss it. The whole of Tucson will be there. Maybe I'll even get me a dance with Candice Carter."

The other man's face darkened.

"Hey, take it easy, McGraw, I was only kidding! After all —she run off with that Kincaid and now she's in mourning. I don't think she'll be dancing, even with you." He laughed.

McGraw swore and left abruptly, knocking over his chair.

Jack looked after him. Who was that? *The whole of Tucson will be there.*

She'll be there.

He drank and fought with himself. He pictured her vividly, and it both aroused and angered him. He imagined her at the barbecue, in the arms of the dark-haired boy named McGraw. Laughing, dancing the white man's dance. Shozkay's words suddenly echoed. *Then change her mind.*

Change her mind.

It would be a foolish thing to do. It was one thing to sit in a saloon in Tucson, another to go to a barbecue at a ranch. But he wanted to see her again.

He had to.

Abruptly Jack got up, tossed a few coins to the girl, and strode out. He paused in the bright morning light, stared across the street at the general store. He crossed the dusty thoroughfare slowly, not thinking now, because he didn't want to talk himself out of it. Two matrons with a young woman hastily veered away from him. He opened the door, a bell tinkling.

A heavy Spanish woman was fingering bolts of cloth. She was the only customer. A lean white man was behind a counter, scribbling in a book. Jack closed the door behind him, and the man looked up.

He looked Jack up and down and closed his ledger. Jack strolled over.

"Yes?" the clerk said.

"I need clothes," Jack said slowly. "I want pants, a shirt. And a new hat, maybe with a scarf. A red scarf."

The clerk folded his arms. "You got money?"

Jack reached into his shirt and removed a money pouch. "Yes."

The clerk smiled, reaching out. "Well, let's see what we can do."

CHAPTER NINETEEN

Everyone was staring.

Candice sat very still on the seat of the buckboard. The barbecue was in full swing. Beyond where they had braked amid the other wagons and horses, a huge steer and a pig were roasting. Two long wooden tables were laid out with all kinds of dishes—tortillas and beans, candied squash and baked pumpkin, loaves of cornbread and bowls of corn pudding. It was early, midmorning, and everyone was standing about in groups. They had been talking and laughing animatedly. Until now.

The Carters had just arrived, and John-John was waiting, hand outstretched, to help Candice down. People had turned to look at her. And whisper. She had expected something, some small level of interest, but not this.

"C'mon, Sis, or are you going to sit up there all day?"

Candice bit her lip and let John-John swing her down. Her father had already drifted off to say hello to Henderson, but Luke and Mark were hanging back protectively. Candice saw Millie whispering frantically to another woman, never taking her eyes off her. Luke took her arm, giving her a smile. "It'll be okay," he said.

Candice lifted her chin. She was in mourning, of course, in gray silk trimmed with black lace and a pale straw bonnet tied with black ribbon. It was too hot for full black.

As they left the wagons and neared the barbecue, individuals shifted uneasily, then quickly looked away. All four ranchers from the Santa Cruz Valley had come, bringing their families. The Bastas were there, of course, as were a few of their neighbors, and Tucson's upper crust—mostly merchants, some freighters, a lawyer, a miner, a driver for the Butterfield Overland mail, their wives and children. There were also two officers present from Fort Buchanan, some forty miles south of the Basta hacienda. Although everyone present was technically American—such citizenship having been conferred upon those who remained in Tucson after '53 —most were of Spanish descent and Mexican birth. Perhaps three or four of every ten men were American born, and the number of such women could be counted on one hand. Almost every woman of marriageable age was wed.

Candice heard someone say the name Kincaid. She realized she was clinging harder to Luke's arm than necessary. Beyond Millie and Theresa Smith she saw Elizabeth Henderson standing with one of her old beaux, Judge Reinhart, his little daughter hovering beside them. She felt a stab of anger, even jealousy. And then, to her surprise, he came striding over.

"Candice," Judge said, taking her hand. He was slim and dark-haired. "I'm sorry about your husband."

Candice felt her mouth quiver. Bless Judge, who was such a gentleman. "Thank you, Judge. Thank you so much."

He held her hand for one more beat, although it was unseemly. "Are you all right?" And she knew he wasn't talking about Kincaid any more.

"Yes." God—would she never escape *him*?

He smiled then. She smiled back.

"Candice, Candice."

She whirled at the sound of Tim McGraw's voice. He was smiling, unable to keep the pleasure at seeing her off his face. She found herself smiling back, and when he took her hand and told her, a touch huskily, that he couldn't say he was sorry, she felt a wonderful relief. Everything wasn't as bad as she had thought. It was going to be all right.

She was just going to ignore the whispered references to a half-breed that were buzzing all around her. But it proved harder to do than she thought—especially when a few hours later, after her brother Luke had tried to raise her spirits by pulling her into a vigorous dance, Judge cornered her under a mesquite tree.

"Candice, do you want to talk about it?"

She held back her anger. "Talk about what, Judge?" She lowered her lashes in a consciously demure gesture.

"It's all over the valley. What happened. That you were captured by a half-breed Apache."

Her eyes flashed. "That's not true! And what else are they saying?"

"Well, I've heard a few different versions," Judge began, looking distressed. *"Are* you all right?"

"I am fine," Candice said vehemently. "But I am sick of everyone thinking the worst!" She turned and strode away.

Remembering the kiss.

And it wasn't just because of Judge's words, or the gossips she was surrounded by. The kiss had haunted her and bothered her and agitated her for the past few days—ever since he had left.

It was one thing to feel compassion for a hurt man. It was another to allow a half-breed Indian to kiss her.

The guilt and the shame were intolerable. If any of her brothers ever found out, they would kill him—and certainly never respect her again. It was too awful to even contemplate. She would never be able to hold up her head around them—and if any of these people knew the truth . . .

She flushed. Furiously. But the anger was directed at herself. How could she have allowed him to kiss her? Why hadn't she fought, struggled, screamed? And—worse—she had been more than passive. She had actually enjoyed his touch.

That was too outrageous and unbelievable to face, so she didn't.

Everyone had assumed Jack Savage had escaped on his own. When Mark had returned, he had been furious over Jack's disappearance. No one had known that Mark had had him tied, but no one seemed too upset over it. Her brother, Luke, did give her one long, thoughtful glance. Candice had forced herself to meet his gaze, but she'd felt her face pinkening. There was no way they could possibly guess that she had set Jack free.

There was one good thing. There was no reward posted for a gray-eyed half-breed, and Candice was surprised at the level of relief she felt. She just wished she could stop thinking about him, stop remembering the shared intimacy—God.

And five minutes later, when she was dancing a jig in Tim McGraw's arms, she looked past Tim's shoulder and thought she was seeing things. She actually tripped on Tim's foot and almost fell on her face except that Tim's strong arms were around her. She stared.

It was him.

CHAPTER TWENTY

He was standing completely apart from everyone, leaning against an oak tree. He was dressed from head to foot in store-bought clothes. Candice could not believe what she was seeing, the transformation. A spotless, brand-new black Stetson, a white cotton shirt, red bandana, and black trousers tucked into spanking new black boots. She looked at his face again. He was staring right at her.

The jolt took her breath away.

"Who is that?" McGraw was asking jealously.

Candice realized she was staring, and she quickly turned away, although she couldn't stop seeing him in her mind's eye. She was about to tell Tim "No one," but knew Jack's identity would soon be known—and then Tim would think she was hiding something. She bit her lip and found herself glancing at Jack again. He hadn't taken his eyes from her. She remembered his body stretched out on top of hers, his mouth hard, sucking and nipping and caressing hers, and she flamed. "That's Jack Savage," she said very softly.

McGraw whirled around, his eyes wide. "That breed?"

Candice had her hand on his arm, darting a nervous glance back at Jack. He had pushed himself away from the tree, watching them. "Tim, let it be. He saved my life. He has a right to be here too."

"He sure as hell doesn't," Tim growled. "And I don't like the way he's looking at you."

"If you make trouble, Tim," Candice said, "I'll never speak to you again."

He stared, then clamped his mouth shut.

Candice led him away, trying not to look back. Her heart was beating wildly. Why was he here? Oh—how could he be so foolish? The High C hands would surely recognize him, even in his new clothes—and if they didn't, Mark would, and he'd be sure to make trouble. She gnawed on her lip and quickly looked around at the crowd. No one was even looking at the man in black and white with the red scarf, standing by himself in the shade of the tree. But she couldn't shake her uneasiness.

Why had he come?

"I can't believe you'd stick up for him," Tim said harshly.

"What? Tim, I'm so thirsty—could you please bring me some lemonade?" She watched him stride off. Her hands were shaking. She pulled out a linen handkerchief and blotted her face very delicately. It was so hot. Still holding the linen to her face, she turned toward Jack and peered over the handkerchief's white lace edge.

He didn't smile, and he didn't look away.

Down came the handkerchief, and Candice began biting her knuckle. He looked so lonely—and alone. So separate from the crowd of laughing friends. Not able to come any closer, watching from afar. And he was extraordinarily handsome.

Her heart twisted.

Tim returned with the lemonade, and Candice was quick to pretend to be inspecting a cut on her hand. She gave him a brilliant smile. "Thank you, Tim." She took his arm and pulled him away.

Jack shoved his hands deeper in the pockets of his new trousers. The sun was moving, and the shadows around him were getting darker. Which was a good thing, because he couldn't seem to take his eyes off her. He knew he should never have come.

All around him there was laughter and camaraderie. It was something he had been very conscious of from the moment he'd arrived. Just like now, alone under this tree, he was very conscious of being apart from it all. The not-belonging was as old as he was, but the way he was feeling it today had never been so new.

Some of the women were dancing to a fiddler and a harmonica player. Candice had been dancing in McGraw's arms not too long ago, just the way he'd imagined, with laughter on her face, looking impossibly beautiful. The jealousy he'd felt then, and the jealousy he was feeling now, was like a clamp around his chest.

Another man had joined her and McGraw, and they were all sharing a blanket and the shade of a tree. Someone else, a third man, came up to her and asked her something—for a dance? She gave him a wonderful smile while declining. He imagined how it would feel to be on the receiving end of that smile. Then he grew angry with himself for even thinking it, for doing this to himself, for being such a fool as to buy all these clothes and using the last of his cash. But he didn't push away from the tree.

She was looking at him.

Jack was very much aware of his heart fluttering when she excused herself from her admirers and started walking toward him. Perspiration gathered under the crown of his hat and beneath his arms. She couldn't be coming this way. She was looking at the ground, stopping to talk to a couple. Laughing, darting him a glance, and breaking free. She *was* coming to him. But it took her a small eternity.

"Hello . . . Mr. Savage."

He tried to sound casual. It was hard, when he couldn't even swallow. "Miss Candice."

She stared at him—big navy eyes that he fell into. He shifted. "You look beautiful today."

She blushed. "It's just mourning gray."

"I know."

"I . . . I don't know if you should be here."

He felt anger, and his tone was sarcastic. "Don't worry— I'm keeping my distance. *You* shouldn't be *here.*"

She was wringing her hands. "I know, but . . ."

"But what?"

"You don't have anyone to talk to. You haven't even taken any food."

"Don't pity me."

"I'm not!" Her eyes flashed. But, oh, she did—in a different way than she'd ever felt pity before. She longed to hold his face and smooth the lines of despair away, and make him smile. Just once, for a short time. She hadn't been able to bear seeing him standing so alone beneath the tree.

He relaxed. She smiled, but he didn't return it. His eyes searched hers unwaveringly. It made her skin tingle and flush. "Would you—would you like me to get you some food?"

"I've eaten." Then he added, "Thank you."

Candice bit her lip. The fiddler was playing, and they were all talked out. But she didn't want to leave him, not just yet. They stood in an awkward silence for a few minutes more.

"You're a good dancer," Jack said unexpectedly. His

mind was on McGraw. He wanted to ask her what their relationship was.

She smiled radiantly. "Do you want to dance?"

He went stiff. His heart was beating too hard. For a minute he couldn't say a thing. Then: "I don't know how."

Her face fell, but only for a moment. She reached out and took his hand. "I'll teach you," she said.

When he didn't answer she moved closer, taking one of his hands and putting it on her tiny waist. She took his other hand in hers. Jack was assaulted by the fragrance of her, the feel and closeness of her. It was almost too much.

"It's very easy," she said, smiling.

"I might step on your feet."

"I don't mind. I hope those handsome new boots don't hurt your toes."

"They don't," he lied. It didn't matter. Nothing mattered—except her.

"Two steps and a skip," Candice said. "Follow me. One-two-skip!"

He was worse than a lumbering ox, filled with self-consciousness and unable to think about much, other than her. He took two steps and a skip; she laughed. It wasn't laughter at his effort, but a happy tinkle of sound. One, two, skip . . . one, two, skip . . . Jack kept his eyes on his feet.

"You're doing wonderfully," Candice said, looking at his brow as he bent his head to watch his steps. "But you don't need to look at your feet. Look at me."

He did.

And he promptly stepped on her foot.

"Oh!"

"I'm sorry," he said, freezing and feeling like a fool.

"No, no, you won't get out of it that easily," she said, urging him back into the dance. "One, two, skip!"

He followed her lead perfectly for two sets, and she laughed, watching the small area of exposed skin on his throat, between the bandana and the shirt. He looked up suddenly, smiling. Candice stared.

It was the first time she'd ever seen him smile, and it was devastating.

"Is something wrong?" His smile was gone.

"No, I—" She stopped when she saw him look over her

shoulder. He dropped her hands and stepped to the side, away from her. Candice turned to see Mark pell-melling his way toward them, his face red with fury, and McGraw behind him—trailed by Luke and a few other men. Her heart constricted.

"I'll kill him!" Mark shouted, breaking into a run.

Without thinking, Candice leapt between them, her hands coming up to Mark's chest. He was so angry he threw her violently off, and she sprawled onto her face in the dust. That was all Jack needed.

Before Mark could even haul off with a punch, Jack landed a bone-cracking right to his jaw—sending him reeling backward onto the ground. He stood, waiting. Candice struggled to her feet, her petticoats twisted and entangled, hampering her. "No! Stop it! Please!"

Mark got to his feet slowly, murderously.

Luke grabbed him from behind and spun him away. "Get over here, Candice," he ordered.

His tone was so hard and authoritative, she moved to him immediately. He pulled her behind him and to the side. "Luke, we were only—"

"I've seen, everyone's seen," Luke said calmly. "Mister, I think you'd better get on that horse and ride out."

"What's going on?" Someone was whispering amid a flurry of excited murmurs. Candice looked around, stunned and dismayed to see that everyone had gathered around.

"Candice and the breed," someone said.

Candice went red and looked at Jack. He was expressionless. But the crowd was changing fast, the sounds going from stunned to angry. Someone shouted, "He touched her, he dies!"

"Yeah!" roared a few men, McGraw among them.

Candice turned. "No! No—we were only dancing—"

"Dancing?" Henderson shouted incredulously. "You'd dance with him?"

Candice lifted her chin.

"Everyone calm down," her father said, stepping beside Luke. He turned to Jack. "Ride on, boy. Now."

Candice gnawed her knuckles, watching as Jack turned, not even looking at her, and strode away. She watched him mount the stallion. When she looked back it was without hearing the heated arguments between her father and some of the other men. Finally everyone dispersed, a few men vowing to teach him a lesson if he ever tried to come around again. Candice was precariously close to tears.

"You all right?" Luke asked with concern, his voice low.

She nodded, her eyes filling.

Luke grabbed her. "Did he hurt you?"

"No!" she cried, twisting away, furious with him, furious with everyone.

"Candice," her father said, "I absolutely forbid you to go near that man again. Do you understand?"

She stared. "Pop—he's not some rabid dog, he's—"

"You are forbidden to go near him. Is that clear?"

She ducked her head. "Yes."

Shortly after that, the Carters left.

CHAPTER TWENTY-ONE

"How could you dance with him?"

It was accusing, and it wasn't even Mark—who wasn't looking at her—it was John-John. Before she could explain he turned his back on her. Her father gave her a short lecture on her reputation. Luke said nothing, merely looked at her intently a few times.

One day after that, when she was saddling her mare, she overheard the hands talking—about her. Red Barton called her a "breed lover." Candice went scarlet—with indignation, anger, and guilt.

She wasn't a "breed lover." She had only felt sorry for him. What harm was there in dancing? It wasn't like they'd kissed. Oh—but they had—could she ever forget? She thanked God that Luke hadn't caught them. Her shame was intense and burning.

Candice resolved to stay away from Jack Savage if she ever saw him again. And hopefully, she wouldn't. After all, she was a lady, no matter if her reputation was now in shreds, and ladies did not dance with savages—even ones who were as handsome as Jack.

They certainly didn't enjoy kissing them.

It was worse in town. The stares, the whispers. Two matrons actually crossed the street rather than walk on the same side with her. In the general store, Frank Smith propositioned her quite directly. He offered her anything she'd like if she went upstairs with him. God knew where his wife was. Candice was so stunned she didn't even smack him. She couldn't move. He grinned.

"Or is it only red-skinned men you got a taste for now?"

She gasped and fled. Out on the street she stood shaking, clinging to the hitching rail. When she had recovered a little, she looked up. It was to see Judge Reinhart staring at her, standing a few doors down. Her eyes went wide, and she waited, breathlessly.

He turned his back on her and walked away.

Candice raised her hand to her mouth to quell a sob. After Jack had ridden off at the barbecue, she and her family had left abruptly—and there had been no time for good-byes. No one had come over to them, however. Not even her beaux—not Judge, not Tim. And now she understood it had been a clear rejection of her. She felt sick.

Instinct made her lift her head again.

Jack Savage stood across the street staring at her.

She closed her eyes. Oh, no, she thought desperately. Please, don't come over here. She couldn't handle it.

But he did. He came slowly, deliberately. He was still wearing the white shirt and black Stetson, but with buckskin pants and moccasins, and he looked more like an Apache than a white man. Candice turned her back intentionally toward him, her heart starting to race. Go away, she thought, fighting imminent hysteria.

She was a vision in blue that had stopped Jack right in his tracks, just as now the sight of her drew him forward like a magnet. He felt it inside—the leaping of his heart in a primal joy. Then he saw her deliberately turn her back to him. In that instant, a hard, cold resolve flooded him. He was assailed with his memories of the barbecue, her whirling in his arms, face uplifted to his, lips curved broadly in a smile. The sound of her laughter, and then that of her horrified protest when her brother had come at him. How it had all ended so ignominiously with his abrupt, forced departure. And now it was like the dashing of ice water. She was purposefully avoiding him, succumbing to the pressure of her family and culture. Jack could not have stopped himself from approaching her if he'd wanted to—and he didn't.

He wanted to be cool, yet there was only a question in his tone. "Candice?"

She didn't turn to face him. "Don't come near me," she warned.

There was a moment of silence.

"Just go away," Candice added on a choked sob.

She hadn't heard him approach, and she didn't hear him leave, but she felt the difference, the emptiness, behind her. She finally wiped her eyes and straightened her spine and turned around. He was disappearing down the block, his stride long and hard and furious.

She wanted to weep.

PART TWO

Abduction

CHAPTER TWENTY-TWO

Candice was wearing one of her best day gowns. Her hair was carefully done in a smooth twist and tucked beneath a blue silk bonnet that matched her dress. She was waiting impatiently on the verandah as Pedro hitched up the buckboard in the quiet of the morning. She was going to pay a call on Judge Reinhart.

It was the day after he had coldly turned his back on her in Tucson. Candice could still feel the shock and humiliation of his rejection. Before she had eloped with Kincaid, Judge had been in love with her—she was sure of it. Of course, he was not the only one, but he was the most successful and respected of all her suitors. Candice was not familiar with rejection. She could not think when she had ever been turned away or disliked or condemned. Especially by a man. She couldn't believe that this was happening, and she had to see him and explain.

To her disappointment, Judge was not at his house, and the housekeeper told her he wouldn't be back until the midday meal. She decided to wait. She curled up on the sofa in the small but charming living room, in front of an adobe hearth that added much warmth in the winter. She tried to pass the time reading a book by Dickens, *A Tale of Two Cities,* but there was no way she could concentrate—not when she was nervous and perspiring with anxiety. She bit her knuckle and remembered that this was really all her fault—for dancing with Jack Savage.

"Hi, Candice."

Little Tommy Reinhart was staring at her with a grin. He was almost six. "Hello, Tommy. Did you have fun at the barbecue?"

"I hated it," Tommy said sullenly. "Tell me a story."

Candice looked at him, realizing for the first time that if she ever married Judge she would become a mother to two children. It was a sobering thought.

"Tell me a story," he said again, sitting next to her.

"Well . . ." Candice began, and then Lisa Anne appeared in the doorway. "Hello, Lisa Anne."

"What are you doing here?" the girl said, staring enigmatically.

Candice was taken aback by the child's rudeness. "I'm visiting your father."

"Are you going to tell Tommy a story?" she asked, approaching.

"Not today."

"Oh, please, please, please!" Tommy screamed.

Candice almost grimaced.

Lisa Anne was studying her.

"You shouldn't look at your elders like that," Candice said. "And it's rude not to greet a visitor properly and offer refreshments. Shouldn't you be doing your chores or your homework?"

"My chores are done, and so is my homework," Lisa Anne said calmly, as if she were twelve and not nine. Tommy was still shrieking about wanting a story. "Shut up," Lisa Anne said to him. She turned to Candice. "You're the one who ran off with the gambler."

Candice stared.

"You're the one who was dancing with the half-breed too. Are you really a whore?"

Candice gaped and clenched her hands to stop herself from smacking the little brat. "I'm going to tell your father about your awful manners," she warned.

"Why? Because it's true?"

She was incredulous and stunned. Just then Judge appeared in the doorway without his familiar, warm smile. "Hello, Candice." He sent the children outside.

Candice was on her feet, biting her lip. "Hi." She tried a smile on him. "I . . . I had to come and see you, Judge."

His jaw was tight. He gestured toward the couch. "Did Lupa offer you any coffee?"

"Yes, yes, she did." Candice sat down. Judge sat in a chair across from her. He didn't say anything. "You're upset with me."

Judge looked at her. "Am I?"

"You're angry."

"If you want to dance with half-breed savages, go right ahead."

"It was only a dance—and he's half white."

"You two were alone for days on the desert," Judge said vehemently, abruptly. "And then you *chose* to be with him again. I think you like his company, Candice."

Candice was pale.

Judge stood. "I think some of those rumors are true. Are they?"

She got to her feet. "No—no."

"We don't have anything to say to each other."

Candice trembled. "I thought we were friends—more than friends."

Judge laughed bitterly. "So did I. Then you eloped with that gambler—and showed up back here with a breed. I thought you were a lady."

It hurt. "Judge . . ."

"I think you had better leave," Judge Reinhart said.

Candice looked at him, feeling a burn starting. "It's not right or fair for you to condemn me for something you know nothing about."

Judge stepped to the doorway.

Candice sucked in her breath and managed to exit with her head held high. But once outside, she stumbled from the house, devastated. He had called her a loose woman without saying the word his daughter had used: *whore.* God—she and Savage had only danced! No—they had done more, much more, and maybe he was right—maybe she was no lady, not in truth. It was a terrible, horrible, wrenching realization, and she was barely aware of the rolling scenery as she and Pedro left the ranch. But about an hour out from Judge's, they both noticed a dark, ominous cloud rising out of the south, from behind them. "Rain," Pedro said.

Candice was about to agree, but suddenly her heart constricted. "No," she said, grabbing Pedro's arm. "It's smoke."

She could feel the cowboy tense beside her. The rising cloud was so obviously smoke that they thought they could smell burning wood and brush. "That must be the V Bar," Candice said, hearing the worry in her voice. The fire had to be huge—to be seen from so far away.

"Do not worry, señora," Pedro said, but there was no assurance in his tone. "Fire—may be all right, this time of the year, no?"

Candice knew he was trying to tell her that a brushfire

could happen for any reason at all. She didn't speak the one word she was trying not to think: Apache.

But after another fifteen or twenty minutes passed without incident, both she and Pedro began to breathe freely again, as the smoke was left almost directly behind them. Candice pulled off her bonnet to redo her hair. Unruly tresses had been teasing the back of her neck, sticking damply. She pulled out a pin and stabbed it back in. Suddenly Pedro gave a scream, slumping over the side of the wagon.

Candice grabbed the reins, about to pull up the team, when the arrow sticking out of the middle of his back registered. She slapped the reins, screaming at the team, urging them into a gallop. Suddenly she heard hoofbeats, dozens of them pounding from behind, getting closer, and frantically, her heart thudding in her throat, she looked over her shoulder. Ten or fifteen Apache were closing in from both sides, red and white warpaint streaking their faces, feathers poking out of their unbound hair. It took just a glance to see they were carrying not only rifles and bows but clubs and lances. A war party! Candice slapped the reins harder, crying out to the horses, fear overwhelming her, taking away all thoughts, her only desire being to escape.

Sweat poured down her face and blinded her. The terrain rose and fell in front of her maddeningly. The Apaches had let loose with their wild, strange war cries, and they echoed sickeningly around her. A rider drew abreast of her, grinning. Candice screamed at the team. The rider was moving past. Another warrior was in his wake. Candice whipped her horses. The first Apache was leaping onto the back of one of the team and already slowing it. The second warrior was at her knee, and then he was in the buckboard, shoving her aside, grabbing the reins. Candice fell on top of Pedro as the team began to slow down. She threw herself off the wagon.

She rolled and rolled, her skirts twisting around her legs. Gasping, she stumbled to her feet, running blindly. A whoop sounded in her ear. Just as the horse drew alongside her, she screamed. The Indian swept her up into his embrace at a gallop, as if she were a sack of flour.

His body was hard and sweat-streaked, and his torso was

greased. He smelled like horse, buckskin, bear fat, and sweat. She struggled in vain, but his grip was iron. He let out a wild, triumphant cry, trotting his pony into a circle of curious, painted faces. Candice closed her eyes and prayed.

CHAPTER TWENTY-THREE

The news spread like wildfire.

Tucson was in an uproar. The Henderson ranch had been attacked by an Apache war party, half of it burned to the ground, two men killed and one captured. And—Candice Carter was missing.

Jack was drinking whiskey in the one-room saloon when he heard the first, and he knew that Shozkay had retaliated—obviously tracking the man he had marked to Henderson's. Then he heard the second bit of information and his guts froze up inside. "What do you mean," he demanded of the Mexican sitting at the other table sharing the news with two friends, "Candice Carter is missing?"

The man looked at him and then turned his back, dismissing him.

Jack was on his feet and flinging him against the wall, his hands on the man's throat. "I asked you a question, *amigo*. What do you mean—Candice Carter is missing?"

Frantically the man told the story. Candice had gone to visit Judge Reinhart in a buckboard with one of the High C hands. That was yesterday. They hadn't returned, and the Carters had found the wagon, Pedro dead, Candice gone. They had clearly run into the war party that had attacked the Hendersons, and the Carters were now out scouring the countryside, looking for Candice.

Jack felt his insides cramp.

Candice was beautiful, blond, and a female—which meant she had been spared and taken prisoner. Unless—*Usen* —unless in the bloodlust of the battle she was mistakenly hurt.

Jack was already out the door and heading for the livery. It no longer mattered what had happened between them the last time they'd met. He'd already buried that encounter in cheap whiskey.

There was still plenty of light left. Keeping the black to a tireless lope, Jack rode out of town. Hours later he found the buckboard.

By then the sun was dipping low past the mountains'

jagged edges, and twilight was settling in. He'd almost missed it. The wagon was lying still and horseless between stands of mesquite and yucca. He approached, reining in.

Jack studied the terrain, squinting hard. The story unfolded. He could see that Candice had fallen, or jumped, out of the wagon, and run a short distance—only to be captured by one of the Apaches. He grimaced.

The thought of Candice at one of the brave's mercy unnerved him, despite the fact that women and children were rarely harmed and usually well cared for, eventually absorbed into the tribe. Only adult male prisoners were taken alive to be tortured and killed by the kin of the warrior being avenged. Now she was the property of the brave who had captured her, to do with as he wished, or give to whom he pleased.

The good news was that the Apaches did not rape. But if Candice did not obey and behave, she could be severely beaten, even killed. A terrible fear rose up in him, and he breathed a quick prayer to Usen and White Painted Woman for her protection. He began to call too on all the *gans*, the Mountain Spirits, for their help. Then he trotted the black away, toward the mountains, following the tracks of the war party.

CHAPTER TWENTY-FOUR

Candice no longer wondered what would have happened to her if she couldn't ride. Her captor had mounted her on one of the team, bareback, her hands tied tightly behind her back. They had ridden all that afternoon and all that night, stopping only once to water the horses. Candice wasn't blind-folded, and at first she had tried to memorize where they were taking her, but it was impossible in the dark. All she knew was that they were heading up, into the Catalinas, end-lessly, all through that first night.

There was another prisoner. A lithe, terrified vaquero, only a few years older than Candice, whom she didn't think she recognized. He had a bandaged shoulder. He knew her. Once, as their eyes made contact—his imploring, desperate—he mouthed her name. Candice understood his fear. The Apaches rarely took prisoners. She had heard all kinds of sto-ries about how they mutilated and tortured their captives. She was too frightened for herself to be frightened for him.

When the sun came up she saw they were traveling in a northwesterly direction. By then she was freezing, the thin silk of her dress providing no warmth, and it was hours before the sun was strong enough to warm her. By midday her face and the top of her chest were burned. She had never spent any time outdoors without some kind of hat, even in the mountains.

Her captor led her horse, never once looking at her. They trailed the rest of the war party. No one seemed to notice her, or care that she was first freezing, then burning, now dying of thirst—her thighs sore and her whole body aching from the endless riding. She was weary to the point of falling asleep, and by the time the sun was past mid-sky, she did, dropping over the horse's neck.

She awoke on the rocky ground, on her back, her shoul-ders aching unbearably, her wrists raw and bleeding. Her cap-tor was yanking her to her feet, and for the first time she really got a look at him. He was above average height, wear-ing nothing but buckskin breeches and thigh-high moccasins. He had a quiver of arrows and a bow slung over one huge shoulder. His shoulders were broad and oversized for his height, his chest massive, his thighs huge. He was an extraordinarily muscular man, just short of being fat. His face was round, high-cheekboned, and flat-nosed. He wasn't ugly, just very Indian. His eyes snapped at her.

"Please," Candice begged through swollen, split lips. "Please, untie my hands." She made a whimpering sound. "I won't run away, I promise." He regarded her diffidently. "There's nowhere for me to go to. Please!"

His hands clamped around her waist, and he threw her back on the mare. Then he turned, about to leap on his own pony.

"Water!" Candice cried. "Please, water!" And because many Apache understood Spanish, she added, *"Agua! Por favor, agua!"*

He was astride, trotting off, leading her and her mount. Candice felt tears of pain and despair trickle down her face.

She had hoped, at first, that she would be rescued. Now, exhausted, aching, thirsty, and weak, she was afraid of her fate, afraid she would never see her home again, never see her brothers and her father. . . .

She thought about Jack Savage. He was half Apache. She thought about how he had cared for her when he had found her dying in the desert. He hadn't treated her like this. Was it possible—and she prayed—that he would know her captors? That she might see him? That he would free her?

But then she couldn't avoid the most important question of all, the one that terrified her. What were they going to do to her? She released a sob. The brave was impervious to it.

They traveled on, through another night. So those stories were true too, about how Apache braves could ride for days at a time without food, water, and sleep. Candice rode in a semidozing state. Every time she fell asleep she jerked herself awake, afraid of falling off. Now they were riding along a narrow path. To her right, rocky cliffs soared, covered with pine, fir, and oak. To her left, it was thousands of feet straight down the mountain into a deep, fathomless canyon, and one fall would be her last.

Another sunrise came, and to her surprise, she realized they were heading down now. They had crossed the Catalinas! This thought gave her new hope. Maybe, one day, when she had her strength back, she could escape and find her way back to Tucson. She had never been a quitter. She would find her way back.

She was dozing again when she realized that her mount had stopped. She forced herself to open her eyes as she sagged low over the pony's neck. There were all kinds of sounds around her, voices, laughter, children. Candice focused. Hide-covered *gohwahs* greeted her, perhaps fifteen or twenty. A creek ran along the farthest edge of the camp. A few deep ovens were smoking. Near-naked children ran screaming playfully, a few pausing to point and laugh at her. Women clad in buckskin skirts and shirts were running out to greet their men, then they too turned to stare at her. Her captor had dismounted and was talking to a husky, square-faced squaw. They both turned to regard her, the squaw talking now, animatedly, gesturing. Candice couldn't understand a word they said. The brave came over, pulling her off the horse. Candice crumpled at his feet.

He pulled her up, and she tottered precariously, then he shoved her back and she tumbled in the direction he was pushing, until she came to a *gohwah*. He pushed her through the opening, and she fell on her face. She couldn't move. Someone cut her ropes, and she sobbed in relief, trying to bring her paralyzed arms to her sides, trying to move her hands. Whoever had cut the bonds left. Candice closed her eyes, falling into a deep sleep.

She didn't know how long she had been asleep when she awoke. For an instant she didn't know where she was, and then the horror of her situation came back to her. She lay in pain in the darkness, her body stiff and throbbing, her face burning—so thirsty, she wanted to die. From beyond the *gohwah* she could hear singing, laughter, drums, and rattles— they were celebrating. She managed to sit up.

She sat very still for a long time, fighting tears of despair and depression and pain, listening to the noises from outside, too numb to think. She began rubbing her sore muscles methodically, despite the discomfort. The hubbub from outside the *gohwah* increased. Movement was difficult, but not impossible, she found, as she stretched tentatively. Her wrists were scabbed and blistered. She realized that she was hungry.

She crawled toward the uncovered entrance of the

gohwah, hesitant and cautious. Lying on her stomach, she peered out.

A group of Apache women were dancing wildly, exultantly, with the young vaquero—surrounded by the singing, celebrating tribe. Some of the women were fully clad in buckskins, but three wore nothing but tiny loincloths and their naked bodies and full breasts gleamed in the firelight. The vaquero no longer seemed afraid and, in fact, was dancing rather avidly with one particular slender, near-naked squaw. Their bodies spoke an unmistakable sexual attraction as they swayed and weaved toward and away from each other. The men were watching and drinking and smoking and singing, some occasionally joining in. It seemed harmless enough.

Candice watched the gyrations of the dancers and became mesmerized by the fluid, graceful movements of the squaws.

After a while the slender squaw led the vaquero away, and Candice wondered if they were going to make love. Then she realized that the other women were following in their direction, and her puzzlement increased. Now the braves were dancing, even more wildly than the women, with much shouting and laughter. They had shed their buckskin pants and were naked except for their traditional breechcloths. Candice became fascinated with the display of their naked, gleaming bodies as they pranced and leapt about the firelight.

A horrible scream split the air.

Candice froze, and then it was repeated. Every hair on her body curled up, as she realized, horrified, that the sound was human. The dancers had stopped and were listening intently. Another scream, even worse than before, came curdling through the night.

The braves started dancing again jubilantly.

Three more screams, each worse than the one before, sounded, making Candice sick, terrifying her into immobility. She lay at the entrance to the *gohwah* completely frozen, afraid even to shiver lest she attract attention. What were they doing to the poor vaquero? And would she be next?

Perhaps an hour later, there was light as someone entered with a torch. It was the square-faced squaw. She placed a bowl and pitcher in front of Candice, both woven of straw and cane, and Candice drank desperately. Then she picked up the bowl and attacked it with her fingers. It was tasteless, almost bitter, some kind of cornmeal. She didn't care. When she had finished, she looked up to see the squaw staring at her with complete and undisguised animosity. Candice shrank away.

The squaw fingered the neckline of her dress, which was covered with dust and dirt, barely blue anymore. She caressed some ribbons at the neckline, at the cuffs. Then she said something. It was an order.

"What?" Candice felt fear rising up in her.

The woman gestured and spoke rapidly.

"What? I don't understand."

The squaw tugged at the dress. Candice suddenly understood. With fumbling fingers, she began to unbutton it. It took her a very long time, but she stepped out of it, wondering why the woman wanted it. The woman gestured at her chemise, which was the only garment between her pantalets and the rest of the world. Candice cringed. The squaw grew angry. Candice pulled it over her head.

The squaw wasn't satisfied—she wanted her underwear too. Sick, humiliated, feeling beaten, Candice pulled off the drawers, hugging herself modestly. The squaw looked at her sharply. Candice covered her breasts with her arms, drawing her knees up. The squaw yanked her arms down and stared at her body assessingly, rudely. Then she stood abruptly and left.

Candice found a blanket on the bed of hides and wrapped it around her. She sank back down, closing her eyes. Another intruder made her jerk them open. It was her captor.

He grabbed her hand, just missing her bruised wrist, and Candice was pulled to her feet, still clutching the blanket, suddenly realizing that he was drunk. He didn't stagger, or even totter, but she could smell the whiskey on his breath. He was smiling as he pulled her out of the *gohwah*. To her horror, she saw that a group of braves, all similarly inebriated, were waiting in a semicircle. He pushed her into their midst.

They stared at her and started talking, grinning, laughing. They were evidently awed by the mass of blond hair, and they touched it repeatedly, sometimes pulling it and hurting her. Suddenly her captor yanked the blanket out of her grasp, and Candice stood there, naked and frightened. She thrust her chin up, gritting her teeth, fighting her first impulse—to try to shield herself—knowing it would be ridiculous. The men had stopped talking and were staring excitedly. Her captor was grinning from ear to ear, and it struck Candice that she was his new possession, and he was showing her off. They all began to speak eagerly, her captor laughing and gesturing, clearly refusing their requests, but happily.

Suddenly they were all silent. Candice looked past her captor at a tall, silent Apache who had materialized out of nowhere. He stared at her, and Candice stared back, hiding her fear and trying to look bold. He was very handsome, as tall as Savage, but leaner, and obviously a man of power. Maybe he could help her. But then he looked past her face, his eyes roving her body, lingering on her breasts, on her womanhood. Candice stood straight and still. Somehow she sensed she would be better off if this man would take her away from her captor.

He spoke quietly, softly, to her captor, who listened intently, then spoke back shortly. They talked for a few more minutes, the handsome Apache becoming persuasive, her captor growing thick with pride, haughty in his replies. Finally the handsome Apache walked over to her.

"You belong to Hayilkah," he said, in heavily accented English. Candice gaped. "I have suggested you are too rare to hurt and my words carry weight. If you obey and work hard, he will not beat you. Someday you may even choose a husband and become one of us." He turned.

"Wait," Candice called. "Please, wait!"

He stopped, turning back to her.

"Please, please help me," she pleaded.

"I cannot help you," he said with pity. "You belong to Hayilkah. Only you may help yourself. You are his prize. He can do with you as he wishes. He can keep you or give you away, or beat you if you disobey."

Candice's heart was pounding painfully. The tall Apache walked away. The other Indians were dispersing. Her captor, Hayilkah, grabbed her wrist, causing Candice to cry out in pain. She wasn't aware of it, but Shozkay stopped and looked back, watching, as Hayilkah shoved Candice back into the *gohwah*, following her in.

To Candice's horror, he dropped the flap closed behind

him. She moved as far away as she could, ducking to stand upright. He stared at her lewdly, assessingly, then spoke to her, but she could not understand. He gestured to her and to the bed of hides.

"No!" Candice spat, suddenly understanding and forgetting everything the tall Apache had said. *He was going to rape her.*

He frowned. With one quick movement he pulled her body against his. Candice found the strength to struggle, but it was useless. His arms were like iron, holding her still, one massive hand pawing her roughly, pausing over her nipples, hurting her. She whimpered in pain. He threw her down and lowered his heavy body on hers. Candice tried to push him off, but his sheer weight pinned her down, and he ignored her pounding fists. He separated her thighs with his own, and she could feel his shaft stabbing her through the breechcloth. She raked his back with her nails.

He smacked her across the face.

Candice's head hit the ground with such impact that she saw an explosion of bright lights. Her face was throbbing, and when her vision cleared, she became aware of what the man was doing to her. He had thrust a finger into her and was exploring her insides. She was overwhelmed with fear, terror, and complete revulsion. He jammed his finger in again and again, so deeply that she thought she would faint from the pain. And then his plunging hand stilled and he said something to her. He was pleased.

Candice trembled and fought her terror and kept her eyes shut tightly, waiting for him to rip off the breechcloth and rape her. Instead, she felt his awful fingers violating her again, thrusting against her maidenhood, making a wave of nausea well up in her.

The fingers were withdrawn. Candice tensed, waited, and heard a grunt. She dared to open her eyes, to see him kneeling there, his face contorted, and then she felt his seed spraying over her thighs.

CHAPTER TWENTY-FIVE

Jack had traveled for two nights and two and half days, making slightly better time than the party he was following. It had soon become apparent that they were crossing the Catalinas, and he was certain he knew the campsite Shozkay was heading for. Still, he didn't dare get ahead of himself and make directly for it, in case he had guessed incorrectly. Like all Apaches, Shozkay's band moved from site to site. Unlike all other Apaches, however, his tribe farmed for about a quarter of their sustenance needs.

Now, in mid-October, they would be in the higher elevations harvesting corn, beans, and pumpkin, and baking and packing mescal cakes, smoking and drying beef, in preparation for the long winter ahead. They would not leave the mountains until they had harvested their crops—except to raid or war.

When he rode into the camp it was shortly after sunrise, the air still chill from the mountain night. There was some activity, but not the usual amount. The women were up and about doing their early-morning chores, and he could smell the acorn soup he was so fond of, but the rest of the camp was in a strange silence, which Jack immediately understood. Last night they had arrived and had had a victory celebration. He went to Shozkay's *gohwah*.

Now that he was so close he was afraid of what he would find. His entire body was tense with anticipation and dread, his heart pounding painfully. He found Luz hovering over a fire. Her eyes lit up when she saw him. *"Shilah!"*

Jack couldn't return her smile or her greeting, and she instantly sobered. "Where is your husband?" he asked.

She pointed toward the creek.

Jack found Shozkay splashing water over his face and down his bare chest. His brother saw him, eyes widening with amazement, and then they embraced, clapping each other hard.

"Shik'isn, I did not expect to see you again so soon."

"The woman," Jack said abruptly, his eyes burning into Shozkay's. "The white woman with yellow hair. Is she alive?"

Shozkay stared in surprise. "Yes, she is."

"And in one piece?" He held his breath.

"I believe so."

Shozkay regarded him questioningly.

"Who has her?" Jack said, his mouth clamping into a hard line to prevent the relief he felt from flooding his features. But he couldn't prevent it from reaching his eyes, and Shozkay saw it.

"Hayilkah."

Jack frowned grimly. There was only one way to free her. "Offer for her."

Shozkay stared in surprise.

"I mean it," Jack said grimly. "Offer the black to Chise and Gahgeh." They were Hayilkah's wife's parents.

"You wish to marry this white woman?" Shozkay was incredulous.

"Yes," Jack said. It was not the truth. The truth was that Hayilkah had captured her, making her his. She was rare. He would not give her as a gift. He would expect many gifts in return for her hand. Or maybe he would want to keep her for himself, as a second wife. It was a thought Jack could not stand.

"The black is a fine stallion," Shozkay said, still staring at his brother closely. "I doubt that Hayilkah will refuse such a gift."

Acceptance of an offering meant Jack could take Candice, and in Apache law, once they had slept together in their own *gohwah*, they would be man and wife. He would not think about those implications, not now.

"How do you know this woman, brother?"

"It is a long story."

"I have all day." Shozkay grinned.

Jack wasn't smiling. "I wish to see her."

"You will have to ask Hayilkah. He is asleep somewhere. Too much *tulapai* last night," he added. They walked back to the camp, and Shozkay put a hand on Jack's shoulder. "I wish I had known," he said softly.

Jack's body was rigid. They found Hayilkah passed out beside a few other warriors. Jack bent and spoke his name, shaking him. After a couple of minutes, Hayilkah opened one eye, saying "Go away, woman."

"It is my brother," Shozkay said, squatting by him. "He wishes to see your slave."

Hayilkah opened the other eye and tried to focus. "Yes, go," he mumbled, then fell asleep instantly.

Jack went to Hayilkah's *gohwah*, where Shozkay left him. Taking a deep breath, he opened the flap. He saw her sprawled on the bed of hides, on her stomach, naked beneath the top covering. It was an old Apache trick to keep captives naked so they wouldn't run away, but a terrible feeling swept him, and he was inside, kneeling beside her, his hand in her tangled, knotted hair. "Candice! Candice? *Shijii*, it's me. Wake up."

He stroked her back, and she moved. He put his arm beneath her, pulling her almost into his lap, cradling her. She moaned, then her eyes shot open, and she cried, "No!" her fingers turning into claws, going for his eyes. Jack grabbed her wrists.

She yelped in pain and he released them, horrified when he saw that her wrists were scabbed and bloody and oozing pus. "It's all right now," he whispered, his hold tightening.

"Jack." She gasped, clinging to him.

He held her tighter, turning his face into her hair. He stroked her hair and rocked her as if she were a child. She clung to him harder. "Jack, take me away from here, please."

"I will get you out of here," he promised, his hands sliding up and down her back. He was too aware of the woman in his arms. He did not tell her just how he was planning to free her.

"I was hoping . . . praying," she said into his shirt.

"What?"

"Praying you would come." She looked up, her eyes glistening with tears.

Of course I would come. "Are you all right?" *Did they hurt you?*

She shook her head, her nose red. A tear fell. "I'm so afraid."

"I know."

She stared into his eyes and suddenly became aware of their position—that she was in his arms, naked except for the blanket, that his hard chest was pressing against her soft bosom and it was all wrong. But it didn't feel wrong. It didn't feel wrong at all.

He read her thoughts and rose, putting some distance between them.

"No, don't go," Candice begged, holding on to one buckskin-clad knee.

Jack's jaw tightened. "I have to go."

"Please," she protested, anguished.

He took a breath, a loud sound in the small space of the *gohwah*. She belonged to Hayilkah, so he had no choice but to leave—as hard as it was.

"Don't go," Candice said, as he walked, stooped, to the entrance of the *gohwah*. "Jack! Don't leave me here! Please!"

Jack tensed and ducked out. He heard her soft, muffled sobs behind him—and they echoed in his mind all day.

CHAPTER TWENTY-SIX

He was here.

And, strangely, knowing that he was here reassured her and dimmed the hysteria that had been growing.

She could barely believe it. The coincidence was too great—that he would appear here after she was taken prisoner. Or, maybe—and she shuddered with the thought—he had been a part of the war party but had not returned with the band, had scouted ahead or lingered behind. She remembered with utter clarity how he had killed the three cowboys who had staked out the Apache boy. How he had said that vengeance was the Apache way. She hugged herself.

It would do not to forget who and what he was.

But . . . before, when he had found her on the desert, he hadn't hurt her. And she was even ashamed now for what her thoughts had been. Not that she exactly trusted him—but neither did she mistrust him. After being treated so brutally and carelessly by Hayilkah, as if she were some piece of meat, the contrast with how Jack had treated her was stunning. He hadn't hurt her, hadn't made her ride for days and days without food and water, hadn't shoved her around, hadn't even touched her—not like Hayilkah.

She couldn't suppress a shiver of fear. He had said he would help her. She prayed it would be soon. She was afraid of Hayilkah, afraid he would come to her again, tonight, and this time rape her. Panic started an insidious creeping.

She became aware of the fact that several Apaches had gathered not far from the *gohwah*—she could hear them talking excitedly, although she couldn't understand a word they said. But she was feeling a little braver because Jack was in the camp, so she crept quickly to the entrance of the gohwah and raised the hide flap.

There was quite a commotion going on twenty feet away. The tall, handsome Apache who had explained her circumstances to her last night, in English, was there, holding Jack's black stallion, which was bridled but bareback. The stallion was prancing in agitation, corded muscles rippling and gleaming, and he champed at his bit, frothing. He lashed out with a lethal hind leg, and someone cried out and jumped away. The Apache and the stallion were surrounded, but cautiously, by perhaps twenty other Apaches, both male and female. One of them was Hayilkah.

In fact, the tall Apache was speaking to an older couple standing next to her captor, and he was grinning and listening avidly to every word. The old, fat woman resembled Hayilkah. His mother? Hayilkah laughed. The tall Apache led the black through the group, which parted immediately before his path. He took the black to a tree, where he tied him. The stallion didn't look like he was going to stay put for very long.

The group of Apaches was dispersing. Candice thought she understood what was happening. Jack was trading the black for her. She had no idea why he had sent the tall Apache as his emissary.

But he was trading his horse for her.

Her heart filled with desperate hope.

CHAPTER TWENTY-SEVEN

Despite the fact that he was exhausted, Jack had a restless night. He was afraid that Hayilkah would change his mind and return the black and take Candice Carter to bed as his wife. He dozed and dreamed of Candice. She was in his arms, and he was making fierce, agonizing love to her. Then she moved him away, laughing. Tim McGraw appeared, smiling insolently, and proceeded to impale her right before his very eyes. In his dream, he wanted to kill McGraw. Now he had his clothes on, while they rutted naked. But he couldn't make his hands move to draw his guns no matter how hard he tried. All he could do was stand there and watch, his body paralyzed.

He even had a brief nightmare about Datiye. He had caught a glimpse of her that afternoon, reminding him of what had happened between them. In the dream, she was giving birth to a child. His child. Candice was there, acting as midwife. He awoke in a sweat, very disturbed. Everyone knew dreams were omens.

At dawn Shozkay found him sitting on his bedroll staring out at the mountains with a harsh forbidding expression on his face.

"Ready for divorce already, brother?" Shozkay teased dryly.

Jack jumped to his feet, his heart pounding. "They have not returned the black?" If the black had not been returned, it meant the proposal had been accepted.

"Come," Shozkay said, smiling. "She is a maiden—you realize that?"

Jack stared in surprise. Kincaid and Candice had never consummated their marriage? And then he felt a swift, hot elation that no man had possessed her.

"You did not know?"

"She is a widow," Jack said.

"How is that?"

"I do not know."

"Well, there is no doubt that she is still a maiden; she was examined carefully, or so Hayilkah says."

Jack grew grim thinking about someone examining Candice to find that out. He clamped down hard on his jaw as anger coursed through him.

Shozkay led him through the camp to his *gohwah,* and behind it there was a buckskin dress, moccasins, and an antelope hide—a kind of dowry. "Well?"

Jack stared, then relaxed and even smiled.

"Are you going to go get your bride?" Shozkay grinned as if he found the whole affair vastly amusing.

My bride, he thought. *My bride.* Now what am I going to do? And instantly an inner voice said—She belongs to you, and you can do what you will. And it was the truth. "I don't want her to know about this," Jack told him.

"I will speak no truths." Shozkay laughed.

"This isn't funny," Jack said.

"I will not even speak to her." Shozkay grinned. "Love, eh?"

Jack gave him a dark look and strode away.

He passed Hayilkah, mounted on a chestnut horse, about to go hunting with a group of men. Hayilkah smiled. Jack smiled too. Had Hayilkah tried to approach the black, much less mount him? The black was an unfriendly horse that rarely allowed anyone but him on his back. Jack thought that Hayilkah had probably tried, and failed, thus his current choice of a mount. Hayilkah was probably intending to break the black another time. Jack wondered if he would be able to do so, and doubted it. He felt a sense of loss, but it was lost among his other careening emotions and the heavy thudding of his heart.

He ducked into the *gohwah.* Candice was awake, still naked, although wrapped in a blanket. Her face brightened with evident joy at seeing him. He looked at her and was swept with a heady flush of pleasure. This woman is mine. "Let's go."

She started in surprise, rising, holding the blanket. "What's happened?" she asked anxiously.

His gaze was level. "I've traded for you."

"Are we going to leave?"

"Soon," he told her. He took her elbow. "Come on. I think the first thing you need is a bath."

She turned fully toward him, one of her hands going to

his bare chest in a natural, importuning gesture. But the moment their flesh made contact, she froze, and he went very still. They both stared at her small, pale hand resting on his hard, dark abdomen. She started to remove it.

He took it in his. "Jesu," he said. Her nails were torn and had been bleeding. Dirt was embedded beneath them. Her knuckles were chapped and raw, her skin dry and leathery. There were scabbing cuts on her palm, and her wrists still looked infected. His touch was very gentle. Their eyes met.

He thought he saw trust, and his heart tightened painfully. "We'll get you cleaned up." His voice was too husky.

"Jack." It was a croak, and she wet her lips, her pink tongue instantly drawing his full attention. He focused on her mouth—the lips cracked and split but so very beautiful. The urge to kiss her was overwhelming. To kiss her and take her and make her his. Why not? She *was* his.

"Did you trade your stallion for me?"

"Yes."

"Thank you."

A slight smile tugged at the corners of his mouth. Her own face mirrored it. It was Jack who finally looked away from her glistening dark-blue eyes.

The hunting party was riding out, a group of fierce-looking braves, rifles in hand, bows slung over hard shoulders. Half a dozen squaws were striding out of camp carrying baskets—obviously some kind of gathering expedition—while the rest of the women were cooking over fires and deep ovens, watching the children. The braves who had remained were sharpening implements, mending harnesses, making weapons.

They walked away from the camp to an area of the creek secluded by thick stands of oak and pinyon. Jack was carrying her dowry—the dress and moccasins. He laid them carefully on some grass, glancing at her. "I'll just walk back a bit."

She clutched the blanket closer but didn't avert her gaze. They stared at each other before Jack turned away, reluctantly, his blood racing thickly. He wanted her, he wanted her now, and he had never wanted any woman the way he wanted her.

He paused beside a large, thick tree, leaning his bare shoulder against it. He could hear her dropping the blanket, and he instantly envisioned her long-legged, lithe, full-breasted body, imagined her turning and walking to the creek. He couldn't help it. He shifted, his manhood rigid and aching now, and glanced over his shoulder. She was wading into the stream, shivering, her long, tangled hair flowing to her waist, stopping just short enough to give him a perfect and tantalizing view of her lush, rounded buttocks and long legs. He groaned beneath his breath but could not for the life of him look away. She bent over and he inhaled, a sharp sound at what she was exposing, and she straightened instantly, whirling, arms across her breasts, her navy eyes wide. Their gazes met.

It took every ounce of willpower he possessed to turn and walk back to the camp.

CHAPTER TWENTY-EIGHT

Standing naked in the sunlight, Candice watched him heading toward the camp. She was very much aware of her nudity and the tightness in her chest. Then, instantly, she dropped into the water and began to scrub herself furiously, darting quick glances around for any unwelcome Apache intruders. How could he have left her there alone? What if a brave appeared while she was naked and defenseless? And why did she keep thinking about the way he had looked at her? She was no longer so naive as to not recognize a look of lust and desire—the expression had been written all over his face when he had kissed her in the barn. Just as it had been now. Candice was agitated.

She dressed quickly in the items he had left. The dress and moccasins were butter-soft, and felt wickedly delightful against her naked skin. She didn't hear Jack returning. She just suddenly knew he was there, and she looked up, getting another glimpse of hot gray eyes. It occurred to her that he knew she was wearing nothing beneath the dress, and she blushed, but she couldn't look away.

"Come here," he said softly.

Candice stared, unable to swallow, unable even to breathe. After a beat he came to her, and for one wild moment she thought he was going to kiss her as he stared at her parted lips. Instead, he picked up one of her hands, and then before she could adjust to the quick disappointment, he was gently applying salve to the rope burns and abrasions. She felt heat rising to her face for her wayward thoughts.

His touch was extraordinarily gentle, the way it had been when he had bathed the dead Apache boy. His hands were large and warm and calloused—dwarfing hers. She was eye level with his naked chest and the heavy necklace he wore. He dropped her hands, and she looked up into his eyes. "Thank you."

He didn't say anything. She followed him, not back to the camp, but into the woods, trailing behind, trying to look anywhere but at his bare back, and wishing she could turn off all her thoughts. He started gathering saplings and brush.

Candice stood watching, until he handed her what he'd collected, filling her arms. He gathered another load for himself, and they started back to the camp.

After they deposited their loads on the outskirts of camp, they went back for more. It suddenly struck Candice what they were doing, and it shook her to the core. There seemed to be no other conclusion than that they were collecting material for a *gohwah,* and if that was the case, did it mean they were going to stay there? He had said they were leaving. Had she misunderstood?

"Jack, are we building a *gohwah?*"

"Yes."

"Does that mean we're going to be staying here?"

He didn't look at her. "Just until you're healed up," he said.

She was afraid to ask what would happen afterward. "Then will you take me home?" Her voice trembled.

This time he did look at her. "Yes."

They spent the morning outside the camp gathering saplings, brush, and bear grass. Around midday Jack told her to stay put by their pile of wood and grass on the edge of the camp, and he disappeared. Candice sat down on the ground and idly picked up stones and tossed them away.

Jack appeared, smiling, two bowls in his hands. "Here," he said, squatting beside her Apache fashion.

She wrinkled her nose. "Ugh. I hate that stuff!"

He looked at her in amazement. "Really?" He raised the rim of the bowl to his mouth and began to eat the thick gruel.

She watched. He is just like them, she thought, staring, as he hungrily devoured the bland souplike food. It was as if he had eaten like this a hundred times, had never needed utensils. He was squatting, thighs bulging in the buckskin pants. He had shed his shirt, and his chest was bronzed almost to the color of oak bark, gleaming with perspiration. The muscles in his forearms rippled with each shifting movement, and his biceps seemed to be in a permanent state of straining, popping thickly beneath his skin. He finished, setting the bowl down, looking at her.

"You need to eat," he said, his tone pleasant. "You need your strength."

"What is it?"

"It's made from acorns," he told her, smiling slightly at the face she made.

She picked up the bowl—she was hungry—and awkwardly drank, or tried to.

"Good girl," Jack said.

"If you pat me on the head I'll bite you," Candice flirted daringly.

He laughed. "I like it better when you wag your tail, *ish'tia'nay.*" He stood. "Watch carefully."

"What does that mean, *ish'tia'nay?*"

He grinned. "Woman."

"Oh."

He used a tool, like a spear, made of mesquite with a pointed, narrow end, to dig six deep, narrow holes in a circle. Then he took a green sapling and inserted one end in one hole. He put another sapling in another hole. He bent them toward each other in an arch, and tied them together with strips of yucca.

"By the way, this is women's work. Braves never build *gohwahs*. So watch carefully, because you're going to finish this by yourself."

"By myself?"

"I'm losing face," he told her cheerfully. "Hand me that *sohi.*"

"That's silly. Hand you what?"

"That sapling."

She did, watching him insert it into another hole.

"Candice, put a sapling in that hole."

"Which hole?"

"That one." He pointed.

"Why are we doing this?" she asked, doing as she was told. "Why don't we just sleep under the stars?"

"Candie, *ti-tonjuda!* Wrong end! The other end—the thicker end—goes in first!"

"How am I supposed to know?" She reversed the sapling. "Why *are* we doing this? It seems like a lot of trouble for a few days."

He tied the saplings together, and now the *gohwah* was almost completely framed. "This is the worst I've ever seen," he said disgustedly. Then he answered her question, "Because, *ish'tia'nay,* it is not appropriate for us to sleep outside tonight."

Candice sighed. "Another Apache custom, I suppose?"

He glanced at her sharply, then away, staring at the frame. "Yes, you might say that." Jack added another arch of saplings and surveyed the frame. "Okay. It will have to do. Now, pay attention. Brush next, then bear grass."

"I think I can figure it out."

"Enju." Jack was smiling and it made the corners of his eyes crinkle. "Have this finished by the time I get back." He turned and started walking away.

"You really want me to do this by myself?"

He stopped and pointed at her. "You build that *gohwah,* woman, or I'll have to send you back to Hayilkah." With that exaggerated threat, he left her standing there.

CHAPTER TWENTY-NINE

He had left her alone with those instructions to finish the shelter. It had taken her a long time to figure out how to fill in the framework of saplings with the brush. At first, the brush kept falling out. Each piece of brush had to be wedged against other pieces and the frame. The fact that squaws and braves kept glancing at her didn't help the situation. The children who came over to jabber excitedly and point and laugh were a distraction—but a welcome one from her tumbling thoughts.

Now, somehow, she was supposed to fill in the brush with bear grass. She was lucky she had gotten this far—the roof had really been impossible.

As she held some grass in her hand and stared at the *gohwah,* waiting for the solution, she became aware of a squaw standing a few feet away, staring at her. Candice looked over at her. The woman was slender and pretty. She was a few years older than Candice, and she stared at Candice with hard, hostile black eyes. Candice could feel her hatred, and its intensity frightened her.

The woman walked closer, and Candice rose to her feet apprehensively. With a look of scorn, the squaw tapped the *gohwah.* It shuddered.

"What do you think you're doing?" Candice asked as calmly as she could, despite the fact that she was sure the woman didn't understand a word she said. "I've spent all afternoon building this, so please keep your hands to yourself."

"An angry wind, it blows away," the squaw said in stilted English.

Candice was surprised. "How did you learn English?"

"Niño Salvaje taught me," she said with a small smile.

"Niño Salvaje?"

"The man you know as Savage."

A sick feeling spread through her veins. "Why did he teach you English?"

"Why do you think he wants me to know his other language?" The woman's smile broadened.

Candice refused to acknowledge her rising comprehension. "I have no idea," she said, but oh, she did.

"I am his woman," the Apache returned calmly.

Candice was very still—except for the pounding of her heart. She could not mistake the avid jealousy pouring through her. She smiled tightly at the squaw. "What's your name?"

"Datiye."

"Well, Datiye, if you are his woman, then why am I building his *gohwah?*" This was said with more confidence and gusto than she felt, even while she knew she was a fool to be competing with this woman for a man she didn't even want.

The woman stared, her face darkening, but didn't answer. It was then that Candice heard his voice and looked up to see Jack approaching with the tall, handsome Apache who had spoken English to her and a stunningly beautiful woman. They were chatting in Apache, the squaw between the two men.

The three stopped, and Candice turned her back deliberately on them, still stunned by the first woman's admission. She was filled with dark emotions, thinking about Jack and Datiye, thinking about Jack looking at her and teasing her that morning while this woman—his mistress?—was here in camp. *I really don't care,* she told herself, and knew it was a lie.

When the tall Apache started to speak sharply, Candice had to look to see what was going on. Jack was inspecting her handiwork carefully, obviously as a means to ignore what was occurring, and Datiye was leaving them with a hard, angry stride, clearly sent away by the Apache.

"This is my brother, Shozkay," Jack said. "And this is his wife, Luz."

Candice nodded, barely able to restrain herself from demanding just what his relationship was with the other squaw. She looked at Luz and was again struck by her sensual beauty. Luz was staring at her too. "You're one of the most beautiful women I've ever seen," Candice told her frankly.

Luz smiled, and she reached out and touched her shoulder. She spoke in Apache, and Shozkay translated. "She wants to tell you the same thing—that you are as beautiful as the sunrise."

Candice was overwhelmed by the compliment, especially as it came from another woman. "Thank you," she said softly, and they smiled at each other.

Jack was inspecting the *gohwah*, pacing all the way around it. "Blessed *Usen*," he muttered, "this is the worst I've seen."

"Fine," Candice snapped, making him jerk around. Her eyes flashed murderously. "You want it built better, you do it by yourself."

Luz and Shozkay looked at each other.

Jack tested the *gohwah*. "Fortunately, the weather is good. Come here. I'll show you how to weave this grass in."

Luz restrained him. "I'll do it," she said, smiling. "Do you speak Spanish?" she said, switching to her grandmother's tongue.

"Yes, a bit," Candice said. "I understand better than I speak it, though."

"I will teach her. After all, she is now my sister." Luz bit her lip, and there was a quick exchange of glances between Jack and the two Apaches.

"What does she mean?" Candice asked Jack, understanding Luz perfectly.

Shozkay answered. "My brother has traded for you. You become our sister the way Luz became his sister through me. It is just a manner of speaking." He smiled.

Candice watched them walk away, her arms crossed over her chest.

Luz showed her how to weave strands of the long bear grass through the brush. She did it quickly and efficiently. Candice was tired of the task and tired in general, and her weaving was loose and shoddy.

"Do you like Jack?" she asked curiously as she picked up another length of grass. The strands were between three and four feet long.

Luz smiled. "Very much. He is brave and strong. He brings much pride to the path he walks, and never shame."

Candice absorbed that. "Why is he called 'Niño Salvaje'?"

"It was the name the great Cochise gave him many, many winters ago."

"Cochise named him?" She was curious.

"Yes." Luz glanced at Candice briefly as she wove the grass into the brush. "It was a great honor to be given such a proud name by such a great warrior—the son of the chief. And he was only a boy."

"Well, it suits him." She yanked out the strand of grass and started over. "Why did Cochise name him? Are they related?"

"No. Cochise gave him as a gift to my husband's parents. They loved him from early on and adopted him."

"He gave Jack as a gift?"

"Yes."

"But, what about Jack's real parents?"

"I don't know. You would have to ask him. They probably died."

Later, after the *gohwah* was finished, hides stretched tautly over the shell, Candice accepted a lesson in cooking. It wasn't that she was interested in how to prepare the bland stew made from acorns—but she did like Luz. Some time later Luz sent her down to the creek with two woven baskets for water.

Candice looked at the baskets doubtfully. "Don't these leak?"

Luz laughed. "No, look inside."

She uncovered one and found that there was a clay urn within.

"We make very little pottery, it breaks too easily," the squaw said. "But sometimes it is necessary."

The creek ran along the entire edge of the back of the camp. She walked slowly through the pines, tired from the day, glad of the time alone. Soon she had left the *gohwahs* behind. She didn't want to think, but she instantly started speculating about the woman Datiye. She was almost at the creek when she heard Jack's voice.

She looked up, stopping short.

Datiye was in his arms. She was pressed against him, her hands on his bare chest. She was talking rapidly in Apache, looking up into his face. He had both his hands on her waist, and his face was unreadable. Candice stood frozen.

Jack looked past Datiye and saw her. Immediately he dropped his hands and stepped away from the slender squaw.

Then he looked back at Datiye and spoke in a harsh tone. Datiye interrupted, throwing her palms back on his chest.

Candice didn't want to see any more, but she didn't move. Datiye stared boldly back. Jack said something to her and she turned and left, but not before throwing a last cold glance at Candice. Jack approached, taking the urns from her.

"I'll do that," he said, his gaze searching her face.

Candice looked at him coldly, trying to remain expressionless and not show him that she felt like murdering somebody. Preferably that *other woman*. "That's all right," she huffed, reaching for the urns.

A tug-of-war ensued. "No, I'll fill them. They'll be heavy."

"Do you fill *her* urns too?" Candice released her grip so abruptly, he momentarily lost his balance.

"What?" he asked blankly, recovering.

"Nothing," Candice said, her nostrils flaring.

Jack gave her a cautious look and started for the stream. Candice glared at his back, then started after him, crashing noisily through the bushes and brush. She pulled up short behind him as he finished filling the urns, and glimpsed a smile he was trying to hide.

"Is something funny?" she asked in an icy voice.

He straightened, and the smile burst, wreathing his face. "No," he said, and started laughing.

"Just what is so funny?" she cried furiously.

"You!" he said, laughing harder. "My God! For such a graceful woman, you move like a hurricane! Candie, *shiji*, I must teach you how to walk."

She stared. She stared at him, laughing. She waited for him to stop, and when he finally did, her voice was as casual as she could make it. "So," she said, "is that woman your mistress?"

CHAPTER THIRTY

"Is Datiye your mistress?" she repeated.

He could see that she was upset, and it stunned him. This was the second time she had asked him that, her tone high and tense. Why would she care if he had another woman? Was she jealous? That thought was intoxicating. She also seemed ready to lash out at him, and now was not the time. The night was looming before them. Tonight they had to share their *gohwah* to seal their marriage, and he didn't want to have to carry her forcibly there—no Apache that he had ever known had taken a wife forcibly; brides made their own choices. Of course, thinking about the deception disturbed him, until he reminded himself it was to her benefit too—it was marry him or be left behind as Hayilkah's property.

"Well? Is Datiye your mistress?" Candice demanded.

"No." His gaze was searching.

"I don't believe you."

"I'm not a liar."

"No? Then why did Datiye say she was your mistress?"

At her tone, his jaw went tight. "She's jealous of you," he said. He put his hand on her shoulder without thinking and felt her entire body go tense. Instantly he withdrew it. "I imagine women have been jealous of you your whole life, Candice, so why let it bother you now?"

She absorbed that with an angry toss of her thick blond hair.

He gave her a sidelong glance and couldn't help the smile or the light in his eyes. "What do you care, anyway, *ish'tia'nay?*" His tone was soft and teasing.

Her hands flew to her hips. "I don't care, Mr. Savage, believe me I don't."

He clasped her shoulder before she could turn her back on him. "You're not jealous, are you?"

Her mouth dropped a foot. "Me! Jealous! Me! Candice Carter?" She laughed incredulously.

He grinned. His forefinger touched her chin. " 'Fess up, sweetheart. I won't tell a soul."

She gave him a black glance. "There's absolutely nothing to *'fess* up!"

"No?" He chuckled. "Then why have your blue eyes turned black—sweetheart?"

She gave him a murderous look, crossing her arms over her breasts. His smile widened. He liked the way that posture crushed and lifted her bosom. She grew crimson. "How you could possibly think that I am jealous of some squaw . . ." she sputtered.

His laughter died.

"I've never been jealous a day in my life," Candice lied furiously, "and certainly not of some squaw!"

A long silence followed her statement, and when Jack finally spoke, his voice was very low and controlled. "How many prejudiced bones are there, Miss Candice," he said, "in that deceivingly beautiful body of yours?"

"Why shouldn't I be prejudiced?" She snapped. "Apaches are savages—they rape and kill and scalp women and children."

"Apaches don't harm women or children."

"No?" She taunted. "No, Jack? I suppose you're going to tell me that Hayilkah didn't *harm* me?"

He grabbed her chin, forcing her to look in his eyes. "What?"

"You heard!"

He pulled her very close. "I know Hayilkah didn't rape you—so just what are you accusing him of?"

She grew red and flustered. His eyes pinned her, his body tensed with foreboding.

"He did rape me," Candice cried out. "But it was with his hands!"

Jack seemed taken aback for a moment, his eyes narrowing.

"He was only examining you."

Candice laughed again, a hard, brittle sound. "He was getting pleasure, and you can't tell me he wasn't—not when he spilled his seed all over my thighs."

Jack didn't move, or even breathe, for a beat. He could very vividly picture Hayilkah with his fingers in Candice, then losing control and coming. The anger he felt was so deep it was completely calm and quiet. He realized Candice was triumphant and waiting for his reaction. He also realized that one day he would kill Hayilkah, and he turned to her slowly. "He's not the first man to lose control around you, is he, Candice?" His words were soft and mocking, the innuendo clear.

She flushed. "You're a savage just like they are, aren't you, Jack?" She spit the words at him. "When you capture a white woman, is that how you *examine* her too?"

There was no point in answering her. "Let's go," he said. "You're going to help Luz with the meal."

"Did you examine me when you found me—when I was unconscious?" she persisted.

"I saved your ungrateful neck, and you know it."

"You kissed me in the barn!" It was an accusation. Tears filled her eyes.

"I guess I'm human after all," he said bitterly. He felt a terrible defeat—how could he have thought for an instant that she was jealous? He supposed she was used to being the sole object of a man's attentions, that her pride was piqued— hadn't she as much as said so? And why in hell did he care what she thought—why in hell did he want her goddamn approval so much?

She wouldn't stop. "How many white women have you captured, Jack? Captured and forced? Or am I the only one?"

"You enjoyed that kiss."

"No, I didn't!"

They stared at each other.

"I saw it with my own eyes once," Candice said. "A scalped little boy who couldn't have been more than ten years old. How much proof do I have to throw in your face before you admit what you are?"

"What I am is a man," he said tersely. "And maybe if you didn't sashay around me like you do, it wouldn't have happened. You can lie to me and you can lie to yourself, but we both know the truth is that you've been itching for me to kiss you since the day you first laid eyes on me."

"That's *not* true!"

"As for the boy—if an Apache did it, he was a renegade. As a rule, we don't harm women and children. Take a good look around you. There are a couple of women in this camp who are not Apache—who are married to Apache warriors and have their children. There's also a little Mexican boy who was adopted by one family seven years ago. Just take a good look around you, Candice." He paused, giving her a scathing look. "All Indians aren't the same."

"If you're trying to tell me that Apaches aren't blood-thirsty killers, then I don't believe you. And not just from the stories. When they captured me there was another prisoner, a vaquero. They tortured him. I heard his screams." She shuddered.

"He tortured the young warrior we found, who died. He was captured and brought back here to be tortured and killed in return. Even your God says 'an eye for an eye.' We do kill, we do torture—we do rape, and we do scalp. But *only* in retaliation." He looked at her, and she felt something race down her spine. "If Luz was captured by one of the ranchers and raped and killed, Shozkay would take that man's wife, or his daughter, or his sister, and he'd rape her, then kill her."

She stared. Her heart was beating way too fast. She knew she shouldn't provoke him. She found her voice. "And you? If someone raped and killed your woman—what would you do? Would you find his woman and rape and kill her?"

He met her gaze calmly, but with steel. "Yes."

When Jack left her with Luz, who was on her knees surrounded by woven mats and rectangular cakes, Candice was still in a state of both shock and anger. Candice felt sick. He was a warrior—he had killed. How many innocent white people had fallen beneath his rifle and his knife? Had he really raped, scalped, and tortured in retribution, in vengeance? And she knew the answer.

It's impossible, one part of her mind cried.

Free yourself from him, he's Apache, she answered back.

It was a relief to turn her attention away from the man who was her new captor, and from his chilling words. "What are you doing?" she asked Luz.

The Apache woman flashed her a warm smile. "Come, look," she invited. She was carefully packing the rectangular cakes in the woven mats.

"What are they?"

Luz smiled and handed her a cake. Candice bit into it,

prepared for the worst, but found it pleasant, almost sweet. "This is pretty good."

"It is made from mescal. From a part—I do not know the name in your words." She held her hands into a rounded shape.

"The tuber?" Candice said.

Luz nodded. "We grind it, bake it. We eat them later, maybe in the winter, if it is bad." She smiled.

"Can I help?" Candice said the words before she had even thought them. Luz was pleased, and Candice watched her carefully, imitating the squaw's actions precisely.

A few minutes later Luz smiled. "You are a good squaw."

Candice actually smiled back. But she couldn't stop thinking about Jack. She needed answers, lots of answers.

"Luz," she said cautiously, after she had regained control, "is Datiye Niño Salvaje's mistress?"

Luz stopped what she was doing to look at her. "I do not know that word."

"His woman."

"Ah, I see." The woman was silent, and Candice felt sick with dread, for she could see her thinking about what to say.

"She is!" Candice cried, horrified.

"No, Sun Woman, not anymore. Once they did share a bed of hides, but that was long ago."

"She was his mis—his woman?"

"Many summers ago."

Candice clenched her fists. She had suspected, but now it was confirmed. She shouldn't care, but she did. *What is happening to me?*

The men appeared a few hours later, as if by magic, just when the thick stew was simmering perfectly. They went inside Luz and Shozkay's *gowhah* to eat. Candice couldn't look at Jack. But she was very much aware of his presence. She sat very still, watching Shozkay smile warmly at Luz while Luz served him. Then he sat down next to her, speaking in Apache. Luz laughed, flashed him a brilliant smile, and handed him a bowl. Candice still didn't move. Jack was standing behind her, so close she could feel his body heat. He murmured his thanks to Luz, then squatted down beside Candice, one warm, callused hand going to the nape of her neck beneath her braid. That was all, one touch, no words, but it conveyed too much—everything.

Later, the instant they were out of the *gohwah*, Candice turned to him as casually as she could. "Luz told me."

"What?"

Her casual air disappeared. "About Datiye. She was your mistress. Luz told me and I know she's not a liar."

Jack grimaced slightly. "That's all in the past."

"Is it?"

"Yes." He sighed. "Datiye was my wife. But that was years ago—"

"What!" She gasped, stunned.

He looked grim. "I said 'was.' We were married. It was my duty. We're divorced."

Her heart was beating wildly, and she could barely hear what he was saying. "You loved her."

"No," he said. "No, I never loved her."

"But . . . then . . . why?" Jack and Datiye had been man and wife. Man and wife . . . it was all she could think of.

"I was married to her sister. She died. It was my duty to marry Datiye. It's our way." He shrugged.

Candice stared. He had been married twice? Why was she so numb? A coherent thought managed to intrude. "Your first wife. Did you love her?"

Jack hesitated. He did not want to talk about this with Candice.

"I see," Candice said, biting her lip. There was no mistaking his hesitation, or the guarded look that had crossed his face, closing his expression. "Did you choose to marry your first wife? Did you love her?"

Jack's mouth tightened. "You don't give an inch." He stood. "We were very young. But yes, I did love her." He shrugged. "What does it matter? She's dead. That was a long, long time ago. Eight years, in fact."

I did love her. The words were a blow. Candice gave him her back and pushed through the hide flap-door. Inside, it was dark. She sank down onto the bed of hides and began massaging her aching feet. He had loved his first wife. He had been married twice.

She heard him enter and purposefully ignored him, her

eyes on her hands as she rubbed her feet. A short while later a small fire blazed, casting a dim, flickering light. She felt his eyes on her and looked up to see him staring down at her. Suddenly the *gohwah* seemed too small for the two of them, and the long night was here.

"Let me do that," Jack said, kneeling and taking her foot in his hands before she could object.

"I don't think . . ."

His hands were large, warm, and gentle. "Stop thinking, Candice. There's no point. What is, is."

He was right. She was there and she had no choice. This man had traded for her, and she belonged to him. She was at his mercy, and probing into his past wasn't going to change anything—except make him angry. And having glimpsed his anger a few times, she would rather not arouse it.

"Feel better?" he asked, his voice husky.

She had heard that tone before, and she looked up abruptly. She had seen that too-bright light in his eyes too. His hand had stilled on her ankle. Her body began a slow throbbing of fear mingled with anticipation. He slid his hand up her calf, its grip tightening possessively.

"You have the most beautiful legs I've ever seen," he murmured.

Her heart was beating erratically. "I . . . I . . ."

His hand moved up her thigh, slowly, moving higher and higher, and Candice's groin was flooded with a hot, hot ache. Oh, dear, she thought, oh, God, what is he going to do?

His hand didn't stop. It kept creeping upward until it had reached her inner thigh. She stared—from his hand, which had pushed up her dress, to his hard, sinewy arm, to his naked chest with the gleaming necklace, to his face, which was gazing steadily at her thigh. She saw the tension there, etched clearly across the sensual mouth and high cheekbones, pinching the nostrils of the straight, classic nose. His hand moved once, closing on her flesh, and she exhaled, closing her eyes. A little higher and he would touch her and she would let him.

"Ahh, shit."

His hand was gone and Candice jerked up to see him

standing with a hard, prominent arousal straining his pants. She flushed. The throb of insistent need increased.

"I'm going to take a walk. Go to sleep." He stared at her with too bright, glinting gray eyes.

Call him back.

He turned and ducked out.

Candice let out another long breath, falling onto her side and clamping her thighs together. She curled up and bit her knuckle. She relived every moment of what had just occurred, then every moment of their relationship since he had found her unconscious in the desert. And by the time she had reached the present, she was crying.

CHAPTER THIRTY-ONE

She imagined him coming home every night to Datiye, sharing a meal with her, sharing his day, a bed. But he hadn't loved her. Oh, no. He had loved his first wife, Chilahe. He had loved her so much he couldn't even talk about it. He must have been more than in love with her—he must have been crazy about her.

It was a long time before she fell asleep.

The next morning Candice awoke to the sounds of a crowd gathered close to the *gohwah.* When she had fallen asleep last night, Jack had not returned, and her last waking thoughts had been that he had gone to Datiye. And now, noticing grimly that he was not with her in the *gohwah,* she was wondering again if he had spent the night with his former wife.

She hurriedly dressed and rebraided her hair, then stepped outside. The black stallion was prancing wildly, and Hayilkah was standing not far away, a rifle aimed and pointed at the stallion. Candice froze, unable to believe what was about to happen—that the Apache was going to kill one of the most magnificent animals she had ever seen. She heard a shrill, eerie war cry.

It was Jack.

He reached Hayilkah and grabbed the barrel of the rifle. They wrestled over it, straining against each other. Hayilkah was wearing only a breechcloth, and his huge, broad body, so unusual for an Apache, rippled with thick muscle. Jack, although powerful and a big man, was taller and not quite as broad. He was bare-chested, and his back rippled as he fought for the rifle. A sharp word from Shozkay made both men pause, still tensed against each other, both gripping the rifle. Shozkay pushed between them and grabbed the gun. Jack stepped back, panting, looking murderous. Hayilkah began yelling angrily.

"What's he saying?" Candice demanded. Everyone was listening intently to the tirade.

"He says Niño Salvaje cheated him," Luz told her. "Trading him a devil in a horse's body. He tried to shoot the horse, but Niño Salvaje stopped him. Hayilkah wants you back."

Candice let loose a sharp cry, causing Jack to flash a hot silver glance at her. "What will happen?" That thought was too terrifying to contemplate.

Shozkay was talking in authoritarian tones. Both Jack and Hayilkah were listening and exchanging angry, hostile glances. It was clear that they wanted to fight.

"Shozkay is chief. He will decide what is fair," Luz interpreted softly. "He will decide by the time of White Painted Woman."

"White Painted Woman?"

"When the moon comes."

Shozkay turned his back on the two men and came over to them. Half the band had gathered, including Datiye, and the sight of her made Candice go rigid—especially when Datiye gave her a hate-filled glance. Shozkay was speaking kindly to her. "Don't worry, Sister. I will decide fairly."

Candice was barely listening. She had been too busy ignoring Datiye. She turned back to Jack and Hayilkah, who were staring at each other. She gasped as the two men stood tensed on the balls of their feet and began to slowly circle and approach each other.

"They're going to fight!" she cried. "Shozkay, stop them!"

Shozkay was watching. "No, this will happen, if not today, another time. It is better that it be now."

Candice was suddenly afraid—afraid that Hayilkah would kill Jack.

The two men were circling each other slowly, intensely. Candice couldn't take her eyes off them, both so powerful and so intent. Suddenly Datiye hissed in her ear, "If he dies, it is your fault!"

"My fault?" She was incredulous.

Datiye turned rudely away, but Luz took Candice's hand, speaking softly. "Salvaje is furious because of the way Hayilkah treated you. That is what they were arguing about just now. He is also angry because Hayilkah examined you, when it should have been his wife or his wife's mother."

As she absorbed that, Hayilkah lunged. Jack easily side-stepped, and Hayilkah quickly regained his balance, facing

him again. Jack danced lightly just beyond Hayilkah's reach.
Hayilkah approached, but was waiting, and the crowd grew
tense. Candice wiped sweat from her brow. Hayilkah suddenly kicked one foot out lethally, and had it caught Jack in
his abdomen, it would have knocked him down easily. But
Jack had anticipated it, deftly moving aside, and the brave's
kick swept empty air. Just as his foot landed, while he was still
off balance, Jack suddenly took two hard, short steps, plant-
ing himself right in front of Hayilkah. He hit him with a
powerful kick to the jaw, then landed lightly on his feet—
while Hayilkah staggered backward, but didn't fall.

Hayilkah was angry. He charged. Jack waited until the
last moment, then stepped aside, one forearm coming out
and strangling Hayilkah's throat, seeking a headlock but unable to find one. The movement caused the brave to jerk
back, and Jack hit him brutally in the kidneys twice, following
with a left to his jaw. Then he jumped back. Hayilkah panted,
but stayed on his feet.

The two men continued to circle. Candice couldn't believe that Hayilkah hadn't even gone down once under Jack's
two attacks, and it sickened her. Jack was covered with sweat,
his chest and face gleaming, but he was barely breathing. She
clenched her fists.

Jack darted in, jabbing with his left, following through
with a right that would have broken through a pine wall. It
connected with Hayilkah's nose, and blood gushed from it.
But as Jack danced back, Hayilkah struck with a kick that
caught Jack in the stomach, and he fell onto his back. Candice screamed.

Hayilkah dove on top of him.

With one hand, he held Jack's hair, with his other, he
dealt a blow to Jack's face while Jack lay gasping for breath.
Jack tried to throw him off, his hands barely affecting
Hayilkah. Hayilkah punched him again. Jack lifted his knees.
He couldn't get them up to kick Hayilkah off. Hayilkah raised
his fist.

Candice didn't think. With a cry, she catapulted onto
Hayilkah's back, sinking her teeth into his shoulder, tasting
sweat, salt, and blood, and she bit with every ounce of
strength she had. Hayilkah yelled, staggering to his feet, Candice still on his back, her teeth still in his flesh. Jack was

already up, but Candice couldn't relax. With a howl, Hayilkah threw her away from him, and she landed flat on her back in the dirt.

The tribe roared with laughter.

Candice sat up, dazed.

She focused, blinking, and thought she saw Jack staring at her in surprise.

Then Shozkay was grabbing her, two strong hands around her waist, pulling her out of the circle. "No!" Candice shouted. She struggled wildly. "Let me go! Stop this suicide! I demand you stop it! He's going to kill Jack!"

Shozkay shook her, hard. Candice stopped protesting because the two men were circling each other again, and she realized there was nothing she could do to stop the insanity. Shozkay said, "He knows now not to get close to Hayilkah."

For many minutes Jack kept to the defensive, dancing away from Hayilkah, keeping just out of his reach, easily dodging his lunges, his charges, playing it safe. Candice started to feel hope. If only he could keep this up indefinitely, he could tire Hayilkah out. But she wasn't sure how long he could hold up. His face was bleeding from a gash over one eye and another at his mouth, and he was drenched with sweat. Now his chest was rising and falling rapidly, and he was breathing through his mouth. His silver eyes were hard with concentration, never wavering from his enemy. But Hayilkah looked every bit as tired.

Suddenly Jack took two steps in and leapt at Hayilkah with both feet. The blow hit Hayilkah high on the chest and sent him staggering backward. Jack kept coming. Another kick connected with Hayilkah's jaw. Blood spurted. Hayilkah went down on his butt. Jack kicked again, to the head, and there was a crack as Hayilkah fell back against the dirt.

Jack backed off, tense and coiled, panting. He waited, out of reach, regaining his breath. Shozkay said quietly, "It is an old Apache ploy to pretend to be hurt and then take the other by surprise." Candice bit her lip. She prayed.

He stepped closer. Hayilkah's hand shot out, reaching for Jack's ankle. Jack barely jumped away, stumbling from the contact, turning just in time to meet Hayilkah's lumbering charge. Hayilkah was tired. He moved with effort, which gave Jack time to get out of the way. As Hayilkah moved past, Jack reached out, yanking his shoulder, and let loose with a right to his head. Hayilkah swayed. Jack hit him again, still holding him, and again. Hayilkah crumpled. Jack stepped back, coiled, and slammed him with a near-fatal kick. He lay very still.

There were shrieks from the Indians, and suddenly Jack was surrounded, being congratulated heartily. He staggered, panting heavily, one hand on his mouth, wiping away blood.

Candice stared, trembling. She couldn't move. She watched as Shozkay put his arm around Jack, speaking softly, only to be shoved aside by Datiye. She threw her arms around him, but Jack held her away. Over her head, he looked at Candice. Their eyes met. His were bold and triumphant. Something primitive and eternal coursed through Candice. She walked forward, not taking her eyes from him. A path cleared before her. Jack watched her approach, his eyes glittering. She grabbed Datiye by the back of her dress, pulling her aside. Candice took Jack's hand. He followed her wordlessly through the crowd, and Candice led him down to the creek, away from the turmoil and excitement.

She could feel the energy, the barely controlled bloodlust crackling in his body, sparking from his hand to hers. She was exhilarated from what had just happened, as the significance of it sank in. Jack had almost killed that warrior, not just because of the horse—but for her.

He sank to the ground, and Candice took his knife and cut a strip from her skirt. With shaking hands and a pounding heart, she soaked it in water, moving beside him, freezing when she met his eyes. His look made her heady—the proud look of triumph, the hot look of lust. She gently inspected the gash above his eye, trying not to tremble. It was as if the primitive fire running in his veins was being transmitted to hers.

"You need to be tended to," she murmured huskily. "Are you sore?"

"Very," he returned. He flinched as she cleaned the gash. "Don't move."

"Just what did you think you were doing?"

She knew exactly what he was talking about. "I was helping you," she said tersely.

He reached out and touched her hair. "Yes, you were,

weren't you?" His voice was husky. "Tell me the truth, Candice."

Candice froze.

"Why did you do that? Because you hate Hayilkah, or because you wanted to help me?"

Candice hesitated. "I owed you," she finally said. And that was true. "Remember? You saved my life, and now I've saved yours. We're even."

He studied her out of intense glittering eyes. "I saved your life twice, Candice. You still owe me."

She couldn't take another breath. From the look in his eyes she knew what he was thinking, and how he was going to have her repay him. She got to her feet quickly, breathlessly. But his hand on her wrist stopped her, pulling her down beside him, the pressure hard enough to hurt. "Jack."

His hand found her jaw, holding her head still, poised to receive his mouth. When he spoke, his breath was warm. "Do you know why I wanted to kill Hayilkah, Candice?"

She managed to shake her head. He had half his body on top of hers.

"No one abuses what belongs to me," he said. "Not my horse. Not my woman." His mouth came down hard on hers, and she was helpless to resist.

"You belong to me," he breathed, running his callused hands over her breasts and her hips. He held her head still again to violently rape her mouth with his tongue.

His words echoed. Her body flamed. She felt a rushing thrill and there was no denying it. Candice had her arms around him, clutching his wet, slick back, her nails digging into his flesh. She thrust her tongue against his, past his, boldly. He groaned and kneed her thighs apart, settling his hard groin against hers. Grinding. Candice found his hips, then his buttocks, pulling him closer, their mouths clinging and clashing desperately, and she arched her pelvis against him, mindlessly, again and again. She heard a wild, primitive moaning as his mouth trailed to her throat, kissing and biting, soothing and hurting, and she was vaguely surprised that she was making those sounds.

"Mine," he rasped, ripping open the front of her dress and pushing up her breasts and nuzzling them. He took a nipple with his teeth and tugged on it before suckling fiercely. Candice cried out, convulsing. Never, never, never had she thought it could be like this between a man and a woman . . .

He knelt between her thighs, pushing her dress up. She moaned, panting, wanting. She felt this hands slide across her swollen, pink flesh and she cried out again, arching against his hand.

"Ahh, God." He groaned, and then he lowered his head and began to tongue her.

Candice grasped his head, anchoring it, and began to sob. Convulsing waves swept through her. Escalating, intensifying. His tongue was so deft, laving the swollen nub, exploring the slick folds . . . she couldn't stand it. . . .

She cried out as her world exploded.

Abruptly he drove into her, again and again, his hands on her hips, claiming her in the most primitive way possible. And then he was collapsing on top of her, shuddering violently, his face buried in her neck, and the groan that sounded said, "Mine."

CHAPTER THIRTY-TWO

He shifted off her, onto his back. She could hear his harsh breathing begin to slow, and she could hear hers. She rolled onto her side, sanity flooding her. *Oh, God.*

She closed her eyes and recalled the magnificence of being possessed by this man. She had wanted him. She had wanted him with an uncontrollable passion. She had been mindless beneath his touch, his mouth. She had enjoyed every minute. No—that word could not possibly convey what she had been feeling. Ecstasy. Physical ecstasy. *What is happening to me?*

She had enjoyed a man's lovemaking, a man who was not her husband and who was half Indian. Oh, dear God. She clutched her hand to her mouth to prevent the choked sound from escaping.

You belong to me.

Mine.

Those words echoed in her mind. They brought a hot flush of shameful elation. She tried to refute the statement, thinking, I belong to no man—and certainly not to him. Then she would remember how he had fought Hayilkah and nearly killed him. She would remember how he had looked at her over Datiye's head, his face wet with sweat and blood, his eyes hot and proud and vitally victorious. Then she would remember how he had pulled her down into the dirt, not caring who might see, and driven himself into her, claiming her, again and again. And she could still hear her own shameless cries of pleasure and surrender.

"Candice?"

His voice was questioning in her ear, his breath warm. His hand closed on her waist. She bit her lip, hesitating, then turned to meet his gaze.

What she didn't expect was the soft look in his eyes, or the way his hand touched her face tenderly. She closed her eyes and pressed her cheek more fully into his palm. She felt his mouth brush her temple, and then he was standing.

She sat up, holding the torn front of her dress together, blushing. He was pulling up his pants and tying the drawstring. She felt the shame again—rutting in the dirt like animals—and looked away. Her heart had picked up its beat. What should she do? How should she act? What in God's name was going to happen next?

What was wrong with her?

"Let's go back to camp," he said without inflection, and when she glanced at him, the softness had gone from his eyes. She could not read his expression. His gaze flicked to her torn dress. "I'll get you a needle and some sinew, thread if I can."

She blushed more brightly.

He left her with Luz and the other women all day. Candice helped them to prepare foodstuffs, but with half her attention on what she was doing. She was utterly distracted. Every time she thought about the morning she grew hot with embarrassment and all kinds of jumbled emotions—including something no lady should be feeling—excitement. She knew only one thing to be true—she couldn't wait to get back to civilization. Back home. And what would happen then?

If her reputation had been damaged before, this time . . .

She didn't dare think about it.

That night they ate with Shozkay and Luz again. Candice found herself looking at Jack, looking and remembering. He didn't return her gaze. It was almost as if he were avoiding the haphazard meeting of their eyes. But once, just once, he looked up and their glances caught, held, locked. The brightness in his eyes almost knocked her backward. She couldn't think, just feel. And anticipate.

They walked back to their *gohwah* in silence. At the shelter he held the flap to let her precede him. She paused, her heart thudding wildly, her skin flushed and warm, and all she could think of—wish for—was that he was going to stay with her tonight—wasn't he? She turned to him.

He met her gaze fully but didn't speak. He held the flap open, waiting. She wet her lips nervously, ashamed, and knew she had hopelessly fallen into sin. "Will you come in?"

His jaw flexed. For one instant he didn't move. "Do you understand what you're asking?" His voice was husky, and it flooded her with liquid heat.

"Yes," she breathed. She ducked in, he followed. She

hesitated, unbearably shy, but her chest was so tight with wanting him that she thought it might explode. He did mean what she thought he meant, didn't he? Or should she take her clothes off?

Like some whore.

She grimaced at the ugliness of that thought, and then he touched her.

Gentle fingertips on her shoulders, but it was enough. She spun around in his arms, he clutched her to him. She raised her face, he lowered his. In perfect tandem their lips met, a soft searching before the storm and the thunder.

His lips grew more demanding, he stroked hard hands down her back and buttocks. She pressed herself fully into the large bone of his erection, and moaned into his mouth. He suddenly drew away from her to press his face in the crook of her neck, his breath warm, so warm. "Candice," he breathed.

"Oh, Jack," she whispered, finding his hair and threading it through her fingers.

"Shijii, darling . . ." He broke off, a choked sound, and lifted her, laying her on the hides. He knelt on the floor above her, she opened her arms wide. The look of anguished pleasure that swept his face made her want to enfold him to her breast all the more. "Come to me," she whispered.

He groaned and stripped off his clothes rapidly, clumsily, tripping over one pant leg. Then he was kneeling over her, pulling her into his arms. "This time, *shijii,* this time," he promised huskily, raining kisses on her mouth and throat, "this time I'll make it so good . . ."

Just having him in her arms, kissing her desperately, his large, swollen member throbbing against her belly, was making her mind reel and her body throb at a precarious pitch. With his tongue thrusting in her mouth he reached down to slide his forefinger between the swollen lips of her groin, and she gasped, arching. "Jack."

"Yes," he said. "I want to watch you, darling, I want to watch you come." Raising himself on his hands, he began rubbing the head of his penis against her, moving it slickly back and forth as her moans grew. She twisted wildly, beyond control and caring. Panting.

"Jack."

"Come, baby, come for me." And he thrust into her, and she came violently, crying aloud.

When she opened her eyes he was lying in her, watching her face with burning eyes, still hard and vitally alive inside her. He took a hank of her hair in one hand with brute strength, and with his other he captured both her wrists—kissing her deeply, fully. His legs pinned hers and she couldn't have moved if she'd wanted to. Hot sparks flared.

She began moving her hips against his, lazily, but with growing urgency. He withdrew. "Jack."

He didn't answer. Still holding her wrists, he forced her thighs farther apart with his powerful legs, keeping her immobile. He was ducking his head to her groin and spreading her flesh, flicking his tongue over it. "Do you like this?"

It took her a moment to realize he had stopped and was waiting for her answer. "Yes."

"And this?" His tongue traced a delicate route around her swollen clitoris.

She gasped, twitching but unable to move.

He raised his head. "Well?"

"Yes . . . please . . ."

"What about this?" He licked her, long and slowly.

"God," she screamed, sobbing, exploding. She felt him thrusting into her again and again and again. . . .

CHAPTER THIRTY-THREE

Where is he? Candice wondered lazily, still half asleep. She sighed and snuggled deeper beneath the heavy Navajo blanket, and all recollection of last night came flooding back to her. She had no choice but to flush furiously.

Jack had made love to her again and again, until they had both fallen into a deep, sated sleep, Candice curled up against his side with her face on his broad, warm chest. Sometime last night, too, she had woken up to find him throbbing against her leg, his hands moving slowly over her breasts, brushing erect nipples. They had made love again, a slow, sensual, dreamlike mating. She smiled with the remembrance.

And then her smile abruptly disappeared. She sat upright. Last night Shozkay would have made a decision regarding Hayilkah's accusation that Jack had cheated him—that he wanted her back. A terrible anxiety rose up in her. She didn't think Jack would listen if Shozkay decided she should be returned—or would he? She really didn't know him. He was so different, so Apache, and she didn't know or understand their ways. Candice got up and pulled on her dress, running her fingers through her tangled hair. She ducked outside.

There was the usual activity in camp. She looked for Jack but there was no sign of him. She started across the camp to the *gohwah* Luz and Shozkay shared. The woman was kneeling over a hide, scraping hairs. She looked up and smiled.

Candice's anxiety must have showed, because Luz said, "He is down by the creek."

Her heart did a funny little flutter. "Thank you," Candice said, and she was off, racing down one of the paths to the stream. She came to an abrupt halt when she saw him standing by a boulder at the water's edge, talking with Shozkay. He was wearing only a loincloth and his knife, and was barefoot like she was. The sun, streaking through the branches overhead, glinted on the delicate veins of gold in his dark hair. His profile was breathtaking and perfect. She had to admire the broad width of his shoulders and the packed muscle of his chest. He turned and saw her and stopped in midconversation, staring.

Candice couldn't look away—but she did blush. The look he was giving her was *that* kind of look.

Shozkay laughed, patted Jack on the arm, and started toward her. Candice managed to tear her gaze from Jack to smile politely at his brother. "Good morning."

Shozkay gave her a warm smile. "Good morning, *niña.*" He passed her and trudged back to the camp.

Candice remembered the reason she had been looking for him—or one of them. She started forward at a run. A smile lifted the corners of Jack's mouth, and she abruptly saw where he was looking—at her breasts bouncing, the nipples hard. She slowed to a walk, giving him a look. "You are no gentleman."

He grinned then, a dazzling expression. "True."

She bit her lip, suddenly shy.

His smile faded and he gazed at her soberly for a long, searching moment. "Good morning, *shijii.*"

Shijii, she had learned last night, meant *darling,* although literally it meant *my heart.* The endearment elated her. "Good morning."

He smiled again, this time softly. "Miss me?" He couldn't disguise the hopeful expression.

She had. She was struck with the knowledge, but afraid to admit it. So she found a new topic. "What are you doing?"

"I came to bathe."

They looked at each other again. "What is it, Candice?"

"About Hayilkah . . ." She trailed off. She wanted to touch him, to be touched. But in broad daylight the intimacy of last night seemed like a dream—except that they both knew it was real. She shifted.

"Hayilkah is very sick," Jack said. "Shozkay has decided I have to bring him, or his family, a mare in foal to the black."

"That means you don't have to give me back to him?"

"That's right."

She felt relief, and it showed.

He lifted her chin. "*Shijii,* did you really think I'd give you to him? Let him touch you again?"

"I . . . I wasn't sure."

That bothered him, and his jaw tightened. Candice saw it and was sorry, but new worries were crowding the old. Were they now free to leave?

She pictured the High C and her family, and she felt a deep sense of dread. This was what she didn't want to think about—her future. Returning. The condemnation, the scandal. And what about Jack?

"Candice, would you run and get me soap? It's in my saddlebags."

"Of course," she said, knowing at this moment she would do just about anything for him. And she was glad of something to do other than think. "I'll be right back."

Five minutes later she returned with the soap and a clean blanket. He was standing in the creek, naked, and she openly admired him, not without being affected by the sight. She was now very much aware of the rise of desire—and what it promised. He turned, and his eyes twinkled. "You make noise like a cow, a drunken cow, moving through the chaparral."

Her eyes widened—he was teasing her! "Mooo!"

He chuckled. "You're also as fast as a tortoise."

"But as soft as a kitten," she purred.

He laughed. "With claws, I know."

She blushed at the reference to her wild passion.

"Give me the soap."

"Step closer to the bank."

"Throw it."

"No."

"No?" His tone was exaggerated.

"If you want it, you'll have to come here and get it."

He grinned. "You are asking for big trouble, *ish'ria'nay.*"

"Very big trouble," she said pointedly, looking at his swelling groin.

He gave her a look.

She giggled.

He charged.

She ran.

He caught her easily and swept her up into his arms. She shrieked playfully and pretended to fight. "Someone else I know needs a bath," he declared.

"No," she cried in mock fear. "The water is cold!"

He waded in and held her a few feet above it.

"Let me down, Jack," she demanded.

"Okay," he said, laughter in his voice.

She tensed, waiting to be heaved.

He released her legs so that her body swung down against his, still suspended, and he began to lower her very slowly, looking into her eyes. Playfulness vanished. Her eyes widened and she slid down his body, the dress riding up. His hands were on her buttocks.

"Put your legs around my waist," he said.

She obeyed and he set her on his straining manhood. She gasped. He laughed. A hoarse, sensuous sound. He had nothing to lean her against, and their position was awkward without support. "Now what?" she breathed shakily.

"I'm going to come inside you," he said.

She gasped and he captured her mouth, dropping slowly to his knees and setting her on her back in the shallow water without ever withdrawing. They began moving together, slowly and rhythmically, reaching a hot climax simultaneously.

"You're insatiable," Candice said, smiling, brushing her hair off his cheekbone.

His gray eyes, sated now and solemn, moved over her face as she continued to toy with the strands. "You make me that way."

She wanted it to be true. Oh, she did. "Really?"

"How can you doubt it?"

Her hand slid to his hard shoulder. "I don't know. You've had others, other women . . ."

"Not many and not often. And never like you."

She inhaled with sharp pleasure, then turned her head to his and sought his mouth with hers. Her lips brushed his softly, and when she pulled slightly back, she saw that his eyes were closed, his expression almost strained. She wondered what dark emotions and darker thoughts wrenched his soul so that he would come to her with unquenchable, fierce need.

"We'd better bathe," Candice said.

He opened his eyes and kissed her breast before sitting. She stood, very much aware of being naked in broad daylight, and she reached for the blanket to cover herself from his gaze. He caught her wrist. "Don't. You have nothing to hide from me."

She colored. "It's just . . ." Her color deepened. "It's

not right . . . the middle of the day . . ." Like some harlot.

"I know every inch of you."

She let him pull the blanket away. "I love every inch of you," he said.

Trying not to feel self-conscious, she walked into the water and began to bathe. He watched her with undisguised interest and pleasure for a while before standing and joining her. He began lathering his legs. "Candice?"

She was rinsing her hair, trying not to think about bathing in broad daylight with a man. "Yes?"

"We could leave today."

She was silent. The words rang, especially *could*. She ducked under the water again and came up pushing her hair out of her face.

"Hayilkah might die. I want to stay here until the danger is past."

Her heart had its own mind and it was jubilant. "That's fine," she said, relief gushing through her.

For the first time, they looked at each other. Neither one wanting to openly bring up the question that they were both thinking. *What happens when we go back?*

CHAPTER THIRTY-FOUR

Candice opened her eyes and realized she had drifted asleep.

Jack had gone to get them dinner and had left her at their *gohwah* to make a fire. She had fallen asleep, day-dreaming about him like an infatuated adolescent. She sat up, rubbing her eyes, and thought about food. At that precise juncture, two rabbits sailed through the air and landed with a thud at her feet, causing her to jump up and cry out in alarm.

Jack grinned, striding toward her.

"You scared the life right out of me," Candice said, but she was smiling because his delight in having frightened her was so boyish. He was showing her a different side of himself, one she was delighted to see.

"That's because you have the hearing of an old, deaf woman," Jack said. "What—no fire? What have you been doing all this time, woman? Here."

Candice wanted to jump back as the knife came flying through the air at her, but she didn't move. It landed an inch away from her big toe, right between the two rabbits, the blade buried in the ground, hilt quivering. She looked up slowly, murderously.

"I've gone too far," he said meekly.

"Too far."

He approached and knelt swiftly at her side. "I'm sorry, *inlgashi.*"

How could she stay angry, with him nuzzling her neck? "You could have killed me!"

He laughed. "Maybe cut off your foot, but killed you? I don't think so."

She hit him in the arm.

He caught her wrist and deftly pulled her between his thighs. "Someone wants more trouble," he purred.

"I want big trouble," she said, and then went absolutely crimson.

His eyes widened, and then he laughed, hugging her fiercely. "Later, *ish'tia'nay,*" he promised.

"I didn't mean—" she began, still blushing.

"Oh, yes, you did."

She was in his arms and she looped her hands around his neck. He was smiling, so relaxed and lighthearted and so impossibly handsome. "What are you looking at?" he asked gruffly.

"You." She was embarrassed, and got to her feet, pulling out of his grasp.

She reached for the game and the knife. He came to her instantly, taking the knife from her hand. "You make the fire, I'll clean the game."

"But cleaning game is women's work," Candice said coyly.

"If you object too hard, I will let you do it."

Candice made the fire. "What happened to your parents, Jack?"

He started. "What's this about?"

"I'm curious. I don't know anything about you."

He grinned. "Now, that's a lie if ever I heard one."

"I was not referring to your baser appetites."

"Baser appetites?" He chuckled. "You mean the fact that I like to make love to you?"

"You have a one-track mind, Jack."

He smiled.

"Your parents?"

Jack spitted the split hare. "My mother died a short while ago. My father, who was a brave warrior, died eight years ago of natural causes."

Candice watched him turning the spit. "I don't understand. If your parents were still alive, how could Cochise give you away as a gift?"

He sat back on his haunches, Apache-style. "I was telling you about the only parents I ever knew—my adoptive ones."

"Oh." She thought about that. "What about your real ones?"

He didn't look at her now, and he was no longer quite so relaxed. "My father was a miner, a white man. I never knew my mother, but she was a squaw. We worked in the streams, panning. He was killed when Cochise and some warriors came to the house. I was about six, maybe seven. Cochise captured me and took me back with him, and later gave me to Nalee and Machu."

"I'm sorry, Jack."

"Don't be. My father was a hard, cruel man and I was better off with the Apaches."

"You don't mean that."

He looked up. "I most certainly do."

She was silent for a moment, absorbing what he'd said and, more important, how he'd said it. "When were you married to Datiye?"

"I divorced her about three years ago." He pulled the hare from the fire and tested it.

Candice was appalled. "You divorced her."

"It's not unusual."

"How long were you and Datiye married?"

Without looking up, he said, "Three winters."

She gasped aloud. Three whole years! She had been his wife for three years!

Jack regarded her thoughtfully, then handed her a section of hare.

"How did your first wife die?"

Jack put down the piece of meat he had just picked up. When he looked at her, every muscle in his face was tight. "In childbirth."

She knew he had loved his dead wife. And she imagined the woman—a dark, ethereal vision. Jealousy ran thickly in her veins, and even though she knew it was wrong, she couldn't help it.

"Do you still live with this tribe? Are you here all the time?"

His tone was clipped. "No."

"But—"

Jack stood, tense and angry. "I left my people three years ago."

She knew she should leave it alone. "Why did you leave them?"

He faced her. "Do you think that sharing my bed entitles you to ask all these questions?"

She felt like she'd been slapped, and she gasped, turning abruptly. Jack threw his dinner down and marched away, into the woods. Candice watched him go and wanted to weep. She had only wanted to learn more about him. It seemed that she knew nothing at all. She hadn't meant to pry. But there had been no call for him to attack her that way—not after all the intimacy they'd shared.

And now the intimacy lay shattered in the night around them.

CHAPTER THIRTY-FIVE

He walked for a long time, and his anger cooled. He hadn't meant to fly off the handle like that. He was sorry. He was more than sorry. He thought about the beauty of last night and today, of Candice warm and loving in his arms, her smile brilliant and just for him, and he felt a physical pain—he didn't want to lose her. As all the gods knew, he would have to give her up soon enough—and wasn't half of his reason for staying behind because he wanted time with her?

In a way, sharing the burdens of his life with her would be a relief. But he wasn't ready. There was too much between them—her white blood, the prejudices he'd already witnessed, her future. He walked for a long time, brooding.

It was midway into the night before he returned, clutching something in his hands, his heart straining his ribs with worry that she wouldn't forgive him. He ducked into the *gohwah* with a torch and set it in the ground. One glance at her stiff back told him she was awake.

"Candice?"

She whipped upright, facing him. Her face was tear-streaked, and it tore his heart. "I suppose you were with your ex-wife tonight!"

He knelt beside her. "You don't believe that."

"It must be after midnight," she cried.

He didn't take his eyes from her face. "I was making this," he said, handing her a woven feather headband. Her eyes went to the beautiful blue, gray, and red band. There were touches of silver and gold in it. "I'm sorry," he said softly.

She looked at him, then at the headband. "It's beautiful," she said.

"I don't want to fight with you," Jack whispered, touching her face. *"Shiji . . ."*

As if on cue, Candice leaned forward, and he pulled her against him. He held her tight, eyes closed, and a long breath escaped him. The feather headband fell to the ground.

Candice clutched his neck, and her mouth sought his wildly. He opened to her, she plunged her tongue into his mouth. He fell backward, she rode him down. On her knees, still kissing him, she began rubbing her bare breasts against his chest. The tips grew hard and tight. She caught a hank of his hair and clutched it almost painfully.

Jack let her be the aggressor, his heart fighting the confines of his chest. He'd never had a woman attack him before. She was biting his neck, all the while rubbing her breasts with their hard, enlarged nipples against him. Then she lowered her naked, wet groin to his and began a rapid, rhythmic grinding. He groaned.

She reached down and fumbled with his drawstring, her breath loud and harsh. He looked at her beautiful, passion-glazed face, the parted lips, the flushed cheeks, the tangled, disheveled mane of hair. "God." He groaned as she grabbed his thick member and rubbed the tip against her swollen flesh. Then she pushed him inside her and impaled herself.

She rode him hard and easy, fast and slow. Jack was spinning out of control too soon. This was Candice, his wife, his beautiful wife . . . he arched upward, shooting his hot seed into her again and again.

When he opened his eyes she was moving slowly, still flushed, so magnificent it took his breath away. She stopped moving and sat panting, watching him in the torchlight.

He pulled her into his arms. "Forgive me, *shijū.*"

"You're forgiven," she said huskily.

"Even for losing control?"

She moaned slightly, rubbing against his thigh, her lips seeking his. "I wanted to watch you," she whispered hoarsely.

Her words knocked the breath right out of him. He rolled her onto her back, nuzzling her breasts, reaching down to fondle the hot, wet flesh between her legs. "Now let me watch you," he said.

CHAPTER THIRTY-SIX

Hayilkah's fever lasted ten days.

On the eleventh day it broke, and everyone knew he would live.

Jack skipped a stone across the creek. There was a constricting tightness in his chest, as if he were wearing an iron band. For a while, it had seemed as if he and Candice would never have to face the future—their future.

After that one terrible time, they had avoided any and all conversation that might lead to a repetition of what had happened. Candice never again pried into his past, and they avoided all topics relating to Tucson, the High C, and her family. They monitored Hayilkah's progress daily, and Jack felt a guilt-laden relief each day that the fever lingered. Candice had spent some time with the women, doing women's chores—mostly preparing food for the winter ahead—and Jack had spent time with the braves, hunting. They had spent their nights together in a frenzied kind of passion. As if there were no tomorrow.

They could no longer avoid facing the inevitable.

Jack's obligation, his responsibility, his honor, demanded that he return Candice to her people and her home. He had married her in the first place to free her. He had never dreamed she would be a willing wife, never dreamed he could ever have a woman like her. Never, when he married her, had he thought they would discover such passion in each other's arms, such intimacy. And, for Jack, such love.

He had known for a long time that he was in love with Candice, but it wasn't something he had been able to face. Until now. And it hurt.

The pain of losing her was almost unbearable.

He thought: But things are different now. True, I married her to free her. But she comes to me willingly, eagerly. She is my wife. *I don't have to give her up.*

Of course, he could not force her to remain with him, it was not done. Women, too, had the right of divorce. Which meant, if he wanted to keep her, he would have to tell her about their marriage and give her a choice. Did he dare even hope she would want to stay with him?

He thought of all the moments they had shared, much of it spent in sex. Still, there were other times, when she cooked his food and mended his clothes and teased and flirted. He thought of how she had come to know all the children by name, and how she had played with the littlest ones, making them shriek with laughter. He imagined her with his children, and it was something he wanted more than he had ever wanted anything, other than her. Hope suddenly reared in his heart, hot and potent. He had a chance. He knew he did. He would will it that she would agree to stay with him as his wife.

Although there was a dark corner of fear within him, he shoved it away and hurried back to their *gohwah* with a light stride. He began thinking of the future. Of course they could not stay there—for all the same old reasons. But they could move away, far away, maybe to California, or the Oregon Territory. They could farm, ranch. They could homestead. Maybe she was already pregnant. Maybe next year, at this time, she would be nursing his son.

She was kneeling over a pot of stew, stirring it. She had become a good cook. She was wearing, as always, the feather headband he had made for her, her hair tied in one fat braid, which was very different from the Apache women's style. He had made matching earrings for her, and they skimmed her cheeks as she leaned forward, shades of blue and red, silver and gold. She had yellow hair the color of sunshine, but she looked like a squaw—his squaw—and he smiled.

She looked up and beamed. "Jack, you're just in time. Come here and taste this. Tell me if it needs more of that funny bark."

He knelt and took her shoulders. "Candice, Hayilkah's fever broke."

Her expression of pleasure faded. "Oh."

He lifted her to her feet. "We have to talk."

Candice bit her lip, a gesture of nervousness he was now familiar with. Her navy eyes were wide and trained right on him. Her heart was pounding urgently. She felt icy despair. "I guess it's time to go back," she said, and wanted to die when she thought about her family's reaction to her return. She closed her eyes, thinking of the ensuing scandal.

"Not necessarily," he said quietly, watching her face.

Her eyes flashed. "It was one thing to be stuck here in this camp," she said, "but I won't be your mistress."

His world started to crumble. "You're my wife."

She stared. "What?"

"I didn't tell you because there was no point. But under Apache law we are man and wife."

She stepped back from the impact of the statement. It was impossible! "I don't believe you," she said.

"It's true. I offered for you and was accepted, we shared the *gohwah*—that's about all there is to it."

Candice's hand went to her winging heart, as if to still it. His words sank in. She was his wife. "But I'm not Apache, Apache law means nothing to me."

He watched her, his jaw flexing, as more of his world disintegrated.

She imagined the scandal. "Candice married that half-breed," she could hear Millie Henderson saying. She went red. She imagined her father—stunned and disbelieving. She imagined Luke, Mark, and John-John—their cumulative shock. Having been in this camp for almost two weeks was bad enough, but actually to be married to an Apache. . . .

She lifted her shocked, frightened eyes to his.

He could barely breathe for the knot that was in his throat. His hand closed around her wrist desperately. "You're my wife," he said with a pleading note. "Whether you think so or not. You don't have to go back. You can stay with me. We could go to California. Wherever you want. We—"

She didn't hear the last, not really. She stepped away from him. "I can't be your wife," she cried. "Jack, are you insane? I can't—oh, God! No one can find out about this!" she cried frantically.

His face turned expressionless, his voice cold. "Fine. I'll take you back tomorrow."

Candice watched him walk away, still dazed. She sank to the ground. She was shaking. It was happening too soon, being confronted with reality, with the future. She was considered married to him? Oh, God. If anyone found out . . .

She covered her face with her burning hands. She felt

something like panic. She remembered the barbecue and the stares and the whispers.

She thought about Jack. A stabbing pain pierced her to her very soul. But now, now she had to face everything—including what she had become. No better than a whore. A lady did not willingly give herself to any man outside of marriage, especially not one who was half Indian. It didn't matter that he was handsome and virile, and all she had ever wanted in a man. What mattered was what she had done, how she had acted, had fallen. The only way she could ever salvage her reputation and atone for her sins would be to marry a white man, become a dutiful wife, and confess all her sins.

She really didn't want to leave Jack.

That, too, she had to face. It stabbed, it twisted, it wrenched, and it hurt. But it didn't matter, because she had no choice. She had no choice but to forget everything that had happened between them. After all, she was not some Apache squaw—but Candice Marilynn Carter.

Why, then, thinking of Jack, did she feel so guilty?

He did not return to share their *gohwah* that night. Candice couldn't sleep. She had been thinking—shamelessly—that they still had a few nights together, and even though it was wrong, she wanted more than his intimate touch. She wanted desperately to lie a few last times in his arms, her body entwined with his, his breath fanning her hair. She imagined him angrily stalking the riverbanks. She imagined him in Datiye's arms. She knew that was not where he was tonight, but soon he would find another woman, and the thought sickened her even though she knew it had to be. Just as she had to find a husband—a white husband.

She was still awake when the first rays of dawn crept beneath the hide flap. Not long after, it opened and Jack ducked his head in. "I'm saddling the black. We'll eat and leave." He ducked out before she could even open her mouth.

She trembled. His face had been devoid of warmth—worse, his eyes were absolutely blank. She took a breath and pulled on her moccasins. She rebraided her hair, which had been left loose while she slept. Her hand fumbled over the headband he had given her, then she put it on with the earrings. She stepped outside.

Jack was already heating up the stew left over from last night, and Shozkay was with him. Candice wished Shozkay would leave so they could talk, but he didn't. Instead he turned to look at her with dark, grim eyes. He spoke urgently to Jack in Apache, and Candice wished she could understand.

Jack replied in a monotone without looking up from what he was doing. Shozkay argued, angry. Finally he gave up and left.

Jack handed her a bowl of stew and bread made from corn and berries. She waited for him to look at her, acknowledge her, say something, but he didn't. He squatted and ate quickly and efficiently. Candice had no appetite. "Jack? What did Shozkay want?"

Jack set his empty bowl aside, standing. "He wanted me to stay."

She bit her lip. "Jack?"

He went into the *gohwah* and came out with all their things—the hides and blanket, his weapons and saddlebags. He dumped everything on the ground, and she watched as he began dismantling the shelter. She felt sick with heartache. She clutched her hands together.

"Take the pot and bowls down to the creek and wash them out," he said without even glancing at her.

The frame fell to the ground.

Candice held back tears and picked up the items and started away. Her vision blurred. It was better this way, she decided emotionally. Better to make a clean break now than have even a few more days.

Of course she was lying to herself, and she knew it.

Luz was waiting back at the camp with Shozkay, and Datiye was there too, talking a mile a minute to Jack. Candice handed Luz the bowls and the pot, which they had borrowed, but she stared at Jack listening to Datiye. She was standing too close to him. She touched his arm, let her hand linger. Jack shrugged, spoke, and turned away.

Candice hated her.

He won't have to look very far for another woman, she thought bitterly.

Luz embraced her fondly. Candice found herself blinking back more tears, then crying. "Usen guard you well, sister," Luz said softly.

"Thank you," Candice said, wiping her eyes. "Usen guard you too—God go with you."

Shozkay and Jack looked at each other, then embraced. Jack had packed up what he wanted and left the rest for his brother. He swung up into the saddle, then dropped his foot from the stirrup, and held out a hand. This was all done impassively. Candice settled behind him, her heart wrenching again. At the touch of her breasts against his back, and her hands on his waist, he stiffened, and she almost gave in to the urge to weep.

PART THREE

Lies

CHAPTER THIRTY-SEVEN

"Get off."

Below the ridge where they'd stopped, Candice could make out the walls and corrals and buildings of the High C, about a mile away. Her hands tightened on Jack's waist.

The past three days had been the worst in her life.

"Candice, get off," Jack said again, in a clipped tone she was becoming too familiar with and hated.

Candice slid off the black stallion. "What—what are we doing?"

He was wearing the battered rawhide hat, and he touched the brim briefly with one finger, a clearly embittered expression on his face. "You know the way."

Her heart twisted violently with understanding—and then began a wild, rapid pounding. "Jack! You're leaving?"

"That's right. It will only take you half an hour to make it down."

She grabbed the horse's reins. It could not end this way. It couldn't. "Wait."

He smiled mockingly. "For what? A fonder farewell? Let go of the reins, Candice." His tone had become a warning.

"Oh, God, Jack!" she replied, reluctantly dropping the leathers. "When will I see you again?"

"In hell, I imagine," he said, turning the black.

She ran alongside him. "I'm not going to see you again, am I?" She panted.

"No." He suddenly looked down at her, his gray eyes icy cold. Candice started to cry. His expression tightened and the black moved into a lope. Candice stumbled slightly, sobbing now, and watched the horse and rider disappear back over the ridge.

She sank onto the ground. She grabbed her knees and sobbed. She rocked and let the anguish and heartache flow. After a while the tears lessened, and the wails ceased, and she wiped her eyes, sniffling. But the sense of loss did not go away. It was potent and stabbing, and nearly unbearable.

She still didn't understand how he could turn from her so completely and abruptly the night before they'd left camp

—when he had told her they were married. He had not thawed for a single instant since then, and now he had her believing he truly couldn't care one way or another about her. Had it all been nothing but a lark for him? While she was willing, she was useful—and once she was no longer willing, she no longer mattered? She didn't want to believe it, but after the past few days she had no other choice.

Oh, God.

The day they left the Indian camp they'd ridden all day in silence. Candice had attempted, finally, to iniate a conversation. She was met with such rude rejection she hadn't tried again.

The nights had been the same. He limited his words to orders, like "Start the fire," "Clean the game." He never looked at her. When it was time to sleep he threw the blanket at her and slept alone, across the fire from her.

It had been that way for three days and three nights.

Candice sniffed again and wiped her eyes and got to her feet. Maybe it was better this way. It would have been dangerous for him to take her all the way back to the High C. This way she could really lie and say she'd escaped her captors a while ago, shortening the time she had supposedly spent in the camp. Yes, this way was better. In time she would forget Jack Savage ever existed.

And she knew she didn't believe that for a second.

She started down the slope, trying not to think about that cold bastard. And to think she had once thought he was warm and loving. Had that tender side of him really existed, or had she imagined it? Instead she focused on her story. And her objective of finding a husband.

She remembered Judge Reinhart's rejection of her because she had danced with Jack at the barbecue. She decided he was out of the running. She was sure she could persuade Tim McGraw to court her, get him to come around if he was still upset about her dancing with Jack. And if not . . . there was no shortage of men. The sooner she was married respectably, the better off she'd be. But why wasn't her heart in this?

It was like the sun had gone out of her life.

It took her more like an hour to reach the ranch. The going was slow, treacherous with rocks and spiky cactus, and she had to keep an eye out for rattlers and copperheads. Once she was out on the flat the sentry saw her coming, and his cries rang out. The heavy wooden gates opened and a rider came out. It was one of the hands.

There was no mistaking his wide-eyed expression. "Miss Carter?"

Candice braced herself reluctantly and thought that the sooner she got out of her buckskins, the better. "Please, Willie, let me up."

"Yes, ma'am," he said, and he swung her up behind him.

He dropped Candice in front of the house. "Everyone's out looking for you, ma'am. They been gone for days, so I imagine they'll be back soon to change horses."

"Thank you, Willie," she said, suddenly feeling overwhelmingly weary. She wanted food, real food, and a bath.

Maria came running out of the house, her arms wide, babbling an incoherent stream of Spanish. Candice was enfolded in her soft, ample frame, and the warmth felt so good she thought she might start crying all over again. "Are you all right, *poquita*?" Maria finally said, clutching her face.

Candice gave her a wan smile, about to say "Yes" when her glance flickered past Maria to the porch. A lean, dark man, impeccably dressed, was standing on the porch—staring at her.

She was seeing a ghost.

"Hello, Candice," Virgil Kincaid said.

CHAPTER THIRTY-EIGHT

Candice fainted, hitting the ground with a thud.

Maria screamed.

Kincaid came running off the porch and swept Candice into his arms.

"I'll get some cool rags and whiskey," Maria said. "You take her up to her room."

Kincaid didn't need to be told what to do. He took the stairs quickly, impatiently. He kicked the door shut behind him, dropping Candice on the bed, staring. Her face was white. Her lashes moved.

He slapped her face, not hard or roughly, but to get her to come to. She moaned. Maria came running in with a pitcher of water, rags, and whiskey. Kincaid stood back to let her minister to Candice. Maria wiped her face, and as Candice moaned again, she lifted her slightly and poured a trickle of whiskey down her throat. Candice started sputtering, and her eyes flew open. She looked directly at Kincaid. "Oh, God, you're not dead."

He smiled tightly.

Candice suddenly closed her eyes, flooded with relief. She wasn't a murderess. She hadn't killed him.

"Are you better, *cara*?" Maria asked tenderly.

"Yes."

"I'll leave you two alone then," Maria said, beaming.

As she left, Candice sat upright—all relief vanishing as she realized Maria and everyone in the valley thought Kincaid was her husband. Oh, God! She went white again. "Did you . . . did you tell them?" Her voice was hoarse.

The bed shifted under his weight.

"Tell them what, *cara*?" He smiled unpleasantly. "That you tried to kill me? Or that you ran off with me and we never married—that what everyone believes to be true is all lies?"

Lies. Oh, God, so many lies. "Virgil, please."

She sat up, trying to control the panic engulfing her.

He smiled a thin smile, and it didn't reach his eyes. "I owe you, my dear."

She tried to twist away from his touch, but his hand

tightened cruelly around her face, and she couldn't move. "I'm sorry," she gasped.

"I'll bet you are," he snarled. "Sorry I'm alive?"

"Please." She whimpered. "No, I'm glad, Virgil, glad you're alive, I didn't mean to shoot you, you have to understand!"

He studied her with a clenched jaw while Candice held her breath. "Did they rape you?"

She gasped. "Who?"

He grabbed her braid and pulled her head back. "Who? You were captured by Apaches. Did they?"

"No! They don't rape women, they're not like the Comanches. I was treated well. I mean I wasn't beaten or anything." She was babbling. "My captor thought I was rare, a prize. He was hoping to marry me off to someone in the tribe for many gifts."

Virgil started to relax. "You look like some dirty, half-breed squaw."

Candice bit her lip. "Did you tell them the truth?"

He understood perfectly. "Relax, dear, everyone believes you are still my wife."

"What do you want?"

"Revenge," he said, removing his Stetson. "And you."

"What are you going to do?" Her heart thudded loudly, painfully.

"You've made it easy," he said. "Telling everyone you are my wife."

His hand touched her jaw, slid down her neck to her shoulder. Candice was frozen. He fondled her bosom. She pushed him away, leaping off the other side of the bed. "I'll scream," she said. She meant it. She would scream, as if bloody murder were being committed.

Kincaid smiled. "I had forgotten just how enticing you are, Candice. Do you know you make my blood race?"

Candice pressed harder against the wall. Why was he there? What did he mean—revenge? And what, in God's name, could she do? And what about the rest of Tucson? He was supposedly her husband. . . .

Kincaid had removed his jacket casually. "It's very convenient that you told everyone we were married, my dear. I think you are stuck in lies of your own making."

"What are you going to do?"

Kincaid sat casually on the bed, pulling off his brocade vest.

"You can't tell them," she whispered, frightened. "Pa would kill me if he knew we didn't get married. And the talk . . . he'll kill you!"

Kincaid grinned. "You mean he'd *try* to kill me. Do you think any of your family has a chance going up against me?"

Candice was horrified. If they ever found out, they would go after Kincaid, and being fair men, they would give him a chance to defend himself. Kincaid would kill them all, one by one. She knew it.

"I still want you, Candice," he said simply. "More now than before."

She was sick.

"After all, it's my husbandly right."

Candice stiffened against the headboard. She was locked in this charade. She could not admit to the truth. She had no choice.

"I don't think you will scream, my dear. In fact, I think you will act the charming, doting wife until we leave here."

Her mind raced. "Leave?" And even as she said the word, she knew she couldn't stay behind if he left, not if everyone thought they were married.

Kincaid stood and walked over to her. He slipped his hand in her hair. "I went to an inordinate amount of trouble to get you away from your family so you could be my mistress." He stared, his dark gaze black and ugly. "Why do you think I went to so much trouble, Candice? Because I wanted you. I still want you, and you will be mine until I'm through with you. Do you understand?"

She understood.

The blow came so quickly, she never saw it, only felt it, as his hand struck her face, sending her head reeling against the headboard of the bed.

"Put it this way. I won't even wait for that hot-headed brother of yours to learn the truth from you and call me out. I will kill him in cold blood if you so much as act like anything but an adoring wife." He began to remove his shirt.

She nodded dumbly.

"Don't worry," Kincaid said conversationally, throwing

his shirt over a chair. His chest was lean and hard, packed with muscle. "The charade as my adoring—*adoring*—wife need last only until we reach El Paso. We will leave first thing tomorrow. But my threat holds. You will obey me until I send you away, at which time you may do as you please."

Candice tried to get her mind to work. Once he tired of her she would be free to go home. She could say he had been killed. Again.

He sat on the bed and reached for her. He was powerful, she thought numbly, as he pulled her close, and she wondered, inanely, if he was as powerful as Jack.

"I may not have wanted to marry you, Candice," he said, his face inches from hers, "but you're an incredibly exciting woman." He laughed huskily, his face coming closer. "The fact that you hate me seems to whet my appetite," he said, kissing her.

Candice tried to turn her face away, tried to push him off, but it was useless. His lips ground into her brutally. He was hurting her on purpose, and she knew it. Instinctively she raked his cheek with her nails. His response was instantaneous. He smacked her across the face—hard, drawing blood from her mouth. She tasted it as tears welled up in her eyes. He stepped back, looking vicious. "Let me give you some advice, dear. I dismiss my mistresses when I'm ready. Don't ever try to leave me again, because I will hurt you seriously next time."

I could go to Jack for protection, she thought frantically. And knew that even if she could somehow send him word, he would not come to her aid. She was trapped, and there was no way out.

Kincaid was on top of her now, his body hot and hard, his manhood swollen and stabbing at her through his trousers. Candice struggled, but uselessly, and he laughed at her efforts.

It hurt. God, it hurt. He freed his manhood and was jamming it into her dry, tight flesh. He smothered her scream with his hand and paused abruptly to stare with disbelief and growing anger into her white, tearstained face.

"I've been dreaming of busting you," Kincaid rasped, furious. "Damn you!"

Candice closed her eyes and bit her lip while his member throbbed inside her.

His fingers dug into her face. "You told me they didn't rape you."

Her eyes flew open and flamed with defiance. "They didn't! I gave myself willingly to one of them!"

His face contorted.

And he slammed viciously into her.

CHAPTER THIRTY-NINE

He groaned.

He opened his eyes and tried to focus. The room was blurred, indistinct at first. He closed his eyes again against the bright, streaming sunlight, and felt the stab of pain in his temples, the unnatural thudding of his heart, the nausea welling in his abdomen. He needed water, desperately. As if he had been traveling across the Sonora Desert for days without a single drop. He opened his eyes and attempted to sit.

His head thundered between his ears.

Jack reached automatically for the pitcher on the floor next to the straw mattress, pouring a mug of the clear, cool liquid, then draining its contents. He drank another glass, then looked around. He was in a partitioned area of what was probably a one-room adobe house. A dirty blanket enclosed the small space he was in. He was lying on a filthy mattress. It was the only item in the room other than the cracked earthenware pitcher, the tin mug, and a looking glass that was propped against one wall.

He had on his pants, but that was it. Where was he and how had he gotten there? He didn't remember retiring—in fact, the last thing he remembered was watching the moon rise through the open saloon door, while he drank himself senseless. He must be in a back room of one of the houses near the saloon. God, did he have a headache!

The blanket moved and Jack tried to sit up. He stared with shock at the familiar face of the half-breed girl who worked in the saloon. She was so pitifully thin and dirty, so lifeless and young. He didn't remember bedding her. He prayed he hadn't.

She didn't say anything, but she smiled slightly and offered him a cup of steaming coffee and a fresh pastry. He wondered how she had gotten the money to pay for it, and felt sick as he understood what must have occurred between them last night—for her to offer him food, for her to smile.

Jack groaned and grimaced, filled with self-loathing. "Do you have any whiskey?" he said, as the pain he had been trying to escape yesterday came flooding back. "What time is it?"

She made signs with her hands, and he remembered that she couldn't talk—someone had cut out her tongue—and he felt nausea rising hard and fast. She set down the coffee and doughnut and turned to go. He grabbed her wrist, his fingers closing over skin and bone. "Wait."

She stopped and looked at him.

"Last night," he said slowly, making sure she understood. "Did we . . . ?" He motioned to the bed. "You and me, did we sleep together?"

She smiled again, and for that instant he thought he couldn't bear himself, not for using some poor abused child, but then she shook her head. She made signs that he had been sleeping next door, his head on the table. She was telling him that he had passed out.

"Thank you," Jack said politely, flooded with relief. He wondered how he had gotten there, to her bed. She left and he rubbed his face. When the blanket moved again, he looked up into the eyes of a heavy Mexican woman.

"You pay for last night," she said in broken English, holding out her hand.

"I didn't bed her."

"No matter. You too drunk is not my business. You sleep here, you pay."

"How much?"

"One bit."

Jack reached into his pocket for a coin and found it was empty. "Damn."

The matron folded her heavy arms across her even heavier bosom. "You have no money?"

"Apparently not."

She scowled, furious.

Jack got to his feet unsteadily. He was sick with a hangover. But at least this novel situation was keeping him distracted. "Look," he said. "I'll bring you a deer."

She stared, unbelieving. *"No stupido,* señor."

"You obviously could use the meat. I'll bring you a deer," he repeated.

She narrowed her eyes suspiciously.

"I give you my word," he said, looking into her eyes.

She smiled. "I believe you. My daughter tell me with sign—you are not bad like the others in that saloon. When?"

"Tomorrow."

She nodded, satisfied. "Maybe a chicken too?"

He almost smiled. "If I can. How did I get here?"

"We wake you with water. You try to walk. You talk loudly about Candice Carter. You are the breed she left Kincaid for, eh?"

"What?"

"I know the story, don't worry, señor. It is all over town. She elope with Kincaid, but she come back with you. She leave Kincaid when she meet you, eh?" The woman laughed. "Now she leave you for Kincaid. The woman cannot make up her mind."

"What do you mean?" he asked, confused. "What do you mean that she left me for Kincaid? He's dead."

"Oh, no, señor. Kincaid ride in a few days ago looking for his wife. Very upset."

Jack leaned against the rough wall. "What? Kincaid's alive? Here?"

"Here, sí. With his wife." She jabbed her thumb behind her.

"They're here now, together, in town?"

"Waiting for the stage," she said.

He was reeling despite his numbed mind. Jack felt his heart pick up a heavy, thudding beat. She was here, in Tucson. *With Kincaid.* Could he never escape her? Where were they going? It was none of his business, he didn't care. She was no longer of any concern to him. Were they leaving on the noon stage west, or the 3 P.M. stage east? Both lines ran late—sometimes by a few hours—but usually by half a day, or even days.

Damn! Where were they going?

And why did he care?

He reminded himself that she had made her choice.

He thought of her in Kincaid's arms.

Had their reunion been joyous? Had she wept with ecstasy because her husband was alive? How would she explain her loss of virginity? Viciously he hoped Kincaid would make her suffer for it.

"You have any whiskey around here?" he managed, focusing on the woman, who was watching him with careful interest.

He tried not to think as he belted down the shot she brought him. He was getting drunk again. After last night, it wouldn't take much. *Where were they going?*

Why couldn't he stop thinking about that heartless bitch?

He had been a fool to think she would stay with him. Damn her! Why did he have to keep thinking about how she looked, how her eyes flashed when she was angry, how they glowed when she was aroused, how they softened when she smiled? How she felt, beneath him, sheathing him, how she responded to his passion in a way that no other woman had, and never would . . . how when they were together, there was something so fulfilled, it was beyond the actual physical act of copulation, giving her a part of himself, and becoming a part of her. . . .

His body moved of its own volition. It wasn't until he stepped out of the shack and onto the dusty street that he realized he was barefoot and wearing only his pants—not even his gun.

Candice sat alone on a bench at the stage depot, right across the street. His gaze moved over her. She was dressed for travel in a blue serge jacket and skirt, a matching bonnet in blue straw. The outfit revealed rather than hid her lush curves, and he felt the stirring of forbidden desire. Her hair was out of sight, except for golden wisps that escaped the bonnet and drifted around her face. She was dark—golden-tanned from all the time she had spent in the sun without protection, much darker than when he had first found her on the desert, dying. For a brief instant he was brought back to that time, when it had all started.

She sat stiff and straight and did not look like Candice. Where was Kincaid?

Jack was halfway across the street, mindless of passersby, when she saw him. Their gazes locked.

He stopped by her side, smiling mockingly. "Well, well," he drawled. "If it isn't *Mrs. Kincaid.* Going on a trip, *Mrs. Kincaid?*"

"Jack!" She was staring at him, her face paling, her eyes huge dark pools, and something in their depths, something he hadn't expected to see, struck him, pulled at him. Why was she sad? Surely his eyes were deceiving him. He shook off the compassion—he didn't care.

"Where is Kincaid?" he taunted, pulling her to her feet.

She didn't shrink away from him, even though he knew his grip had to be hurting her. Instead she stared into his eyes, searchingly. He tightened his hold until she grimaced.

"Aren't you going to beg me to leave you alone?" He sneered. "Aren't you afraid of being seen with me in public? What's wrong, Mrs. Kincaid, has the cat got your tongue?"

He yanked her. Still, she didn't protest, didn't cry out. "Well? Are you happy now, Mrs. Kincaid, with your white husband?" His face was very close to hers. Why did she just stand there and take his abuse? "Can you even tell the difference in the dark?" He threw her off.

She stumbled against the post, then straightened. Her eyes never left him. "Jack, you don't understand . . ."

"Oh, I understand, Candice, I understand perfectly the bigoted little bitch that you are," he said disgustedly, grabbing her shoulders again.

She whimpered.

"Get your hands off my wife!" Kincaid rasped, striding down the street toward them.

Jack dropped his hand and stepped aside instinctively to move away from Candice, so she wouldn't be hurt in the gunfire that followed. His hands were already tensed at his sides when he realized he had no gun. Not even his knife.

Which was unfortunate, because he itched to kill the man who was Candice's white husband.

"No, Virgil," Candice cried with panic, rushing to him, grabbing his arm. "He's drunk. We were just talking. Please."

"Is this the one?" Kincaid demanded, livid. "Is he the one?"

"No!" Candice lied, clinging to him. "No, I swear it, no!"

"Step aside, Candice."

"No!" Candice shouted.

"Get away," Jack said to her, fighting to clear his head. He wasn't frightened, but he knew he was in trouble. He was hung over and drunk, and Kincaid could kill him with such an advantage. He fought to sharpen all his senses, concentrating with an effort fed by adrenaline.

"Virgil, he's drunk and unarmed." Candice clung to him. "Virgil, please."

Jack watched as Kincaid glanced at her. She was pressing against him, her breasts crushed against his side, one of her hands on his chest, her lips parted, her look partly seductive, partly pleading. She lowered her voice and was speaking rapidly. Jack strained to hear her words. He knew he would have been able to discern them if he weren't so numb from alcohol. And then Kincaid relaxed, placing his arm around her, and with a last warning look, he pulled Candice away.

Not once did she even look back.

CHAPTER FORTY

Traveling by stage was endless. The first day Candice sat numbly in the crowded coach of the Butterfield Overland Mail, which ran a semiweekly service from Tipton, Missouri, to San Francisco, by way of El Paso, Tucson, Fort Yuma, and Los Angeles. The stage covered only fifteen or twenty miles a day in this kind of country. At times the trail wound across rocky, flat, mesquite- and sage-studded valleys, rimmed in the distance by brown, jagged mountains. At other times the trail became difficult if not treacherous, winding up in soft, dry arroyos as they made their way through rocky mountain passes where juniper and pinyon cast great shadows and the air grew slightly cooler.

At the worst of times, all the passengers had to get out, the women walking as the men pushed the stage when its wheels sank into sand or got caught on rocks or in ruts. For Candice, walking was a vast relief. The wagon bounced incessantly, until her back was stiff and her neck paralyzed, and it was hot and malodorous in the coach from the clustering of unclean bodies. The conversation was idle and monotonous, yet no one slept throughout the long day—no one dared. The fear of the passengers bordered on the psychotic. It was contagious.

Apaches.

Candice did not care. She was devastated, and not just because of Kincaid's abuse. Her heart was broken, and the pain she was feeling vanquished all other considerations. She was wondering more and more if she was in love with Jack. She knew Jack had to become a part of her past—her forgotten past. She couldn't be in love with him, because it would be hopeless. There would be insurmountable problems, not the least of which was her family, and they would surely disown her. She wanted to cry but it was pointless. Savage's hate-filled words and his hate-filled eyes, his cruelty—*"bigoted little bitch"*—kept haunting her, torturing her. He had meant every word. He hated her. And the worst part of it was that he was right.

Then there was Kincaid.

He was ruthless. She did not doubt for a second that if she tried to escape or betray him, he would come after her—and then punish her. The other day he would have murdered Jack in the blink of an eye while he was too drunk to defend himself, if she hadn't stopped him. She had no doubt. And she knew there was only one solution.

She would have to bide her time and wait for the perfect opportunity to kill him.

She had almost murdered him once. This time she would have to succeed.

At times this cold, deliberate scheming, mixed with the pain she felt over Jack, kept her from thinking about last night, about Kincaid's brutality, about the horror of rape. At other times the horror resurfaced, making her tremble, making her feel sick. All she wanted to do was close her eyes, find sleep, and escape reality.

Because there were five other passengers besides herself and Kincaid, he treated her courteously and did not assault her at night, where the sleeping arrangements were communal. Yet she was always aware of his too-intimate touch and his hot eyes—his lust. She dreaded reaching their destination —which was, after all, El Paso—not San Francisco, as Kincaid had told Maria and everyone else. He hadn't even let her wait to see her family.

At least for now she had a respite. If he fondled her occasionally when no one was looking, or stole a hot, hard kiss, it was better than being raped.

On their fourth night they camped at the way station at Apache Pass. By this time the only other woman on the stage was a zombie from fear, and nothing her husband could do could take away the corpselike pallor of her skin or still her trembling body. *Apache Pass.* It was almost eight treacherous, narrow, rugged miles long, and every inch of the way afforded the Apaches the perfect opportunity for an ambush. Tiny gorges and arroyos and canyons fell off the pass, and in one of these canyons, to the north in the Dos Cabezas Mountains, it was rumored that Cochise often camped with his warriors.

The pass cut through the Dos Cabezas Mountains and the Chiricahua Mountains, connecting the Sulphur Springs Valley in the West with the San Simon Valley in the east. For as long as settlers had been using the pass, and the trappers and trailblazers before them, it had been a dreaded place. Its name, Apache Pass, was synonymous with death. Apache attacks, murders, massacres . . .

Now, of course, Cochise protected the stage and the whites traveling through the pass. It was not unusual for Chiricahua warriors and squaws to trade at the trading post established at the way station. Still, everyone knew about the other murderous Apaches, just east of the pass, led by Mangas Coloradas, and that other crazed warrior, Geronimo. And even Cochise could not be trusted. He was Apache—wasn't he?

The station consisted of a stone corral built in an L-shape. At the southwest corner of the corral were the kitchen and sleeping quarters. At the west end, built on the inside of the corral, were the storage rooms for grain and food, firearms and ammunition. The springs, which were the reason Indian and traveler alike used the pass, were located about a quarter mile east of the station. The station was located halfway through the pass, on the north side of Siphon Canyon.

Candice ate in silence and retired for the night. She was aware of Kincaid's hateful presence on the pallet next to her, but he left her alone, and she fell into a sleep brought on by emotional exhaustion. The night passed uneventfully, and the stage set out at the first light of morning.

It was still early, and just warm, but soon it would be stifling hot, and the narrow, rocky, rutted descent from the pass was barely behind them. They were emerging from Siphon Canyon, and ahead of them stretched out a sea of brownish grass, gnarled mesquite, and yucca trees. The mules plodded steadily, untiringly. They were a little over halfway to El Paso.

The attack came with no warning.

At one moment everything was calm and peaceful, and there was nothing but the sound of idle conversation, the squeak of wheels, the jangling of harnesses. And then the air was split with that wild, weird Apache war cry—a cry Candice had heard not too long ago and that even now filled her with terror.

The stage was stopped as the Apaches rode at a gallop

around and around it, firing, at random, both bullets and arrows. Candice was on the floor, having been yanked down by Kincaid, who was firing back through one window. But she had seen one of the drivers tumble from his seat above the stage, and she had seen the painted, frenzied faces of the warriors before she was pushed down.

"How many are there?" the passenger Davis said tensely. He had taken up a position on the opposite side of the coach from Kincaid.

"Maybe twenty," Kincaid replied, as another bullet tore into the coach. "Wilson's shot."

"Where's Harris?" Davis was asking about the other driver as he carefully fired out the window.

"He's safe—beneath the coach."

Candice recovered her wits and sat up. "Virge—give me a gun."

He glanced at her briefly, then fired again.

"Here, lady, take this," Davis said, grabbing a frightened passenger's derringer from him as he lay huddled on the floor.

Candice took it, checked to see it was loaded, met Kincaid's glance coolly, and carefully crawled up onto a seat, inching toward the window. Her heart was pounding and she was terrified, but she had a weapon—and she knew how to use it.

"Use your ammunition carefully," Kincaid told her.

She nodded, fired, and missed. "Damn it." She wouldn't miss again. And she didn't.

Ten, fifteen minutes passed, and the Apaches were tireless, seeming to come from all directions, unyielding and almost erratic in their onslaught. Two other men and a woman passenger huddled on the floor, whimpering in fear, while Davis, Kincaid, and Candice took careful shots. It was difficult to hit the Apaches. They would come in for a shot hanging over the far side of their horses' bellies, shooting from beneath the neck. It was a losing battle, only a matter of time, Candice thought, before she and the rest would run out of either ammunition or courage.

Davis screamed, and Kincaid and Candice turned as one to see him being pulled out of the other door of the stage by a painted warrior, his throat slit and blood pouring out of his carotid artery. Candice screamed, but Kincaid was faster, firing at the warrior, who either ducked or collapsed simultaneously.

And then she felt hands clasp her from behind, as she was pulled out of the coach from the door on her side. She staggered as the slim warrior pulled her into the battle. The noise was terrifying. There was the sound of more firing, the pounding of galloping hooves, and the never-ending war cries, but the din had escalated by many, many levels. Candice realized she held the derringer in the folds of her skirt, and she raised it and shot her assailant in the back of the head. She ran.

There were no longer twenty Indians, but hundreds, and she had no idea where she was running, but she heard Harris cry "Cochise!" although it didn't register. There was no escape—there were Indians everywhere.

She stumbled between racing, plunging horses and warriors and fell to her knees, her breath coming in gasps, before she realized some of the Indians were fighting each other. And then she saw the Apache riding at her, his lance poised, a second from running her through. She froze, still on her knees, clutching the gun tightly in her hand, hiding it in her skirt. Time stood still. He came closer and closer. It was like a dream, in slow motion. And still closer. He was upon her. She could make out his harsh features. She could see his eyes, and the jagged design of the red and white paint. She could see sweat on his brow. She raised the gun steadily.

Before she even fired, the warrior collapsed on his pony's back and tumbled to the ground, shot from behind.

Then everything happened so fast it was a blur. The person who had shot the warrior was another Apache on a big bay and he just kept on coming at a gallop. He was a blur of bronzed, gleaming flesh and flying black hair, and he wore no warpaint. She thought he was going to run her down. Before she could move out of the way the stallion veered, and she was suddenly being lifted effortlessly, placed in front of the warrior on top of his mount, at a dead gallop. She twisted to fight, raising the derringer she still held.

The Apache grabbed her wrist so hard that she dropped the gun. She looked into black, unreadable eyes, and then he was shoving her off the big bay stallion, onto the ground, where Candice fell to her knees, panting. He reined in abruptly. Candice gazed up at him, waiting for him to kill her. His horse moved restlessly as he sat staring down at her, and she became aware of many things at once—the sudden silence of the canyon except for the sound of creaking leather, the coach that wasn't far from her, the near-naked, lean Indians ringing this man, and the fact that no one was wearing warpaint. The fighting had stopped.

"You will not be hurt, *pindah*," the warrior said, in a slow, stilted speech, his bay prancing in place.

Slowly Candice got to her feet. She knew who this was— it could only be Cochise. Everyone knew Cochise was very tall and good-looking (it was something that seemed to amaze white people), but there was also no mistaking his aura of power. It explained why he and his warriors had stopped the attack on the stagecoach.

"You are very brave for a *pindah* woman," he said, a smile touching his eyes.

She wondered if he would let her go—or if he would abduct her. "You're Cochise."

A breeze lifted his long, wild black mane, which grew to his shoulders. "You know me?"

She was completely mesmerized by him, unable to tear her gaze away. "Yes," she said, then flushed. "No. I know of you. But I do know Niño Salvaje."

He stared with obvious interest. "Ahh. A brave and fierce warrior. For a brave and fierce woman. Is he your man?"

She flushed again. "No. He saved my life also."

Cochise's expression was enigmatic.

"We're friends," she added, feeling uncomfortable beneath his assessing gaze. "Thank you for taking me out of the fray and for saving my life."

"Geronimo has an angry heart."

Thinking that it had been that crazed, murderous renegade attacking them made Candice shudder.

"If the great burden I carry were not so heavy," Cochise said, speaking very slowly as he chose his words with care, "I would take you as my third wife."

Candice gasped in complete surprise. She stared, wide-eyed, frightened and speechless.

As if reading her thoughts, he laughed. "Do not fear me, *ish'tia'nay*. Perhaps, if Usen wills it, we will meet again."

Candice watched him turn away and lead several hundred mounted warriors thundering back into the mountains ringing Apache Pass.

CHAPTER FORTY-ONE

They reached El Paso four days later. It was almost twilight when they pulled into the dry, arid town that was part adobe and part wood. Candice was exhausted, and followed Kincaid numbly from the coach, not paying attention when he led her past the shabby hotel.

The moment she was in the door of the establishment Kincaid had led her to, Candice gasped. She was in a whorehouse. She had always wondered what the interior of these houses must be like, and this one fulfilled some of her expectations. The salon just visible from the entry was garish in red velvet and silk, and the women lounging among men were in states of undress—scant costumes, sequined and feathered, that revealed entire lengths of leg and arm and nearly exposed entire breasts. Kincaid's hold tightened warningly, and Candice could only stare as an older, statuesque woman approached.

Unlike the women in the salon, she was clad in a full-length, although daring, gown. Her shoulders and most of her bosom were bare, and the skirt split up the front to reveal a glimpse of long legs as she walked. She would probably be handsome, Candice thought—fascinated despite herself—without the rouge and painted lips, the heavily kohled eyes. Her hair was blond, lighter than Candice's and piled high on her head. Brilliantes dazzled at her throat and ears.

"Virge," she purred huskily, and they embraced without him releasing his hold on Candice.

"Lorna, you look very fine." Kincaid smiled, his eyes caressing her openly.

She laughed, touched his cheek with the tip of one painted fingertip, and glanced at Candice. "What's this?"

"I'll explain," Kincaid said, "later. We're going to be staying awhile. First Candice needs a bath."

Lorna looked at Kincaid, and Candice was puzzled over the gleam in her eyes. "Take her up to the room at the end of the hall. Suzie's old room. I'll have Carla bring up hot water and a tub."

"Thank you, dear." Virgil smiled again, kissing her cheek.

"I take it you'll be occupied tonight?" she asked archly.

"Most definitely. But there's always tomorrow, dear." He turned and pulled Candice up the stairs.

"This is a bawdy house," Candice protested.

"Quite right, my dear. We'll be staying here for a while, until I finish some business in the area." He strode down the hallway, Candice hurrying to keep up with him. She heard the pounding of a bed against a wall and went scarlet. A woman's high-pitched moan sounded, and then a man was saying hoarsely "That's it, baby, that's it." His cry followed. Candice wanted to turn around and run. Or at least clap her hands over her ears. And hearing the couple made her think of being in Jack's arms, writhing with her own passion.

"Virgil, do we have to stay here?"

"Yes." He grinned. "Relax, darling, you'll get used to it." He opened a door to a bedroom.

Candice glanced around. The room was ordinary, except for a large bed. The floors were pine planks, there was a small throw rug, an oak table with two chairs, and a crude pine wardrobe.

"I'm going downstairs to have a drink. Get undressed. The serving girl will be up with your bath. Relax. I'll join you for dinner in a bit."

She stared as the door closed behind him and fought a feeling of despair that was rising rapidly. Don't bother hurrying back, she thought, needing belligerence as a refuge. If she didn't keep her spirits up, he'd defeat her. If she caved in to the desperation she was feeling . . . No. Keep calm, she told herself. Don't think about what's going to happen later.

She sat on the bed, grateful for the feel of the soft mattress, and pulled off her shoes. It was then she noticed that the one window in the room was boarded up.

With a start, she went to the door and tried to open it. It was locked. He's going to keep me a prisoner here, she thought angrily. She went to the window and tested the boarding. Tight as a drum. She would never get the boards off without a crowbar. Had someone else been kept there before her as a prisoner? She paced and worried.

The sound of a key in the lock drew her attention, and

she quickly sat down, waiting. A burly man entered with a big brass tub, followed by a slovenly young girl carrying two sloshing buckets of hot water. The man glanced at her lasciviously as he set the tub down, and he left. The girl poured the water in the tub and told Candice she'd be back with more. She left, closing the door behind her. The lock clicked.

The maid returned with two more buckets of water. Candice began to undress. "What's your name?" she asked, thinking the girl could be an ally.

"Carla," the maid said, studying Candice with open curiosity. "You came with Kincaid."

Candice stepped out of her skirt and petticoat. "Yes, that's right. Do you know him?"

Carla smiled, moving toward Candice's clothes. "He's so handsome," she said.

Candice had shed her chemise and stood naked. Kincaid no longer seemed the slightest bit attractive to her, just menacing and evil. "Are you going to launder those?" she asked as she stepped into the tub and sighed.

"They told me to take them," Carla said. "And to tell you anything you need is in the wardrobe." She left, and again Candice heard the lock turning.

The water was heaven. She closed her eyes, sank in deeper, and tried not to let her thoughts go in their inevitable direction. What was Jack doing this very minute? she wondered. Other than hating her? She tried to move her thoughts away from him, but couldn't. She had spent most of her time in the stage dreaming of him, of how he looked, how he walked—with the grace of a treacherous mountain lion—how he sounded when he laughed, or when he was whispering heated love words to her. How his eyes gleamed silver with passion, how his hands felt, roaming her body. Vivid visions of their lovemaking danced before her mind's eye, teasing and thrilling her. God, she missed him—and she might as well face it.

And then, inevitably too, she remembered their last encounter at the depot in Tucson. She fought a feeling of hysteria. He had been drunk, red-eyed, reeking of whiskey, but he was still magnificent. And full of hate for her. She would never forget those words spoken in hatred. Had he been with a whore just then? He'd had nothing on except his pants—

not even boots. A sad kind of jealousy swept her. He was so quick to find solace elsewhere.

She knew she was only torturing herself. There was no point. Even if she admitted her attraction to him was deep—what then? *But it is deep,* she thought in anguish, and I have to admit it. I think I love him, and I miss him terribly. Despair brought hot tears to her eyes.

She should have stayed with him as his wife.

She tested out the notion. She couldn't imagine living in an Apache camp for the rest of her life. But that brought another thought to mind, one she hadn't wanted to face either. She hadn't had her monthly flow since before she'd met Jack, and she was overdue. It was possible that she was pregnant with his child.

Her mind was evil. It spoke the thoughts she didn't want to hear. The child was conceived of a half-breed, out of wedlock. A bastard and part Indian.

Candice slammed upright in the tub, her heart speeding. Never would she allow anyone, if she was pregnant, to cast slurs on her child. Not even her family.

Would Pop accept his grandchild, or disown it—and her?

What alternatives did she have? To marry Jack and live like an Indian, turn her back on society as she knew it, raise her child in Jack's heritage, not hers. She rejected that instantly. Even if Jack would marry her for the child, he hated her—and that was too much to bear.

Another solution presented itself. She could marry a white man—it was early yet—and pass the child off as his.

No one would know the child had Apache blood, and he would be spared the horrible prejudice that had followed Jack through his life.

Oh, God.

She was trembling, and her bath was cold. She should pray that she wasn't pregnant. But she couldn't. Another fact to face. Despite all the problems, she wanted this baby—she wanted this part of Jack.

CHAPTER FORTY-TWO

Candice watched as the big, red-bearded man set a dinner tray down on the table. He straightened and studied her. Candice was sitting on the bed, and fortunately there was only one light in the room, but she knew the night rail she was wearing hid little, if anything. She stared back defiantly. She refused to be intimidated because Kincaid wouldn't let her have decent clothes. The man grinned and left.

Candice was off the bed and racing to the table. A knife! She was trembling with excitement at her success. As she ate quickly, because she was famished, she began to plan. Would Kincaid come back tonight? Tonight would be perfect. The room was mostly dark, and if she extinguished the one kerosene lamp, hid the knife under her side of the mattress . . .

Someone had included a bottle of wine with the meal, but Candice ignored it. Wine always made her tipsy, and she needed all her senses as keen as they could be. She pushed aside the plate. And waited.

An hour later the red-haired man appeared, grinning at her. Candice was in bed, pretending to sleep. He bent over the tray, then set it down. "All right, lady, where's the knife?" He reached her and pulled her upright. "Gimme the knife, now, 'cause I ain't leavin' without it."

"What knife?" Candice feigned innocence. "There wasn't a knife on the tray."

"Liar."

For an instant she tensed, sure he would hit her. Instead he threw her off the bed, hard, and she landed on her hands and knees, watching as he proceeded to check under the pillows, under the mattress—she wanted to shriek in frustration.

He tucked the knife in his belt. "Kincaid ain't gonna like this."

Candice leapt to her feet. "Wait! Please." Her tone softened. She smiled. "What's your name?"

"Jim." He eyed her suspiciously.

"Jim," she repeated, and swayed closer to him, provocatively. "Jim, won't you be my friend?" she breathed.

He stared at her, mostly at her breasts and at the dark

in fact, sometimes I think she prefers women," Kincaid said, smiling when shock crossed her features.

Candice turned to look at Lorna. "No, I don't believe it —it's not true."

Lorna smiled, her eyes bright with a light that Candice understood now, and reached out, one smooth hand cupping Candice's face. When Candice tried to wrench away, Kincaid held her firmly in place, against his chest. Lorna's hand lingered. "I could pleasure you, my dear," she said huskily. "I have no doubt about that."

Candice was momentarily stunned.

"If you don't behave," Kincaid said into her ear, his breath warm, "I may give you to Lorna for a night."

"Virge," Lorna said, glancing at him breathlessly, her hand still on Candice's face, "please do. I'm no threat to you."

"Never!" Candice cried, twisting her face away. But Lorna's hand followed it. "I'll kill you!"

Kincaid laughed. "She can always tie you up," he told her. "In fact, I would make sure that she did."

Candice stood panting against Virgil's iron hold, dazed and panic-stricken.

Kincaid laughed.

Lorna's hand slid down to Candice's shoulder, and she glanced at Kincaid as if for a sign to stop. Candice twisted again, but uselessly. Lorna smiled, and both her hands came up and cupped Candice's breasts, rubbing and squeezing, seeking out her nipples with dextrous fingers.

"Virgil!" Candice cried, bucking against him. She had to escape Lorna's hands! Worse, as she pressed away from Lorna, against Kincaid, she could feel his male response to her. There was no mistaking it.

"Enough," Kincaid said quietly. "Leave, Lorna. Another time."

Lorna dropped her hands immediately, and with a hungry look at Candice's pale face, she was gone.

Candice's heart was pounding wildly. Dear, sweet Jesus! God help me! She felt nauseated and, worse, almost hysterical from despair. She closed her eyes as Kincaid lifted her and carried her to the bed.

"Let go this time, Candice," Kincaid whispered huskily, pulling off her gown. "Let me pleasure you."

Never, Candice thought, trying to hold back a deep, wrenching sob. Never.

CHAPTER FORTY-THREE

Jack slammed the glass down and reached for the bottle. His hand closed with exaggerated precision around it. He lifted the bottle and poured, managing to spill as much as not. He didn't give a damn. He banged the bottle down, raised the glass, and drained it.

It had been two weeks.

Two weeks since she'd left on the stage with her white husband. Fifteen days since he'd told her she was *his* wife and asked her to marry him. What a fool he was.

The saloon was busy even though it was only midday. A few wranglers, many drifters, some miners, and two baby-faced soldiers from the fort. The bartender was serving a steady stream of drinks. Nadi, the young half-breed, was busy serving and avoiding grabs to various parts of her anatomy. The buckskin skirt clung to her young, high buttocks and was the most sought-after target on her person.

He should have left town days ago, but he hadn't the ambition to do so. Where would he drift to now? Sonora? Texas? West, to California? Shit, he didn't give a damn.

By now he'd heard all the gossip. Rumor had it that Candice had jilted Kincaid in Arizona City for him, then had jilted him for Kincaid. It was amazing how the perverted gossipmongers could so totally twist the facts. There was a lot of head-shaking. Men and women alike believed that Candice was that kind of woman, a scarlet woman, a hussy, a breed lover. She was ruined, irreparably.

Was she happy?

He didn't even want to consider that thought, not when he was so damn miserable. But whose fault was that? It was his, for being foolish enough to marry her—worse, make love to her, fall in love with her. Even now, he didn't hate her as much as he loved her. And the whiskey only dimmed the pain.

He was sitting there brooding when suddenly—or not so suddenly—a miner was standing before him, a tall, brawny shadow, and the next thing Jack knew, his chair was kicked out from under him. He went flying back onto the floor.

"Hey, breed," the miner laughed. "Hear you got a taste of a white woman."

Jack was badly drunk. He shook his head to stop the floor from spinning. He knew he was in serious trouble. He leaned up on his elbows, trying to focus on a pair of thick calves clad in moccasins.

"You know what I think of breeds who fool with white women?" the miner asked. "This!"

Jack saw it coming, the hard, vicious kick to his face. It was one thing to see it and another to react. He tried, and managed to move his head slightly aside, but not enough to avoid the stunning blow. His head slammed against the floor, and he saw stars.

He was still seeing stars when he was being lifted to his feet by many hands.

"What should we do with him, boys?" the miner roared.

"String the no-good bastard up!" someone shouted.

"That'll teach him," a wrangler declared, and a round of laughter greeted this.

"He won't never touch no white woman again," agreed one of the soldiers.

"Yeah!" It was a chorus.

Jack's legs refused to work as the miner began dragging him outside, followed by the crowd in the saloon. He was done for. He was so drunk he barely cared. He heard Nadi trying to scream for help. He smiled, thinking, Poor, foolish girl.

Someone threw a rope around his neck. Panic set in, and his heart started to pound, clearing his head a bit. Things were more in focus. His mouth was bleeding from the kick.

"We'll take him around back where there's a nice tree with his name on it," the miner shouted, and everyone laughed and roared their approval.

The cocking of a gun sounded. "I don't think so."

Jack knew that voice, but he couldn't place it. He turned his head, blinking, trying to focus on the rider on the rangy bay.

"Stay out of this, boy," the miner said.

"What's his crime?" Luke Carter asked coolly.

"You asking what his crime is?" the wrangler asked incredulously. "He stole your sister from Kincaid."

"My sister," Luke said calmly, "was dying in the desert after leaving her husband for dead in Arizona City. This man saved her life. Untie him."

The miner hesitated, but held at rifle point, he had no choice. He slipped the noose from around Jack's neck and stepped away, muttering angrily. Jack stood swaying while Luke dispersed the crowd. He wiped his sleeve over his mouth and looked up at Luke Carter.

Nadi came running up and grabbed him, and he leaned on her gratefully.

"You'd best sober up," Luke said, slipping off the horse. He walked over. "You need a hand with him?" he asked the girl.

"Please," Nadi's eyes seemed to beg, her face tense with anxiety.

"Shit" was all Jack managed, and Luke threw an arm around Jack as he stumbled along. He found himself falling onto Nadi's straw pallet. "Thanks," he mumbled, groaning.

Luke stared down at him, glanced around without expression at the squalid little room, nodded to Nadi, and left.

Jack had flung his arm over his eyes. Nadi crouched beside him, pressing her face on his chest. As his world did another spin, he groaned again. Nadi made a funny noise, something that sounded like she was crying. One of Jack's hands came out and he patted her head.

Later, and how much later he wasn't sure, but the room was in total darkness, so he knew he had passed out, he became groggily aware of a warm, naked body curled beside his. He was naked too. He remembered what had happened that afternoon and cursed himself for his idiocy in getting so drunk that he couldn't defend himself.

The woman's slim, hard body moved on top of his. At the sensation of soft, warm skin and hot groin, his body stirred. He recognized Nadi with a start, despite the numbed, half-inebriated state he was in. "Nadi? What are you doing here?"

She began kissing his throat, and his groin swelled.

"Nadi, no."

Her hands slid to his jaws, holding his face, and as she kissed him, she rubbed hard little nipples against his chest.

"No," he tried to say, into her mouth, but now his groin was aching and full, his rigid penis straining against her belly.

He was still half drunk and barely awake. He groaned, opened his mouth, closed his arms around her, and surrendered. She was warm, and she was woman. He knew he shouldn't. It was in the back of his mind. She was too young, and a prostitute for the patrons of the saloon. None of that mattered now. What mattered was sheathing himself in her warm, wet flesh. He flipped her and drove into her, groaning.

She moved her hips in rhythm with his, returned his kisses, ran her hands up and down his back. Because of all the alcohol, it was some time before he found release, but he wasn't too drunk to tell that he hadn't aroused her—even halfway. He rolled off her and stared at the ceiling. She instantly curled against his side.

He turned to look at her thin face with the too-big black eyes, which were shining with adoration. Her expression made him freeze. "Nadi, this wasn't right."

She smiled, took his hand, and placed it on her heart. The look she gave him was as eloquent as words she seemed to want to say but could not: "I love you."

Jack looked at the ceiling, feeling awful. He felt her kiss his hand before releasing it. A change of topic was always safe. "How old are you?" Her fingers moved too rapidly, and he grabbed her wrist. "Slow down."

She smiled, held up ten fingers, then five and two.

She looked fourteen. "Is that the truth?"

Still smiling, she nodded vigorously. She was so sincere, and so pathetic. He had just used her, and even though she had offered herself, he was grim with remorse. He stared again at the ceiling.

She smiled and stretched out alongside him.

He looked at her.

She stroked his chest languidly. He watched her get up and pull on her calico blouse and the buckskin skirt. Her clothes were much mended and could use a wash. He was aware of the heavy odors in the room. He recalled how her hair had felt in his hands. He glanced at the soiled pallet he was lying on.

She returned with coffee and whiskey. His head pounding with an immense headache, Jack reached for coffee and pushed the whiskey away.

CHAPTER FORTY-FOUR

Three days later Jack rode into Cochise's stronghold in the Dragoon Mountains late at night.

Nadi had wept and tried to convince him not to go.

He felt no small amount of guilt. Although he had stayed in Tucson for a few more days, because he needed the time to pull himself together, he hadn't touched her again. She had offered herself hopefully. But Jack had nothing left to give, and he could not take from her again.

Earlier he had sent a smoke signal up that had been answered, or he would have never gotten past the two sentries that guarded the mouth of the stronghold. The stronghold was actually a canyon with a very narrow gorge as the sole entrance to, and exit from, Sulphur Springs Valley. The stronghold was completely defensible, because even if troops could find the entrance, which hadn't happened yet, they would be annihilated by just a few warriors as they tried to enter through the gorge. Inside the stronghold, the entire Chiricahua tribe was nestled among mesquite and juniper and scrub oak, cholla and prickly pear and agave. A stream wandered the whole length of the canyon.

Nahilzay, Cochise's lieutenant and finest warrior, greeted him. "Welcome, my friend," he said, smiling. He was tall and lean, about ten years Jack's senior.

Jack returned the greeting as he dismounted.

"Cochise wishes you to share his fire," Nahilzay said, taking the reins of the black. "It is my honor to tend to your horse."

Jack didn't say thank you, it was not the Apache way, although he was very pleased that Nahilzay thought enough of him to see to the black. They had ridden together only once, many years before, on a war party against Mexicans. Jack made his way through the camp and found Cochise's *gohwah* without difficulty. The tall chief was sitting in the moonlight outside, and he stood as Jack approached. He embraced him.

"Come in, my cousin," he said, his eyes traveling over his face carefully, intently.

Jack followed him into the *gohwah* and sat beside Cochise. He accepted a cup of *tiswin* from Cochise's first wife, a woman Cochise's own age, some forty-five years—but who looked closer to sixty. Tesalbestinay smiled and left.

"White Painted Woman has kept you in her embrace," Cochise said.

"And Usen rides with you," Jack returned.

They both smiled and dropped the formalities.

"Many winters have passed since last we rode together," Cochise said. "It is good to see you again. I know when we ride together I can turn my back and have no fear. That is no small thing."

Jack remained serious and did not smile at the high compliment, for that would be undignified.

"We have a mutual friend."

"Who?"

"A woman more beautiful than many mountain sunrises. Her hair is the color of the midday sun."

Jack choked on the *tiswin*. "Candice?"

"I do not know her name," Cochise said, watching him with amusement. "She is very brave. I almost wanted to take her as my third wife—but I have enough problems with the two I have." He was laughing.

Jack started. She had worked her wiles on Cochise too. "She already has two husbands," he said. "And I'm one of them."

Cochise chuckled. "Is this a new white custom? A man may have many wives, yes, but a woman many husbands?"

"No." He didn't see any honor in the situation. "No. I married her only to take her away from my cousin Hayilkah. He captured her. She thought her first husband was dead." He grew grim as he thought about Kincaid.

"If you still want her, why do you not go and take her, as is the Apache way? You were married to her last—she is yours."

He frowned. "I gave her a choice. Where did you see her? At the pass?"

Cochise nodded. "You gave her a white man's choice. An Apache husband would cut off her nose. Or at least beat her for her infidelity."

Jack didn't answer.

"You also look like a White Eyes," Cochise said disapprovingly.

"How so?" Jack smiled grimly. "Am I not dressed in the Apache way?" He gestured at his buckskin-clad body, at his warrior's necklace.

"Buckskins do not make an Apache."

Jack grew somber.

"Riding free with the wind makes an Apache." Cochise drank the beerlike *tiswin.* "Your actions speak the white man's language, not Apache."

"Yes and no," Jack said.

Cochise smiled. "So you try to sit on top of the thorns? Foolish man! You must stand on the ground, on either one side or the other."

"That's easier said than done."

"One cannot ride in Dos Cabezas and the Chiricahua Mountains at the same time."

"I understand your point. I ride neither place."

Cochise smiled sadly. "Look around you, my brother. Look with care and tell me what you see."

"I see many brave Apaches."

"Brave once. You did not look carefully enough. Once we were hunters, now we are herders. Have you not noticed the white man's cattle we nursemaid?"

Jack wisely refrained from commenting. The government had given Cochise's tribe some cattle, and although it was beneath all Apaches' dignity to tend animals, it was done because Cochise willed it so. The settlers, troops, and travelers had disturbed the big game, driving them away—making a gift of the cattle necessary, and acceptance even more so. To tell Cochise he herded cattle would be a grave insult.

"I read your thoughts. The cattle are a gift from the United States." He shrugged. "My heart is heavy. My people are unhappy. We are no longer free. The white man comes in numbers so great, I know in my heart that if we do not learn the white ways my people will vanish off the face of the canyons and mountains for all times. I seek to learn. To learn I give my word I will protect the white man, and even fight my brothers to do so. I am hungry for knowledge. Hungry to know the white man."

Jack nodded. "What you do is good. The white man is

very powerful. His power comes not just from guns and cannon, but numbers and wisdom. I think it is a good path you chose."

Cochise sighed, as if even the discussion of the topic that ruled his entire being was a great burden. "Why, Niño Salvaje? Why did you choose to ride with the white man?"

Jack tensed. He could not refuse to answer, for Cochise had used his name in framing the question. "It was the time of the Earth Is Reddish Brown," he said slowly, drinking. He told Cochise about the cattle raid so many years ago and the subsequent encounter with the armed white riders—how he had killed his first *pindah*. "Then, soon after, two of my cousins were betrayed by whites who invited them to share their fire. They were given much firewater and then murdered. I rode with the war party to avenge their wandering souls."

Cochise studied him in the firelight. "But you were a seasoned warrior. You rode the warpath many, many times before."

"Against Mexicans. Against the Papago, the Pima, the Pawnee." Jack looked up. "Never against the white man."

A heavy silence stretched across the *gohwah*, broken only by the crackling of the tinder.

"We burned the entire wagon train. Only the women and children were spared, and we did not take them captive. I killed many men that day. I took many scalps—as they had taken my cousins' scalps. But I was no warrior." Jack met Cochise's dark gaze across the fire. "The bloodshed sickened not just my heart, not just my soul, but my body. I was weak as a woman from the battle and gore. No one knew—but I knew. The sign was so clear, it was sent from Usen. I could not ride against the people of my blood." Jack stared. "Yet I cannot ride with them either."

"You walk alone." It was not a question. Cochise's dark gaze was unwavering.

"Yes."

"A difficult path, perhaps impossible. The day will come soon when you must choose your path again."

Jack tensed. "No."

"All around, the white troops chase and hunt down the Apache, sending them to reservations. Your people are still free—but for how long?"

"Shozkay has not been bothered," Jack said.

"Have you become so white that you no longer read the smoke? To the north, many Apaches have been enclosed upon the earth with a fence upon it. Many Apache."

Jack had heard that a few bands from the White Mountains had been sent to a reservation, but he had not given it much thought. The different Apache tribes were not close.

"Where did you go when you left your people?"

"East," Jack replied. "I kept drifting east, through Texas. I finally reached a big city called New Orleans." Jack grimaced. "Never have you seen so many *pindah* in one spot."

"Tell me," Cochise urged, leaning forward. "Tell me everything."

They sat up drinking *tiswin* and talking all through the night.

CHAPTER FORTY-FIVE

She had been imprisoned in the whorehouse for almost two full weeks. She spent her days in a restless, angry state, planning an escape or a murder—whichever opportunity arose first. When she wasn't plotting, she found herself daydreaming of Jack. Sometimes Lorna came to visit. The second time she had come—after that first visit with Kincaid—Candice had smacked her when she had tried to touch her, and now Lorna kept a wary, hungry distance. Once she offered to help Candice escape if Candice would let her come to her bed. Candice had managed to laugh in her face at the absurd and disgusting proposition, but she was shaken.

Lorna hated her as much as she lusted after her, and it was another thing for Candice to have to worry about. She was afraid that her rejection of Lorna would make the other woman do something to hurt her in some scheming way. About the only bright side to her life was that Kincaid hadn't passed her around—yet. It was his latest threat, to tie her up and let Lorna at her. It worked—and it didn't work. It would temporarily make Candice submissive. But submission wasn't in her nature. Soon she would be fighting him again, tooth and nail.

Once she had bitten him. He had beaten her soundly for that, leaving her body black and blue. It had been four days before Kincaid had forced himself on her after that, so in a way, the beating was worth it.

Kincaid enjoyed seeing her submissive. Sometimes the threat of Lorna—combined with a few hard slaps—brought Candice temporarily to her knees, obeying his whims. He forced her to do the things she hadn't even done to Jack, taking him in her mouth until she choked on his seed. Even if she escaped first, one day she would return to kill him.

It was the dream that sustained her and kept her spirit alive.

And she still hadn't gotten her monthly flow.

She could feel the life growing in her, and it strengthened her resolve, made her determined not just to survive, but somehow to extricate herself from the situation she was in. She had the baby to think of. It nourished her.

It was midafternoon when Kincaid entered her room. Candice stiffened every muscle and looked at him, hating him. He was unperturbed. "I've ordered you a bath." He walked to the wardrobe and flung it open, riffling through the costumes within. "Tonight I want you downstairs. You're going to entertain a friend of mine."

"What?"

He threw something crimson and black on the bed, facing her. "Tonight I want you downstairs, dressed like a whore, acting like a whore—charming my friend until he can't see straight."

"Charming him? And what about later—when he wants to take me to bed?" She was horrified, thinking that her worst fears were going to come to pass—Kincaid was letting Lorna use her as a whore for the customers.

Kincaid grabbed her chin cruelly. "Perhaps, darling, if you showed a little enthusiasm in bed, I would be more inclined to keep you as my private stock. To be totally honest, raping you is like fucking a board, and it bores me." He turned away.

Candice couldn't react for a flat second, and then she was lunging after him frantically. "Virgil! You don't mean . . ."

He laughed. "I do mean it, Candice. You're beautiful and clean—I can make a lot of money from you. Tonight we start with Dick Anderson."

"I won't do it."

"No?" He raised a brow. "Do I have to beat you to make you behave?"

She thought of her baby. She stared at the floor, her eyes swimming with tears. He laughed again and shut the door.

Candice sank onto the bed in despair.

Her worst fears were coming true.

"Dick, this is Candice," Kincaid said, smiling, his hand tightly clasping Candice's elbow.

"You were right," Dick Anderson said, staring at Candice unblinklingly. "She's gorgeous."

"And feisty." Kincaid grinned, his hand moving to her hip.

Anderson grinned. Feeling horribly self-conscious in a scarlet satin corset and a black beaded skirt that came to mid-thigh, Candice could not smile until Virge stared at her—and then she had no choice. Kincaid led her into the salon, already full with patrons and prostitutes, and set her in a chair. He and Anderson each took one on either side of her. Anderson was in his late forties, husky but not fat, with a weathered face and gray hair. His hand settled on Candice's knee, kneading her flesh. Feeling Kincaid's warning look, Candice managed to smile again.

"Why don't you sit here, honey," Anderson said, patting his lap.

Kincaid was signaling for drinks. Candice got up and settled gingerly on Anderson's lap. The man promptly placed one hand low on her abdomen, fingers spreading. They dug into her flesh.

"Have you talked to Arnold?" Kincaid asked.

"Sure have. He says he'd sell out for two thousand, not a penny less."

"Hmm." Kincaid sipped his whiskey.

" 'Course, what with the rustling and Indians, he might feel obliged to change his mind soon," Arnold said, his hand sliding up to lift Candice's breast. She stiffened. He began fondling it, his fingers searching out her nipple and stroking it to hardness.

"Why don't we make sure that he does?" Kincaid said.

"To partners," Anderson agreed, raising his drink. Glasses clicked and they drank. "Honey, you are so quiet. How about a whiskey for the lady," he called to Lorna. He nudged her neck with his cheek. "You like that idea, honey?"

"Just fine," Candice managed.

The next half hour passed at a snail's pace. Anderson kept stroking and pinching her breasts. The two men discussed business and the current news, especially the latest slaughter led by Geronimo and his renegades. Anderson shifted Candice off his lap and excused himself. "But I'll be back." He grinned at Candice and gave her a kiss on the lips. She kept her mouth shut.

Kincaid grabbed her wrist and twisted it. "You're not living up to my expectations of you," he warned menacingly.

"You're hurting me," she protested.

"Do I have to take you back upstairs again?"

"No."

He pulled her closer, then glanced down her bodice reflexively. "I have some business to attend to. I'll be back in two hours. Don't think of doing anything foolish—Jim is going to keep an eye on you. You are going to let Anderson drill you tonight, Candice. I don't expect you to show enthusiasm—just spread your legs." He released her.

Candice forced down her hysteria.

Kincaid stood as Anderson sat, pulling Candice back on his lap. "Dick, I have something to attend to, but I'll be back later."

"Fine." Dick beamed, wrapping his arms around Candice's waist. "We don't need him, do we, honey?"

Kincaid walked out.

"Mmm, you smell good," Anderson said, nuzzling her neck. Candice sat stiff and willed herself not to cry. His hand plunged into her bodice and lifted out a full, ripe breast. He squeezed and nibbled her neck. Candice closed her eyes.

When she opened them, she thought she was dreaming. Standing in the doorway of the salon was Jack Savage. And he was staring right at her.

CHAPTER FORTY-SIX

Candice stared back, feeling as shocked as Jack seemed to be, and then her heart started pounding painfully in her chest. Jack's gaze dropped, and suddenly she was ashamed. Ashamed he was seeing her like this. He stared at Anderson's hand on her bare, exposed breast, kneading the lush flesh. His gaze went back to her face, and their eyes met. His were blazing with fury.

Anderson released her breast, standing and pulling her to her feet. He had one arm clamped around her waist. Candice frantically began to tuck herself into the snug bodice, and Anderson laughed. "What's the bother, honey? I'm just gonna pull it down in another minute. You shy about showing your tits?"

It was a nightmare. She watched Jack stalking toward them, his face so tight and strained it looked like it might crack. Anderson followed her gaze, then stiffened when he saw Jack and his obvious anger. "Who's that?" he hissed.

"Take your hands off her, *pindah,*" Jack said in a low, controlled voice.

Anderson scowled. "I paid for her, she's mine. Find yourself another gal."

Jack did not spare another glance at Candice. "Take your hands off her now," he said, his tone softer but more ruthless.

"Oh, Christ!" Anderson cried, dropping his arm. "No two-bit whore is worth getting killed for." He looked at Candice. "I'll be back for you, honey." He turned.

Jack grabbed him by the shirt and spun him around and backward. Anderson crashed into a table and landed on his back on it, spilling drinks and causing the occupants to cry out and leap to their feet. Jack leaned over him, a hand on each of Anderson's arms, his face inches from his. "No you won't, *pindah,* not if you know what's good for you."

He jerked upright.

Candice was trembling—with relief, elation, and anxiety all at once. She saw Lorna approaching, and she moved closer to Jack. He still didn't look at her. His gaze was cold and controlled when he turned its full force on Lorna. "How much for the whore?" he asked.

Lorna opened her mouth and closed it. For a full minute she did not speak.

"Jack," Candice croaked.

"Shut up. How much?"

"Five dollars."

Jack stared at her. "She's a little overpriced. Or does she have some special talents I haven't tried yet?"

"Five dollars. She was otherwise engaged."

"I saw how engaged she was," Jack said. He removed one of his guns from his holster and handed it to her. "That should cover it and then some."

Lorna looked as if she were about to protest, and then changed her mind. She gingerly took the gun and handed it to Jim. "Take this to my office, Jim."

"But—"

"It's all right."

Jack turned to Candice, who knew he could not be serious. This was a scheme to free her—it had to be. She took his arm and gave him a tremulous smile. There was no warmth to greet her in his eyes. "Let's go—whore."

CHAPTER FORTY-SEVEN

He dragged her down the corridor, despite the fact that she kept stumbling in her high heels, and threw her into the room, slamming the door behind her. "All right, whore," he began.

Candice bit her knuckle and shrank away from him.

Jack leaned against the door and hated himself, hated her, hated the way he felt. He closed his eyes, knowing he couldn't take her in violent anger even though a part of him primitively wanted to.

Then the last thing he'd expected happened. She catapulted herself at him with a small sob. Clinging, pressing against him, crying out his name, again and again. "Jack, God, Jack, oh, Jack . . ."

And then there were the hundred questions racing through his mind, and the damning evidence of his own eyes. He wrenched her hands away from his neck and threw her backward. She landed on the bed and stared at him, wide-eyed, propping herself up.

"I came here to find a whore," he said hoarsely. "And it looks like I found one."

"No," she whimpered. "It's not true."

"A whore who's also my wife," he said, and the pain almost knocked him over.

She stared, her eyes huge, her mouth open, breathing just as hard as he was. "Jack—"

"God," he cried, an anguished, wrenching sound. He turned his back to her and leaned panting against the door. *"Usen."*

Candice flung her arms around him from behind, and he went stiff and rigid. Her breasts were soft against his back. He heard her sobbing his name. And he felt her shaking against him with the force of her weeping.

He turned.

It wasn't premeditated. It was the most natural thing in the world to turn and open his arms and close them around her, pressing her face in his chest and burying his mouth in her hair. She moaned, lifting her face, and he stared for an instant at her navy eyes, laced with pain and hope, at the tears tracking her cheeks, and he was lost. His mouth brushed hers. She clung and opened. Their tongues touched. He groaned in complete capitulation and kissed her hotly, deeply —frantic and demanding. "Candice," he cried, "Candice," and he was pressing her as close as he could, rejoicing in the perfect fit of her body, throbbing with a wild, explosive need for her, kissing her uncontrollably.

They were falling onto the bed.

Jack wrapped his hands in her hair and held her face still so his mouth could plunder hers, everything forgotten, all the anger and hate. She arched frantically against him, her long legs going around his waist, drawing his bulging manhood into the warm valley between her legs. An electric desire coursed between them.

He couldn't stand it. Never had his need been so uncontrollable and so frenzied. He tore off her scandalously short drawers and yanked open his fly, his mouth still plundering with a savage desperation. He could feel her body shuddering beneath his, and he raised himself briefly and plunged violently into her.

The union took his senses up and away.

Right now, this instant, she was his and no one else's.

He moved hard and fast, in that frantic, steady, wild climb toward ecstasy, and she moved with him, insistent, demanding, her nails clawing his back, shredding his shirt. Her tremors began first, and he felt them immediately, the tight, sharp spasming of her sheath, and then another contraction followed, and another. . . . Candice gasped, wrenching her mouth away from his. In that one instant, Jack saw her face in the throes of release, and then he felt his own explosion as he surged even deeper within her, deeper, harder, exploding again and again.

He lay on top of her, in her, panting, his heart beating wildly. Remembrance and reality returned. Candice. Candice, who had betrayed him. Candice, who had chosen Kincaid over him. Candice here, a whore in a whorehouse. Without moving his body, he raised his head and looked down at her.

She was so damn beautiful. He watched as she breathed unsteadily through parted, swollen lips, black lashes fluttering against her golden skin. Her eyes opened, and she looked right into his. Tears shimmered. "I love you, Jack."

CHAPTER FORTY-EIGHT

Candice lay beneath him and held him tightly, closing her eyes, her cheek pressed in the smooth joining of his neck and shoulder. She wondered if he had heard her; he was so very still. Her heart was still racing, and an exultant joy was coursing through her. How could she have ever given this man up? She turned her head to press her mouth against his flesh, which was musk-scented and wet from exertion. She inhaled his scent deeply, listening to his heartbeat.

He slipped to her side, onto his back, placing a small breath of space between them. Candice felt his withdrawal on an emotional level. She immediately curled against him, her arms going around him, refusing to allow him to pull away, either physically or emotionally. "Oh, Jack," she said, her voice unsteady. "God, I've missed you." Tears threatened to overwhelm her but she fought them back.

"Right." He sat up, pulling away from her.

Candice sat too, grasping his arm. His eyes were ice cold, like the desert frozen with a dusting of frost in winter, and the glitter in their depths was dangerous. "Jack? Wait. You don't understand."

He laughed again. She hated the sound of this laugh. It was full of contempt. "You're right. I don't understand."

"Let me explain."

He stood, tightening the drawstring of his pants. "What kind of explanation could there possibly be for a man finding his wife in a whorehouse?" He looked at her. "How many men do you sleep with every day? Three? Six? Ten?"

She felt as if he had punched her in the chest, and for a moment she couldn't breathe.

"Do you enjoy it?"

"No! Jack, I'm not a whore," she cried.

His jaw clenched. But his gaze roamed over her costume and her bared breasts.

"No, I'm not," she cried, yanking up the bodice, grabbing him. Tears filled her eyes. "I didn't want to go with Kincaid. I had no choice. He forced me and hurt me. He promised me he'd let me go when he was tired of me—except he's lied!" Her voice was high, and she could feel a wild hysteria threatening to engulf her. "Tonight he was going to make me sleep with Anderson—he said he was tired of me, that I bored him. Tonight was the first time, I swear it." She moaned, and tears trickled down her face. Why was he just looking at her like that? Like she was a freak and he couldn't care less? There was no compassion or comprehension in his eyes, just coldness.

"More lies?"

"No, it's the truth! Jack, dammit, aren't you listening? I love you! But it's hopeless for us, and I didn't want to be in love with you. But now, with the baby—"

He grabbed her. "Baby? What baby?"

She bit her lip, managed a smile, eyes glistening. "I'm going to have your baby, Jack."

He stared. "Is this another lie, Candice? So help me, if it is, you'll live to regret it."

"I haven't had my monthly time since before we met. I know I'm carrying your child." And she smiled, fighting the tears.

He swung away and cursed.

She could feel him fighting her. "Jack, will you help me get away from him? Help me get home?" Her voice was tense and low. When he didn't move, she said, "If you don't believe how bad it is, look at that window."

Jack turned his head, but his expression remained hard and unreadable as he stared at the boarded-up window.

"Jack—listen. Virgil will be back any time now. Jim, that big red-haired brute, is guarding me. We have to do something soon!"

His face was a dangerous mask. "I'll kill Kincaid for you, Candice."

"Jack!" She was on her feet, clinging to him. "No, Jack, I'm afraid!"

He looked at her as if she were an annoying nuisance and a stranger.

"He'll shoot you in the back," she cried. "Jack, just help me get out of here."

He grabbed her and shook her. "This had better not be a lie, Candice," he rasped. "You have some feelings left over for Kincaid?"

"No," Candice said. "But I'm afraid for you. Please don't confront him, you don't know how cruel he is. Let's just run away."

"How cruel is he?" Jack asked impassively, still clasping her shoulders.

She met his gaze directly. "He likes hurting me. He likes raping me."

Jack's jaw tightened. "A man can't rape his own wife."

Candice bit down on her lip, hard. She was afraid to tell him the rest of it, that Kincaid was not her husband. Oh, God, she was afraid. "Jack, please."

He released her abruptly. "I'll wait for him downstairs."

"No! Didn't you hear me? If he sees you first, he'll murder you without thinking twice!"

That stopped him, the hysteria in her voice, and Candice saw by the way he was looking at her that he was wondering if she had really meant what she'd said before—that she loved him.

"Don't take the chance," she begged, clutching his shirt. "Jack, how I feel about you isn't a lie. I love you, and I don't want you to die."

An expression of unbearable intensity swept his face briefly. He was at the door, opening it. And then he was gone.

CHAPTER FORTY-NINE

The tension in Jack was coiled and strained, explosive. He paced deliberately through the salon and found a chair, which he promptly placed against a wall. He sat, his back to the wall, facing the entrance to the salon and, beyond that, the foyer and the stairs.

Even if Kincaid used the back entrance, there was only one way up those stairs to Candice's room.

Candice. God, he couldn't believe his passion for her.

It hadn't died—just the opposite. It had grown even hotter.

And a baby. Usen had willed it—she was carrying his baby.

He was filled with fierce resolution. The urge to protect and comfort her had nearly choked his breathing. But fighting that urge, equally strong, was his pride—and she had wounded it mortally.

He wanted her and their child more than anything, but he vowed she would never again make him feel powerless.

And he was glad to have any excuse to kill Kincaid.

One question tormented him. If she really had been forced to leave with Kincaid against her will, then why hadn't she come to him for protection? It wouldn't have mattered to him that Kincaid was her husband. But she hadn't turned to him for help, when she damn well knew he could end Kincaid's life in the hair's breadth of time it took for him to draw his two Colts. He glanced down at his one empty holster grimly.

The answer was too obvious. In front of her family and Tucson, Candice would not and could not acknowledge her relationship with him. He smiled tightly. He no longer cared what she wanted or what she was afraid of. His child was not going to be born a bastard.

He would gladly kill Kincaid. Kincaid had taken *his* wife, and it didn't matter whether it was against her will or not. Kincaid had taken his wife, and he had used her and possibly abused her. For that he would die.

The salon was crowded and noisy now with drinking

customers. A pianist was playing a hearty tune, and one of the half-clad girls was singing along, the others roaming and entertaining. Jack was aware of every movement around him, his senses tuned in to nothing but Kincaid's arrival.

At that precise moment, she appeared in the doorway, looking beautiful despite her whore's clothing. She saw him and made her way purposefully toward him, her face stricken and determined. She shoved through the crowd, ignoring men who touched her and tried to pull her into their laps as she passed. Jack steeled himself against her.

"Jack," she cried, her face strained, eyes huge. "Please don't do this."

He was too aware of her hands on his arm and chest, her fragrance, her nearness.

"I'm afraid." She moaned. "What are you going to do? Call him out?"

"You're in my line of vision," he told her coolly.

She gasped and stepped aside, glancing worriedly at the doorway. "What should I do?" she asked tersely.

"Stay out of my way," he told her, his eyes on the doorway.

He watched her walk away, agitated. He imagined her with Kincaid, their bodies slick and wet, Kincaid driving into her. He wanted to believe her—that tonight was the first time she'd been playing the whore, just as he wanted to believe that Kincaid had forced her. *You fool,* he thought. *Your preoccupation with her is going to get you killed one of these days —as it almost did in Tucson.*

He was Apache. He could sit motionless and wait for hours, if need be. Two hours passed, and it was well after midnight. Jack was not stiff, not sore. Two hours was nothing. He was as alert as ever while he waited for his enemy to appear. And even though his eyes were fixed on the stairway, he always knew where Candice was. He could sense her hanging back by the bar, her anxiety communicating itself even across the room to him. And no one made a move toward her.

It was half-past two when Kincaid appeared. Jack caught a brief glimpse of the man before he disappeared up the stairs. Jack stood, moving the chair away from his legs with one booted foot, waiting for Kincaid to return.

He appeared in the entry of the salon looking as immaculate as ever in a dark suit, the jacket unbuttoned. His gaze ran quickly, excitedly, over the salon, and Jack saw his eyes gleam as he found Candice. Then he saw Jack, and his countenance froze as their gazes locked.

"Kincaid," Jack said coldly. He was standing in a draw stance, legs slightly spread, thighs tensed, hands ready at his holsters.

Kincaid had opened his jacket and moved it aside so as not to interfere with his draw. Already, people had noticed both men and what they intended, and were clearing away. "So you've come for her," Kincaid said, smiling with no humor.

"You stole my wife," Jack said softly, but his voice rang out in the sudden silence. Then there was no one between him and Kincaid. Only chairs and tables separated them as they faced each other at a distance of twenty feet. "You will die for that."

As soon as the words were out of his mouth he sensed Candice coming closer, could feel her nearness, and saw her out of the corner of his eye. "Candice, get back," he said, never taking his eyes from Kincaid.

"No," she cried. "Stop, please, stop this!" He could feel her coming.

And he saw Kincaid reaching.

But it was all over before it began.

He drew his Colt before Kincaid had even cleared his holster. Two, then three red flowers blossomed on Kincaid's white shirtfront, and he staggered, fell, the gun clattering across the floor.

Candice screamed and grabbed Jack's arm.

A heavy silence fell over the salon.

Jack turned to her furiously. "I told you to stay back."

"Are you all right?" she cried.

People began to shift and whisper in hushed, excited tones. Lorna came swiftly forward to kneel by Kincaid. "He's dead," Lorna said.

CHAPTER FIFTY

"They say Casey O'Brien just up and left this place one day last spring," Jack said.

Seated behind Jack on the black stallion, Candice cautiously surveyed the adobe house that was one of the last in town, just off Main Street. The door was open and swinging slowly in the breeze, half off its hinges. The rawhide windows were cracked and coming loose, hanging drunkenly. There was a corral, which was half completed. A broken bucket, a horseshoe, nails, a tin plate, and a few other items littered the dirt front yard. Candice bit her lip.

After swinging his front leg over the horn, Jack slid down, then lifted her to her feet. He immediately dropped her hand, as if avoiding contact, and Candice, although still stunned and exhausted from all that had happened in the night, was disappointed. She squinted through the dawn light and felt her heart sinking. Were they really going to live here?

"I can fix things up in no time," Jack said.

Candice followed him inside, and her dismay increased. The floor wasn't even packed, just loose dirt. A pallet lay in one corner, and the suspicious odors coming from within seemed to emanate from that location. One rickety table and a stool stood in front of the fireplace. The kettle hanging there was black and encrusted. A blanket lay crumbled halfway between the bed and table, and a few rats scurried for cover. Candice shuddered. "Do you really think we should stay here?"

Jack lifted his gaze. "Where would you like to stay? Tucson? With the Apaches? You name it, we'll go."

Tears welled in her eyes. Jack was angry with her. Ever since they had made love—no, ever since she had refused to remain with him as his wife in the Apache camp, he had been cold and angry. She hated him this way. She brushed her eyes with the back of her hand.

"What's wrong?" he asked sharply.

"Nothing."

"You sit down, and I'll get this place cleaned up."

"I can help."

"I want you to rest."

"I'm no invalid, just pregnant—possibly two months. I can help."

Jack gave her a quelling look. "I said stay put."

She wanted to scream at him, but instead her voice was low and taut. "Is it always going to be this way?"

"What way?" He wasn't even looking at her.

"What way? This way! Damn you, Jack, are you trying to punish me?" She fought tears because she wasn't going to give him satisfaction now.

He turned to her, his face expressionless. Then he began collecting odds and ends, clearing the room. Candice clenched her fists. She wanted to pound his back, hurt him. "I've already been punished enough, damn you," she said, and her voice cracked.

His shoulder stiffened, and he froze momentarily in the act of moving a rusty bucket. Candice watched him, waiting desperately for him to come to her and set things right. But he didn't. Instead he gathered the pallet, blanket, and kettle and carried them outside. Candice sat on a stool and fought to come to grips with her overwrought emotions. Maybe he hated her. *I will not cry,* she vowed, blinking furiously.

Jack returned and began sweeping with water, until the floor was hard and packed and spotless. The awful moment of utter despair had passed. She was strong, she would survive this too. She began rubbing her aching back. Jack laid out fresh straw and made a new pallet with his bedroll, then ordered her to lie down and get some sleep.

"Jack?" She sat on the pallet cautiously.

He paused in the doorway. "What?"

"Do you think it will be okay? For us to stay here?"

"If Casey comes back, we'll find another place."

"No, I mean, after what happened."

"I doubt anyone will think much of my killing a man who stole my wife. And Lorna doesn't want that kind of trouble."

"I'm afraid."

"Don't be." He left.

She lay on her back and fought fresh tears. Was it only hours ago that he had been making love to her as if he really cared? How could she stay with this cold, angry man? And what were they doing? Was she supposed to live with him as his mistress? He may think they were married, but the Apache ritual meant nothing to her—or to society. And what was the alternative? A Christian marriage?

I do love him, was her only answer.

And she fell into an exhausted sleep.

The savory, mouth-watering aroma of a stew simmering awakened her around midafternoon. Candice opened her eyes and turned her head. The first thing she saw was Jack, shirtless, bending over the gleaming kettle, bringing a ladle to his lips. In the glow of the firelight his arms and back rippled, and his perfect profile was cast into vivid relief. Her heart clenched and she sat up.

He looked at her. "Feeling better?"

"Yes," she said truthfully, smiling.

"Hungry?"

"Starved."

And he smiled. It lit up his face and made her heartbeat quicken. Then he was all business, ladling out a dish and bringing it to her. When he squatted beside her to hand her the bowl, their gazes met. He was the one to look away first, breaking the intimate contact. Candice took the bowl, dismayed.

Jack stood. "I'm going to go hunting. If I'm not back by nightfall, don't worry. Tomorrow I'll trade for some chickens and a milk cow, and whatever else we need. Come spring I'll round up a few wild longhorns. I can even build us a place outside of town. But we'll stay the winter here—close to the doctor."

Candice wondered who he wanted—her or the baby.

Somehow, she didn't think it was herself.

CHAPTER FIFTY-ONE

Jack was not back by the next morning.

Lorna had returned Candice's clothes, apparently motivated to do so by Jack, but everything seemed wildly inappropriate for the hovel they were living in. She slipped on her most casual cotton dress, and it was like a slap in the face. The careful stiching, lace trim, and bright blue were a startling contrast to the squalor of their home. Home. It was not a home, just a shack. She hated it. She could become very depressed there, especially if Jack kept on acting as if he hated her.

Looking at her pile of dresses, Candice had an inspiration. She knew just what the house needed—a woman's homey touches, her touches. There was a needle in Jack's saddlebags. She spent the morning making curtains in a cheerful yellow from two of her gowns, a cotton and a silk. There were only two windows, so it was not a huge chore, but she was already imagining a cranberry bedspread and cheerful floral tablecloth.

She trimmed the curtains with lace. She had nothing to hang them with, so she decided to borrow a hammer. If they were going to be spending the winter there, she might as well get to know her neighbors.

If only she had some money—they needed so many things. Inspired anew, she took two of her taffeta dresses and bundled them up. Surely someone would trade her soap, blankets, a hammer, and a few others things for them.

She was feeling positively cheerful when she stepped outside into the bright morning. A Mexican woman next door was washing her laundry in a big tub outside, stirring the clothes with a huge stick. Candice smiled, her bundle firmly under her arm, and called out a frienldy greeting, starting over. The woman looked up, then looked back to what she was doing.

"Hello," Candice said again. "Good morning. My name is Candice Car . . . Savage, and we're neighbors."

The woman ignored her.

Candice had a terrible suspicion. Her chin lifted, the

smile faded. "Excuse me. We're neighbors. I thought you might be interested in—"

The woman looked up and spat at Candice's feet. *"Puta. Salgate."* She spat again.

Candice stepped back, shocked. "I only wanted to trade, I have these dresses."

"Whore's dresses," the woman hissed.

Taking a deep breath, her face flaming, Candice turned and hurried away. Once on Main Street she paused, feeling sick and nauseated. Everything had happened so fast, she hadn't stopped to think that probably the whole town knew she'd been at Lorna's. She gritted her teeth. What the hell did she care what some middle-aged, fat, Mexican woman thought? She strode down the street.

A piercing wolf whistle sounded.

Startled, Candice searched for the whistler, and her gaze settled on a young rider, grinning at her. He moved his horse alongside her. "Howdy, gal. You sure look pretty in that dress."

Candice stiffened. She knew that smile—it was lewd and disrespectful. Looking away, she crossed the street. He moved his horse to her side.

"Cat got your little tongue? My name's Abe. What's yours?"

She reached the other side of the street and began walking down it. He rode alongside.

"Aw, c'mon. Don't play shy with me. I know who you are. You're Candice—that mystery girl of Lorna's."

Candice sucked in her breath, then restrained herself from responding. She knew it would do no good.

He leapt down and placed his hand on her shoulder. "Let's go back in the alley. I got a dollar. What d'ya say?"

Candice stopped. "I say get your hand off me—you bastard!"

He laughed, and didn't remove his hand. "My money's as good as the next one. 'Sides, you'll like it, they all do."

She didn't think. She struck him, a ringing slap across the face. His expression went from grinning lewdness to shock, and then to anger. He grabbed her before she could avoid him and began kissing her. Candice lifted her knee and jammed it as hard as she could into his groin. The breath left him in a whoosh, his face went white, and he crumpled to his knees, clutching himself.

Candice was shaking. "My husband will kill you if you ever come near me again," she warned with bravado she didn't feel. She had no weapon, and she resolved never to leave the house again alone without a gun or knife. She hurried away, leaving him lying there, groaning.

There was one general store and trading post, a few doors down from Lorna's. Still shaken from the encounter, Candice took a breath and entered. A little bell tinkled over the door. A heavyset bearded man was behind the counter. Two old men sat before a stove, warming themselves and drinking whiskey. A woman was inspecting bolts of cloth. Everyone stopped what they were doing to stare at Candice.

She could feel the censure, and she blushed.

Head held high, she walked to the counter. The owner stared. Candice strove to remain composed, placing her bundle on the counter. "Good morning," she said with false cheer. "I've two taffeta dresses here, and I thought I might barter for a few items my husband and I need."

The man scrutinized her face.

Behind her, she heard one of the old men saying loudly "That's the half-breed's woman."

Candice wondered if she might faint.

The matron came rushing over, shoving aside the dresses. "Ben Matthews, you can't possibly be thinking of trading with this—this—trollop!"

Matthews looked at the enraged woman. "No, Missus Adams, I ain't."

Behind her, the other old man said, "You think she's a breed too? She sure looks white."

And his companion answered, "What does it matter? She lives with a breed, that makes her a squaw."

Candice's voice was quavering. "This is fine material. Surely we can work something out."

"No, I'm sorry we can't," Matthews said.

The matron gave a snort of satisfaction and moved back to the bolts of cloth.

"Do you mean," Candice said, "you won't trade with me because of my husband?"

Matthews smiled. "Nope. I don't care who you live

with. I won't trade with you because I got no demand for dresses like this."

Candice began to gather up her things. She couldn't leave the store soon enough, but she was desperate. She *had* to sell the dresses.

One of the old men said, " 'Course, they're probably not even married."

She was not going to cry.

Bravely she looked up at Matthews. "I'm sure you could sell these dresses to Lorna and her girls for a nice profit."

Matthews blinked in surprise. Behind him, Mrs. Adams gasped in shock and outrage.

"I'll sell the lot for twenty dollars," Candice said. She was trembling.

Matthews smiled. "You got a deal."

CHAPTER FIFTY-TWO

He heard the hammering before he'd even entered the yard, and his lips set. He urged the black forward and swung off, reaching the house in two strides and throwing open the door. Candice was standing on a stool, hanging curtains—curtains, for God's sakes!

"Damn it," he shouted. "Are you crazy, woman?"

Candice yelped and slipped.

Jack reached her and wrapped his arms around her waist before she could fall.

"Jack," she breathed, "you scared me!"

A heavy anger began to fill him. He lifted her off the stool. "What in hell are you doing?"

Her expression of pleasure disappeared. "I'm finished. I made curtains."

He grabbed her face. "What if you fell? You could have killed the baby!"

She pulled away, her lips going tight and hard. "Don't touch me!" she shouted. *"Don't you touch me!"*

"Start using some sense," he said, turning away, guilt replacing the anger. He looked at the curtains. They certainly brightened the room, and they did something strange to his insides—made him tingle. She had done this for their home. It was a heady thought, one he instantly tried to shove away.

Candice was slapping a bowl of beef stew and some coffee on the table. Jack sat down. "Where'd you get the coffee and coffeepot? Are those potatoes I see in here?"

She didn't answer. She slammed another bowl on the table and pulled up a sawhorse that had not been in the yard. She sat and began eating angrily.

"Where'd you get the sawhorse?"

No response.

"The curtains look nice," he finally said, glancing at her downturned face.

She put her spoon in the stew with such force it splattered all over the table. Then her shoulders started to shake. Amazed and then horrified, he saw that she was weeping.

"Candice, I'm sorry," he said. "I just don't want anything to happen to the baby."

She leaned her head on her hand and kept crying, barely making any noise.

"Damn," Jack said softly. He hesitated, then got up and went around the table to her. From behind, he awkwardly put his hands on her shoulders, rubbing them. *"Tu-inchú-da,"* he whispered. "Don't cry, sshhh."

She pushed him away fiercely. "Don't touch me!"

He cursed and encircled her with his arms. She was so soft and warm. It affected him. She affected him. For a brief moment, she was in his embrace, her wet face against his chest. He touched her hair. He had begun by comforting her, but his groin grew heavy.

He knew she felt it, because she braced her palms hard against his chest. "No!"

He wanted her; he needed her. His hold tightened. "Candice," he breathed, nuzzling her hair. His hands slid to her buttocks, cupping them, pressing her against his thick arousal.

"Damn you!" she snapped, wrenching abruptly away.

She managed to take only a step when he caught her roughly by the wrist, pulling her back to him. Her fists came up and banged down on his chest. He ignored it, his arms already around her. He was lost, undone, and he groaned, hugging her fiercely. She fought helplessly within his embrace, but his arms were steel bands. His mouth touched her temple, her cheek. He was shaking. She went still.

Candice raised her tear-streaked face and looked at him with wide navy eyes. It was his complete undoing. He groaned and captured her lips with his. He caught great hanks of her hair. She opened, and when he thrust his tongue into her, she met it tentatively, slowly. He swung her up into his arms and carried her to their bed, laying her down carefully. She smiled at him through glistening tears and held her arms wide.

"Love me," she choked. "Love me, Jack."

He almost told her that he did.

"Damn," Jack said huskily, looking at her beautiful face, her parted red lips, her thrusting breasts and tiny waist. Her skirts were spread wide on her opened thighs. He tore off his shirt and moved on top of her.

She moaned with uninhibited pleasure, wrapping her arms and legs around him and kissing him aggressively. His heart was threatening to take flight. Her hands moved down his bare back, to clasp his buttocks and knead them. He gasped as she pulled him harder into her crotch. He gave up her lips to find her soft white throat. She cried out, arching for him.

"I want to see you naked," he said huskily, kneeling, his fingers fumbling with the buttons on her dress.

"Make love to me," she demanded breathlessly. "Now, Jack, now."

"Let me get your clothes off." Cursing because there were thirty buttons, he ripped open the last few, and pulled her dress over her head, then her petticoat, chemise, and pantalets in rapid succession. She lay spread and white, voluptuous before him. *His wife.*

He caught her face in his hands and began nibbling her lips, her nose, her jaw. He moved down her throat, lingering on the rapidly beating pulse. He lifted her breasts, crushing them, and buried his face in their silken warmth. His tongue darted around one hard, large nipple, and then he was sliding down her belly, pushing her thighs up over his shoulders. He groaned when he buried his face between her legs, groaned at the potent scent of her, at the soft-slick feel. With his thumbs he held her open and began to plunge into the moist pink depths with his tongue. She shuddered and writhed, and began keening in ecstasy. He didn't stop.

When she lay still he moved up alongside her, to stare at her face in the soft aftermath. She opened her eyes and smiled. He didn't smile back.

She leaned up on one elbow and touched his chest, running her fingers over it. The heavy aching of his erection grew almost painful. She slid her hand down slowly to his belly, then paused. Instantly his hand covered hers, guiding her further, until she was enclosing his shaft, squeezing its pulsating length. He fell onto his back, breathing harshly and raggedly as she began to stroke him.

His eyes flew open when he felt her lips closing over the large head. "Candice."

"Sshh," she said, and began sucking, her tongue swirling around the tip.

Moments later he grabbed her head, hard, to pull her up. But she wouldn't move, and then it was too late. His hard arms crossed over her head, locking her in place, as he convulsed violently inside her, his harsh cries ringing out.

She snuggled happily against his chest.

He stared tensely at the ceiling.

Where had she learned that? Had she done that to Kincaid? He couldn't help it. Not the anger—nor the jealousy. He raised himself up. Her expression dissolved when she saw his. "Did Kincaid teach you that trick?"

She sat up, moved away against the wall. "That's not fair."

"He did."

"He forced me."

Jack's jaw clamped hard. The man was dead. He had killed him. He wanted to kill him again.

"You'd better listen to me," Candice said vehemently. "Kincaid forced me every time. I hated him. It wasn't my fault. He beat me too. He liked hurting me. Lorna hates me, so she'd probably lie, but if you ask the other girls, I imagine they'd tell you how it was. Then you could stop accusing me of being a liar."

He folded his hands under the back of his head. "I never said you were a liar."

"Do you think I liked being raped? Worse—taking that pig in my mouth?"

He stared at her, judging her, and felt guilt again. The truth was on her face and in her eyes. He hated himself for his uncontrollable jealousy.

"I want to tell you something else, Jack," Candice snapped. "I can't take much more of your attitude. You have no hold over me. Yes, I'm having your baby. But I'm not the first unmarried mother the world has seen."

"Are you threatening me?" he asked, sitting up.

Her chin went high. "I'm telling you."

Their gazes locked.

Jack swung to his feet. "I have game to see to."

She grabbed his arm. "Jack, I want a gun."

He looked at her. "What for?"

She hesitated. "I didn't like being here alone."

"What happened, Candice?" he demanded.

"A cowboy on the street made some lewd suggestions, that's all."

Jack grabbed her arm. "Tell me all of it—in exact detail."

"He wanted me to go in the alley with him for a dollar," Candice said.

"Who was he?"

"It doesn't matter," Candice said. "I took care of it."

"What does that mean?"

"I kicked him in the groin."

Jack stared. "He touched you?"

She hesitated. "Yes."

"What was his name?"

"Abe."

"I'll get you a gun," Jack said, dressing. "From now on, don't go out without it."

As he buckled on his gunbelt, Candice took his arm. "Don't do anything, Jack. There's been enough trouble and talk with your shooting Kincaid."

His gray gaze pierced her. "I can't let him get away with it," he said levelly.

At the door he paused. "After today, no man in this town will dare even talk to you."

CHAPTER FIFTY-THREE

Five days later, Candice was outside in their yard doing wash. Her sleeves were rolled up to her elbows and the top three buttons of her shirtwaist were undone, a kerchief wrapped around her head. Her face was flushed from the steam rising from the boiling water. Her hands were red and chapped.

It wasn't their wash. She was taking in laundry from outside to help make ends meet. Soldiers from Fort Bliss in Magoffinsville would be her best customers. This was only her second load, and when she'd decided on this as the only way of raising some cash, she hadn't realized just what hard work it would be. She'd never done laundry before in her life.

She stopped what she was doing with relief, straightening and pressing her hands against her back as she saw Jack walk into the yard carrying something big and white and made of shiny wood. She squinted.

He carefully opened the door with his back and disappeared into the house.

"What is that?" Candice mused, starting for the house.

In the doorway, she froze. Jack had been carrying the object upside down, and now he'd placed it in one corner of the room, on its four delicately wrought legs. It was a cradle.

A magnificent, ornately sculpted, intricately hand-painted cradle. Designs of birds, butterflies, flowers, and vines were etched along the legs, the sides, and head and footboard. "Jack! It's beautiful!"

Jack looked up and smiled.

Candice didn't notice the rare smile, she was running her hands over the smooth, silky wood, exclaiming, "Where did you ever find this? Oh, Jack, we can't afford this!"

"You like it?"

"I love it," she said enthusiastically, finally looking at him.

Nothing had changed in the past few days. He was reserved and withdrawn—except when he turned to her in the night with desperation and urgency. His smile was devastating. Not just because of the physical change it wrought on his features, but because she did love him—and it was a smile that reached into his soul. Reflexively Candice reached out and cupped the side of his cheek. He stopped smiling. She felt him fighting her, felt his confusion, and maybe—fear. He pulled away. Candice dropped her hand.

Their bed now stood on a frame with four legs—Jack had made it. Her cranberry satin gown had been made into a spread that covered it. A tablecloth covered the table, and Jack was adding shelves and a work space to the right of the hearth. He'd bartered for a chair. Soon they would get a thick Indian rug for the floor. He'd already obtained four chickens and a rooster. Candice was anticipating roast chicken with delight.

"I'll be back later," Jack said, his gaze moving over her flushed face.

She gave him a bright smile. "Okay."

"What are you washing, anyway? All my things are buckskins. You look tired."

"Just a bit achy," she said, biting her lip and averting her glance. It wasn't that she was hiding what she was doing from Jack, but she knew he was proud, and she didn't think he'd approve. He wasn't even supposed to be back until later.

"Why don't you lie down for a few minutes," Jack said.

"All right." She flashed a smile, relieved he'd forgotten his question.

Her image lingered with him, long after he'd gone. Even dressed like a washerwoman, she was beautiful—it made him ache right to his soul. He hated seeing her in homespun and rags, hated seeing her hair hidden beneath that gray kerchief. He hated the feel of her work-roughened hands. Candice was a lady. There was no doubt in his mind, as, in truth, there had never been. She didn't deserve this kind of life. She deserved a rancher like Judge Reinhart who could afford maids and cooks and laundrywomen. She deserved the finest silks and lace-edged underwear. But just what in hell was he supposed to do?

She was carrying his child. The doctor had confirmed she was about six weeks along. That ended any and all doubt as to the child's paternity—only he could be the father. He was thrilled. He couldn't wait for the birth of their child, and he was doing what he had to do—taking care of his wife the best way he knew how.

After the baby was born, things would be different. They would set out for California—he'd already decided. But he needed a stake, and the next year was going to see him accumulate enough for the move and a few head of cattle. The first few years wouldn't be easy, of course. But one day he would build her a fine home, with huge white pillars and a verandah that went all the way around the house. And a garden full of roses. His children would be sent away to school once they were old enough, to get the education he'd never gotten. His wife would have whatever she desired.

His dreams did not ease the guilt he felt about their current situation.

Because, despite the baby, he knew his motivations were more selfish than pure. No matter how hard he fought her web, he had already lost the war—and he just couldn't ever let her go.

CHAPTER FIFTY-FOUR

Ten days later Jack saw the preacher and couldn't believe his luck.

This was what he had been waiting for. Like most towns, El Paso didn't have a preacher, and the townspeople waited for one to travel through to hold services and weddings. If too much time elapsed between visits, couples would often forgo the legality and move in together, then make things right when the preacher did appear. Jack had never forgotten Candice's threat that she wasn't the first unmarried mother-to-be—with its implication that she could and would leave him if she felt like it. He had been intending to tie her to him with a Christian wedding from the moment he'd found out she was pregnant, although he hadn't mentioned it because he was afraid she would balk. Now he would make her say her vows at gunpoint, if necessary. Nothing was going to stop this ceremony from taking place.

It didn't matter that the preacher hadn't shaved in weeks, or, from the looks of him, washed either. It didn't matter that he was standing outside the saloon, swaying slightly, obviously drunk. Jack approached with rapid strides, his heart pounding, calling out. The man didn't even turn his head, not until Jack called out again and laid a hand on his arm.

The man jumped.

"Sorry, Padre," Jack said. He could smell the whiskey on his breath. "I've been waiting for a preacher to ride into town."

The man nodded. "An' whut—whut ken I do fo' you—my son?" He slurred.

"I need to get married. We've been living in sin."

The preacher hung on to the doorpost. "S'fine. My pleasure, an' God's. Yuh got five dollars—son?"

"Yes. You think you can perform the ceremony now, Padre?"

"Yeah," the man said, and smiled.

Jack took him by the arm and led him to their house. Candice was in the yard doing laundry again, and this was the

second time he'd seen her doing so much—looking so flushed
and fatigued, the strain etching lines on her forehead. His gut
was tight. He had one set of clothes other than buckskins.
Just what in hell was she washing?

"Candice."

She turned, saw him and the inebriated preacher, and
her smile faded to a quizzical then nervous expression.
"Jack?" Her look was uneasy.

He forgot about the laundry when the truth hit him
with a painful blow—she didn't want to get married. "Padre,"
he said, "why don't you go on inside and have a whiskey.
We'll be right in."

The preacher grinned. "Than' you, son, than' you."

Jack watched him begin an unsteady walk to the door
before turning to Candice. "We're getting married."

Her navy eyes went wide.

"As far as I'm concerned, you are my wife, but I won't
have the *pindah* saying my son is a bastard." His voice was
soft, ruthless. "Do you understand?"

Candice overcame her initial shock. Things had gone
too far—she was pregnant and his mistress, so this was the
only solution, and it had been what she had secretly hoped
for. She did not want her baby called a bastard either, not
ever. And she loved Jack—although she'd never told him
that, not since the first time, because she didn't think he felt
the same way about her.

She was momentarily disappointed. She knew he was
marrying her because of the baby, not because of herself.
Then she realized she didn't care. One thing Jack had was
honor—he would never abandon them, and marriage would
tie her to him forever.

He reached out and his hand closed too firmly over her
wrist. "I'm not giving you a choice," he growled.

She looked up, startled, realizing he'd misread her reasons for hesitation. "Let's get married," she said, too lightly.
Then she added, "Is he too drunk to perform the ceremony?"

"I don't really care," Jack replied, "just so long as it's
legal."

When they entered, the preacher stood, knocking over
his chair and looking foolish. "That's all right, Padre," Jack
said, picking up the chair.

"Sorry."

"Are you Catholic, Father?" Candice asked. Jack kept calling him Padre.

He looked confused. "No."

"Oh."

He reached inside his jacket and produced a small, worn Bible. Jack stepped to Candice's side. Candice hastily yanked off her kerchief and stuffed it into her apron pocket. She had a flash of every woman's fantasy—of herself as a bride, gorgeous in white satin and lace with a veil and a ten-foot train, walking down a real church aisle, with Jack waiting for her—resplendent in a black suit. Her father giving her away.

Tears came to her eyes, and she blinked them away. She would not compare this ceremony to what she'd always imagined her wedding would be. She wouldn't.

"In sickness an' in health, to love an' to cherish?" the preacher was saying.

"I do," Jack said.

"An' do you, er—"

Candice felt panic. He needed to know her name, her real name. She was frozen, not even able to breathe.

"Candice Kincaid," Jack supplied.

Oh, my God, I should have told him. She heard herself inhale loudly. "Candice Carter," she corrected, her voice a bare whisper.

Jack's gaze swung to her, hard, incredulous, burning.

"An' d'you, Candice Kincaid, take this man to be your husban', to love an' to cherish, in sickness an' health, until death do you part?"

She didn't dare look at Jack. She could feel the heat of his gaze. "It's Carter," she said, forcing herself to speak up.

"Carter?" The preacher looked infinitely puzzled. Then his brows drew together. "Can't you make up your min'?"

"Candice Carter," Jack reiterated, his voice low and menacing.

"D'you, Candice *Carter,* take this man to be your husban'?"

Candice had never heard such an abbreviated ceremony, but more important was Jack's burning gaze on her. *I should have told him the truth.* "Yes, I do."

"You got a ring?"

Jack had a ring. He'd acquired the plain gold band weeks ago, and he saw Candice's surprise when he slipped it on her finger.

"There." The preacher grinned, snapping the Bible shut, and Candice saw it had been upside down. "I now pronounce you man an' wife."

Candice's mind raced.

Jack paid the preacher, thanking him, offering him coffee and something to eat. He refused, and Jack escorted him to the door. "Thanks again," he said, closing the door firmly and turning slowly to face Candice. Her face was flaming.

"You were never married to Kincaid."

"Jack, I can explain."

His eyes were flat and cold. "If you weren't his wife, then how could he force you to go with him?"

"Jack, please let me explain."

"I'm waiting."

"We eloped—but in Fort Yuma he refused to marry me. He told me he only wanted me to be his mistress. We fought. He tried to rape me. I shot him. I thought I'd killed him."

Jack stared.

She swallowed because her throat was dry. "I was afraid they'd hang me as a murderess, so I stole a horse and ran away. After that, you found me. When Kincaid reappeared I was trapped. My reputation was already in shreds. I couldn't let my family know we'd run off together and never been married—I just couldn't. I'd already lied—already told everyone we were married. Don't you see?" she pleaded.

There was a long silence. "What other lies have you told me?"

Instantly she thought about the laundry. "None—not really. I mean . . ." She flushed again.

"There's something else you're hiding from me, isn't there?" He reached her in two hard strides and pulled her to her feet. "What is it, Candice? Is it about the baby?" His eyes flashed.

"No!"

"Is that baby another man's?"

"God—no! It's about the laundry!"

He instantly relaxed, looking incredulous and relieved all at once.

She touched his face. "Jack, the baby is ours. Yours and mine. I swear to it."

He released her. "What kind of lie could there be about laundry? What in hell are you washing, anyway?"

She bit her lip. "I'm taking in laundry, from the soldiers and the hotel."

He stared.

Not a sound could be heard in the dim room.

Candice tried a smile. "We need the cash. It was all I could think of."

He exploded, his face turning red, veins straining. "You're taking in laundry? My wife a washerwoman?"

She took an instinctive step back. "Jack, it's not so bad—"

"Even if you weren't pregnant, I wouldn't let you do it!" he shouted. "You get that garbage out of my yard and give it back to whoever it belongs to. You, woman, are out of business!" He jammed a finger at her.

"What am I supposed to do? How can we live? We need the money, damn you, Jack—damn your pride! I can't live on eggs and squirrels! We need flour, sugar, coffee, ham, soap, cloth, thread—the list is endless!"

"You return that laundry, Candice. You return every bit of it today. You're not taking it in again, and that's that."

"I am your *wife*," Candice said, so furious her voice cracked. "Not some squaw! You can't order me around!"

"You return that goddamned laundry today, Candice," Jack warned. His hands closed on her shoulders.

Candice tried to twist free but he wouldn't let her. "I'm only doing what has to be done. We have nothing!"

His eyes widened, while a muscle tightened in his jaw. "Jack!" she gasped. "I didn't—"

He released her and slammed out of the house. The frame around the door trembled long after he was gone.

Candice sank onto the bed, trembling, fighting tears. She hadn't meant to say that, she knew how proud he was.

And that night, when Jack came back, he didn't even reach for her in the dark.

PART FOUR

War and Betrayal

CHAPTER FIFTY-FIVE

February 1861

Candice heard the door opening and looked up, smiling. "You're just in time." Seeing Jack's grim expression, her smile faded. "What's wrong, Jack?"

"I just heard some news," he said grimly. "There are troops up at Apache Pass way station under siege, along with two stages full of passengers. Two men have been killed, and more are wounded. The rumor is Cochise has taken three Americans prisoner."

Candice paused, carving knife in hand, the succulent roast chicken forgotten.

"Apparently," Jack said, "Cochise has gone on the warpath."

She searched her husband's smoky gaze. "Are you all right?"

"I've heard that Oury's going to rendezvous with troops from Fort Breckenridge at Ewell Springs. They're rounding up volunteers in Tucson. They also sent soldiers to Fort Buchanan for medical aid and supplies." Oury was the agent for the Butterfield Overland Mail.

"How did this happen?"

"Remember the kidnapping of John Warden's boy this fall? The troops were sent to find him." Jack sat down and stared at the fire.

"I heard you say a long time ago that Cochise didn't take the boy," Candice said, sitting also.

"Warden says he did." He briefly met his wife's gaze and was struck by the compassion he saw there. She couldn't know what he was going through.

"Jack?" Her voice was high and uneasy. "Is this war?"

"Yes."

Jack's face was expressionless. He knew, without having to be told, that if white men had been killed and taken prisoner, it was war. And the only thing that would make Cochise break his word was betrayal. Cochise betrayed would

be a warrior who would wreak devastation the extent of
which no one could imagine except for himself. He was grim
and pensive. And afraid.

"Do you want to eat?" Candice asked gently, thinking
fearfully about her brothers and father. They had never been
at war with the Apaches, not since they had moved to the
Territory almost eleven years ago. Raids and skirmishes were
one thing. But war? God, no.

"You eat," Jack said. "I'm not hungry."

He walked outside, alone—but not to do chores. He
mounted up and rode out of town, giving the black his head,
thinking. His thoughts were dark.

He respected and admired Cochise above all other men.
He was proud that Cochise had given him his childhood
name, and had been proud, too, to ride with him and be held
in respect by the Chiricahua chief. He understood what was
happening better than most men, white or Apache. Cochise
had sought to make peace with the white man to insure the
survival of his people. The Apaches were few, the white
many, their ways superior, more powerful—ways built on wisdom and technology. The whites had guns, cannon, glasses,
maps, supplies, and, most important, endless numbers. Only
in peace could the Apache hope to survive, by living side by
side with the Americans.

The war would be one of survival . . . freedom . . .
life and death.

Jack knew in his heart that the war was lost before it had
begun. Cochise knew it too. It was why he had wanted peace
with the white man, why he had hung on to it so tenaciously
in the face of contempt from the Mescalero, the other
Apache chiefs—Mangas Coloradas, Geronimo—and dissent
even from his own warriors, who ached to fight for their way
of life, their land, and their freedom.

How would it end? For how many years could the
Apaches hold off the whites? Already, as Cochise had pointed
out, many Tonto and Coyoteros had been herded like animals and confined to reservations. Not a bodily death, but a
death just the same. A death of a way of life. Of a people.

Jack knew as he rode back to town that there was only
one decision to make. He had no choice. He untacked the
black, then rubbed him down, giving him grain and lingering

—to put off the inevitable. Finally he turned and went into the house. Candice was throwing another stick of wood on the fire. He looked at her in the pink lace nightgown with the thin silk wrapper and felt an overwhelming need for her—a need that went beyond mere desire. He wished, in that instant, that he could take back all the walls of silence between them, redo and relive every moment he had ever spent with her.

"Come on," he said softly.

"What is it?" she asked with worry, as he led her across the room.

He didn't answer. Standing so close to her that his thighs touched hers, he stared at her face, flushed from the fire, and thought: I don't want to leave her, I love her. How come I've never told her that? His hands went to the belt of the robe and loosened it. He slid the wrapper from her shoulders.

"Jack?"

He couldn't smile, not when this was good-bye.

"Jack?" she asked again, this time with panic as his arms drew her against him.

He was thickly erect already, the aching need coming from desperation. He kissed her softly, tenderly, his mouth slanting over hers, ignoring her stiff, unyielding form and her hands on his chest. Again, in a more panicked voice, she said, "Jack?"

And then she melted. Her arms went around his neck, fingers threading through his hair. Her response, wild and instinctively urgent, displaced the soft tenderness of his kisses, turning them hard and insistent and demanding.

He turned savage. The urgency in his heart overtook his body, and he grabbed her hips, pulling them against his long, hard arousal, rubbing against her. He invaded her mouth with his tongue, seeking, frantically seeking. He needed her, now.

It might be the last time.

They fell on the bed together, and she was caught up in his urgency and passion, tearing at his clothes. Within a moment they were naked, and he thrust into her, hard, and she cried out in surprise, but was wet and ready and eager. Jack stroked her rapidly, his mouth on hers, harder and faster, holding her, lost in this one moment, making this one memory . . .

"What is it?" she whispered afterward, looking up at his glazed face.

"Sshh," he said as he kissed her.

He rolled to his side and held her, but did not relax, did not close his eyes. Instead he studied her face, drinking in her flushed beauty, the dark fans of her long lashes, the smoothly sculpted planes of her face, the swollen, red lips, now slightly parted. He leaned forward to kiss her lightly.

Her gaze became focused and worried. "Jack, what is it?"

"Sshh, *shijíi*, not now," he hushed, his mouth covering hers again. Tonight was theirs, and nothing could change that.

The next morning Candice awoke to the unfamiliar sounds of Jack moving back and forth across the room. She sighed, stretched, and instantly remembered last night— Jack's urgency and insatiability. She was immediately awake, sitting, the fear rushing back.

Jack was standing in the center of the room, fully dressed and fully armed, right down to the crossed ammunition belts. On the table were his saddlebags and an extra change of buckskin clothes. Completely frozen inside, she watched him toss a cloth headband and his warrior's necklace onto the pile.

"You're leaving," she stated flatly.

He looked at her, and his gray eyes were luminous with something akin to pain. "I'm riding up to Apache Pass," he told her.

She stared. Her heart began to thud wildly and hurtfully. "Please don't go."

He had flint, his loincloth, some jerky, and an extra blanket in his saddlebags. He rolled up the clothes, then donned the necklace, tucking it beneath his shirt. "You don't understand," he said levelly.

"Why are you going?" she said. "What are you planning on doing? How long will you be gone?" Her voice cracked.

He tied on the headband. "I'm going to see Cochise."

She gasped. "It's too dangerous! Are you crazy? Please— *Jack!*"

He faced her squarely. "You don't understand, Candice. Cochise has been betrayed. I am riding with him."

She stared, thoroughly stunned.

He came to her and sat on the bed, touching her arm—she pulled away violently. "I'm sorry," he said. "I wish there was another way."

"You can't do this!" she cried. "What do you mean? You're going on the warpath with Cochise?" Her voice was shrill.

He nodded.

"You can't—you'd leave me here, pregnant, to go ride with those damn Apaches?"

He almost flinched. "I have no choice."

"No choice?" she shouted. "Every man has a choice!"

"God!" he cried. "Candice, I have no choice—it's my duty—there's honor and loyalty involved."

"Honor and loyalty?" She gasped. "Duty? Your duty is here—with me!"

His expression hardened. "I'm taking you back to your family."

It took a full second for the import of his statement to sink in. "No. No, I won't go. Jack, don't leave, please, there's nothing you can do up there."

"I have to go, Candice, don't you understand?" He pleaded.

"No! I don't understand! You're my husband and I'm having your baby! We need you here!"

"That's why I'm taking you to the High C."

"No!" she cried. "No, Jack, I won't go!"

He took her cold hands in his, his eyes searching her face. He couldn't help the bitterness in his tone. "Afraid to face them while you're carrying my child?"

"Yes!" She flung back the truth furiously, hoping to devastate him. "Yes, I'm afraid to face them, afraid of what they'll say, what they'll think—damn you!"

He stood up, his expression as hard as granite, and moved to the table where he began packing his things in his saddlebags. He heard her muffle a sob. He hefted the bags onto his shoulder. "I'll have the Santana boy see to your heavier needs. Here's forty dollars. It will hold you for a few months if I can't get back sooner."

She said nothing, staring at the sheets, twisting them in

white hand, tears falling. He waited for her to look at him, and when he realized she wouldn't, he walked to the door.

She reached him at the door, grabbing his arm and hanging on desperately. "Don't go—I need you here!"

"I'll be back as soon as I can, and as often." He tried for a reassuring smile and failed miserably.

"No," she cried, but it was half a wail. Her eyes were filled with horror.

He paused and kissed her, but she was frozen into immobility, her lips like stone. He didn't look at her again as he walked out the door, leaving her standing there naked and shocked.

Candice closed her eyes. What if he was killed? God, I love him, and he's leaving me—what if he's killed? What if I never see him again?

She shrugged on her wrapper, not even bothering with the nightgown, sick and hysterical because her world was falling apart and the man she loved was riding off to war—against her own people. And then she was flying as fast as she could outside, barefoot. He was leading the black out from the corral, and she cried out his name, running across the yard. He hesitated as she came, then swung into the saddle.

"No!" she cried, grabbing his ankle. "Jack, don't go! You can't!"

"I have to." He looked down at her, but his face was masked. "Get back inside, Candice, before the neighbors see you."

She stood, tears streaming down her face. "Don't go, Jack, damn you, don't go!"

He closed his eyes briefly. "I love you," he said softly, then urged the black into a trot, breaking free of her.

She clung to the fence, weeping, watching his shadowy figure until the night swallowed him up.

CHAPTER FIFTY-SIX

Three days later Jack reached Apache Pass. He had pushed as hard as he could, and the black was exhausted and lathered. After using a smoke sign to announce his arrival—for he had no intention of being killed by his own people—he rode up to the summit and was greeted by six warriors who led him to Cochise.

Cochise's camp was in Goodwin Canyon, about a mile and a half from the way station. Jack saw that Cochise did, indeed, have the station under siege—heavily armed warriors were atop all the surrounding ridges. He dismounted with the other warriors and promptly saw Nahilzay striding forward. The tall warrior's eyes were black, intense, and wary. He stood watching Jack without speaking for a long moment.

"I come as one of the people, a brother, and a friend," Jack said slowly.

Nahilzay was inscrutable. Jack knew he was not pleased to see him there, and that he was suspicious of his intentions. That irked him. He turned and Jack followed, leaving the black drop-reined. His horse needed water and feed, but no one moved to care for him. Jack was keenly aware of the difference between this greeting and the one he had received a couple of months before.

Cochise was sitting outside his *gohwah* in grim silence. He rose slowly as Jack and Nahilzay approached. His face was expressionless, but his eyes were angry and determined. He waited.

"The thorns are too prickly," Jack said, referring to Cochise's opinion that he would not be able to straddle the fence between the white world and the red one indefinitely.

Cochise smiled then. "Welcome," he said, with complete understanding.

They embraced, but Nahilzay did not relax. "Forgive me," he said to Cochise. "But he is a White Eyes."

Cochise was no longer smiling. "Do not insult my brother," he said. "Tend his horse." It was a dismissal, and his lieutenant left, his face hard and angry.

"Tension runs high," Jack said.

"Sit," Cochise said. "Eat. Drink. I need only to see you here and look at you to know you are Apache in your heart and soul. We know blood is of little importance." He gestured at his camp. "I could count on four hands Apaches with no Apache blood, but they are Men of the Woods."

Jack drank from a gourd of *tiswin*, draining it, and it was promptly refilled by Cochise's first wife. Then he ate hungrily, and Cochise did not speak, but sat staring at the distant ridges as twilight deepened the sky to a starless purple. It had snowed some days ago, and the ground was crisp and white underfoot, making the sky seem violet in contrast.

"What happened?" Jack asked, when he had finished.

"My word has been doubted. I have been called a liar. I have been betrayed—my people have been betrayed."

Jack listened intently, and Cochise told him the story. His voice was emotionless, but his eyes were furious.

Four days ago troops under the command of Lieutenant Bascom had ridden into the pass and made camp not far from Goodwin Canyon. Cochise had gone down to the station to ask his friends, the men who were the stationkeepers, what was the meaning of the troops. Culver had told him they were on their way to the Rio Grande, but that Bascom wanted to meet him and would like him to visit; he would be flying a white flag. Cochise knew now that he should have been suspicious—the white flag was not necessary because Cochise was not at war with the white man. But the thought hadn't crossed his mind.

Cochise had gone down to the camp with his second wife; his eight-year-old son, Nachise; his brother, Naretana; and his other brother's two grown sons. Bascom was flying a white flag atop his Sibley tent. They had been invited inside the tent. It was a trap.

Bascom had asked Cochise for the return of Warden's son and the oxen that had been stolen during the kidnapping—which was the same thing as an accusation of the crime. Cochise had ignored that insult, denying calmly that he had taken the boy, but offering to help find him and buy back his return. Bascom became angry and called Cochise a "damn liar" twice, and then informed him that he and his family were prisoners, to be held as hostages for the release of the boy. Immediately Cochise had whipped a knife out from beneath his loincloth, slit the tent, yelled for his family to follow, and had broken past the soldiers, making a wild dash up the hill. Gunfire followed, and he was hit in the back of the leg, but not seriously. No one else had escaped.

"I was still not inclined to war with the white men, understanding Bascom to be an arrogant, unwise young fool," Cochise said. "I came down to the station with several warriors to take the station men hostage for an exchange. I called them by name. Because they are my friends, they came out. Culver and Welch and Wallace." He frowned. "One betrayal begets another. We talked, we tried to take them. Culver was shot in the back escaping, but only wounded. Welch was killed by the soldiers accidentally as he tried to flee over the corral wall. We took Wallace, then retreated."

Jack listened grimly. Cochise was not finished.

Since then they had tried to negotiate twice for the release of the Indians in a prisoner exchange, but Bascom was adamant in his refusal unless the Warden boy was included—even though the Apaches had attacked nine wagons camped in the pass and taken two more Americans prisoner.

More skirmishes had occurred when an eastbound stage from Tucson had been attacked as it tried to get through the pass. Two of the mules were hit, the driver and conductor wounded, but the stage made it to the sanctuary of the station. The westbound stage arrived unmolested a few hours later. All the stage passengers were well armed.

The next day it snowed, providing the besieged Americans water. The springs were six hundred yards from the station and controlled by the Apaches. On the following day, out of desperation, an armed military escort took half the stock down to the springs. They were attacked, one soldier killed, two wounded, and all the stock stampeded west.

Cochise stared into the fire.

Jack sat silent, his lips in a thin line. Cochise's wife and son, brother and nephews were the prisoners—and there was no way to get them out of the station, which was a small stone fortress. For a moment he imagined what he would do if it were Candice and their child being held hostage. Bascom was a fool. And asking for trouble—lots of it. "And now?"

"Tell me, Niño Salvaje, what you would do."

Jack knew Cochise wasn't looking for advice, that he had already decided. "You have more patience than I," he said angrily. "Bascom is a fool. He seduced you into his tent under the white flag. He has insulted your honor many times over. Now he holds your family. If I were you? It is a hard choice. All Apaches are your family. Still, they have your wife, your son." Jack smiled coldly. "One more try," he said fiercely. "Then show them the wrath of the Apache."

"You are very white," Cochise said, "to suggest one more attempt at trade. My warriors long to spill white blood in vengeance already. But it is more important to think of not just the Apache prisoners, but what will follow if we kill more Americans."

"Yes."

"War."

CHAPTER FIFTY-SEVEN

The next day Jack got a look at the three prisoners. He had accepted Cochise's invitation to share his *gohwah*, not because it was cold—something he could have easily endured —but because it would still all doubts within the tribe as to whose side he was on. He rose early, shared a light breakfast of mule meat and beans, and walked through the camp to his stallion. He knew if he stayed he would have to build himself a *gohwah*—women's work, which brought to mind an image of Candice, whom he missed already. He imagined her at that precise moment weeping over his having left her. His gut constricted painfully. Even if she weren't pregnant, how could he have brought her here when they were in a war? He forced her out of his mind. Then he saw them.

They were tied, standing, to stakes. Two wore leather coats, but Wallace—whom Jack recognized as one of the Apache Pass stationkeepers—wore nothing but a shirt and pants, and was blue from cold. The men were exhausted, too, from spending the night on their feet. Each time they would fall asleep they would sag until the ropes bit into them and forced them awake. A quick stab of pity went through Jack.

One of the men he didn't know saw him approaching and stared, trying to determine if he was white or Apache. Except for his coloring, his short hair, and his eyes, he looked every bit the Apache, dressed and armed as one. "Help us," he cried in a low voice. "Good God, help us."

Instantly the other man and Wallace saw him, Wallace's eyes growing huge with recognition. "Savage!" And then he took in every detail of his dress.

Jack's face was carefully without expression. He reached them and kept walking past. For some ridiculous reason, he wanted to stop and at least give Wallace his buckskin jacket.

"Savage, stop!" Wallace called. "Help us! We're freezing! We ain't eaten in days! Savage! Please! Help us!"

His back very stiff, face set, Jack didn't break stride until he found his horse. He began to saddle him, then saw Nahilzay and another warrior approach. "You're leaving?" Nahilzay asked.

Jack met his gaze coolly. "No. I want to scout the area, see what the situation is for myself."

"I will come with you," Nahilzay said, clearly indicating he did not trust him.

Jack's expression did not change. "Once you trusted me," he said, refraining from breaking the other's nose only because it was stupid to fight each other when they had to fight American troops. "Or is your memory short?"

"Then you were Apache." Nahilzay answered. "Many winters ago you left the Apaches to join the *pindah*. Now you come to us in time of war. Perhaps to spy?"

Jack couldn't let it go. It was a direct insult. He dropped the black's reins and moved a few steps from the horse's haunches. Nahilzay moved with him, and Jack threw off his jacket, tossing it away. This was not the way to regain acceptance with his people. But too much was at stake.

Jack lunged at him. They grabbed each other and began to wrestle Apache-style, straining against one another. Nahilzay was tall but lean, and Jack was by far the bigger of the two. However, Nahilzay was a formidable opponent. Every time Jack made a move to get him off-balance, Nahilzay anticipated and deftly avoided the snare. Soon they were sweating and panting, neither one able to get an unbreakable headlock on the other, neither able to flip the other, or gain advantage.

"Cease!"

Both men recognized Cochise's voice, but it was a moment before they pulled apart to stand facing each other, panting, perspiration beading their faces, steam rising off their bodies in the sunlit morning. A small group of warriors had gathered.

"Do I have to chastise my best warriors as if they were little boys who knew no better than to waste their strength fighting each other? Fools! You want to fight, and soon you may fight—but not each other." Cochise was angry and imposing, and had succeeded in shaming both men. "What is the reason for this ridiculous match?"

The two men stared and started to speak at once. Cochise looked at Jack. Jack said, "It was my fault. I lost my temper."

Cochise looked at Nahilzay. "No, it was mine. I accused him of being a spy."

Cochise did not hesitate. "Listen well. Niño Salvaje is my brother. He has proven himself time and again a warrior worthy of the name I chose for him many, many winters ago. He rides with me. Any who doubt my wisdom in this must come to me." He had been looking around the crowd, but then he looked at Nahilzay, making the man cringe slightly. "Speak now or hold silence."

"I do not trust him," Nahilzay said. "He left the people many winters ago to walk with the White Eyes. Now when our trouble is greatest, he comes back. I have not the wisdom of you, great chief, but still, I am no fool."

"In this I think you are a fool," Cochise said harshly. "Has he not ridden with us before? Has he not acquitted himself as a brave warrior? Has he not had Apache wives? Has he not returned when our time is darkest, when our need of mighty warriors is greatest? Has he not found his heart now, after much turmoil? Do you, Nahilzay"—Cochise's voice lowered—"after so many winters and even more harvests, decide to doubt my wisdom? Do you now choose to insult my ability as your chief?"

"No," Nahilzay said, looking shamed.

Cochise walked away.

Jack looked at Nahilzay, and the warrior met his gaze enigmatically. "Time will show that the great chief speaks the truth," Jack told him. "I am going to scout the situation. Join me and explain to me how we stand." It was a peace offering.

Still inscrutable, Nahilzay nodded, and soon appeared astride his mount, a chestnut stallion of blue blood, obviously stolen from a white man's ranch. The two men rode off in a strained but accepting silence.

The way station was in Siphon Canyon, surrounded almost completely on four sides by hills. Siphon Wash ran past the station going north and south. Cochise's warriors had surrounded the station from three hills, which was all the situation warranted to keep the soldiers and passengers under siege. In so doing, they also guarded the springs.

Looking down, Jack saw not a single person outdoors. The soldiers were huddled in the stone corral with the stock, behind the twelve-foot-high stone walls. He assumed the passengers probably numbered a total of twenty men, including drivers and conductors if the stages had been full. They were obviously barricaded inside the station house. Soon they would need water, even as they must need it now. They would be slaughtered if they made the attempt.

He was grim. The incident with Nahilzay had gotten his mind off the three prisoners, but now Wallace's image came back to haunt him. He shoved the small seed of compassion deep within himself and buried it. He had been too long in the white man's world. There could be no compassion in war.

That night, through luck and error, a small escort slipped up to the station.

Cochise was furious. As it turned out, his scouts had seen several companies of dragoons heading east about twelve miles north of the pass on Old Leach Road. Thinking the troops were being sent to attack the Apaches from the east, the scouts had abandoned their posts guarding the west entrance to the pass and gone to the east entrance, where just a few men could hold off the several companies. The small escort had thus slipped in through the west entrance, racing the last leg of the way to the station. Although taken by surprise, the warriors on the hills saw them and opened fire. However, when they saw that the soldiers had three Indian prisoners with them, they had stopped firing, amid much confusion. The Indians were clearly Coyotero Apaches.

Cochise was grim as he sat with Nahilzay, Jack, and two of his other best warriors. Now the Americans held eight prisoners, including Cochise's second wife and small son. Because the small cavalcade had been driving about thirty ponies and as many or more cattle, it was obvious to everyone that the Coyoteros had been returning from a raid when they had run into the troops and been engaged. The night was grim, and Cochise asked each man in turn his thoughts on the matter.

The three Chiricahua warriors wanted blood. They wanted to torture and kill the American prisoners to show the troops what betrayal of their chief's word and honor meant. Jack again said he would offer one last time to trade prisoners. Nahilzay snorted in disgust. Then Cochise spoke.

"Eight Apaches, when our numbers are so few, and less

every year. Five of whom are irreplaceable warriors. My brother, Naretana, is irreplaceable for his wisdom, the keenest of any man's. Tomorrow we send Wallace down. It will be my last offer."

The next day the sun was bright, the snow crisp and white underfoot, the sky blue and cloudless. It was bitterly cold. Wallace was untied from the stake; Nahilzay held a lariat around his torso beneath his arms. A hundred warriors in full war dress rode to the top of the hill, with Nahilzay and Cochise in front, Wallace walking alongside. Jack rode a bit behind and to Cochise's left, two of the top warriors between him and the Chiricahua chief. Like everyone else, his face was painted red, black, and yellow.

Nahilzay was on Cochise's right. He played out his rope, and Wallace, already instructed by Cochise, walked partway down the hill until he was gazing over the dry wash running between him and the station and corral.

"Lieutenant Bascom," he called.

The door to the station house opened immediately. Obviously someone had seen the Apache on the hill. Several men stepped out, three in uniform. Jack picked up his field glasses.

Lieutenant Bascom was about twenty-two or -three, deeply red from the sun, small, slender, and tense. A sergeant stood next to him, clearly a grizzled veteran, and a man wearing a uniform with a surgeon's markings on it also stood with them. So did John Warden, the big, red-haired Irish rancher, and a man Jack recognized from Tucson, William Buckley, superintendent of this section of the Butterfield line. Jack passed the glasses to Cochise, who refused them.

In the incredible quiet of the snow-laden mountain morning, sound traveled easily up the hill as Wallace and Bascom shouted back and forth at each other.

Wallace began. "Bascom! We're all in bad shape. We're starving, we ain't had anything to eat in days. We're freezing. They won't give us blankets or nothing. Cochise will let us all go if you release the Indians. He says this is his last offer!"

Bascom spoke. "Bring the Warden boy down with the two other Americans, and we'll release the Indians."

Wallace and everyone else turned to look at Cochise for his response. His lips were set in a grim line.

At that moment, Wallace started running for the station. Nahilzay smiled and caused his horse to rear up, making Wallace go down on his back. He was almost at the bottom of the hill, and Nahilzay urged his mount forward, fast. The rope went tight. Wallace went onto his stomach, grabbing foolishly onto a rock. Tension strained the rope, then Wallace was being dragged over the ground, face downward. At a gallop, Nahilzay raced back and forth across the hill, dragging the man behind him, and then the Apaches turned away, disappearing back over the hill—Nahilzay following, still dragging his inert burden.

The screams started shortly afterward.

Jack stood in the ring around the three prisoners, who were still tied upright to stakes. He was motionless and without expression. It took all his Apache training to control himself. Cochise and Nahilzay were beside him. A hundred warriors had gathered around, one-fifth of the warriors Cochise had. With spears in hand, several warriors ran forward at once, lances raised at the ashen, stricken prisoners. Screams of agony rang out, again and again. Soon the snow was no longer white but crimson. Cochise walked away.

Jack gazed at the bloody victims, heard their screams for mercy, and controlled his expression, did not even blink. *I have become too white,* he thought impassively, using an iron will to remain detached. He had never had the Apache capacity for torture. And although the Apaches never tortured except in vengeance, in that they were cruel beyond description. The torture sickened him.

He wondered, now, as he heard the men's screams and saw them with a part of himself completely separated from feeling, if it was because of his white blood. The white man did not torture except in isolated instances; it was not a part of American culture.

He walked away, and as he did so, he saw Nahilzay looking at him through narrowed, knowing eyes. Jack did not care.

CHAPTER FIFTY-EIGHT

She was angry.

Her back hurt. She had a fierce headache. It was cold out, too cold to be outside doing laundry. She'd taken on more wash. Jack had left her with a brood of chickens, true, and a milk cow, and plenty of smoked game, but she had the baby to think of. The baby and their future.

And right now she wasn't sure that Jack Savage was a part of it.

And forty dollars wasn't going to take her as far as she intended to go.

This was not the future she wanted for her child. As soon as the baby was old enough to travel, they would leave. She couldn't go to her family. She would make sure she had saved enough to rent a place for herself and the child while she looked for work. If she had to, she'd clean floors—but one day her baby was going to have everything he needed.

She stirred the laundry angrily. Her breath made vapors in the air. Her nose was red, and she sneezed. Her hands were frozen and redder than her nose. She needed to bring in wood before nightfall if Louis Santana failed to show up again today. She needed to feed the stock. She needed to bring a side of venison in from the smokehouse Jack had built. And she wanted to bake a loaf of bread.

His declaration of love for her had come a little bit late, she thought angrily, tucking wisps of hair back into her kerchief. What man loved a woman then left her pregnant and alone? Damn him. She had the insane urge to weep—something that was quite common these days. If he really loved her he wouldn't have left her to go to war. To go to war on the wrong side. Even now, as she was thinking, was he scalping whites, torturing them? Dear God, what kind of man had she married? How could he talk of honor and loyalty in the same breath with the Apache? What about her? What about her and her baby?

"Howdy, Candice."

Candice straightened and turned eagerly, to face Corporal Lewis. "Henry—is there any news? From Apache Pass?"

His eyes moved over her. They were laced with a combination of admiration—she knew he found her attractive despite how she was looking—and pity. It had only been two
weeks, but everyone in town knew her husband had disappeared. Candice had not confided in anyone. It was all she
needed—to be lynched by the Apache-hating townsfolk now
that emotions were running so high. Henry pitied her, she
thought, because she was working so hard, living in poverty,
deserted by her husband. He admired her because he was
hoping she would let him in her bed—just like all the other
soldiers. It was why she always carried the derringer Jack had
given her—even when she locked the door at night and went
to bed.

Thank God her pregnancy wasn't showing yet, and that
Doc Harris was a decent man and not a gossip.

"Lots of news. You look tired, Candice. How about inviting me in for a cup of coffee?"

She smiled wearily. "Of course. I see you've brought me
some laundry."

He smiled too. "Sure thing."

Candice wasn't afraid of Henry Lewis, not like some of
the other soldiers who brought her laundry. He was from
New York, the third son of an upper-class merchant family.
He was young, well educated, but just plain starved for a
white woman. She knew he hated the army and would leave
the instant his tour was over. She didn't blame him.

As she poured coffee, Henry unfolded a square of linen,
revealing fresh, still-warm pastries. Candice began to salivate.
She was always hungry these days, and never had time to
make something sweet. He saw her expression and laughed.
"Oh, Henry," she said, turning away to get some plates. She
had the insane urge to cry again.

"You work too hard," he said when she sat, taking one of
her callused hands in his.

Candice gently withdrew it. She smiled slightly but
didn't answer. "Tell me about Apache Pass."

"Good news," Henry told her, his face lightening.
"Cochise's rancheria has been burned to the ground."

Candice went white and felt faint. *Jack.*

"Candice? Are you all right?"

She closed her eyes and hung on to the table. Please,

God, no. I love him, I do, let him be all right. She opened her eyes and blinked through tears. "What happened?"

"Troops from Fort Breckenridge made it through. Two companies of dragoons under the command of Lieutenant Morris. It was real quiet. Turns out the rancheria had been abandoned . . ."

Candice didn't hear any more. Abandoned. *Thank God.* "Abandoned? They were gone? The Apaches were gone?"

"Every last one. What we did find was three badly mutilated bodies. Poor bastards," he said, his face darkening.

Candice was too relieved that the Apaches had deserted the rancheria before it was burned to think of the American prisoners who'd been murdered. Henry continued. "Oury identified one of the corpses as the stationkeeper, Wallace, from his gold teeth. They hanged all the Indian prisoners, including three Coyoteros they'd run into on their way to the pass. Except for the squaw and the boy, who were taken to Fort Buchanan. They hanged them over the graves of the dead men." He paused, sipping. "Three of the hanged Apaches were related to Cochise, or so it's said. They also say the squaw and boy are his."

Candice couldn't eat, and she couldn't drink. The enormity of what had happened sank in. She raised her eyes to Henry's. "There won't be any turning back now, will there?"

"I doubt it," Henry said. "Looks like we're in the middle of a damn war with the Apaches."

Later, at the door, Henry took her hand and squeezed it, looking into her eyes with unmistakable urgency. "Candice," he said, his tone too hoarse.

"Thank you for bringing me the news," Candice said politely. He didn't release her hand.

"Candice—he's gone." It was a statement and question all at once.

Instantly Candice froze and removed her hand from his. "I'm tired, Henry, it's been a long day and I've still got a dozen things to do before dark."

He stared at her for one more moment with obvious longing. "You deserve better," he finally said. "Better than a husband who'd leave you here, like this, alone. Better than a ha—"

"Don't you dare say it," Candice warned. "Good-bye,

Henry. Your laundry will be ready in three days, if the weather holds."

He opened his mouth to speak, then shut it.

Candice closed the door and leaned against it, waiting until she heard him riding out. All she could think of was Jack. It was all she could think of the entire time Henry had been there, and the visit had seemed interminable. Jack was riding with the Apaches. Was he holed up in some secret canyon, preparing for another strike against the white man? Or was he ambushing some innocent wagon train, right now? Was he all right? Even if he wanted to come see her, how could he do so now? God only knew where he was—and how far away.

She closed her eyes and prayed for his safety.

Then she went out to finish the laundry.

CHAPTER FIFTY-NINE

Scouts had been left behind when the Apaches abandoned the camp in Goodwin Canyon for Cochise's eastern stronghold deep in the Chiricahua Mountains. One returned with grim but not unexpected news of the hangings. Jack had ridden out with Cochise and a dozen other warriors to cut down and bury the bodies. There was little danger, for they knew the troops and passengers had all left the pass.

The six bodies swung gently in a whispering winter breeze beneath a huge oak, over the fresh graves of the three Americans. The party approached, and they came close enough to make out the fact that the bodies looked untouched except for their broken necks. Jack's glance swept over the six Apaches, grimly, sadly, then his gaze was drawn like a bolt to the third man.

Shozkay.

No!

He stared, frozen. *No! It couldn't be!*

But it was. There was no mistake. Shozkay, his brother, twirled in the breeze—his head tilted completely to one side, so his chin touched his shoulder. His eyes were open, staring, unseeing, lifeless. The breeze lifted his shoulder-length hair, and strands of it touched his face, catching on his mouth.

Jack made a sound. It came from deep inside, tearing its way upward, a pain so unbearable, so vast, that for a moment he wondered if he might not die and join his brother. He fought to steady himself. He couldn't move. He was not even aware that everyone else was slipping off their mounts. My brother, he screamed inwardly. My brother! *Not my brother!*

He dismounted. It was one of the hardest things he had ever done in his life. He went to Shozkay, his breathing labored, his vision skewed from blinding tears. He cut the rope, catching Shozkay in his arms, and went down to his knees, cradling him gently. He sobbed, huge animallike sounds that burst free of their own accord. He sat there and held him for a long, long time.

He didn't know how long he sat before the tears finally

stopped. He took a few deep breaths, still holding his brother on his lap, and regained a precarious degree of control.

He removed the noose from Shozkay's neck and smoothed the raw red welts with his trembling fingers, as if to take away the blemish. His skin was already cold, lifeless. *No!* The huge pain welled from deep within again, choking him, exploding. He put his arms around Shozkay and held him, closing his eyes, pressing his cheeks against his hair, unable to move. So cold, so stiff . . . he had to move, had to bury him. He looked up, blinking, to see that he was alone. The morning was very white and very quiet, marked with the silence of death. He stood unsteadily and lifted his brother, very gently, despite his great size and weight. He carried him to his horse.

He rode to the springs where the burial preparations were already underway. No one looked at him, or in any way intruded upon his grief. Numbly but tenderly, for it would be the last time he would be with his brother until they met in the afterlife, Jack washed him. He could not believe it, He could not believe Shozkay was dead. Hanged. Not even a warrior's death. Shozkay, whom he had grown up with. Whom he had wrestled with and run with and played with and loved better than a brother, as a best friend. Shozkay, whom he would have gladly exchanged his own life for. Shozkay, whom he loved more than anyone else in the world, except his wife and their mother. A different kind of love. A love that ran so deep it made them a part of each other.

Jack redressed him, then gave him, from his own person, everything he needed for his journey to the other world—for Shozkay was unarmed and possessed nothing except his clothes, his necklace and war amulet. Jack armed him with his own Colt and knife and gave him his jacket and a blanket. He buried him carefully, in a crevasse on a hilltop shaded by juniper, killing the horse that had been brought for just that purpose. The tears had come again, sometime as he was burying Shozkay. He wasn't sure exactly when. He walked away, desperately seeking numbness.

Much later, bathed, steamed with herbed smoke, his hair cut, and his anger rising, he rode back to the stronghold with the rest of the party. He had one coherent thought emerging through the heavy mists of his grief: *revenge.*

Revenge.

It nourished his heart, body, and soul and kept him sane through a week of isolated mourning. Jack spoke to no one, stayed apart, could not eat, and grieved deeply. The camp was quiet except for the intermittent sobbing and wailing of women whose kin had been buried. Everyone waited for Cochise's period of mourning to pass, wondering how long it would last. The chief saw no one, spoke to no one, and no one saw him.

Exactly one week after Shozkay's burial, Jack came out of his shell of grief. He was still alive. There were other things he had to do. He ate for the first time in days, almost becoming ill from the shock to his system. Then he found Nahilzay and told him he was taking the bad news to Shozkay's kin. He rode out of the stronghold at first light.

He reached the San Pedro River the next morning, after stopping to sleep and rest that night. He was sorely tempted to head east—he was only two and a half days from El Paso. From Candice. He needed her. He needed her so much it was like an ache. He wanted to lose himself and his grief in her. Just for a little while. But he turned north and rode up the San Pedro Valley. Using smoke signs, he located Shozkay's band that afternoon, camped in a creek in a canyon west of the valley.

He knew Luz would be hoping for the best, but aware of the worst. The rest of the raiding party would have returned over a week ago. Had they seen Shozkay and the others captured? There was no way of knowing. There was also no way of breaking the news gently. He rode into camp with the sun hanging golden just over the hills, spreading the day's last warming rays.

A cry went up that he had arrived. He dismounted, looking past the men who converged, shouting greetings and eager to hear the news of war. The Apaches communicated with each other over long distances through smoke sent up by scouting party after scouting party, like a chain letter. By now Apaches from the New Mexico Territory to west Texas, as far south as Mexico and north as the Jicarilla and Kiowa in Colorado, knew that Cochise had taken the warpath against the White Eyes. But Jack merely responded to the greeting by rote. He saw Datiye approaching, then saw Luz, behind her.

Luz froze and stared. Their gazes met. Jack reached inside himself for strength and courage. Luz paled. Her mouth opened. He couldn't hear the words, but he knew it was a denial. He strode through the crowd to reach her and grab her shoulders.

"No! Do not tell me . . . do not!" Tears swam in her eyes. She shook in his hands.

"I'm sorry," he said hoarsely, a fresh wave of his own grief rising in him. "He's dead . . . I've buried him, Luz."

She screamed and twisted. Jack let her go. She turned and ran, and, after briefly meeting Datiye's worried gaze, he went after her. He found her on the ground beside her *gohwah,* beating it, clawing herself, her cheeks and arms, tearing out hunks of hair. He knelt beside her, placing his hand on her back. He did not stop her from inflicting pain upon herself, because it was the Apache way to grieve. When her beautiful face was gouged and bloody, she crumpled onto the dirt, weeping wildly. Jack knelt there beside her for a long time.

She cried for hours, then fell into an exhausted sleep. Jack carried her into the *gohwah* and laid her upon the bed of hides she had shared with her husband, his brother. He was once again choked with his own grief. He looked up as Datiye entered, carrying a woven pitcher of water. She knelt beside Luz and began to bathe her face and arms. Jack went outside.

He sat at the cooking fire and was left alone. Other women in the village were already wailing for the loss of their leader and their relatives. It had been too short a time since he had heard that anguished female wailing, and he hated it.

Luz would mourn the full year. Of that he was certain. A year was a long time away, but then it would be his duty to marry her and provide for her—unless, of course, she chose a different man. A lot could happen between now and a year, but what if he was still with Cochise, Candice still in El Paso? And he were to marry Luz? He knew Candice would not understand, just as she hadn't understood his having to ride with Cochise. He wouldn't even think of it until the time came.

Still, from now until then it was his responsibility to provide for Luz. Her people were Chiricahua, a happy coincidence. He thought her parents were dead, but that she had cousins and a married brother. When he left to return to the stronghold, he would take Luz with him. Depending on the situation, he would be glad to care for her if her family was too encumbered to do so. He looked up vaguely as Datiye came out of the *gohwah* and moved to sit down across the fire from him. Then he looked at her again, hard.

She was no longer so slender; in fact, her breasts were full and her belly protruding slightly. He found himself staring at that slight swelling, and then looked up at her smooth-skinned face, serious now, but flushed with good health. Her dark gaze was on him. "I am so sorry," she said softly.

"Datiye, you are pregnant." It was an accusation.

"Yes." She smiled faintly.

Of course it wasn't his. But he felt uneasy. His own wife had conceived some time in mid to late October—two weeks to a month after that one drunken time he had lain with Datiye.

Datiye looked at him. "Ask."

"Who is the father?"

"You."

He felt a choking sensation. "It's impossible, Datiye," he said harshly.

"Not impossible."

"It was one time."

"I have been with no one else since my husband died. That is common knowledge among this band." She was serene.

He refused to believe it, and said so. His heart was beating too quickly.

"All the men have tried—many times—to take me to their beds. They become angry because I always refuse, even offers of marriage. They say I am foolish. Then they say I think I am too good for them. But when I say I am with child, they all leave me alone, as is the way. Ask everyone," she said. "There is no man here who can claim this child as his own. Except you."

"How many months?" His words were stiff.

She smiled. "Four and a half."

He could count. He had lain with her then, exactly. Four and a half months ago he had taken her, too drunk to care, knowing even then he would regret it, that she would make demands, interfere in his life. "I am married now," he said angrily. "My wife is with child too."

Datiye shrugged.

Jack frowned. He had so many thoughts at once. "Who brings you meat?"

She looked toward the *gohwah* where Luz was sleeping, not wanting to mention the name of the dead. Jack understood. Shozkay had provided for her. "Now who hunts for you?"

"I do not beg," she said proudly, lifting her chin.

Datiye's parents were dead, and she had no brothers, no sisters. She was alone. He felt the weight of his responsibility toward her as the mother of his child. It was a responsibility he did not want to feel. It made him angry. "You should have married four months ago," he said.

"You can have many wives," she reminded him.

He stood, walking away to think. Datiye needed care, and she needed it from now until the child—his child—was born.

How could this have happened?

Had she planned their night together knowing she was fertile—to trap him?

Did it even matter?

If Candice ever found out about this, their marriage was finished. He knew it instinctively. She would not care that a man had the right to more than one woman—an Apache to more than one wife. Further, the time of conception was so close for both women, she would believe he had slept with Datiye after being with her. He was sure of it. He was in a bind, and no matter which way he turned, he would feel the noose tightening. And once again he had no choice.

He found Datiye by the fire. He squatted. "I will return in seven days. Be ready, both you and Luz. I am riding with Cochise, and I will take both of you with me." He grimaced at her smile of satisfaction, and turned and walked away. Tonight he would sleep. Tomorrow he would ride east—to El Paso.

To his wife.

CHAPTER SIXTY

She was showing.

It was eight days into March—and Jack had left exactly one month ago. Candice was four months' pregnant and already beginning to show. However, she was careful to hide it, and so far her secret was safe. She'd let out two of her dresses and was constantly draped in a dark-green shawl that effectively hid the swelling of both her breasts and her belly. She had never been more tired in her life—or more lonely and afraid.

There had been no more news since Henry's visit ten days ago. That frightened her. She didn't believe that no news was good news. She had to find out what was going on —and there was no way for her to do so.

It was a bitterly cold, gray day and it looked as if more snow would fall. Just my luck, Candice thought bitterly. She had laundry to do. But today, because of the weather, she would wait just one more day, and hope tomorrow would be warm and sunny. Honestly, she was just too tired to do the backbreaking work, and Doc Harris had warned her a few days ago not to push herself so hard. He had been kind enough to bring her half of a roasted turkey with blackberry stuffing. She wondered if it was true—that he was living out of wedlock with a young, very pretty Mexican woman. If so, she was a wonderful cook.

Louis came running in with the morning's eggs, a tall, gawky boy with a missing front tooth. *"Buenos dias, señora.* Today is very good, *si?"*

"Oh, yes, it is," Candice replied with real delight, counting the precious eggs. "Thank you, Louis. Please bring me in some water before you go."

He left as quickly as he had come and Candice sighed, setting the eggs aside carefully. The wind had picked up, indicating a storm, and the doors and shutters shook and rattled against the house. Doc Harris had also split some wood for her—which happened to be the least of her problems because, with a fetching smile, she could always get one of the soldiers to do it for her too.

There was a sharp rapping at the door.

Candice, who was kneading dough (and even that made her tired) got up, instinctively patting the gun in her apron pocket before pulling her shawl more securely over her breasts. She peered out one window, then smiled when she saw a red-nosed Henry Lewis standing on her doorstep with more laundry. She had just seen him last week, and she knew he was not there because he had a passion for clean clothes.

"Hello, Henry, come in, it's cold out."

"That it is," he said, shivering despite his army greatcoat. "Who would have thought it's like this in winter out here? I thought the sun always shone in the desert."

Candice laughed as he came in. "So did we when we first came out here."

He looked at her, removing leather gloves. "You and your husband?"

"No, me and my family. They're in Tucson." The instant she said it, she regretted it. She had been keeping her identity a secret.

"Really? I didn't know that."

"Let me take your coat," she said. When she reached for it her shawl slipped, but she didn't notice it as she hung his coat on a peg. She turned back. "How about—" Seeing his expression of shock, she froze.

Then went red. His eyes were on the protrusion of her belly, and she immediately dragged the ends of her shawl together.

"My God," Henry said, stunned.

Candice decided to make light of it. "Surely I'm not the first pregnant woman you've ever seen?" She laughed and went to the coffeepot. "I just made fresh coffee, Henry."

He was behind her, his hands closing over her shoulders. It was the first time he'd become so intimate. She stiffened as he turned her abruptly. "He deserted you while you're pregnant?"

Candice felt the old combination of anger and hurt rising. Hurt and anger that Jack had deserted her. But she felt compelled to defend him. "You don't understand."

"You shouldn't be doing laundry!" Henry cried passionately. "You need a man to care for you, my God!"

"I'm doing just fine," she said, but she knew he was

right, she did need a man—she was too tired to bear her burden alone.

He cupped her face. "I'll help you, Candice. I'll split more wood and do your chores before I leave."

"Henry . . ." She was overwhelmed with his kindness—but frightened by it too. Would a man who simply lusted after her go to such trouble? She didn't want him to fall in love with her. But, God, she needed someone. . . .

"Don't say a word. Let's have that coffee and then I'll go out, milk the cow, split the wood, fetch the eggs, and bring you water. Okay?"

He was still holding her face. Tears sparkled in her eyes. Damn you, Jack, she thought miserably, for putting me in this position. Then she blinked and knew Henry was going to kiss her.

His lips were light and tender, and so very gentle. Candice wanted to be held—she needed it. The kiss meant nothing to her, stirred nothing within her, but she leaned against him and he wrapped his arms around her and held her, and she closed her eyes, sighing. If only she were in Jack's arms.

After a cup of coffee, Henry got up and went outside. She could hear him splitting wood. She was feeling dangerously emotional, and very low. But the rhythmic sound of the ax was reassuring and comforting. When suddenly it stopped, Candice waited for it to resume. When it didn't, something pricked at her, and she got up and opened the door.

She almost fainted.

Jack sat on his stallion, dressed from head to toe in buckskins, fully armed with two revolvers, a knife and rifle, ammunition belts crossed over his chest. He was staring at Henry, who stood in his blue-and-black army unifrom, ax in one hand, staring back.

The stallion shifted restlessly.

Jack turned his gaze to her.

Candice didn't think, she reacted. She smiled, a dazzlingly brilliant smile of profound joy, and ran down the two steps and across the yard, arms open. He slipped from the horse and then she was in his embrace—his warm, hard embrace, cheek to cheek.

He set her back, gave her a long, hot look—the kind of

look that told her he hadn't had a woman since he'd left her
—and he turned to Henry, who was flushing furiously. Candice clung to Jack and he put his arm possessively around her.
"Thanks for chopping wood for my wife," he said levelly.

Henry dropped the ax and came forward, still highly
colored. "You're the one who should be here doing this! Not
me!"

Candice bit her lip. "Henry!"

"And just how is it you're on such close terms with my
wife?" Jack asked, with no inflection except to the last word.

"I—"

"We met through Doc Harris," Candice cut in, using the
first lie she could think of. She gave Henry a warning look,
then flamed when she saw Jack reading it.

They stared at each other.

Henry broke the silence and awkwardness. "Candice, I
guess I'll go." With that he turned and retrieved his coat,
shrugging it on. Jack didn't move, his arm still around her
until Henry had mounted and was riding out.

"You go inside," Jack said, looking at her with piercing
eyes. "I have to rub down the black."

"Jack . . ."

"We'll talk inside." He led his horse to the covered remuda.

Candice turned and went into the house. There was no
mistaking her joy. She was apprehensive, too, because of
Henry. But if Jack had never left her, she wouldn't have the
need for another man to do her domestic chores. She was just
praying that he wouldn't think it meant something more.

And then there was the anger. Even though it had taken
a backseat to her happiness at seeing him again, he had left
her at a terrible time, and that wasn't something she could
forgive him for so quickly. Even now she could feel her body
tensing.

But maybe he had come back to stay.

She was standing with her hands on a chair when Jack
entered, tossing his rawhide hat onto a peg. Their gazes
locked. Nervously Candice said, "Jack, Henry only helps out
because of my condition."

He unstrapped his gunbelt and hung it on a peg, then
turned, eyes blazing. "He's in love with you."

Candice went red. "I don't think so. It's not what you're thinking. . . ."

He removed the ammunition belts, tossing them on a chair. "No?" His tone was as cold as ice chips.

He had left her. If he'd stayed, she wouldn't have needed Henry's help, and now, now he was making accusations . . . "How dare you!" she cried. "What are you accusing me of? Are you calling me a whore again?"

His fist smashed down on the table, making it jump, knocking a pitcher and bowls to the floor, where the pottery shattered. "Has he touched you?"

"You left me. You abandoned me, you have no right coming in here demanding—"

He grabbed her, pulling her up against him. "I have every right. You're my wife. Did he touch you?"

Candice could feel the entire length of his hard body, and it was trembling with fury and jealousy. She herself was shaking, enraged and sick. "Damn you, Jack, damn you! I needed his help, you left me, and Henry was kind."

"How kind?" Jack gritted.

"You bastard!" she cried. Tears welled up in her eyes. "All right, he kissed me once, damn you, once, and if you were here he wouldn't have. It's all your fault!"

For one instant Jack stared into her eyes, and she thought she saw it all, the anger, the hurt, the jealousy, the love. Then his mouth came down, hard and abrupt, on hers. Candice tried to turn her face away, but he held her jaw. "Did he kiss you like this?" He claimed her lips again.

"No." Candice sobbed. "Don't. Not like this."

Jack froze, eyes squeezed painfully closed, his big body rigid. She felt him fighting with himself, felt him begin to relax, felt his hands slide up her arms. Their gazes met, and the agony in her own heart was clearly mirrored in his eyes. "Don't cry, *shijii,*" he said, his voice husky. "I'm sorry." He kissed her, slowly and sensually, and she could feel him trembling with the restraint of his pent-up passion.

"Don't leave me again, Jack," she said, tears streaking down her cheeks.

He groaned and his arms went around her. "Darling." He kissed her again, this time with urgency, and she opened to him, just as urgently.

After a long time he lay her on the bed and began removing his clothes. She stared at the necklace of turquoise and silver lying on his broad, muscled chest. Need for him rose up in her, swelling her painfully. It pounded through her veins. It throbbed in every pore. "Oh, Jack."

He straightened before her, magnificently naked.

She looked at him hungrily, unable to turn her gaze away. So powerful, so beautiful, muscles rippling beneath bronzed skin. His manhood was thick, erect, eager. He came to her.

She enveloped him in her arms while he kissed her like a starving man, hard and frantically, his hands roaming desperately down her body, over her lush, swollen breasts. She loved him, needed him, badly. She locked her arms around him and probed his mouth wildly with her tongue. She bit his mouth, his jaw, his throat. She tasted blood. She held his head still with both hands and devoured his mouth.

He removed her dress and chemise and she heard a seam ripping but didn't care. His mouth came down hard and unceremoniously on one nipple, and she moaned. He started to suckle wildly. His teeth almost hurt. He was frantic, as frantic as she. Through the haze of hot, pulsing desire, she knew he had missed her the way she had missed him. And she felt a thrill of elation in knowing that he needed her—still wanted her with a desire and passion that matched hers.

"Candice, you're even more beautiful pregnant," he said huskily, nuzzling her swollen breasts. He had removed her pants and undergarments, and now stroked his hand up and down her hips and thighs, again and again. He moaned, a choked sound, and rose up over her, parting her thighs with his knees. He paused to look down into her eyes.

His face was rigid with desire, his eyes glazed with lust. She captured his head with her hands, trembling uncontrollably, pulling him down so she could tear at his mouth with her own. He thrust into her.

His thrusts were hard and fast, and she arched to meet him, clamping her legs around his waist, nails digging into his shoulders. It was only a moment later that it came, their simultaneous release, bodies arched, convulsed, exploding, the one into the other. And then he dropped to lie drained and wet on top of her, still entwined, still as one.

CHAPTER SIXTY-ONE

She held him. She wrapped her arms around his back as he lay on top of her, their bodies wet, their heartbeats subsiding as one, and held him to her. Tears came beneath her closed lids. She fought them. She loved him so much it hurt.

He stirred, rolling off her, but she snuggled against him. She kept her eyes closed, wanting to keep out the ugliness of reality. In her arms his body was warm, damp, and hard against hers. She pressed her face against his broad, muscled chest.

"Candice." His voice was like spun sugar.

She opened her eyes, and too late, moisture seeped out. Her gaze met his silvery, shining depths. He touched a forefinger to the tear on her cheek. "Why are you crying?"

"I'm not," she lied.

He propped himself up on one elbow, his gaze sweeping over her, lingering on her breasts, her thighs. She watched his expression, soft, slightly hungry. He reached out to cup one of her swollen breasts, playing languidly. "You've put on weight," he said.

"Most pregnant women do," she returned evenly.

He stroked her, the length of her body, from her breasts to her knees. His callused touch was possessive, lingering. She sighed. He caressed her hip. Then he met her gaze again. She saw the growing lights of desire.

"How did you meet the soldier?"

She was enjoying what he was doing yet she tensed. "He's a gentleman, Jack."

"How did you meet him?" he asked again, his hand roaming over the curve of her buttock, roaming too low for comfort.

She didn't want to lie. But she didn't want to start another fight. Not now. This was too precious. If only she hadn't told him the truth earlier. "Doc Harris and Henry are friends," she lied.

"And he kissed you." It was a flat statement.

Jack rolled her beneath him. He was already hard against her thigh, hard and hot. She met his gaze bravely. "Tell me,"

Jack commanded, and she heard the low note of restrained anger.

"It was for all of two seconds," Candice said. "Oh, Jack, please. He surprised me. If you were here none of this would have happened. But now we don't have to worry about Henry any more, do we?" Her tone rose hopefully and she held her breath. "Now that you're back."

His answer was a hot, demanding kiss.

Candice tried to resist. She tried to ignore the warming of her body, and the new evidence of his passion for her. She failed.

"I need you," he said hoarsely, before taking her, claiming her, loving her. He made love to her all afternoon, knowing full well that he might not be able to see her again for a long while, and determined to fill himself up with her and her with him. His love and need drove him to frenzied desperation at times, at other times to languorous, tender sensuality. Hours later, they both fell asleep in each other's arms.

He woke first. The sun was rising outside in a hushed display. He gazed upon his wife, enjoying her beauty and the serenity of her features in sleep. He smiled tenderly, but inside he was hurting. He wished for a moment that she wasn't pregnant, then he would take her with him. He instantly knew he didn't wish that at all. In five months Candice was going to have his child. He smiled again and touched her belly gently, not wanting to waken her. A slight, slight swelling. Their child. It warmed him. Thrilled him.

Silently he rose and dressed. When he had done so he paused to gaze at her again, drinking her in, not wanting to leave. He could not stay any longer. He had his responsibility, not just to Cochise, but to Luz and Datiye. Worse, if he stayed a few days he might forget his duty, not just to his people, but to Shozkay as well. He might not leave. Even now he didn't want to. He stared out the window.

There was snow on the highest peaks of the Organ Mountains to the east, peach-colored in the first rays of sunlight. He thought of his burdens—Luz, Datiye, Candice. He heard her stir and turned to find her on her side looking at him.

"You're leaving," she said, alarmed.

"Yes." He met her gaze and saw the undisguised hurt,

the bitterness, the sadness. He didn't want her to be any of those things. Why couldn't she understand?

She sat, hair parting like two curtains to reveal all her splendid nudity. "Were you going to wake me, or were you just going to leave?"

"I was going to wake you. Candice . . ."

"Don't! Is this the way it's going to be? You ride in and bed your wife whenever you feel like it? Or did you just happen to be passing through town?"

"I told you I would come as soon as possible," he said carefully, refusing to be drawn into an argument.

Her tone didn't change. "And when should I expect another magnanimous appearance?"

He frowned. "I don't know."

"Don't even bother!" she cried with rising hysteria.

"Are you telling me I shouldn't stop by?" he asked calmly, but inside he was frozen like a winter lake.

"Very astute, Jack Savage! You expect me to manage by myself, pregnant, without a husband while you ride off to war on my people? No! I won't do it!" Tears came. She swiped at them. She was standing. "I want a divorce, you bastard. I want a divorce!"

He felt like she'd kicked him in the groin. "You don't mean that."

"Just go," she said, her voice breaking, turning her back to him, her shoulders shaking. "Just go and get out! And this time—don't ever come back!"

He couldn't leave like this. He went to her and put his arms around her, to comfort and reassure her and make peace between them. But she writhed away like a furious spitting cat. "Just go," she said vehemently. She was crying. "Just go and don't ever come back!"

He hesitated, then took her roughly in his arms and kissed her, his mouth hard—a brand, not a lover's kiss. "I'll be back," he said. And he left her there, crying, as he went through the door.

CHAPTER SIXTY-TWO

Luz came to him shortly after he arrived back at the Coyotero camp three days later. He tried to keep the pain and sadness he felt from leaping into his eyes at the sight of her. It was hard to believe that this was the same woman he had known. Her face and forearms were scabbing where she had gouged them deeply with her nails. Her hair had been cropped raggedly at ear length. Her skirt and shirt were torn and dirty. Jack grieved with her, and for her.

"What happened?" she asked evenly. It was the first time she had questioned him about the way Shozkay had died. Her green eyes were glazed with anguish.

With a deep breath, Jack told her. Luz listened without expression, then turned away. "Wait," Jack said, catching her. "Luz, I know you're mourning, but can you be ready to leave today?"

She looked at him blankly.

They left a few hours later, Jack on the black, Luz and Datiye each mounted on Shozkay's ponies, a mule packed with hides, supplies, and gear. They rode at a walk because of Datiye's condition, and made camp that night in the San Pedro Valley, almost where the Butterfield Trail crossed the river.

"How are you feeling?" Jack asked Datiye.

"Just tired. I am all right." Her gaze held his searchingly, making Jack feel grim.

She wanted him, wanted to be his wife, wanted to bear more of his children. She was the noose, one he couldn't remove. At least, not until the child was born. He looked over at Luz, who had ignored her food and was staring toward the east.

Datiye followed his glance. "She won't eat. Except to ask you what happened, she doesn't talk. There will never be another man for her."

Jack frowned. How long should he let her go on starving herself? The problem was, he knew it was true. Luz would never love again the way she had loved Shozkay. Few were fortunate to experience that kind of love in a lifetime.

He thought about his own wife. Before Candice, he had not understood Shozkay and Luz's relationship. Now he could understand what Luz was feeling—it was what he would have felt if Candice should die. And thinking of her, as always, brought with it the pain of having had to leave her. Once again he wondered if he shouldn't have brought her with him, and then instantly knew she would never come—not of her own free will, not to live with her enemy.

"Eventually Luz will remarry," he said. "It is the way of things." His words sounded hollow even to his own ears.

"No," Datiye said.

Jack was startled.

"Soon she will join Shozkay."

"Don't say that," Jack snarled. He walked away and sat down to eat dried venison and dried beans. There was no fire, for the last thing he needed was to have to defend two women, one deep in mourning, the other pregnant, against scouting soldiers. But the moon was half full, shining, and the sky was lit with a million glinting stars.

Jack put his plate down and looked up into red eyes.

For a moment he froze, then reached for his gun as he realized he was staring into the eyes of a coyote, one that stood not fifteen feet from him, and an even shorter distance from Luz. The starlight turned the animal's coat a silvery white—or was it a white coyote? "Don't move," Jack said, slowly drawing his Colt.

"Shozkay," Luz breathed, and the coyote, hearing her voice, turned to look at her, his ears up.

Chills swept Jack's body, and he hesitated. A lone coyote did not wander into a human camp, ever. Was she right? He held the gun, prepared to kill the small beast if it so much as moved toward any of them. His heart was thumping. The coyote's eyes were so damned unnatural, like red coals, burning with an almost human intelligence. He had never seen anything like it.

The animal stood there for a minute at the most, but it was a long minute. Then it turned and raced off silently. Jack looked at Luz. She was trembling, tears spilling down her face, clutching herself with her arms. He wanted to hold her, but it was totally improper. He was relieved when Datiye did, comforting her as one would a child.

Disturbed, Jack sheathed his gun. Had it been Shozkay? For a moment, he closed his eyes. Of course it had. Between him and Luz, they were thinking about Shozkay continuously, and spirits always delayed their journey to linger under such circumstances. More so in this case, for there would be no journey to the afterworld for his brother. Shozkay would wander the face of this earth forever, crying with a need to be avenged.

How could his brother be avenged? Kill Bascom? Kill Warden? Kill the lieutenant in charge, Morris? Or all three?

Morris, he thought savagely, and knew his own war would never be over until Morris had died in retribution for ordering the hangings. Then his brother could leave this world and find peace for eternity in the next.

Three days later they rode into Cochise's stronghold. It was a sea of *gohwahs*, for the Chiricahuas numbered some twelve hundred men, women, and children. On the outer edge of one side of the village, Jack stopped and dismounted, helping Datiye down carefully, then Luz. "I'll start cutting juniper immediately," he told Datiye. "You supervise the unloading and the animals."

She nodded.

It was some time later, when he had brought the last of the tall juniper logs to the site where he would erect the *gohwah,* that he saw Nahilzay watching. Jack ignored him and began to dig holes, then to erect the frame. Datiye came over and protested.

"That is my duty," she said, placing her hand on his.

"No," Jack returned. "You can weave in the bear grass." She met his implacable gaze, then nodded. Jack began to secure the juniper poles with pliable branches of desert willow. He didn't look up as Nahilzay came over, but stepped back to view his work. It was certainly better than the last time, and a pang struck him as he thought of that day he had shared with Candice.

"The woman should do it," Nahilzay said, referring to Datiye. He knew Luz, of course, though he probably didn't recognize her, for it had been years since she had left the Chiricahua to marry Shozkay and join the Coyoteros. But anyone who saw her knew she was deep in mourning and would both shun her and respect her grief.

"I prefer to protect the babe," he said, looking at him for the first time.

"Is she your wife?" Nahilzay asked. It was a natural conclusion.

"Yes," Jack said. She was now. He was providing for her and she was pregnant with his child, and under Apache custom that was enough to make her his wife. "My second wife," he added. "My first wife is white and I left her with her people."

"You divorced her?"

"No," Jack said shortly. "I do not want to endanger her child."

"Two pregnant wives," Nahilzay said, his lips turning into a smile of amusement. "May they both be sons."

Jack nodded curtly, but did not thank him for the compliment, for that would have been considered ungrateful. He thought that Nahilzay was softening toward him with the addition of Datiye and Luz to his household.

"Tomorrow we ride the path of war," Nahilzay told him.

Jack watched him walk away, then turned to the task at hand.

CHAPTER SIXTY-THREE

Some five hundred warriors in full war dress thundered across the Sulphur Springs Valley, turning north to bypass the Dragoon Mountains, where Cochise's west stronghold was hidden. Jack was fully armed with a quiver of arrows and bow, a lance, his rifle, Colt and a knife. The bow, arrows, and lance he carried were Shozkay's, which Datiye had wisely packed in the Coyotero camp. Brown and black white-tipped eagle feathers hung from the end of the lance and the black's bridle. Jack's face was barely distinguishable beneath streaks of red, yellow, and black paint. Before he had left, Datiye had pressed a war amulet upon him, and he did not know whose it was, or if she had made it for him overnight and gone to the shaman for blessings. The mass of warriors veered south down the Sonoita Valley.

Their target was the Warden ranch, just twelve miles north of Fort Buchanan.

They bypassed the other ranches in the valley, and when they surrounded Warden's, it was still dark, the sky turning from black to slate and then mauve gray in the east. An owl hooted. The signal to attack. With wild war cries from every direction, the Apaches attacked.

Jack was riding at a gallop amid dozens of warriors toward the back of the ranch house, a wooden one-story cabin with one chimney, smoke wisping upward. He urged the black on until he reached the front ranks of the riders, then surged ahead, alone. The cabin was only twenty yards away . . . fifteen . . . ten. He wanted Warden.

He let loose a bloodcurdling scream.

He rode the black straight at the house, and when a rifle protruded from the window that was the focus of his attention, he drew his Colt and fired. The rifle blasted with a puff of smoke, but a second too late. The barrel waved loosely, aimlessly, in the air before slipping out of sight behind the windowsill.

Jack sawed hard on the reins. The black reared, then came down and was turning for another pass at the window. All around him Apaches were attacking the cabin, the bunkhouse, the cookhouse, and torching everything they could. Flames were starting to lick at wood, smoke curling almost lazily. The stock that had been freed from the corrals were stampeding, horses screaming, a donkey braying. Jack reached the window at a gallop, pulled up hard, and leapt off, dropping the stallion's reins. Gun and knife in hand, he threw himself against the wall and peered through the window.

To meet the startled gaze of a man.

They both lifted their guns simultaneously, but Jack was quicker, and he blew the man's face apart, flesh, blood and brains splattering his shirt and face. He climbed through the window, dropping agilely to the floor. He paused, eyes searching the dark interior, to wipe his face with one sleeve.

He was in a small bedroom the size of a large closet with one bed and a table, the door partly ajar. Already he could smell smoke, even see wisps—five hundred warriors could do great damage against a dozen unsuspecting men in a very short time. He could even hear the crackling of flames, and when he looked back at the window he had come through, he saw a tendril of fire snaking into the house. He pushed through the door.

A woman screamed, raising her rifle.

Jack fired instinctively and she fell, blood flowering on her chest. But he wasn't looking at her.

"Warden!" he shouted.

The big rancher was at the window across the kitchen, where flames were moving rapidly along both walls converging upon him. He had already turned at the sound of the gunshots, had already raised his rifle, was already pulling the trigger.

The front door burst open with a splintering of wood. Cochise, Nahilzay, and another warrior burst in. Warden and Jack were firing. Jack knew the woman had cost him the draw, and felt the burning sensation of the bullet as it tore into his side. Simultaneously three rifles boomed, and Warden fell backward, blood gushing from his neck, his chest, his ribs. He screamed as he fell into the flames, and was engulfed in the inferno.

"Come, Niño Salvaje!" Cochise ordered.

Jack realized he had staggered backward until he was sitting on a chair. With effort, holding his hand over his side, sticky blood pouring through his fingers, he tried to stand, and barely managed. Dizziness swept him. Nahilzay reached him first, grabbed him, threw one arm around him, and half propelled, half dragged him out.

All around him the Apaches were looting and destroying the ranch. Jack looked around for his horse and whistled feebly, then again with all the effort he had. The black came galloping around the corner of the house, eyes white and rolling, ears pinned back, nostrils flaring. Jack grabbed the reins, placed one foot in the stirrup, clinging to the pommel, trying to heave himself up, failing, and was pushed upward from behind. He managed to find his seat and hung grimly on. He nudged his horse slightly. The black needed no prodding to follow amid the rest of the galloping horses. Caught up in the herd of thundering warriors, the black ran, while Jack fought to stay on.

CHAPTER SIXTY-FOUR

It was too late.

She miserably regretted every word she had said to Jack. She had wanted to hurt him. She had ranted at him in a combination of hurt, anger, and hysteria. She should have known better. He was a man of determination, and nothing she could say or do could change his mind from doing what he thought was right. But what about her? What about the baby?

A little over a week had passed since Jack had been home, and although she regretted her rash words, her bitterness had not faded. If anything, it was stronger than ever. She couldn't help making an ugly comparison. His Indian heritage was more important to him than his own wife and baby. That hurt unbearably. He had said he loved her. Well, he wasn't capable of it. She wanted a divorce.

It seemed to be the only solution. Maybe, with time, she could forget Jack and fall in love again. But this time with a man who could provide for her and the baby. A St. Louis businessman, or a lawyer, or even a merchant. She could pass herself off as a widow. Of course, she had saved only ten dollars from the laundry, and that certainly wasn't enough to get to St. Louis.

Damn Jack!

She knew she was only fooling herself if she thought she could ever forget him—if she thought there would ever be another man for her.

But exactly what kind of man was he? Did she even know him? And what in God's name should she do? Sit there in El Paso until the baby was born? It looked as if she had no choice.

She wondered if Jack would come back.

She wondered if he was all right.

News had come from an outrider about the devastation and carnage that had occurred throughout the Sonoita Valley. An estimated five hundred Apache warriors had gutted Warden's ranch, then proceeded to attack every ranch in their path as they rode north to the safety of the mountains. Basta's spread had survived, but not without casualties, and one man had been killed in the fighting. Fortunately, most of the ranch buildings had been saved, but Basta had lost his entire remuda. Three other ranchers had been attacked as well, with about the same results. The troops had lost the Apaches' trail at the foot of the Chiricahua Mountains. The huge war party had just seemed to disappear.

She wondered if the next attack would be on the High C.

If Jack rode against her family, it was over. She would never forgive him. Never.

Candice knew it could take years for her to get a divorce. She would probably have to go to California or Texas to get one. The New Mexico Territory not only didn't have statehood, it had no judges (or law for that matter), and while it belonged to the United States, it didn't even have the status of a federal territory. Another problem was that she didn't know if Jack had to be present to obtain a divorce. If he did, she might never be free of him.

And the thought of being free of him made her want to weep.

Why couldn't they stay together and just be a family? Go somewhere far away where there were no Apaches? Where no one knew them—so they could live in peace and raise their child together, happily. Why couldn't Jack come to his senses?

Candice didn't think things could get worse, but they did.

The sun was high and bright. Buds had appeared on the saguaro and octillo in the yard. It was warm enough to go without her shawl, and Candice had even rolled her sleeves up. She bent to pick up wood for the fire when a hand from behind restrained her, and a familiar voice said, "Let me get that, little lady."

Candice turned with a smile, then saw, with surprise, that it was the preacher who had married her and Jack months ago. He had left town shortly afterward, and she hadn't known he'd returned. "Good morning," she said, "and thank you."

He grinned. "You're welcome." Although there was

whiskey on his breath, he didn't seem drunk. "Hear tell your man's gone and left. Looks like you could use some help."

Candice's skin crawled. It was wrong, he was a man of God, but he repulsed her. She had never seen a preacher so slovenly and ill-kempt. "Yes, well, thank you." She would have to offer him food and drink, but for some reason the thought of inviting him alone into her house made her terribly nervous.

"I smell fresh coffee." He grinned, picking up the wood.

Candice bit her lip. "Won't you come in and sit a spell?"

"Why, sure," he said, and chuckled. He shifted the wood and followed her into the house. "When's the little one due?"

Candice froze—it was not a question a man asked of a pregnant woman. "Four and a half months. Could you put the wood over there?"

He complied. Candice turned away to get the coffeepot, hoping he wouldn't stay long. Her pulse was racing. She was pouring when she felt his hands close around her thickened waist. "What!" She grabbed his wrists. He laughed and tightened his hold, turning her around and pulling her against him.

"Bet you sure miss a warm, hard man at night, don't you, a gal like you?"

Candice opened her mouth to protest, her hands bracing herself away from his chest. His mouth came down hard on hers and she gagged, trying to push him away. He might be thin, but he was strong, stronger than she was, and it was like trying to budge a stone wall. His lips were wet and repulsive, and she twisted her face away frantically, panting from the effort.

"I've had a hankering for you since I saw you," he breathed into her ear, then squeezed her breast.

"Stop it, stop it this minute!" Candice struggled.

"Don't play pretend with me. I know you was at Lorna's before you found your man. Come on, honey, it'll be real good." He grabbed her face and held her head still, then began kissing her again.

He was a preacher. But she didn't care. She reached into her apron and drew out the derringer and pressed it against his chest. He froze.

"Back off," Candice gasped.

He did. His expression was one of shock, then it became calculating. "Come on, honey. Put that toy away."

"Get out before I blow off your head," Candice said.

He stared, then raised his hands and smiled helplessly. He started backing to the door.

"Don't you ever come back," Candice cried, her hand steady by sheer force of will. "I'll kill you if I ever see you setting one foot in my yard!"

He left.

Candice ran to the door and bolted it, then ran to the window and watched him walking away. Her hand began to tremble, her body began to shake. Sweat was running in rivulets down her face and between her breasts.

Three days later the preacher was arrested for the murder of a man in Corpus Christi by a Texas Ranger. El Paso was buzzing with the news. The "preacher" was a murderer, wanted in New Orleans as well. His name was Benjamin Grady, and he had never been a minister of God. That had been a disguise he'd used to avoid his pursuers.

Which meant that she and Jack weren't even married.

CHAPTER SIXTY-FIVE

Jack was still too weak to get up, but he insisted on trying to feed himself. The fever, which had lasted three days, had broken the day before yesterday. He didn't remember the ride back. Someone—Nahilzay, Datiye said—had tied him to his saddle. By the time they arrived back at the stronghold he was unconscious from loss of blood. Today was the best he'd felt since the fever, and he wanted to get up, but Datiye wouldn't let him.

He was in the *gohwah,* on a bed of hides and blankets, one wool blanket pulled up to his hips. The bandage was clean, changed yesterday, and free of blood. The wound was healing nicely, Datiye said, but the next time she changed the bandage he would inspect it himself, to make sure. Propped against his saddle, he spooned the stew made of beans and squirrel into his mouth. He was ravenous. "Who got the squirrel?" he asked.

"The great chief sent it, and more." Datiye smiled. "You bring me much pride. Your fearless bravery and desire to avenge the hangings is well known."

"I didn't kill Warden."

"You were first inside, alone." Her eyes shone. "Both the chief and his most trusted warrior spoke of your bravery, in the dance."

Jack didn't smile, but he was pleased. She was referring to the victory celebration that followed a successful battle or raid. After the shaman thanked the spirits, each warrior got up in turn to dance out the story of the battle as they had seen it, in pantomime. Datiye told him that Cochise and Nahilzay had included what he had done in their renditions.

When he was finished, Datiye took the bowl and disappeared. She returned with a large pitcher of water and a cloth. He had closed his eyes, tired after eating, but when he felt the cool cloth on his face he stopped dozing.

"I haven't bathed you since the fever broke," she said.

He closed his eyes and let her bathe him. There was nothing like a sponge bath by a woman, he decided, which of course made him think of his wife. As soon as he was able, he would go to see her. He missed her. But damn, he didn't want to fight with her. He knew she hadn't meant it when she said he should never come back. At least, he didn't think she had meant it. And even if she had, she was his wife. He would merely give her no choice in the matter.

It had hurt when she said it.

He asked Datiye about the rest of the battle, and she began telling him about the exploits of different warriors, many of whom he knew. She wrung out the cloth and wiped down his chest, his abdomen. She told him of how Cochise's oldest son, Tahzay, had taken thirty warriors, covered the major party's tracks, and led the troops following into a box canyon. There they disappeared up a steep, seemingly impassable slope of rock and pinyon. She flicked the blanket down to his feet. "It was very bad. They had to lead the ponies up what was nearly a cliff on foot, and three broke their legs and had to be shot and hidden so the troops would not see. But even if they did see, no White Eyes would dare to climb that mountain. Except you."

Jack didn't smile. She was bathing his genitals, and he knew he was better because he was having an unavoidable reaction. She sucked in her breath and looked at him. He sighed. "It's been too long," he said.

"There are many widows and divorced women. As soon as you are stronger, you should take one to your bed. It is not right you deny yourself." She spoke matter-of-factly. Jack was relieved when she moved to his thigh, but the fullness in his groin did not go away. Datiye could be objective about his taking another woman because Apache men did not sleep with their wives from the time of pregnancy until they had finished nursing, and Apache women nursed their children until they were two. It was expected that widows no longer in mourning—and divorced women—would pleasure themselves, and men, in Jack's situation. Usually such casual, out-of-wedlock couplings occurred during victory celebrations.

The Apache believed in moderation in all things, including sex. An Apache man, in fact, was supposed to show the height of good judgment and not impregnate his wife more than once every four years. A man whose wife had children spaced less far apart was considered imbalanced because of an obviously too lusty nature. Two pregnant wives at once was even more of an indication, and remembering Nahilzay's carefully guarded expression when Jack had told him that his first wife was also pregnant, he smiled.

He would not tell Datiye he had no intention of bedding a divorced squaw. Instead, he would ride out and visit Candice, the only woman he wanted.

Besides, he wanted to make sure she was all right.

CHAPTER SIXTY-SIX

"Candice, I'd be a bit happier if you put on more weight."

Candice sighed. "I'm eating quite a lot, Doc."

"Try to slow down," Doc Harris said, glancing pointedly out the window at the Confederate gray uniforms hanging to dry in the sun. Fort Bliss had surrendered to the Confederacy on March 31, with little ado, but it meant nothing to Candice, not as long as she still had soldiers who needed their laundry done. The War between the States seemed very remote and very far away.

"I'll try," Candice said, thinking bitterly that if her husband were there she wouldn't have to be pushing so hard; she wouldn't have to be preparing to pack herself and her baby up to start a new life. Then she realized her slip. He wasn't her husband anymore.

Oh, Jack.

"Have you heard from him at all?"

Candice didn't mind Doc Harris's question. It was asked out of concern, not malicious prying. "Not in almost a month, since he came to visit." She saw the pity in the doctor's eyes too.

After the doctor left, Candice sat down heavily and thought about Jack. Every week there was news of attacks. So far, all the activity had been east of the High C, and while she knew the Apaches would be foolish to attack that ranch, it was inevitable that they would start marauding in the Santa Cruz Valley. Candice was waiting with dread and apprehension for the worst, and every time a soldier brought her laundry she prayed he wouldn't be bringing her news of an attack upon her family's home.

By now rumor in town had it that Jack was riding with Cochise. He was considered a traitor. When she went to the general store for supplies, townspeople made a point of letting her overhear them discussing Jack with venom in their voices. She was openly shunned, and still called the "breed's woman." And she was more than a little afraid when she left the safety of her house. More often than not, her hand was

on the little gun in her apron. She hated this town. It was
another reason to leave as soon as her baby was born. Back
East no one would be able to call her baby a breed and a
bastard. East—they would head east, and if they didn't have
enough money to get to St. Louis they would go as far away
as the money she was saving would take them.

She stretched and rubbed her back. It ached—more than
ever. And the discomfort had become steady. So had her
crying. She had become incredibly emotional. The littlest
thing set her off, mostly thinking about her husband—or
rather, Jack.

She heard the horse's hooves and went to the window,
thinking Doc Harris had forgotten something. She stiffened
and nearly fainted.

So he had come. So he had finally come.

He sat very still and erect on his stallion, looking pale
and thinner. As the light-headedness eased, a warm flush stole
over her. She was not and would never be impervious to him.
He was magnificent, and angry as she was, she was glad he
had come—not that she would ever let him know. He was
staring at the gray uniforms waving in the breeze like so many
banners.

He dismounted.

Candice opened the door.

Jack looked at her steadily, his gaze hard and angry, and
Candice braced herself. As she watched, she saw the changes
—the cold hard light warming as he stared at her, silvery
points of light glittering in his irises, becoming hot and
bright. She swallowed and took a step back, knowing she was
already lost. It didn't take much—his presence, a look. Why
did she have to love this man?

He approached slowly, steadily. "Candice."

She took another step back. "Dammit, Jack. You can't
just come riding in here . . ."

His hands closed over her shoulders, and the look he
gave her was so poignant, all words fled. "Ahh, God," he
said, and kissed her.

She closed her eyes and let him do as he would, not
returning his kiss, not opening, but her heart was beating
madly. When he lifted his face she opened her eyes and saw

the burning, the aching in his. "Is this my greeting?" he asked huskily.

"You don't deserve a greeting," she said tersely, meaning it.

He hesitated, his hands still clasping her shoulders. "I'm doing the best I can," he said, a raw edge to his voice.

And in that instant she felt his pain and wanted only to comfort him, hold him, chase it away. "Jack."

But he was looking at the uniforms. "Is that what I think it is?"

She twisted free of him. "Yes."

"That's why that corporal was here before," Jack stated, his eyes cold and hard again.

"Yes."

A murderous look crossed his face, and she was frightened. She stepped back again, this time hitting the door.

He grabbed her chin firmly, without hurting her. "What should I do with my disobedient wife?" The question was level.

"I'm not your wife."

If she'd slapped him, she couldn't have made his face drain so suddenly of color. "What?" And he was thinking: *She got a divorce. She's left me.*

Candice bit her lip. This wasn't how she had meant to tell him, in the middle of a fight.

"What did you say?" he demanded.

"Damn you!" she cried. "We're not married, we never were. That preacher was arrested a few weeks ago by the Rangers for a murder. He wasn't a preacher, Jack, it was a disguise. He was an outlaw."

Jack released her and stared.

Candice turned and ran into the house, fighting tears. She brushed at them wildly, then heard his slow footfall as he entered. "Is this a joke?" he said, dazed.

"No," she shouted, turning. "It's no joke, it's the truth, ask anyone!"

Jack's mouth tightened. "You are my wife, Candice, just like that's my child you're carrying."

"No! I don't want to be your wife, not anymore!" She began sobbing.

Jack turned to stare out the window. There was a long

pause, silent except for the sound of her weeping. He looked at her shaking back. "I'm not giving you any choice," he finally said.

"How dare you," she cried, whirling to face him. "How dare you abandon me—*us*—and then tell me you're not giving me a choice?"

"Do you think I wanted to leave you?" he demanded.

"You left me here *alone.*"

"I offered to take you to the High C and you refused."

"I didn't want them, I wanted you."

They stared at each other with fiery eyes.

"Are you going back to Cochise?" Candice finally demanded.

"Yes."

"Fine," she said, and flung her back at him. She started to cry again.

He moved to her. She tried to shrug him off when his hands tightened on her shoulders. "But this time you're coming too," he said.

Candice froze. She turned to face him slowly. "What?"

"I was a fool," he said bitterly. "A woman belongs with her man. I should have never left you. I thought I was doing what was best, but I wasn't. You're coming with me."

"To live in an Apache camp?"

His face tightened. "Yes."

"No."

His smile was bitter. "I told you—I'm not giving you a choice."

Her eyes widened. Her heart was pounding. "The Apaches are murdering my people. And you expect me to live with them just because you have some kind of insane notion of loyalty and honor?"

Jack turned away. He went to a small straw chest, opened it, and dumped the contents on the bed. He began going through her things.

"I'm not going," Candice said again with real apprehension. "First you make me your mistress, now you want me to be your squaw? I won't have this child in an Apache camp!"

Jack didn't answer. He bundled a few of her things into a blanket. He placed the blanket by the door. "We have a half day of light left," he said, looking at her. "We may as well start now."

Candice didn't move. "I changed my mind," she said. "I want you to take me to the High C."

He ignored her. "Let's go, Candice."

"I'm not going, Jack. I'm not going to be a part of this —I'm not going to live with the enemy."

He walked toward her. "Do I have to tie you up?" He said it painfully.

She drew her derringer and trained it on his chest. "Yes," she said. "Because kidnapping is the only way you'll get me to go."

He stopped, looked at the little gun, then at her flashing eyes. "Do you hate me enough to hurt me, Candice?" he asked softly.

"I don't hate you," she said, her face cracking with the threat of more tears.

"I didn't think so," he said, and started toward her again.

"Jack, don't make me shoot you," she pleaded. "I won't have my baby in that camp."

"If you have the hardness in your heart to shoot me," Jack said, stopping in front of her, "then go ahead—I don't want to live."

She emitted an anguished sound, half a sob.

He took the gun from her drooping hand, then placed it back in her apron. "Let's go, Candice," he said gently. "From now on, you'll be where you belong, where you should have been this whole time—with me."

CHAPTER SIXTY-SEVEN

They weren't halfway down Main Street, riding double, when they saw the mob.

Candice saw the guns and knew, with clawing, icy terror, that they wanted Jack.

Jack saw the guns and knew with cool certainty that he would do whatever it took to protect his wife and their unborn child.

He halted the stallion.

"What are we going to do?" Candice whispered.

Jack drew his rifle out of the scabbard. He looked over his shoulder. More townspeople, the men with more guns, the women with stones.

"Drop it, *breed,*" a big burly man called. "Drop it right now."

"My wife is pregnant," Jack said calmly. "Leave her out of this."

"Pregnant with your Injun kid!" someone shouted.

"A white woman who beds a breed deserves to die."

"Let's string her up too!"

The crowd roared its approval.

Candice was afraid.

Jack leaned against her. "When I hit the ground and start shooting, you ride like hell dead west. If I can, I'll find you."

"No, Jack. You don't have a chance."

But he was already sliding off the horse, shouting "Ride, dammit!" and slapping the animal's flanks.

The stallion took off.

Jack was diving for a water trough as someone shouted, "Stop the whore, she's getting away!"

Candice, taken by surprise, clung to the horse as it galloped down the street, scattering the people in their path. She regained the reins and began to try to bring the powerful horse to a stop as gunshots sounded. She had to go back. She heard shouting. The stallion had the bit in his teeth and fought her, still running as Candice sawed futilely on the reins. She glanced back, but could only see the blurred figures of the townsmen firing, the women having run to shelter.

The stallion slowed, shaking his head in frustration. Once he was under control, Candice instantly turned him down a side street, doubling back, the sound of gunfire intermittent and growing louder. There was a lot of shouting. She reined up two blocks behind Main Street, panting, her heart thudding, a cramp taking her unaware and making her gasp from pain. She had to help Jack. She had to. She couldn't leave him alone to be murdered.

Someone screamed, "He's making a run for it!" and there was a barrage of gunfire, a simultaneous booming.

Candice jammed her heels into the stallion and he shot forward, toward the shooting.

It was at that precise instant that she saw Jack, running like lightning down the side street, the mob a half block behind, firing on his heels. He was an open target. It was suicide.

"Jack!" she screamed, galloping forward, toward him.

He was diving toward a building, and Candice thought he was hit. "Jack!"

He was on his feet, running toward her and the thundering horse. Candice pulled hard on the reins but the frenzied horse wouldn't stop. Jack grabbed for the saddle and missed as they shot past him, toward the mob. His hand clung to the heavy wood of the stirrup as he half ran and was half dragged alongside.

Candice shifted the reins into one hand, pulling back with all her might and reaching for her derringer with her other hand. A bullet whistled past her, and another. She felt the sting of something on her cheek. The stallion screamed while she took careful aim at a man who was reloading his gun. She fired. He fell. The stallion reared wildly. When his front legs hit the ground, Jack was suddenly behind her, his hands on the reins, twisting the animal's neck around. They took off at a gallop in the opposite direction, away from the shouting, furious mob.

They rode like the wind.

It wasn't until they were out of El Paso that Candice became aware of the throbbing in her face and the stickiness running down the side of it. They were disappearing in the rolling swells of the desert. The stallion was slowing, obviously tired. Jack's arms were around her, supporting her. She became aware of the feel of him behind her. *They were alive.* She leaned against him, felt another cramp, and moaned reflexively.

"Candice, you're bleeding," Jack cried. He pulled up the horse.

He was on the ground, lifting her gently down. "Usen, it's your face," he said, helping her to her knees.

He touched her cheek and she whimpered.

"It's only a graze," Jack breathed. "Dammit! I told you to ride like hell! Do you ever do what I tell you to?"

"Oh, Jack" was all she could say.

He fell to his knees beside her and took her in his arms, holding her tightly for a long moment. He released her. "Let me clean this up."

She nodded, waiting with a terrible fear for another cramp. With her hand she began massaging her belly, praying it wouldn't come. Jack had gone to the horse, and she heard him exclaim in dismay, then curse audibly.

"What is it?"

"He's hurt," he said. "Easy, fella, easy, sshh," he said, and then began soothing the beast in soft Apache words.

Candice looked past him and saw the horse's heavily bleeding hindquarter. "Oh, Jack, he's been shot."

"It's just a graze, but it probably hurts like hell." Jack's hand stroked down the stallion's neck. "This horse has more courage than any I've ever seen."

He left the animal and returned to her, tenderly wiping her face of blood, then holding a strip of cloth in place to stop the bleeding.

"Will he be able to carry us?"

"Yes, but not far. He needs rest, and more important, so do you. You look very pale, Candice. Are you all right?"

Tears came to her eyes. She touched his face. "I was afraid they were going to kill you."

"And keep me from you?" he said with attempted levity. "Never."

"Jack, I've had a few cramps."

Jack sucked in his breath harshly. "I want you to lie down. Now. How do you feel?"

"Weak. Relieved. All right."

He cursed, again and again. "I should have never left you there in the first place. We'll stay here the night."

"We're too close to town," Candice said.

"I won't jeopardize the baby. We have some natural protection, and I'll keep watch. Besides, a mob is a coward. They want to take what is easy. I wounded four of them, and unless I saw wrong, you got one too. I doubt they'll come after us, and if they do, they'll regret it."

Candice found herself closing her eyes. Jack laid out his bedroll and lifted her onto it. His hand was gentle on her hair, smoothing it back from her face. She turned her cheek into his palm. She was exhausted, so exhausted. She fell asleep.

It was while he was salving the stallion's flank that Jack's hands began to shake. He glanced over at Candice. If anything had happened to her . . . He would have never forgiven himself. Never.

In making the spontaneous decision to take her back to the camp with him, he had acted without thinking, responding to the male instinct of possession and territoriality. Candice was his, whether that preacher was a fake or not, just as the child she was carrying was his. Nothing and no one could change that. But now coherent thought returned. He was in deep water. Almost drowning.

How in hell was he going to explain Datiye's presence in his *gohwah*?

Things were bad enough. The mob had only delayed the conflict between them. He knew she had meant it when she'd told him she would not give birth to her child in an Apache camp. He knew she was with him unwillingly. But it was too late. Circumstance had forced his hand. He was no longer giving her a choice—he couldn't.

He needed to think his way out of this predicament. It wasn't easy. He thought up a dozen different ways of telling her about Datiye and her pregnancy, and in each his relationship with Candice was irrevocably ruined. He decided to put off telling her about who would be sharing their *gohwah* until the morning—or the next evening—or the day after that.

He kept watch all night, repeatedly checking on Candice, who slept heavily and undisturbed. Then, just before the first flush of daylight, he crawled into the bedroll with her. He wrapped his arms around her and fell asleep.

CHAPTER SIXTY-EIGHT

Candice awoke to an early-morning sun that promised more of spring. She was in Jack's warm embrace. Instinctively she snuggled closer, then remembered where she was, and why. Jack had come back, as she'd known he would—only to take her with him. Now, in the light of a new day, with the terror of the mob behind them, Candice felt grim and sad. Nothing was right. Nothing was as it should be. There was no way she could live with the Apaches, who were at war with her people. It was impossible. She sat up.

She gazed down at him, and although she suspected he hadn't joined her until very recently, his eyes were open and alert. She could see tired lines etched around his mouth. "Come back here, *shijii,*" he said softly.

She looked at him, with sorrow she couldn't hide in her eyes. She pulled her shawl more tightly against her and walked away, to relieve herself and to think. When she came back Jack was saddling the stallion. He didn't look at her.

"I want you to take me back, Jack," Candice said. "Take me home, or take me east. What you're asking of me isn't fair."

He turned to her, his mouth hard. "Do you think I don't know that?"

"It's not fair to our child either."

"That's why I didn't take you with me to begin with," he said harshly, with ill-concealed anger. "But now fairness doesn't matter."

"Yes, it does."

"War isn't fair," Jack said. "That Shozkay was killed isn't fair. There are worse things than your coming with me—your rightful husband."

"Shozkay is *dead*?"

Jack turned his back to her and began tying on their saddlebags. "Yes."

"Oh, God." She stared at his rigid back, feeling him withdraw. "I'm so sorry, Jack."

He didn't turn and didn't answer. Candice approached and laid her hand on the tense muscles of his spine. He quickly moved away—away from her touch. She stood there helplessly. They had never been intimate, except physically. Why now, when there were more walls between them than ever, did she expect him to open up to her, turn to her with his heavy need?

Now was not the time to bring it up, but when they stopped before dusk that night, Candice did. "Jack, if you won't take me to the High C, why won't you consider letting the Apaches wage their war without you? You're half white. You have a family to think of. We could go away, the three of us, go where no one knows us, where no one will call the baby names."

He stared at her. "And leave my brother's soul unavenged?"

She wanted to weep.

That night there was no need for Jack to keep guard. Candice curled up in the bedroll and began to feel warm as she watched him carefully put out the small fire they'd cooked over. She wondered if he would try to make love to her. Then she instantly chastised herself. Of course he wouldn't—she was too heavily pregnant, and there was so much stiffness and anger between them—the bricks of insurmountable walls. She pretended to be sleeping when he crawled in beside her, but couldn't fool herself. She wanted him. That was the only way they were close, the only time they were like one, the only time reality became irrelevant. She ached for him desperately.

His hand settled on her hip, stroking slightly, and desire filled her groin. When she didn't move away she felt him press against her, and there was no mistaking the throbbing erection against her buttocks. His hand moved over the swell of her belly, so very softly.

"Candice," he said huskily, his voice heavy with need.

"Jack." She moaned, arching back into him.

He held her buttocks tight against his manhood with a long, slow groan. She felt his mouth against her hair. He began rubbing his cheek there. She turned her face toward him, rolling onto her back, and his mouth came down on hers.

She wished he would tell her again that he loved her.

He didn't.

"I don't want to hurt you," he whispered, his hands

splaying over her full breasts, rubbing her large nipples into erectness.

"You won't."

"You're so beautiful."

"I've become a cow."

"A beautiful cow," he said, smiling slightly, and she laughed just before he abruptly bared a breast and took the peak in his mouth. Then her laughter died.

It had been so long for both of them. Jack rolled onto his back, rolling her with him, on top of him. His hands were at her skirts, shifting them out of the way, and at his pants. She felt him the moment he was freed, straining against her bare thigh. His finger slid into her and Candice arched, dazed and mindless and ready for him. "Please."

"Yes, darling, yes."

He lifted her hips, then pulled her down onto him. They gasped together at the sensation of their tight, throbbing fit. His hold on her hips never ceased as he instructed her in a rapid rhythm, until Candice exploded, collapsing in Jack's arms. Jack's own cry was harsh and guttural in the night.

Afterward he held her tenderly in his arms until she fell asleep.

They rode for three more days at an easy pace, keeping an apparent truce between them although nothing was settled. And at night there was always the bittersweet lovemaking. Candice began to take an interest in being outdoors and riding again. She was also curious, and Jack soon told her what had happened at Apache Pass and the raid down the Sonoita Valley. He edited the version as he told it. Since the attack, he had tried not to think about what had happened at Warden's ranch. Now he remembered the woman. He kept seeing her, terror etched on her face as she raised the rifle at him. His own gun's report, and the blood blossoming on her chest. He felt sick.

"Is something wrong, Jack?"

"The Warden boy's real father is a Coyotero," he told her, changing the subject. "From one of the White Mountain bands. Cochise found out about two weeks ago. The boy's father kidnapped him and has no intention of giving his son back, and I can't say I blame him." But he couldn't get the woman's image out of his mind. He would never forget her

face, her look of fear. He would never forget that he had
killed her.

"Was it really Cochise's wife and son that the troops had
taken prisoner, Jack?"

"Yes."

"What happened to them?"

"They were taken to Fort Buchanan and later released.
They returned on foot."

Candice thought about a young mother and a boy walking all the way from Fort Buchanan to the Chiricahua Mountains. It was incredible. "Did they . . . hurt her?"

"You mean, did the soldiers rape her? If she's told anyone what happened, she's told Cochise. And he certainly
wouldn't spread that kind of news around."

Jack put off bringing up the subject of Datiye. While
Candice wasn't exactly warm, she wasn't cold or aloof, and
she accepted his ardent attentions at night with the same
need as his. He didn't want to upset the precarious state of
their relationship. It felt so good to be with her again. But
. . . he wished they could have more. Maybe it would never
be like that.

"Do you expect me to live as a squaw forever, Jack?" she
asked on the third day, quietly.

"Of course not."

"So you do see an end in sight. You don't intend to die
fighting with Cochise."

"Wars always end, Candice," he said heavily. What would
happen? Cochise had vowed he would never stop fighting the
whites over their betrayal, not until he was dead. What if a
peace could be worked out? Cochise would never accept a
reservation for his people. Even if by some miracle the government gave him Chiricahua territory, Jack couldn't imagine
him accepting a circumscribed area for the Apache. It would
be the end of their freedom, and this Cochise would never
agree to.

On the fourth morning, when they were breaking camp
at the foot of the Dragoons, just fifty miles from Cochise's
eastern stronghold, Jack decided to tell her. He couldn't put
it off any longer. He wished he were still making love to her,
as he had been doing a few moments ago. He dreaded this.
He felt like a coward. He watched her rolling up the bedroll.

When she stood, he took it from her and threw it across his saddlebags, tying it in place. "Candice, Datiye is at Cochise's camp."

She looked at him blankly, then her eyes grew wide. "What?"

"Let me explain," he said.

Her face had paled with a terrible anticipation.

"Her family is dead. There was no one to provide for her. And . . . she's pregnant. So I brought her to the camp."

Candice didn't move, couldn't move, for a long, stunned moment. "I take it you're the father." Her voice was curiously low and calm.

"Yes."

She turned her back to him, shocked. It couldn't be . . . this was a dream . . . he couldn't do this to her. . . .

"Candice, there was one time—before we were ever together, after I went to the ranch to get back my horse. I was with her then, just that once."

There could be no greater betrayal. There *was* no greater betrayal than this. Another woman, another child. His mistress. She wanted to laugh and cry at the same time. All this time, while she was alone . . . thinking of him . . . missing him . . . waiting for him to come visit her. . . .

He was with Datiye. With his Apache mistress.

"Candice?" he said uncertainly. Her back was to him, held stiff, and the lack of fireworks truly frightened him.

She turned to face him, her face rigid with control, but he knew she was on the verge of tears, that her control was precarious. Her mouth was turned downward. "I will never forgive you," she said evenly. "And I demand you take me home now."

"Candice, I had to take her with me. Soon she'll be too big to hunt for herself. For the baby's sake," he pleaded.

She looked at him with cold contempt. "Don't hand me those lies. Datiye told me a long time ago that she was your mistress, and I should have believed her, not you. I truly detest you, Jack." She couldn't believe this was her—so calm, so controlled. She knew if she let go, she'd sob with all the intensity of a woman with a broken heart. Because that's what he had done. Broken her heart.

"She's not my mistress," he said angrily. "Candice, believe me! Apache men don't sleep with pregnant women, not from the moment they know the woman has conceived. It's not done."

She stared. "Is that so? You sleep with me. You seem to think you're Apache—after all, you're fighting with them. But tell me, if she's not your mistress, then what happened? An immaculate conception?"

"It was that one time," he said harshly.

She felt weak, dizzy, numb, faint. She turned away.

He watched helplessly, his eyes grim.

Candice closed her eyes, fighting to shove the pain down, deep down inside her, in some secret place. Huge sobs wanted to rise up and choke her. She took a deep breath and opened her eyes. "Will you take me home?"

"No," he said, and he turned away too.

CHAPTER SIXTY-NINE

Candice ignored the stares and obvious speculation as they rode through the Apache village. She was sitting in front of Savage, trying to look indifferent—trying to *be* indifferent. She was numb. But not numb enough not to be stricken with painful grief.

She grimly watched the activity around them, and it was no different from Shozkay's camp. Women were cooking, mending buckskins, or preparing foodstuffs. Children ran, shouting and playing. Men were cleaning their guns, replacing arrows, sharpening knives and the stone points of spears. She saw the back of one tall man and instantly recognized Cochise. Although it was a cool spring day, he was wearing only thigh-high moccasins, completely plain, and a loincloth that reached almost to his knees. His hair had been shorn. It reached only to the nape of his neck. He turned and immediately saw them.

Jack stopped the black when the tall chief approached.

"Now I understand," Cochise said, smiling at Candice and then Jack, "why you are gone so many days."

"I decided her place was at my side," Jack said easily.

Candice stared boldly at Cochise. He was handsome, and compelling. She realized she was sorry he was on the warpath. And she wondered if he would help her.

"A good choice," Cochise said. "A woman should be with her man."

She knew then that he wouldn't.

"Welcome, Sun Daughter. I am glad this man has seen his foolish ways. Now perhaps he will stop mooning after a woman and prepare to fight." Cochise smiled at her and walked away.

Jack nudged the black forward. They had ridden in absolute silence all day. Jack had made several attempts at necessary conversation, such as: "Would you like to stop for a rest?" But Candice had not spoken a word. He was beneath her attention, she had decided, and she intended to ignore him forever, if she could. More important, she was afraid that if she opened her mouth to speak, great sobs and moans would come out instead of words.

They moved to the outskirts of the rancheria, and Candice recognized Datiye in front of a *gohwah,* doing something with what looked to be the stems of yucca plants. Candice stared at her with pain and jealousy and the beginnings of anger.

Datiye was larger than she was, but not much. Everything suddenly dawned on her. The two women were both equally pregnant, so that it was even possible Candice had conceived first. Candice was no fool. She knew the odds of Datiye conceiving from just one night with Jack were minuscule. Of course Jack would tell her he had slept with Datiye before they had discovered each other. She blinked away tears. The more she thought about it—the more she remembered Datiye's words in Shozkay's camp and her jealousy— the more she was positive Datiye was and had been his mistress. The pain was unbearable.

Jack slid off, reaching up to help her dismount. Candice ignored him, trying to slide off by herself, but he cursed audibly and pulled her into his arms before setting her down as if she were a china doll. She lifted her nose into the air and spoke distinctly. "Don't touch me."

"Candice," he warned.

Datiye rose. There was no mistaking the expression on her face, one of complete dismay and surprise. She came forward. "I worried, you were gone so long," she said to Jack in Apache.

Jack looked at the two women, who were doing their best to ignore each other. Candice was looking past and through Datiye. Datiye was looking at him. Their neighbors were watching with great interest. It was not an unusual thing for wives to be jealous of each other, and even hate each other and fight—viciously—until their husband grew sick of it and beat one or both of the culprits.

"Datiye, arrange another bed in the *gohwah.* Today Candice will rest, but tomorrow she can help you with your chores."

Candice turned to look at him. "I'm sorry, Jack," she said calmly. "But I have no intention of helping your whore with anything."

Datiye seemed stricken, then furious. Jack reached out and grabbed her wrist to prevent her from attacking Candice with her nails. He looked at Datiye, who was waiting for him to defend her. He felt it was the honorable thing to do, but he didn't want Candice to know that she was considered his second wife. "Datiye is not a whore, Candice. Datiye, there will be no fights between you and Candice. That is my law. There will be peace between you." He knew that she, at least, would obey him.

Datiye's look was incredulous.

"I will be very displeased if you do not follow my wishes," he added.

He hesitated. Candice was bound to find out the rest, and it would be better if he told her himself. She had been looking at him, and now she quickly looked into the woods to avoid his regard. "Candice, when a man provides for a woman and lets her sleep in his *gohwah,* that woman is considered his wife."

She turned to stare at him disbelievingly.

"Datiye, leave us."

With an indrawn breath and a hateful look at Candice, she left. Jack was grim. This was never going to work.

"You fornicating bastard sonuvabitch prick," she hissed. "That whore is also your wife? Is that what you're telling me?"

"I don't love her," he gritted. "But it's my baby, and taking care of her is my responsibility."

"I want to be alone," Candice said. How could he do this to her? *How?* Didn't he know he was breaking her heart irreparably? She couldn't take any more.

"Candice." He took her shoulders. "I intend to find Datiye another husband after the baby is born. I swear. Just bear with me. Bear with this. Just for a little while."

She couldn't answer. There was no answer to make. She shrugged him off and strode into the *gohwah.* Datiye was there arranging a bed of hides. "Get out," Candice said.

"Don't order me around," Datiye returned, her eyes flashing.

"Get out before I kill you!" Candice shouted, all her frustration and fury spewing.

Jack opened the canvas door. "Come on, Datiye, leave

Candice alone for a while." He pulled her out. His brow was wet with perspiration.

"I don't want to sleep with her in there," Datiye told him rigidly.

He couldn't take it. "Fine," he said. "Sleep in the woods for all I care!"

Datiye sat down in a huff, grabbing the basket of yucca stems, rootstocks, and tule shoots. She began sorting them angrily.

"Here," Nahilzay said from behind him, laughing. "You need this."

Jack started, then saw the proffered gourd. He took a few heavy drafts of the *tiswin,* wishing it were the stronger *tulapai.* "Christ!" he said, wiping his mouth.

"Forget the white god. You better say some prayers to the *gans.*" Nahilzay grinned. "Maybe the shaman knows a dance to help you."

"I don't think prayers will help me through this one," Jack said. He looked at Nahilzay. "Hey, my friend. How would you like a wife?" Nahilzay was in his thirties and unwed.

Nahilzay's grin grew wider. "Sun Daughter would warm my bed of hides nicely."

Jack shot him a look. "No. Datiye. She is obedient and eager to please." He stole a look at her, but he had lowered his voice and she hadn't heard. "Very good to look upon. Good in the bed of hides too." He smiled encouragingly.

Nahilzay just laughed and walked away.

CHAPTER SEVENTY

Candice knew she still loved him.

Just as she knew he was not worthy of her love.

She had stopped crying, finally, and lay on the third bed, her face pressed against the fur of one of the hides. She didn't know how her heart could be so stupid. Worse, even her mind was trying to betray her, thinking, What if he was telling the truth?

She couldn't sort it out. Bringing her there against her will, where the evidence of his infidelity—or at least his virility—with another woman was before her very eyes? It was too much for any woman to take. He had deserted her, turned against her people. He was the enemy, and the father of her child—his bastard. She didn't know what to do.

Get rid of Datiye, she thought viciously.

He had said that after Datiye's baby was born he would marry her off to another man. Had he meant it? Still, that didn't resolve the problem of now, or all the other problems. She would not share even his name with Datiye. She didn't give a damn if that was the Apache way. She would be better off at home than to be so humiliated by Datiye's pregnant presence.

Or would she?

The thought of going home pregnant, with his child, still frightened her to no end. But now the prospect seemed infinitely preferable to biding her time until she could get to St. Louis. In fact, St. Louis had been the farthest thing from her mind since Jack had returned. God, what should she do? What could she do?

She knew her mind could go round and round all night over her dilemma, but it wouldn't change anything. She was stuck in this godawful Apache camp, behind enemy lines, pregnant, with a rival, and that was that. If only she could turn her love into hate—or indifference.

She started when the canvas flap swung open and someone stepped inside the *gohwah*. At first she thought it was a stranger, and she stared at the gaunt, bony woman with the ragged cropped hair. The squaw was obviously ill, and did not even look at her, but lay down on her back, staring up at the ceiling with vacant eyes.

Candice stared. The woman's face was scarred with thin pink lines from temple to jaw on either side, as if she had been clawed. There were the same kinds of scars on her forearms. Then she realized the woman had green eyes, and she cried out in shock, for it was Luz.

"Luz, what's wrong?" Candice cried, dropping to her knees at her side. "Luz? Good God, what happened? What's happened to you?"

Luz finally looked at her, briefly, but did not speak. Then she closed her eyes.

Candice got up and stepped outside. Datiye was at the cooking fire, and an aromatic smell of some kind of stew rose up and made her stomach grumble. Jack was sitting on the other side of the fire with a gourd by his leg, whittling a piece of wood. He looked up.

"Jack, what happened to Luz?" she said, aghast that the once-beautiful woman had turned into a haggard skeleton.

He stared at her for a moment, then looked away. "Leave her be, Candice. She's mourning."

"Mourning? She's dying! Jack, she needs a doctor."

"A doctor can't help her," Jack said, meeting her eyes. And she saw the pain in his.

Candice's heart turned over. She wasn't even aware of crossing the distance that separated them and kneeling by his side. "We can't let her die because Shozkay died."

He looked up briefly, then returned his concentration to his stick. Candice bit her lip. When she thought of Shozkay dying she felt not just saddened for the fact that he had been a fine, handsome man. Her heart went out to Jack, for the grief he must feel but wouldn't share with her. Then she realized that Datiye had probably comforted him, and she fought her feelings of compassion. In a cooler tone she said, "Jack, she needs to eat. I think she needs to see a doctor too."

"Nothing will help her," Jack said quietly. "She's dying. She wants to die."

"You can't just let her starve herself to death!"

He looked at her levelly. "After much thought, I can and will. It's better this way. She'll join Shozkay, and their spirits will wander these mountains together—until he is avenged and can find peace in the afterworld." He reached for the gourd and drank.

She stared. "What kind of nonsense is that? Spirits wandering . . . the Apaches believe in heaven?"

He was calm, but he didn't smile. "I suppose you could say so. Hell is not being able to journey to the afterworld, but to wander the earth forever, hopelessly. Heaven is attaining the peace of the afterlife." He shrugged.

Candice believed in heaven and hell herself, and was amazed at his interpretation. She was even more amazed at how dissimilar the Apache concept was to the Christian one —how could he even think there was a similarity? Everyone knew that to be in hell was to be burning forever, not wandering around the earth as some lost soul. "So you're letting her die so she can join her husband?"

He nodded.

He's a romantic, she thought, stunned. She turned away, shaken with that revelation. What else didn't she know about this man who was her lover, her Apache husband, and the father of her child? "She still should be forced to eat. It's not right not to try to help her live."

"We tried that at first. She fought like an animal and had to be tied down. Then her body rejected everything we'd forced down her. She wants to die, Candice, and nothing will hold her back more than temporarily."

Candice felt tears and hugged herself. Beautiful Luz and handsome Shozkay. It was too awful. At least there were no children. "Jack, how did it happen?"

He took a deep breath and forced his voice to be steady. "They were coming back from a raid south. They ran into troops sent from Fort Buchanan to relieve the besieged at Apache Pass. He was captured and hanged with the others."

Candice stared at his hard, downturned face. Shozkay was one of the first casualties of this war. She knew now that Jack had even more reason than before to ride with Cochise. He was completely Apache when it came to vengeance. That horrible feeling of hopelessness rose up in her again.

Supper consisted of the stew, made from venison and chunks of vegetables that were similar to potatoes, called *tule*, and wild onions. Datiye also served a dense bread that was sweet and tasted faintly of berries. Jack told her it was made from a paste of acorns and hackberries. Candice was famished, and even the day's devastating events didn't detract from her appetite. She didn't move to help Datiye clean up, and eventually the woman spoke softly to Jack in Apache and retired into the *gohwah*.

"It's getting late," Jack told Candice, rising. "Good night." His eyes held hers for a second. Candice knew he had been drinking all night from that gourd, which Datiye had constantly refilled, and she knew the substance was alcoholic. She didn't move. He seemed to want to say more.

"I never wanted to hurt you," he finally said. Then he moved past her and slipped into his bedroll by the side of the *gohwah*.

Candice didn't want to sleep in the *gohwah* with Datiye.

But more than that, Jack's slightly inebriated, woebegone expression pulled at her.

With her decision made, she stood and walked over to Jack, and before he could say a word, she had lain down beside him. On her side, her back to him.

Wisely, he didn't say a word, didn't try to touch her.

Candice didn't think she would ever be able to sleep with his presence—so warm and compelling—just inches from her back. But she did fall asleep—in exhaustion. Once she awoke, however, in the middle of the night, startled by some alien sound. She found that Jack had curved his body around hers, his arm around her waist, his hand splayed protectively over her belly.

CHAPTER SEVENTY-ONE

Candice awoke the next morning to find Jack gone. She had no idea where he had disappeared to, and would be damned if she'd ask Datiye. Nor would she offer to help the woman who was busy roasting hundreds of stems from the yucca plant.

Luz did not move nor speak, and Candice ate leftover stew and bread, absorbed in her thoughts. She was piqued that Jack had disappeared without a word, and even more irritated that he hadn't even tried to kiss her last night or this morning. Not that she would let him touch her . . . but at least he could show some interest.

Datiye finally said, "If you help, it will go twice as fast."

"Help?" She raised a brow. "I'm not a squaw, Datiye." And she walked away.

She brought Luz food and tried to get her attention, knowing even as she did so that it was hopeless. After half an hour of futile efforts, she gave up. There was still no sign of Jack. She wandered through the camp.

Everywhere she went, conversation stopped, and men, women, and children stared, then started talking about her. Even though they spoke in Apache, she knew it was her they discussed. She stuck out like a sore thumb. With her hair so yellow gold, it was like walking around waving a flag and asking for attention.

She noticed that some of the squaws were clearly not Apache, but Mexican. The difference was in the shading of their dark skin tone, and in the texture of their hair, their features. Yet they acted just like squaws, clearly belonged to Apache braves, and had half-Apache children at their breasts or running underfoot.

Despite everything, she was interested in all the activity going on around her. It was hard to believe that these people were her enemy. But they were, and Candice didn't forget it for a second. Since coming to the Territory eleven years ago, she had practically been reared on stories of Apache atrocities, which were a part of life in the Southwest. She had never actually encountered a hostile Apache party until her capture awhile back, but both her brothers had crossed paths with raiding parties on several occasions over the years. She herself had seen the little boy who had been scalped and shot. Mark wasn't the only one to have suffered directly with the murder of his fiancée. Almost every neighbor had suffered in some way. She knew ranchers whose stock had been stolen and who had lost hired help in ensuing encounters. She knew men whose partners had been killed, scalped, or staked out. She even knew of children who'd disappeared, never to be seen again. Like Warden's boy.

War. Shozkay's death brought it home even more than Jack's riding away. The New Mexico Territory was in a state of war, and her husband was on the wrong side, and now so was she. What ending could there possibly be for her, Jack, and their child, even if there weren't Datiye to consider?

Had Jack actually killed white men in battle? She didn't want even to consider that thought. It was too horrifying, too hopeless. Maybe there was no solution.

"So sad," someone said. "So lost. Are things that bad, woman?"

Candice started and turned to see Cochise. His countenance was both questioning and sympathetic. She wondered how much she dared to say. His gaze searched and held hers, and she was unable to look away. "Yes," she finally admitted.

"Let's walk," he said, gesturing, and they strolled ahead. "There is a beautiful place up ahead where the water falls over rocks and the sun shines through trees. It is a good place to think, to pray, to talk." He smiled.

Candice smiled back. Instinctively she trusted this man. "I'm sorry about what happened to your people at Apache Pass," she said sincerely.

He glanced at her. "An Apache never speaks with a double tongue. The white man always does." He added, "Except for your man. His tongue is Apache, not white."

Candice sighed. "Maybe to you," she said.

Cochise looked at her seriously. "You accuse your husband of lying?"

She lifted her chin. "I do not know if he has lied to me or not," she said. "But it is more likely than not that he did."

"He could beat you for your words."

"I would kill him."

Cochise smiled. "Your spirit deserves his. Look, we are here."

He was right, the spot was beautiful. A waterfall careened over a cliff, forming a pool in the basin below, then rushing on down the canyon. Tall pines provided a fragrant canopy, broken by streaks of dazzling sunlight. Above, a bird sang, and a faint breeze eddied Candice's skirts about her boots.

"Do you wish to tell me what is wrong?"

She hesitated. "Would you help me?"

"It depends on what you ask."

She sighed. "Is it true that Apache men don't sleep with pregnant women?"

Cochise was truly startled, then he laughed. "You are angry your husband denies you his attentions?"

She blushed. "No, no. I am white. I do not share what is mine. If Jack has slept with Datiye since we were married . . ."

"I see." He studied her. "Apache men do not sleep with pregnant women, no. Not once they know a child's soul has been born."

That was a relief, she thought.

"Whatever Niño Salvaje has told you, I would believe. He is a man of great honor. He tells lies to no man, no woman. His word is even good to his enemy. If that is so, it is surely good to the woman who holds his heart."

She stared at him. "You think I hold his heart?"

"I know so," he said. "Once we talked long into the night." Cochise suddenly smiled. "It was some time after I had seen you at Apache Pass with another man." He scrutinized her.

Candice blushed. "I had no choice."

"A woman with many husbands is a rare thing," Cochise said, chuckling.

Candice wisely did not respond.

"Some time later Salvaje shared my *gohwah*. He talked of you. He did not have to say in words what his heart put in his eyes. It was easy to see."

She took a deep breath. Even if it was true, it wasn't enough and it didn't solve anything. "It is still humiliating for me to share my husband with another woman, even if it is in name only. It is not done." Her eyes flashed. "I have pride. It makes me want to kill them both!"

Cochise laughed. "It is the Apache way. But, more important, he would lose all face if he did not feed and shelter a woman carrying his child. Whether he chooses to later bed her or not makes no difference. He owes her his care, that is his duty."

"How do Apaches divorce?"

Cochise became wary. "Why do you wish to know? Will you divorce your husband?"

"I might," she said, very seriously. "Is it easy for a wife to divorce a man? Or is it usually the other way around?"

"Wives rarely divorce husbands, because there are fewer men. I do not think I should tell you how it is done. This is something for your husband to tell you."

"But it's common knowledge to an Apache!"

"And you are not Apache," he said easily.

Candice knew he had made his mind up and no amount of wheedling would get him to change it. Yet she felt uplifted by their discussion. She was sure now that Jack hadn't bedded Datiye since their Apache marriage at Shozkay's camp, and that did mean something. At least he had been faithful to her since then. Except for the time she was with Kincaid. That she would never hold against him, except to feel disappointed that he had been so quick to find solace elsewhere.

Maybe there was hope.

If she could just hang on until this war ended—if it would only end.

CHAPTER SEVENTY-TWO

When she returned to the *gohwah*, Candice saw that Jack was there. He had brought fresh game, an opossum and two cottontail rabbits, which Datiye was cleaning. He did not look pleased. In fact, he looked at her intently. "Where have you been?"

"With Cochise," she answered smartly.

Jack's eyes grew narrow. "Don't push me," he warned.

She wondered if he was jealous, and the possibility delighted her. But she hid her smile. "I'm not pushing you. Cochise and I are friends. He is a pleasure to be with. And— he's honest."

He strode over to her. "Wives do not keep company with men that are not kin, without their husbands present."

"Apache wives," she retorted. "But I'm not Apache."

"Don't even think of trying to make me jealous," he said darkly.

She managed to hide her smile, because he reeked of jealousy, and it served him right. She couldn't resist. "Cochise wanted to make me his third wife when we met at Apache Pass." Her eyes were wide and innocent.

His nostrils flared. "That will happen only over my dead body—or would you like to be a third wife? I thought you were having enough trouble being a first one!"

"I share my husband with no other woman," Candice said. "And you'd better keep that in mind, Jack, if you expect to save this marriage." The moment she'd said it she wanted to bite her tongue, but he pounced.

"Ah, so you admit it, that we're married," he said, smiling.

"I think you'd better focus on the rest of what I said."

"I heard you, and I've already told you, it was one time with Datiye, before we met. I'm not going to bother repeating myself again." He gave her a long look. "Most women would look the other way and be happy their husband had stayed with them."

"I am not most women."

"I fully realize that. Look, Candice, no more games, and don't even think of flirting with Cochise."

"I don't consider this a game," she flared. "Being abducted, carrying your child, living with the enemy—with another woman pregnant by you? It's no damn game, Jack!"

He strove for control and found it. "I don't know how we got on this topic," he said tightly. "I can't stop this damn war, but I would if I could. You know the rest of my plans— it's just a matter of time. Maybe if you try to trust me you'll see things aren't so bad—and they could actually get better."

Candice kept her mouth shut. He would have to work to win her trust, and that was that. He didn't deserve even that much from her.

"I expect . . . no, I'm asking you if you would mind helping out around here. There's plenty to do. Food needs to be prepared, dried for extra rations, buckskins need to be mended, hides tanned. It's not right that Datiye work to feed four."

Candice was about to protest, but decided against it. She needed to occupy herself. "I'll help, but I won't do anything with her. Just point me in the right direction."

"I suppose that's fair," Jack muttered.

She spent the next week doing various chores—including a full day boiling white flowers from the yucca that Datiye had collected on a communal gathering expedition. The flowers were boiled with meat and bones. Some was for immediate consumption, and the rest were dried and stored, as were almost all surplus foodstuffs. Other yucca buds were opened and dried to be used as sweeteners for the herbs Apaches used as tea.

Another gathering expedition went out at the end of the week. The women were on foot; a few braves—including Jack —on horseback, to provide protection if necessary. Extra pack animals accompanied them. Both Datiye and Candice went. The stalks and crown of the mescal plant were gathered on this trip. Candice stayed away from Datiye, and while the other women could not speak her language, they were neither friendly nor rude, making signs when necessary to communicate when she had missed a plant. She actually enjoyed herself. The sun was warm and felt glorious. She relished the feel of using her strong body again, for she had never been one to be idle. And she was aware of Jack's eyes almost always on her. Protectively. She actually looked forward to the next gathering expedition, which Jack told her would be for sumac berries, locust tree blossoms, and wild onions in the summer.

The mescal were roasted or pit-baked, Datiye preferring the latter, before being sun-dried and preserved with mescal juice. This reminded Candice of the afternoon she had helped Luz wrap cakes made of ground mescal at Shozkay's camp, and it saddened her. There was no change in Luz. As for Datiye and Candice, their duties threw them together gradually, and while they never spoke to each other, they found themselves working side by side on more than one occasion.

Candice slept with Savage every night in his bedroll. They seemed to be in another delicate truce. She longed for his touch. She was a woman meant to be loved, in all senses of the word, and at night her need for him kept her up long past their bedtime. But he didn't make love to her. In fact, he would not even hold her until after she had fallen asleep, and Candice knew that he sometimes did so only because if she ever awoke in the middle of the night they were firmly ensconced in each other's embrace. Yet, when she awoke in the morning, he was always up and gone.

She hadn't exactly forgiven him for forcing her to live with his people, or for Datiye, but she had come to accept what could not be changed, for the time being. Then, about ten days after her arrival in the Apache camp, Luz died.

CHAPTER SEVENTY-THREE

Jack was relieved. It had been so hard watching Luz slip away bit by bit, day after day. She passed on in her sleep. It was Datiye who found her that way. Two women, Luz's cousin and sister-in-law, came to help Datiye prepare her for burial. They took her away to bathe and dress her.

"Are you all right?"

He turned to look at Candice. He wanted comforting, wanted her to hold him, love him. Instead he nodded abruptly and walked away. To think and grieve, although in truth he had little grief left to give.

He wandered down to a secluded glade by the creek, clad only in a loincloth and moccasins, and perched on a boulder, the sun warming his bare torso. It was still hard to accept that Shozkay was gone—that was harder than accepting Luz's self-willed death. He thought of his wife. Incredibly, she had adapted, or appeared to have adapted. He knew she hadn't forgiven him for getting Datiye pregnant, but she seemed to have accepted it, and he was hopeful that that was the first step in the direction of understanding and forgiveness. Somehow, someday, he wanted them to be able to put all this behind them and live as friends and lovers, man and wife. And he wondered if it would ever be possible.

Of course, she still hated Datiye. Or maybe hate was too strong a word. He always felt uneasy when he left the two of them alone at some task, dreading that he would return to find a dead woman and a battered victor. He wondered how long they could go on not speaking to each other.

And, of course, Datiye hated Candice. Even more than vice versa, although Candice didn't realize it. Datiye knew her position as Jack's wife was solely because of the child, while Candice was his wife because he loved her. There was also the fact that Candice chose to make blatant her claim on him by sleeping with him in his bedroll every night. Now, that was torture. And getting worse day by day. He was afraid one night he'd wake up and find himself coupling with his wife in the middle of the camp. It would be the height of bad taste, worse, a loss of face.

Just thinking about it made him hard.

He had carefully kept away from several divorced women who had made it known they would be only too happy to cheer him up while he was burdened with two pregnant wives. Not that he wanted any of them, he truly didn't, but the last thing he needed was for Candice to stumble across him while he was being propositioned, as he had been yesterday by Gaage. She was very young, recently widowed, but apparently not grieving. She had given him coy looks on several occasions. Yesterday she had intercepted him on his way back from bathing and had engaged him in a conversation. When he had cut it short, she had grabbed him and rubbed herself against him. There were some things a man couldn't avoid, especially after a couple of weeks of denial, and a physical reaction to a warm female body was one of them. Thank all the *gans* Candice had not chosen that moment to appear. He had sent Gaage away with unequivocal words, but he had the unhappy feeling she would be back.

He heard a noise behind him and felt himself grow grim. He was sure it was her, come to tempt him again. He started when he saw Candice.

She paused uncertainly at the base of an ancient oak. He tried not to look at her as if he were starving, but she was incredibly beautiful, and he could not be unaffected looking at her. Especially when she was carrying his child.

"Jack?" She came forward.

He wanted her touch. He stiffened. "Candice, I need to be alone," he said, but his voice was husky. He stared out at the creek, but was intensely aware of her having stopped behind him. He felt her hands on his shoulders. They slid up to his neck, firm, kneading, then dropped. She walked around the rock to his side. Her eyes were big, navy blue, sad.

"I feel sad too," she murmured.

He looked at her. Then, simultaneously, he reached out for her and she leaned against him, wrapping her arms around him. They held each other, rocking slightly, hearts beating together. He closed his eyes and pressed his face against her silken hair. Somehow she was standing between his thighs. She leaned fully into him, her thigh pressing against his thick arousal.

She looked up.

He caught her face in his hands and kissed her. The first touch was soft, then exploded into urgent need. His lips tore hers. Biting, nipping, pulling, and slanting down with an insatiable possessiveness. She moaned. He invaded with his tongue. He needed her . . . now.

He picked her up effortlessly and carried her away from the creek, into the woods, deeper and deeper, until he was sure no one would stumble across them. She was clinging to him, her face against his bare chest, her lips moving, caressing his skin, finding a nipple and teasing it with her tongue. With a groan, he sank to his knees, lowering her on a natural bed of pine needles, and with trembling fingers he began to unbutton her blouse.

She strained toward him, catching his face in her hands, kissing him hard, demandingly.

"Damn." He groaned, fumbling with her buttons while she poured kisses on his mouth and jaw and throat. He pulled away, finally getting the last button open to reveal her white, swollen, blue-veined breasts. With shaking hands he pulled off her shirt, then her chemise, clutching her lush flesh and lifting it up for his intent gaze. "Candice," he said, "God, Candice."

She whimpered.

He took a large, darkening nipple in his mouth and tugged with his teeth.

She reached out and deftly untied the loincloth, letting it drop, exposing the swollen length of him. She stared for one long moment, then lifted her eyes to his. When she looked back down it was to reach out one forefinger and touch the quivering tip, removing a drop of semen. She touched it to her lips. Jack groaned.

She lifted her skirt up to her waist, spreading her thighs to reveal glistening pink flesh.

He was breathing too loudly, too raggedly. He rolled onto his back, pulling her up on top of him in one movement. He held her hips immobile as he thrust upward, deeply, while she eased down fully on his length, trembling, the sensation of fullness exquisite. He reached for her breasts.

She moved.

He slipped one hand beneath her skirt, finding her moist, slick flesh, sliding his finger over her clitoris, around it, beneath it, lifting it. She whimpered, and he watched her, knowing she was close, so close . . . She fell forward with a cry. He surged up into her, letting himself go, exploding harshly, uncontrollably, ecstatically. Then he sank into bliss, with Candice embraced firmly in his arms.

"Oh, Jack," she said.

He stroked her face. Then he cupped the back of her head with one large hand and pulled her closer, kissing her. When he opened his eyes he saw that hers were closed. He kissed her again. "I love you," he told her hoarsely, then felt himself go tense with expectation.

She looked at him solemnly. Then she smiled slightly, brushing a lock of his hair from his forehead. "No need to deny ourselves, just because the Apaches do."

He kept the hurt from showing in his eyes.

But he wanted to know, had she fallen out of love with him? Or had she ever even loved him? They were not thoughts he liked. "We should try," he said, then pulled her closer and began moving slowly inside her again.

CHAPTER SEVENTY-FOUR

After they returned from the woods, Jack disappeared. It was not unusual. The men were always preparing for war. The cleaning, replenishing, and mending of weapons were constant duties. Hunting was even more important. Game was always being supplied to the camp, and what was not consumed was dried and stored. Jack had told Candice that the Apaches had hidden caches of food throughout the Territory in caves, for emergency purposes. But it was even more important that the rancheria be adequately supplied. "The women and children of the Apaches are the future," he had said.

Jack often kept counsel with Cochise and the other leaders of the Chiricahua. Candice could not believe that all the time he spent with the great chief was in deliberations over war.

Now she carried with her the pleasant aftermath of their exquisite lovemaking. It had been too long. And it was more than that. The intimacy between them had been something that she had missed sorely before. She needed the reassurance of his need for her, even if only expressed in the physical act of union.

She remembered his declaration of love. It had taken her completely by surprise, and had thrilled her. Candice, however, could not forget easily. Jack's words did not wipe everything out between them and expunge him of the wrongs he had done. But she knew that he had meant it, and his words left a tingling warmth wrapped around her heart.

That night was the first of four nights of ceremonial dances by the masked men who, Candice was told, impersonated the *gans*.

"Would you like to attend?" Jack asked.

Some of the tension was back, Candice could see it in the cautiously formal manner he used to address her. "I suppose so. Who are these *gans* again?"

"Mountain People," Savage said easily, as they walked toward a huge clearing in the center of the camp, already surrounded with Apaches clad in their best buckskins, which were painted and beaded heavily. "The *gans* are very, very powerful. They can move mountains if they wish. Some are more dangerous than others. There are regular *gans*. But the clown is dangerous, and the Black One very dangerous."

She gave a snort.

"If you see the Black One tonight, do not touch him or talk to him, Candice. I mean it."

She laughed. "What will he do—strike me dead?"

"Just obey me," he muttered in exasperation.

"But these are Apaches impersonating the so-called Mountain People," Candice objected later. Four men wearing blackened buckskin masks with slits for their eyes, woven floor-length skirts, and elaborate headdresses made of wood slats with pointed ends, some two feet wide and high, were dancing in what to her was a typically Indian fashion. Drums beat, and there was a strange whistling noise.

Savage frowned. "The *gans* come and join in their human forms—if they feel like it."

"Jack, be honest, do you believe in the *gans?*"   He smiled slightly. "Mountain spirits exist."

The dance was interesting, and it was entertainment, Candice decided. She was enjoying Jack's company, though, even more than the dance. His shoulder pressed against hers in the throng of Indians surrounding the dancers. She remembered the afternoon. After that first, frantic joining, he had taken her gently and tenderly, as if to prove there was substance behind his unexpected declaration. She glanced at his handsome profile out of the corner of her eyes. He was so handsome, his presence so commanding. Her heart swelled with love, even if her mind tried—unsuccessfully—to rebel. He glanced at her, saw her regard, and smiled, taking her hand and squeezing it. When he released it, she clung to it, felt his surprise, and then his large warm hand closed over hers again. They stood that way, hand in hand, watching the dancers for close to an hour.

"What is this dance for?" Candice asked, leaning against him.

He hesitated, and she felt it clearly. "One of the shaman had a powerful dream last night. The time for the Apaches is now. These four nights we pray for strength and victory."

She pulled away. "You're going on the warpath."

"Yes."

The delight of the evening crumbled into shreds around them. "When? After the fourth night of dancing?"

He nodded, watching her closely, if not a bit grimly.

She looked at the *gans* dancers without seeing them. She had been there almost two weeks, wondering, but afraid to ask when they would finally take to the warpath again. In four days Jack was going to ride away, into battle, against her people. It was too incredible, too distasteful to believe. Why? Why did it have to be this way? Would he attack her home? Fight her family? Kill someone she loved?

"Look, Candice, there's the Black One," Jack said, trying to distract her.

She didn't care, automatically glancing at the figure ominously garbed in black buckskin who stood apart, forbiddingly. "Where are you riding? Who are you attacking?"

"Lower your voice," he said. "The High C will not be attacked."

She felt an immense relief. "Are you sure?"

"Cochise knows it's your home, and I married into your family."

She was confused and he saw it. "Candice, typically a man marries into his wife's family, and not the other way around. Cochise has promised the High C will not be touched. Besides, it could never be taken, not unless it was besieged until the inhabitants were starved out. That is not the Apache way."

Her relief was short-lived. "Then who?"

"I do not know," he said tersely.

She had the feeling he did but would not tell her. She turned away. She was almost glad this had happened to remind her of where she was and what he had done. This afternoon had made her forget and forgive too easily. Nothing had changed. If anything, she realized something now that she had not realized before. He was her enemy. Her husband was her enemy, and this was war.

CHAPTER SEVENTY-FIVE

He avoided her.

It was hard enough to prepare to do battle this time, without her accusing gaze and silent condemnation. Or not so silent condemnation. He tried not to think of the woman he had killed at Warden's—but it was impossible. She was haunting his waking moments and his sleep. He made sure not to bed down for the night until after Candice was asleep, surprised she should still be sharing his bedroll, but he knew she was stubbornly doing so only to defy Datiye and keep her in her place. If it weren't for Datiye, Savage was sure he would never get near her at night.

There was another reason why this time it was even harder to prepare for battle than it had been before. Their target was the Santa Cruz Valley. They would bypass Tucson, which would be too well defended, and hit the ranches down-valley. Savage was grim. That meant the TR—Judge Reinhart's spread, as well as Henderson's, ranches that belonged to Candice's old friends. The two places were close enough together that they would attack both simultaneously, dividing their force. Then they would run for the mountains.

He reminded himself that this was war. He reminded himself of his brother's death, which helped steady his resolve. He thought of all the Apaches, who numbered an ant-hill among the mountains of the whites. This was war for survival—for a way of life, for freedom. It was probably the last chance for his people.

But my people are white too.

This was a time when a man needed his wife's gentle touch, her love, and her support. He had none of those things. If he gave her a choice she would leave him without hesitation, and he knew it.

After the fourth night of ceremonial dances and prayers, Savage returned to his *gohwah* with a strange sadness. When going into battle there was always the prospect of death. He was not afraid of death, for he had the Apache attitude, which was somewhat fatalistic. He did not think his time had come but one could never be sure. In any case, there was always the possibility that he might never return—might not see his sons born, or see his wife, ever again.

She was sleeping on her side. Her rounded abdomen was hidden by the blanket, but he longed to stroke their child, encased in her flesh. He wanted to make love to his wife too, and be given some sign that she cared for him, even worried about his departure into battle. With a sigh, he slipped into the bedroll beside her. Lying on his side, he pulled her against him, nestling the curve of her buttocks against his groin, her back against his chest. He closed his eyes.

He would never be able to sleep that night, this he knew. The heat from her body was inflaming him, and his loins were already full, tight, achingly so, his penis stiff and throbbing with life. He shifted onto his back to stare up at the starless night. He could hear a baby begin to cry, then silence as its mother fed him. A man's voice, inaudible, drifted on the breeze, and with it, a feminine tinkle of laughter. Excited laughter—at least one husband was saying a fond good-bye to his wife.

Candice rolled against him, full breasts pressing against his arm. She was wearing only her chemise, and a bare knee touched his thigh beneath his loincloth. Then, taking him by surprise, she moved her hand and lightly touched the length of his arousal.

He had thought she was asleep.

"What are you doing?" he whispered.

She closed her fingers over him, while freeing him of his loincloth. He grabbed the roving culprit. "Candice," he began, a feeble protest. Datiye was sleeping nearby and there were still people up. The mountain air carried sounds—the nearest *gohwah* was only thirty feet away and occupied by a family of five.

She threw her thigh over his and mounted him gracefully, wrapping her arms around him and kissing him. He relaxed. He wanted her. He was thrilled she wanted him. He held her head, coiling her hair around his wrist, and accepted her prodding tongue.

They should not be doing this there, he thought, but didn't care. This could be the last time. Her chemise had ridden up, and she was wet and moist on his belly. "Turn onto your side," he whispered in her ear. "No, your other side."

She obeyed in some confusion, so her back was to his chest. "Jack," she protested in a soft breath.

He pressed his hardness against her buttocks and, with a creeping hand, found her breast. He nibbled the nape of her neck as he rolled a nipple into hardness between his thumb and forefinger. Then his hand swept down, over the delicious curve of her belly, and lower still, into the warm, wet delta where she throbbed in invitation. She gasped and bit off the sound. He stroked her rhythmically. She arched against his hand.

He raised her upper leg, then slipped his hand between her thighs from the rear, fingers invading her moistness, showing her the way he would enter her. She whimpered in understanding. He removed his hand, clasped her hips firmly, and slowly prodded toward his goal. He plunged into her. Gripping her tightly, moving with growing rapidity, he brought them both to a stunningly quick and intense climax. He managed to clasp his hand over her mouth as she cried out, while he drained himself into her, riding her to the end of their surging crest.

He held her in his arms and needed to find the right words. He nuzzled her neck, thinking desperately. At the very least she should know she would be taken care of if he didn't come back. "Candice," he whispered softly. "I want you to know you don't have to worry."

She didn't answer. Because she still had her back to him, he didn't know what her expression was. He ran his hands over the firm curve of her belly, then up to her breast. "If I don't come back, Cochise will see that you return to the High C."

There was still no answer.

He sighed. Did she even care at all about him? Or was it only the pleasure he could give her? His thumb touched her jaw and stroked it idly. Tonight he would keep her in his arms all night, and make love to her again and again. It was such a small yet such a large token. His thumb moved higher, then stopped, paralyzed. Her cheeks were wet with tears.

"*Ya-tethla?*" Then, realizing he'd spoken in Apache, he said softly, "What's the matter, *shijii?*"

She shook her head wordlessly.

He turned her over despite her attempts to remain facing away from him, and peered at her face. The dying fire not far from them shed little light. He tasted the salty tears with his mouth, kissing them away.

"Love me again, Jack," she said brokenly.

CHAPTER SEVENTY-SIX

The past three days had been a nightmare, filled with nothing but anxiety. She couldn't help it. The war was there, filling up her life with the possibility that Jack would be hurt or killed. Three days. What had taken them so long? A day and a half of restrained riding to reach the Santa Cruz Valley (Datiye had told her their destination), several hours of battle, a day of pell-mell galloping back. Where were they? Had they encountered troops? And was Jack all right?

She didn't want to live this way.

Worse, what about after the baby was born?

She had been thinking about that a lot lately.

Almost overnight, the physical signs were becoming pronounced. She didn't think she was due until August, but if she had conceived the first few times they had lain together, she could be due in mid-July. And what if she gave birth early? She realized, then, that she could go into labor as early as the end of June. Less than two months away.

Having a baby became as real as the war and the danger Jack faced when he rode out to go into battle.

And her resolve to leave Jack and take the baby East and make a new life for them was stronger than ever. She fully realized her predicament now; that she would need help from her family. There was a dark, bitter sadness at the eventuality of leaving Jack. But she had no choice. She was determined to avoid thinking about never seeing him again.

In the late afternoon of the third day that they had been gone, a cry went up from the sentries left behind to guard the entrance to the stronghold. They had returned.

For days the camp had been preparing for the return of the war party. A huge feast had been in the making. Now the women hurried to don their best, most elaborately decorated buckskins to greet their men. Children ran screaming with delight up the canyon to greet their fathers. Candice stood by the *gohwah* in tense anticipation, waiting.

Datiye came out clad in a white deerskin dress that, despite her bulky form, was beautiful, beaded and fringed. Her moccasins matched. She wore a necklace of colored beads, and a silver and leather bracelet, beaded earrings. Candice was dismayed. The woman had decked herself out in finery to greet Jack, while she stood clad in her single woolen skirt, which was brown and ugly, and a plain white blouse, which was ragged from being washed so many times. She felt dowdy and unattractive as Datiye hurried off.

She refused to be outdone. She changed her clothes furiously. Her petticoats were clean and white, lace-trimmed and ruffled. She slipped on two with a lacy camisole that buttoned down the front and was trimmed with pink ribbons. She felt a smug satisfaction. The Apaches would not even know the difference, would probably think she was wearing a fine dress. And Datiye would be green with envy. Candice unbraided her hair and brushed it with a wood comb until it gleamed. She removed a white ribbon from her underpetticoat carefully and tied it around her throat. She wished she had a mirror. She placed a hand on her belly for a moment. She was obviously pregnant, but she no longer felt like a cow. She felt beautiful. She smiled, thinking about how she had felt like a cow when her belly had barely protruded, months ago.

She pulled off her boots, refusing to spoil the effect, then washed her feet, her hands and face. She stepped outside.

The rancheria was alive with excitement and welcomings. A heavy, frightened anxiety was strangely interwoven, though, with the excitement, which Candice understood as she made her way across the camp. Not toward the entrance to the stronghold, which was already jammed with the throngs, but toward a knoll from which she could overlook their arrival. She sat down on an outcropping of boulders, watching the riders walking in single and double file down the canyon.

She saw the black first, then Jack, sitting easily, tall and magnificent, and her heart tightened with relief. A parade of five hundred warriors took some time, but once in the stronghold the men dispersed, rushing to greet their waiting families, lifting shrieking children in the air, kissing beaming wives.

And then there were those who did not see the men they were looking for, and turned away, crying and tearing at their hair.

Candice moved down the knoll toward the *gohwah* after Jack had ridden ahead in that direction. She moved easily through a section of woods, then paused when their *gohwah* was in sight. Datiye was handing Jack a gourd filled with *tiswin*, which he drained. Her hand lingered on his shoulder. He still wore the warpaint, now smudged, and his body gleamed with grease. Candice did not like the familiar intimacy between them. She gritted her teeth and moved forward.

He saw her, but gave no sign that he was glad to see her. She realized he was exhausted. He didn't even speak, but took the clothing Datiye handed him and went toward the creek. Relief warred with anger at his failure to greet her.

Datiye stared at her clothes, and Candice flashed her a warning glance. Damn Jack, she was thinking. Tired or not, he could at least say hello. Or didn't he care that she was there anymore? Or had he expected her to be waiting, like every other squaw in the rancheria? His presumptions were too much. She strode back into the woods, back up to the knoll. This was the last time she would go out of her way to greet him, or even show him that she was worried. He didn't deserve her concern.

Already the celebrations had started. Warriors were drinking and bragging about their exploits, flirting with their women, being waited on by their wives. There was much laughter and shouting. Children ran playing, dodging adults. Drums beat, and rattles shook. Men and women were dancing. Candice watched it all with a brooding interest.

Cochise came, resplendent in full dress, with two eagle feathers in his headband, his face repainted, carrying his weapons. He sat in a spot clearly reserved for him, elevated by hides, and his best warriors surrounded him. Candice straightened when she saw Jack join the central group on the dais, sitting cross-legged on a single blanket at the edge of the group. Someone spoke to him, slapping his back and handing him a gourd, and even from this distance Candice could see his white teeth flash.

She was angry. She was up here, alone, on this damn knoll, and he was down there, surrounded by men, enjoying himself thoroughly.

It was getting dark, but huge bonfires made it easy to see

everything and everyone. From where she sat she had a better view than if she was down on the flat with the huge crowd—she could even make out the expressions of Cochise, Jack, and their cohorts if she concentrated. Jack hadn't even seen her, or looked her way, not once.

She didn't know how he could miss her, not when she was sitting up there alone and clad in white like some virginal, golden-haired bride.

The revelry ceased abruptly, and a man Candice recognized as one of the shamans came into the center of the crowd, walking first to the east, then to the west, then north and south. He said something, a prayer of thanks, Candice supposed. He sprinkled pollen in the four directions, then Cochise rose, and was blessed by the shaman with more pollen. The shaman left and Cochise remained standing.

The crowd started to roar. Candice didn't know what they said, but they were shouting Cochise's name in a chant, over and over. They grew silent. Cochise moved.

He was dancing.

As she watched his lithe, graceful movements, Candice realized he was enacting a story. The dance was a pantomime of the battle. It was hard for her to follow, but the crowd was going wild, apparently having no trouble interpreting his movements. And then, with a twisting movement and a downward plunge of his hand, which Candice understood as an act of stabbing a man, he returned to his elevated seat.

The men around him followed in an apparent order, first Nahilzay, who, though graceful, looked clumsy after Cochise, then five others. Some of the men were very inventive and got carried away, leaping wildly around the clearing, chasing foes, throwing imaginary lances, wrestling in hand-to-hand combat. Others were clearly reluctant to dance their tales. One of the men's dances was so brief the crowd roared with laughter. He grinned foolishly, and Candice realized he was drunk—as drunk as the entire tribe was getting.

She was about to leave when Jack stood. She gasped.

The crowd grew very quiet, waiting. He was wearing only a loincloth and moccasins, and his torso gleamed in the firelight. He put his hand to his head, looking, searching. He ran . . . gracefully, corded muscles standing out on his thighs and arms. Galloping into the fray. Someone shouted for help. He jumped from his stallion, searching. All around him was the confusion of bloody battle. He warded off an attack. He leapt over chaos and carnage. He was attacked from behind. He fell, twisting, and brought his opponent down. They wrestled, back and forth. Jack got the man beneath him and, with a savage motion, slit his throat.

He returned to his place with the others.

He was magnificent, she thought, awed. Graceful, powerful, as fine a dancer as any of the others. She was stunned.

Other men got up and began to dance, no longer singly, and in no particular order. Women came into the circle, dancing. Candice was shocked again. Some were fully dressed, but others wore nothing but tiny loincloths. They danced unashamedly.

One of the near-naked women gravitated toward the dais, and Candice watched fixedly—with growing anger. The woman was slender, her body perfect. Long black hair fell loosely to her hips. Her breasts were full but young and firm. Dark nipples were taut. She was very graceful and very sensuous, and she had the attention of half the men on the dais, then all of them. She moved directly in front of Jack.

He watched her dance with full attention. Candice wanted to slap the half-smile off his face. The woman swayed closer to him, her message unmistakable. For what had to be five long minutes she undulated in front of him, for him, and he never once took his eyes off her. Then she beckoned with her hand, turned, and disappeared into the crowd.

The men on the dais started laughing, and one of them pummeled Jack on the back. They gestured after the girl, encouraging him. He rose, amid hoots, and started after her. Candice was frozen with disbelief. He disappeared in her wake into the crowd.

Her heart was pounding furiously. She picked up a stone and stood. Should she bash her head in, or his? She strode grimly, purposefully, down the knoll. How in hell was she ever going to find them? They had probably gone into the woods. She would never find them. She vowed to kill Jack when she next saw him—and hoped that would be very soon.

Away from the firelight it was dark. She skirted the woods instead of going through them. She walked right into a pair of powerful arms, and started to twist free. He laughed.

"Looking for me?"

"You bastard!"

He pulled her against him and silenced her with a kiss. His lips were hard and demanding. She could feel his arousal. She was furious. "Stop it, you bastard! Just stop!"

"You look beautiful," he breathed, lifting her easily into his arms. "I've been waiting for this moment all day." He began walking into the woods.

"What about your little squaw?" Candice hissed, but her body was melting rapidly.

"Who?"

"Don't 'who' me!"

He chuckled. "You sound like a jealous witch. *Inlgashi shijii*. Witch of my heart!"

"You're not funny," she cried, but he dropped to his knees and kissed her again. Candice wrenched away. "Who is she?"

He slid his hand up her arm, his eyes smoking. His tone was husky. "Nobody. Trust me. Come here, *shijii*, kiss me . . . greet me properly."

She pushed herself out of his arms. "Greet you properly? You couldn't even say hello when—"

He caught her with a chuckle and kissed her again. "I'm saying hello now." He urged her gently backward, until she was lying on her back. The ground was damp.

"Jack . . ." she started.

He smiled and slipped his hand beneath her petticoats, instantly silencing her. She closed her eyes and was lost to waves of dizzying pleasure. And when his mouth followed the path of his hand, and his tongue started seeking her sweetest, slickest recesses, she clutched at his hair and forgave all. A tidal wave of pleasure soared over her, again and again.

Then he took her and claimed her as a man claims a woman, fiercely, intently, purposefully. That night his harsh cries mingled with hers, unheard beneath the din of revelry.

"Who is she, Jack?"

He smiled. "Her name is Gaage and she's a widow. Have no fear. I have no intention of making any more trouble for myself, I have enough as it is."

"You certainly enjoyed her dancing," Candice said jealously.

He stroked her hair. "I was imagining my wife dancing naked in front of me, dear heart." He chuckled.

"You liar."

"I was also imagining the very delicious things I intended to do to you tonight—and I assume you're satisfied?"

She had to smile. "Just stay away from her," she told him.

"I give you my word," he said, biting off laughter. She was jealous, and while he meant every word he said, he was thrilled that she should be so green. A jealous woman was a woman who cared.

"What happened, Jack?" She peered up at him.

He stiffened. "I don't want to discuss that now. Let's make love again." He began unbuttoning her camisole.

"You rode on the Santa Cruz Valley," Candice persisted. She had to know. His hand stopped, then slid negligently into her bodice, cupping a breast. "I want to know what happened. Did you attack Tucson?"

He withdrew his hand and sat up abruptly. "You have great timing," he said harshly. Silver eyes were bitterly angry. "Do you really want to know all the ugly details?" He stood, reaching for his loincloth. "All right. Reinhart's place is gutted. He won't be able to rebuild. Henderson's is gutted also. At least ten men died yesterday. Four were Apache. Is there anything else you want to know?"

She sat, clutching the ends of her camisole together. "Yes. Is Judge Reinhart all right?"

He stared, his mouth tightening. "I don't know."

"Oh, God," she said.

"Do you still fancy yourself in love with him?" he snarled.

"Oh, grow up! Judge is a good man! My neighbor!"

"You were practically engaged to him, remember? You seemed to be in love with him!" His eyes were flashing shards of ice.

"I can't believe you could attack a man like Judge," Candice said. "How could you?"

He stared, furious. "Don't you dare condemn me—or even judge me." He strode away. But even as he did so, he knew his anger wasn't directed at her, but at himself, and the whole damn war.

CHAPTER SEVENTY-SEVEN

Candice decided she would not bring up what was obviously an extremely sensitive topic for Jack again. She found him at their *gohwah*, drinking *tiswin*, alone and brooding. She was exhausted, still very disturbed, but no longer agitated about the slender squaw. It was what had happened to Judge Reinhart that held her attention—she hoped fervently that he was all right. She slipped into her usual place in Jack's bedroll, thinking about Judge and his children, her husband (in Apache law), and their unborn child. It took her a long time to fall asleep.

She found him the next day packing his stallion's foreleg with a poultice of mud and herbs. "What happened?" she asked, pretending their disagreement yesterday had not occurred.

"He's a bit sore," Jack said, apparently in the same mood as she. He patted the black and straightened. He smiled. "I never asked yesterday, but why are you running around in your petticoats?"

"To make Datiye jealous," Candice said truthfully.

He burst into laughter. "Were you looking for me?" His gray eyes had become warm and tender.

"Yes, Jack, I need some buckskins."

"For what?"

"To sew. For the baby."

He was startled and pleased. "Can you sew clothing?"

"Of course. Will you get me the material?"

"You'll have to tan the hides yourself."

"Will you show me how?"

He smiled. "Gladly. I'll go hunting today. For a doe. Doeskin is softest."

Candice frowned. "Make sure she doesn't have a fawn."

"I'll do my best."

He came back empty-handed that day, but brought her a doe the next morning. Candice was filled with excitement and determination; the urge to prepare and provide for their baby, now that its arrival was imminent, propelled her relentlessly. She would prefer to see her child clad in fine clothing, but soft buckskin would do for now.

Jack spent the next two days showing Candice how to make buckskin cloth. He was still surprised and amused at her eagerness. And knowing the material was for their child warmed him thoroughly. He was truly enjoying helping her in her efforts over the past few days. They weren't quarreling. They were working side by side, and it was more than companionable. It was the way it was supposed to be between a man and a wife, sharing their endeavors, working toward a mutual goal. He liked his wife's company. He liked her determination, her pleasure at work performed well, her smile and her laughter. Most of all, he liked seeing her absorbed in a task that involved care for their unborn child.

In the afternoons, toward dusk, he took her up the canyon to a secluded glade by the creek where they bathed, played, and made love. At night she slept in his arms, and when he awoke from taunting nightmares—visions of the Warden woman's face just before her death haunting him, or the sounds of battle and human death knells ringing in his brain—he would turn to her and take her urgently, before she was even awake—stroking her with a need to lose himself in her and escape guilt and torment. When her moans became audible he silenced them with hot, hard kisses. If anyone knew he was bedding his pregnant wife, no one gave any sign. He no longer cared. He needed her too much to care.

"Datiye, I want you to rest," Jack said. His voice was firm. He took the basket, which was too heavy for a pregnant woman, away from her. "I mean it."

"I am not tired," she said, but he could see she was exhausted.

"Rest, now," he said with a touch of anger. She was somewhere in her eighth month, and she was trying to do too much. It made him feel guilty. He knew it was because he gave all his attention to Candice, but, dammit, he hadn't wanted a second wife. He was coping with a precarious situation in the best way he could. If he showed Datiye any more interest than he already did, he would jeopardize the tranquillity between him and Candice. That, he was not about to do. He was lucky, he knew, that she had accepted things as much as she had.

He watched Datiye waddle away and disappear into the *gohwah*. Then he turned as Candice came up to him. She was frowning, watching him. He gave her a smile.

"Jack, she's so big. Has it ever occurred to you that her child isn't yours?"

"It's mine, Candice," he said, more sharply than he meant to. "I inquired around of the men in the camp. From the time of her husband's death, Datiye went with none of them—except me. A man who thought the child was his would be only too eager to claim it. Apaches love children."

"It was just a thought," she said contritely. Then, surprising him, she smiled and produced something from behind her back. She held up a buckskin dress. "What do you think?" she asked, a bit shyly.

He carefully kept himself from laughing. It was a good try. The sewing was awful. The stitches were large and childlike, but he pretended not to notice. "It's fine," he said. "But, *shijii*, don't you think it's a bit large? Or are you planning on birthing a twenty-pound baby?"

She was dismayed. "Is it too large? Well—he'll grow into it."

"That he will," he said, chuckling. "I take it you've never seen a newborn baby?"

"Of course not. I was guessing as to the size."

He grinned, handing her back the garment. She inspected it ruefully. "Sewing was never my favorite pasttime. Before El Paso I hadn't picked up a needle in years."

He carefully bit back a response.

She looked at him. "It shows, huh?"

"No, no, it's really a fine dress."

"You're lying," she said, smiling because his eyes were filled with mirth.

"No, I swear I'm not," he said, putting his arm around her. "Let's take a walk."

"I wanted to do some more sewing," she protested, strolling along with him anyway.

He laughed. "Babies do grow quickly."

"I get the message," she said. Then, earnestly: "Jack, I . . ."

"What?"

"Damn! I want our baby to have things, Jack, real clothes, and toys, and candy and a pony and a damn house! With a garden!"

He stopped, placing his hands on her shoulders. Her words tore at him. He was torn up inside as it was. "I want to give you those things," he said finally.

"Then let's leave here!" she cried.

He stared. "You want me to run away like a coward, don't you?"

"You have your family to think of!"

"Apache children grow up very happy. I think you're thinking of yourself, not the child."

"No, I'm thinking about both of us—all of us! And the child isn't a damn Apache—can't you get that through your head?"

"I thought you were happy."

"Well, you thought wrong," she said bitterly. She turned away.

"I know you care for me," he said a bit desperately. "Don't you?"

She didn't answer. She strode away, clenching the dress in one fist.

Jack stared after her. He knew she was right. Their child was three-quarters white. And he wanted to give her everything she wanted—but how could he? When his duty lay here? Or did it? Maybe his duty was not to the people who had raised him, but to his family, their future.

And then there was Shozkay. His spirit still cried out in anguish for revenge. Jack turned and walked to an oak tree, leaning against it. He had known from the start that this life was not right for his wife and child. That was why he had ridden away to join Cochise without taking her with him. He had abducted her in anger and jealousy. He was glad she was there; he wanted her with him. He couldn't imagine living without her there by his side, and he thought that if she truly loved him, she would gladly make the sacrifice.

Yet it wasn't fair to ask her to live like an Apache.

And if he was less selfish, he would let her and the child go.

The realization was too painful. He quelled it. But he knew it would remain now to taunt him, no matter how hard he tried to chase it into the shadows.

CHAPTER SEVENTY-EIGHT

Her look was accusing.

The black moved restlessly beside him. "We won't be gone long. A couple of days."

Candice looked sick. "How can you do this? You're killing your own flesh and blood!"

His mouth tightened. He refused to be drawn into this topic. He mounted gracefully, gave her a hard look, and wheeled the black, cantering down the canyon to catch up with the war party. He could feel her eyes on him. Accusing and dismayed, even repelled. Her emotions seemed to be an echo of his own.

They rode steadily throughout the day, only two hundred strong this time, and Jack rode beside Nahilzay, who was in charge. They rode north up the Aravaipa Valley, toward Fort Breckenridge. They wouldn't go that far. A supply convoy had passed ahead of them, marked by Cochise's scouts yesterday. They would ambush the convoy. They needed guns and ammunition.

Jack kept thinking about Lieutenant Morris, the man who had ordered the hangings in February, the man responsible for Shozkay's murder. Almost a lifetime ago. He was still at Breckenridge. Thinking about him filled Jack with a bloodlust, a murdering rage. His need for vengeance was completely primitive and completely Apache.

They ambushed the convoy at dawn the following day. The convoy was foolishly camped in an arroyo, but the whites liked traveling in dry arroyos. They had yet to learn the Apache way of traveling across the ridgetops—which was safer, although slower. Arroyos were perfect for ambushes, meandering between hillocks and buttes. Two hundred warriors descended screaming at once upon the fifty infantrymen mounted on mules.

The troops quickly turned over the wagons and made a barricade, returning their fire. In the initial onslaught, three of them had been killed, a few others wounded but dragged to safety. Jack pulled up the black as the Apaches circled the barricade at a racing gallop, firing bullets and arrows at the soldiers, coming from all directions at once. For a moment he just watched. It would have been a slaughter if the troops hadn't overturned the wagons so efficiently. Now the skirmish could go on for hours, until the Apaches grew tired or ran too low on ammunition, in which case, if they didn't fulfill the goal of the attack, they were worse off than when they had started. . . .

He urged the black into a lope and into the melee. He quickly became absorbed into the battle. When a rifle was pointed at him he had to fire to defend himself. The cycle was swift, comprehensive, and vicious. He wounded a soldier, seeing his head disappear from over the edge of the wagon. A bullet missed his horse's flank narrowly. Still cantering, he circled, fired at a soldier, missing. He hated wasting ammunition in this kind of fray.

Something made him turn.

Nahilzay's horse was hit and floundering. The tall warrior leapt off and escaped being crushed with the reflexes of a cat. Jack moved the black toward him to provide protection to the man on foot. Nahilzay saw him, smiling fiercely, running toward him. Jack and Nahilzay saw the crouching figure in blue at the same time. Nahilzay had no gun; it had been crushed by his horse, as had the bow. The soldier was drawing his weapon, Nahilzay reaching for his knife. Jack saw the soldier's face. He was a baby-faced boy. His eyes were blue, his skin badly sunburned. He was terrified. Nahilzay threw the knife before the boy drew, but missed, losing his footing as he released it, jostled in the melee. The boy raised the gun. Jack was frozen.

"Niño Salvaje," Nahilzay shouted, looking at him with an unmistakably urgent message.

Jack drew. He was as fast as lightning, and both guns went off simultaneously. The boy fell, killed instantly. Jack rode the black hard to the warrior, who leapt astride behind him.

They galloped up the hill, where Nahilzay slid off, unhurt. He stared, every muscle in his body corded with fury. He didn't have to speak—what was on his mind was self-evident. But he did. "Go home, White Eyes. There is no place here for a man who cannot kill his enemy."

Nahilzay strode off, furious.

CHAPTER SEVENTY-NINE

Nothing could shake her mood, which was terribly sad.

She walked slowly through the woods from the creek, where she had bathed, rubbing the small of her back. The baby had been very active today, and it fascinated and awed her. Even now, she could feel him kicking. As a woman pregnant with the child of the man she loved, she should be ecstatic—not heartbrokenly sad.

She was so absorbed in her thoughts as she came out of the woods that for a brief moment she thought Datiye was merely standing against a tree. Then she realized with horror that her arms were tied to branches way above her head, and her legs were spread wide and tied that way, too. It took Candice a second to realize that she was in labor. She was wearing only a cloth shirt, and her awkward body strained against it. An ancient squaw was encouraging her as Datiye, silently, pushed. Her face was contorted with pain and concentrated effort. Sweat dripped from her chin, and there were huge wet patches under her arms. She was wearing something funny around her waist—a loose belt of many different colored hides. Candice screamed and ran forward.

"Stop it," she shrieked, grabbing the old woman. "Stop this torture, let her down. This is inhuman!"

The old woman babbled angrily at her in Apache and gave her a gentle but firm push that meant go away.

"I'll get a knife," Candice said to Datiye, who was grunting, sweat pouring down her cheeks. It was the first time she had spoken directly to her since her arrival at the rancheria months ago.

"No," Datiye panted. "Just . . . go."

She's crazy, Candice thought, watching for a moment as she strained against the ropes. Damn Jack! He should be there! Candice turned and ran a few steps toward the *gohwah*. She found a knife and hurried back as fast as she could.

Datiye's eyes were closed and she was straining with all the effort she had, making Candice pause, suddenly uncertain. The old woman was on her knees, reaching between Datiye's legs. Candice thought of the strange singing and chanting she'd heard last night. She hadn't asked Datiye what was happening, but had known it had to do with her baby, especially when the woman had been blessed with pollen and the belt of hides that was now tied around her waist. She had recognized two of the men as shamans, and had guessed the other two were also medicine men. Gripping the knife, she strode resolutely forward.

Datiye gasped, and the old woman gave a triumphant cry.

Candice stared at the slippery red bundle that the woman was pulling out from between Datiye's thighs. She was amazed. The squaw reached up and slit the umbilical cord. The red-faced infant let loose a howl. Datiye sagged against the tree. Her shoulders slumped in what appeared to be exhaustion.

The old woman put the baby down in the grass and stood, scowling.

"What's wrong?" Candice cried. "Is he deformed?" She stepped closer, to look. The baby was wailing now. The old woman glared and spoke sharply to Candice, then picked up the infant and marched into the woods. Candice had only gotten a glimpse of the child, but it had seemed like a normal baby. He certainly was a lusty thing, she thought, for she could still hear him howling. "Datiye? Are you all right?"

Datiye opened her eyes, and Candice saw to her shock that tears were streaming down her face. She cut her down, and the woman slumped on the ground. "Are you in pain?"

"No," Datiye said.

"Is the boy deformed?"

"He is a crier," Datiye said simply.

Candice didn't understand. "What? All children cry!"

"Apache children do not cry," Datiye said.

Candice had a sense of imminent danger. "What is that witch doing with your child?"

"Putting him to death," Datiye said.

Candice stared, then was running, as fast as she could. She didn't understand. She couldn't believe it. But that child was Jack's. Were the Apaches so cruel as to kill a child because it cried?

She found the woman at the creek placing the wailing

baby in a small hole that had been freshly dug. "No!" Candice screamed, panting.

The woman looked up, glared, and began throwing dirt on the crying baby. Candice picked up a rock and threw it at the woman. It hit her shoulder, stopping her efforts. Candice fell to her knees and picked up the boy, still wet and covered with a whitish afterbirth, still wailing lustily. She cradled him against her breast, feeling a twinge in her side. "Get away," she hissed at the woman. "Get away, you sick old witch!" She clutched the baby closer still.

The woman said something, rose, and stomped away. Candice started to cry. She couldn't believe it. The woman had been about to kill this baby, a sweet, innocent, helpless baby—and Datiye was going to let her do it.

The baby's mouth was working against her breast. "Damn," Candice whispered. "You're just hungry. How could they kill a baby for being hungry?"

She stood unsteadily. Her heart was still pumping. Her side ached, but it most definitely wasn't a labor cramp—or at least she didn't think it was. She walked down to the creek and quickly bathed the crying baby, singing to him to try to make him stop, drying him with her petticoat, which she then wrapped around him. His eyes were an unusually pale gray-blue. "So you really are Jack's son," she crooned. She felt overwhelmingly protective toward this tiny creature.

She strode back to the *gohwah,* the baby suddenly quiet. Candice said a quick prayer of thanks and paused at the edge of the woods, looking around. What if someone forcibly took the child from her and killed him before Jack returned? And how would she get milk for the baby? Could she talk Datiye into nursing the child? The baby had to eat!

Cochise.

Resolutely she walked through the camp to his *gohwah.* Miraculously, the baby had fallen asleep. Cochise was not in sight, but his first wife, whom Candice knew only by sight, was stirring the contents of a large iron pot. She stared at her with interest.

"I must see Cochise," Candice said. "Cochise."

Without a word, the woman stood and shouted something. Candice saw a boy of about nine, listening, then he turned and ran off. The woman smiled and said something to her. Candice realized she had offered her a seat. Gratefully she sank down, wondering if she would ever be able to stand up again. Her back was starting to ache terribly.

She took a moment to study the baby's wrinkled, red face. Did all babies look so funny? Even so, there was something incredibly beautiful about him. She stroked his downy head.

She saw Cochise coming a few minutes later, tall, broad-shouldered, his face expressionless, his black eyes dancing with interest. "You seek me?" he asked, staring at the baby.

"Cochise, I need your help," she said, knowing full well she was asking him a favor in such a way he could not refuse.

He regarded her. "This is the second wife's son."

"Yes. They tried to kill it. I think because he cried."

He did not seem surprised. "A crying baby can jeopardize the safety of an entire tribe, not just his own family."

"So babies who cry at birth are killed?" She was appalled.

"Usually."

"I need milk. This boy will not be killed. I will not allow it."

A faint smile touched the corners of his mouth. He turned to his wife and spoke in Apache. She nodded, looking interested, and turned to do his bidding. The baby woke up and started to cry. Candice frowned, realizing he wasn't a crier but a howler. She rocked him, afraid to look at Cochise. But she did.

"He is very loud," Cochise noted.

She didn't answer. She made soothing sounds, a little awkwardly, but out of instinct. Please stop crying, she begged silently. Please!

"There is no danger here," Cochise told her, his voice so stern and laden with authority that Candice looked up. "But if the day ever comes that we must leave this place and run from the soldiers, should the baby cry like that—his throat will be slit instantly."

Candice bit off a gasp.

"One death is preferable to many," Cochise said.

Candice was horrified. She understood, but that didn't make it any more palatable. She was overwhelmed with relief when his wife appeared with a teat of buckskin and a gourd of milk. "Thank you," Candice said, and began feeding the baby.

He is a greedy boy, she noted, fascinated. Like his father, she thought tenderly. She glanced at Cochise. "Will Datiye reject him even now?"

"I do not know," Cochise said. "You may tell her I extend my protection until the day we leave this stronghold. With the help of the gods, that day may never come." He seemed to be slightly amused. He turned and walked away.

After the boy had fallen asleep, Candice stood, the older woman assisting her. Cochise's wife sent his son with them, carrying the rest of the milk and the teat. Candice wondered what Datiye would do. She found herself hoping fervently that she would accept her own child.

Datiye was on her knees, slicing wild onions and tossing them into a pot as if she hadn't given birth that day. When she saw Candice and her son she went very still. Her face turned white. "What have you done?"

"I won't let you kill him," Candice said, rocking the sleeping baby. He was still wrapped in her petticoat. "He needs his mother. Will you take him?"

Tears came into Datiye's eyes. Candice was afraid to trust her, but when Datiye held out her arms, she handed the baby to her. Datiye clutched him to her breast and began to weep silently.

CHAPTER EIGHTY

He was as tired as the rest of the war party, but his mood was low, while everyone else was jubilant. They had captured the wagon train of supplies. They had lost two warriors, with several more wounded, but the whites had lost five times that number. The warriors were elated. Jack knew better. If every time there was an engagement the Apache lost a man or two, in no time they would have too few warriors left to fight. It saddened him immensely.

And he was angry with himself and torn up inside.

Jack was rigid with self-loathing. Nahilzay was lucky to be alive—and had he been shot, it would have been Jack's fault. His fault for hesitating. There was no place in battle for a man whom his friends could not trust to come instantly to their aid. No place at all. His hesitation had almost cost a great warrior his life.

He was realizing his priorities might be confused. It was a difficult understanding, one he fought. He still felt that his duty lay with the Apaches. But he knew he was worthless to them if he could not conduct himself bravely and ruthlessly in battle.

The black was tired, and walked in a subdued manner through the camp. There was much rejoicing all around him, but Jack was in no mood for a celebration and had no intention of taking part. He looked forward to seeking solace in Candice's arms. He would be happy just to be with her. He spotted her the minute his *gohwah* emerged into view amid the other lodgings.

She saw him too, and his heart leapt at the excitement that crossed her face. She dropped what she was doing and came rushing toward him, half running. He urged the black forward, then jumped off. "Foolish woman," he cried, grabbing her. "Don't run!"

"Jack!" She threw her arms around him. He smiled, holding her tenderly. Embracing her was awkward now that she was so large.

"How are you feeling?" he asked gently, after he had kissed her thoroughly.

"Fine. Jack—" The baby's loud wail cut her off.

Jack started and stared toward the *gohwah*. Then he looked at Candice.

"You have a son," she said, regarding him closely. "A beautiful boy."

Jack sucked in his breath. The boy was quiet now. "Is— are they both all right?"

"Now they are," Candice said enigmatically. "Why don't you go see them, because afterward I intend to give you a piece of my mind." She glared at him.

He ignored the threat and hurried forward and into the *gohwah*. He stopped short at the sight of Datiye nursing the baby. She met his gaze and smiled softly. Jack strode forward and stared down at his son. An overwhelming sense of love flooded him.

"His eyes are so pale," he said, startled. And then he felt joy, for he knew the boy had to be his.

"Like his father," Datiye said.

Jack studied him. His skin was swarthy, and the few wisps of hair were blue-black. He felt a sudden grimness—the boy was too obviously a half-breed. He remembered all the times he had been called such, and how he had hated it. It would be a painful cross for his son to bear, one he wished he could spare him, but knew he couldn't. "He has a healthy appetite," he remarked. He touched the boy's silky head. The baby seemed to look at him, while still sucking greedily. Jack smiled.

"We will call him Shoz," he said. "Little Shoz." He looked at Datiye. "He is beautiful. Thank you."

Datiye hesitated. "He is a crybaby, husband."

Jack's jaw tightened. "How so?" He knew very well what happened to crybabies, and didn't understand. If his son was a crier, why was he alive?

Datiye hesitated. "Candice would not let him be killed. She fought for him. I—I let them take him away. But she saved him. It is to her you should give thanks."

Jack was stunned. He couldn't believe it; in fact, he didn't. "Are you sure?"

"She went to Cochise for protection. He gave it for as long as we remain in this safe place."

The baby had finished nursing, and his little fist clenched

against his mother's breasts. Jack touched it. The baby made a noise, and his hand tightened around Jack's finger. Jack took Shoz gently into his arms. He smiled at him. "Little Shoz," he said, gazing at him. He had had no idea he would feel so fatherly toward a child, any child, except maybe Candice's. "You must learn not to cry, Shoshi."

Datiye stood. "Do you want me to take him now?"

Jack nodded reluctantly. Datiye turned her back, and Jack placed Shoz in the cradleboard she was wearing. Shoz smiled and fell asleep.

Outside, Jack found Candice waiting impatiently. Before he could say anything, she tore into him. "Why didn't you tell me how cruel the Apaches are? Jack! They tried to kill your son! Because he cried! No one is going to kill my child, Jack, I warn you!"

He pulled her close. "Thank you, sweetheart, for what you did. And no one will kill our child, I swear. I'm not leaving your side from now until you have the baby, I promise."

"And I'm not going to be tied to a tree either!"

"It's not as bad as it looks . . ." he began.

"No!" There was panic in her tone.

"All right," he soothed. "You won't be tied, I swear."

She relaxed somewhat. "Jack, would you have let them take him away if you were here?"

He grimaced. "I—I don't think so," he said.

"Datiye let the old witch take him."

"Why did you protect Shoshi, Candice?"

"Is that his name? Shoshi?"

"Shoz. His name is Shoz. Shoshi is an endearing form of Shoz."

She smiled. "Shoshi. That's a good name for a child, but what happens after he's older?"

"His name will be Shoz," Jack said firmly.

"You're naming him after Shozkay," Candice said.

"Yes. Candie, you didn't answer. Why?"

"I'm a human being, Jack, it's that simple." She frowned. She didn't tell him she somehow had come to love Shoshi, that she wished she could hold him. But she didn't dare ask Datiye. After not speaking to her for five months, how did one start? Candice didn't want to be friends with her anyway. She still hated her—well, disliked her. The woman was her rival. The woman had borne Jack a son. That would never change—although Candice had realized very recently that all this was Jack's fault, not Datiye's. Datiye was a woman, and what woman could resist Jack's seduction? If Jack hadn't been such a horny bastard, she wouldn't have to share him with Datiye right now. But, no matter what, Shoshi was innocent.

And now Datiye owed her. Candice knew that when the time came, Datiye wouldn't be able to refuse aiding her in her escape. The thought should have been uplifting. It wasn't. It was disheartening.

CHAPTER EIGHTY-ONE

Datiye was cleaning up after their dinner. Jack held Shoshi, making faces and sounds. The baby gurgled and smiled back. He flailed his little arms, catching Jack's chin. Jack laughed. Shoshi ga-gaahed, smiling in that peculiar way young infants do.

He looked up. Candice, bigger than ever now, was watching, standing a short distance away, to the side. He felt a bit guilty, but studied her for signs of jealousy and didn't see any. Datiye got up and left with the pot to wash and sand it. Candice approached slowly, then, awkwardly, sat down by his feet. Their eyes met.

"I guess I look sort of silly," Jack said sheepishly.

Candice smiled, but she wasn't watching him. Her eyes were fastened on the baby. "Can I?"

He started. "Sure."

He handed her the baby. He watched, amazed, at the soft smile that spread over her beautiful features. She cooed to Shoshi, rocking him gently against her breast. He felt overwhelmed by the sight of her there, holding his son.

Later that night Jack climbed into the bedroll beside her. She still insisted on sleeping with him, which was fine for her. She practically passed out these days. But he was so afraid to disturb her, he could barely sleep. Now, however, he saw that she was awake. He leaned over to kiss her mouth lightly. Her arms came up, clenched him, and her lips opened, inviting him to deepen the kiss. He did. Incredibly, surges of hot desire swept him. Even with her due in a few weeks, he still wanted her as much as ever. No, more.

"Jack?"

"What?"

"Promise me something."

"If I can."

She turned her head to look at him. "Don't let them tie me to a tree like they did Datiye." There was a tremor in her voice.

"Candie, it helps, it really does."

"No!" she cried.

"All right," he soothed, taking her in his arms and propping himself into a sitting position. "I'll hold you up myself. Not all women are tied. Some squat. But believe me, trust me, it's easier than lying down."

She didn't answer. He looked down and saw fear on her face. He suddenly was overwhelmed by a dread sensation and an image of Chilahe lying dead in a pool of her own blood after giving birth to their child. God, he didn't want to even think it! He hugged her harder. What if Candice had a hard time? No, she was as healthy as a woman could be. "Don't worry," he whispered, but he was suddenly sick with anxiety himself.

"I'm not worried," she said, and they both knew she was lying.

His fears wouldn't leave. As the days passed, he became obsessed with memories of how Chilahe had died after hours of agonizing pain and awful, heart-wrenching screams. He reminded himself that the shaman had said her passage was too narrow, her hips too small. He had Candice examined by a medicine woman against her will. The shaman was cheerful and optimistic, assuring him that Candice was healthy and should have no problems. When he had asked about the size of her hips and birth canal, the woman had laughingly told him to leave well enough alone. He couldn't help it. He was terrified with the thought he might lose her. He wished he could stop remembering Chilahe's death.

He knew he was being completely foolish. One had only to look at Candice to know she was meant for bearing children. She was a woman built strongly. Her hips were wide without being overly large. Her breasts were full now with milk. She was the picture of health, but he was obsessed with fear.

It was early July. Jack was down at the creek, fishing. Not for food, for the Apaches never ate fish. But for sport and amusement and to stay distracted. He heard Candice coming a mile away. These days she waddled, making her even noisier than before. Someday, he thought, I *will* teach her how to move quietly. He turned his head to see her emerge from the woods. She smiled at him, her face flushed. "I thought I saw you coming down here," she said, breathing a bit hard.

He dropped the spear he had been using and stood. "You look overheated," he said worriedly. "You shouldn't be tramping around like this."

"You've become a mother hen, Jack," she said with a smile. Then she winced.

"What is it?" He felt panic.

"Jack, I think I'm in labor."

"You think?"

She smiled wanly and suddenly winced again. "They were so dull before, I thought I was imagining . . ." Suddenly a spasm took her. She gasped and sank to her knees.

Jack was at her side instantly. "Candice, damn it. Are you—"

"Oh, I think so." She moaned as another spasm took her.

"Candice, another pain?" He was aghast. They were coming too quickly, one right on top of the other.

"Jack," she cried out, grabbing his shoulders and digging into them. She moaned.

"*Usen!* Candice, I'll go get help! Don't do anything until I get back! When did the pains first start?"

"A few hours ago." She moaned, panting, pushing, straining, as she slid to her back.

"A few hours ago!"

"I didn't know they were labor pains! Jaaack!"

"Oh, shit." He groaned, kneeling, afraid to leave her. Her legs were bent at the knees, spread. He pushed the skirt up. "How could you not know, Candice?" he cried.

She was panting. "They were . . . so slight. Just a . . . discomfort—oohhh!"

"You have to squat," he said, lifting her up.

"No, Jack—oohh."

"Squatting is easier, trust me." He panted, his arms around her, forcing her up.

"How would you know? Ohh—God!" Her hands, covering his, gripped and clawed.

"Believe me, I know," he cried. "Are you pushing? Are you breathing? Breathe and push!"

"I'm breathing, I'm pushing," Candice cried. "For God's sake, Jack, you're holding me too tightly . . ."

"You should be tied, dammit, you should be tied!"

"Don't—oh!—you even think it!" She started to press away from him, and taken by surprise, he slipped, and they went tumbling down, Candice in his arms.

"Look what you did!" Jack panted, stumbling to his knees and lifting her back up. Sweat ran down his face.

Candice grabbed Jack's hands and removed them. "I am lying down now, Jack," she announced calmly, placing her bottom on the ground and then her back.

"No, trust me." Jack gasped, his arm going beneath her to lift her. Then: "Shit!"

"Ohh!"

"Usen give me strength," he muttered, forgetting all about his wife being in the wrong position, because suddenly he could see the baby's head. "I see the head, Candice, push, hard!"

"I'm pushing." She panted, and she pushed.

"It's coming," he cried, and then before he knew it, a white-coated baby had slipped into his hands.

Candice closed her eyes and lay gasping for air.

"A girl, Candice, it's a girl!" he cried, awed, thrilled, relieved, and exhausted. He wiped sweat out of his eyes and reached for his knife. He cut the umbilical cord.

"Oh," Candice whispered. "Let me, Jack . . ."

"Let me wash her first," Jack said, staring at the red-faced baby. She was bald, her eyes screwed shut. He hurried down to the creek and washed her, then removed his loincloth to dry her and wrap her in it. She opened her eyes and blinked. He smiled, then, drinking the sight of her in. Her eyes were blue. He noted that she wasn't completely bald, there were a few dark hairs above her forehead. She opened her mouth, turning her face against his belly, searching. He hurried back.

Candice reached out, her face glowing. Jack knelt and placed the baby in her arms. "Oh," she whispered. "She's beautiful."

"Like her mother," Jack said softly, then started laughing. A rich, warm, relieved laugh. "You did better than any Apache woman I ever saw, Candie. I can't believe you didn't know you were in labor," he said.

"But I didn't," she said simply, stroking the baby's soft, downy head.

"Do you feel all right?" he asked softly.

"Wonderful," she murmured. "Hello, Christina. You are so beautiful. My little lady."

"Why do you want to call her Christina?"

"It's a real lady's name," she said, never even looking at him. "A Christian lady's name. And she's going to grow up to be a fine Christian lady."

Jack looked at her, absorbing her words, watching as Candice freed her breasts, moving Christina closer to one soft nipple. A fine Christian lady, he thought, the words echoing disturbingly. Then his attention became fastened on his daughter as she found her mother's nipple and began to suck. He felt incredibly proud watching this scene. His beautiful wife, his beautiful daughter. He sat behind her and propped her head up on his leg. "Better?"

She smiled contentedly.

CHAPTER EIGHTY-TWO

Jack watched Candice grinding the seeds into flour from wild berries, which would then be made into bread. He didn't smile. The sight of her like that, their daughter in the cradleboard on her back, asleep, should have made him smile —at the very least with the warmth he felt for them, or even because she looked so adept, as if she had become a squaw.

But Candice would never look like a squaw. Her hair was plaited in a thick, fat braid, which she had draped over one shoulder carelessly. Wisps of golden-yellow hair curled around her golden face. He felt a pang of desire, but refused to entertain it. It was still too soon. And something was wrong. He could sense it. He wondered if there was such a thing as a woman becoming melancholy after having a child.

He left, striding rapidly through the camp, his mind made up. The resolve had formed on that last disastrous war party up the Araviapa Valley. So close to Fort Breckenridge . . . what if Morris was no longer there?

Cochise greeted him with a smile. "What brings my brother and causes him to leave such a joy-filled family?"

Jack frowned.

"How are your wives, your children?" Cochise asked with some concern.

"Fine. I'm riding out," he said smoothly, although abruptly. "Up to Fort Breckenridge. I intend to kill Lieutenant Morris and give my brother's spirit the peace he needs to leave this world."

If Cochise was startled, he hid it. "That is a very dangerous mission for one man. How will you get into the fort?"

"I considered using treachery, being white-skinned, but I decided against it. At night I will scale the wall. I will slip into Morris's quarters and slit his throat as he sleeps. I will leave the same way I came in." He shrugged. His face was grim.

"What you do is a good thing, for all our people. I think, if anyone could do it, you can."

"If I do not return, I wish you to see that Candice and Christina return to the High C under escort."

"It will be done, if you do not return."

"Also, I do not want anyone to know of my mission. I do not want Candice to find out and worry. I'll tell her I'm scouting, nothing more."

Cochise nodded, then embraced him. "Tonight, and until you return, the *gans* will dance and offer many prayers. The people will think it is for another war party, but I shall know it is for you."

"Thank you," Jack said.

He strode back to his *gohwah* with only his mission on his mind. He hadn't told Cochise the rest of it. That if he returned, he was intending to leave the Apaches and never return. Shozkay would be avenged. It was the best he could do. His staying and fighting in the Apache cause was no longer something he could do, nor was it fair to the warriors he rode with. And it wasn't fair to Candice, or Christina.

He refused to think about leaving Shoshi behind with Datiye. It would just have to be done.

He was clad in his buckskin pants and shirt, and he wore no warpaint. He saddled up the black, taking only his rifle, his Colt and knife, and his bow and arrows. The latter wasn't for the purpose of his mission, but because it was a convenient way to kill game without being heard if the need arose. He finished and went around the *gohwah*, to where Datiye was pounding a rawhide she was tanning, Shoshi on her back.

He said a brief good-bye to her, not bothering to tell her anything except that he would be back in a few days. He patted Shoshi on the head, his hand lingering. The baby woke up to look at him out of silvery eyes, then started crying. Datiye began to nurse him.

"Where are you going?" Candice asked, her voice very still.

He straightened, taking one last look at his son, and moved to her. "Scouting. I'll be back in a few days, three probably, maybe four."

She stared, her eyes huge and stricken, and he thought she was afraid for him. "Come here, *shijii,*" he said, pulling her into his arms. She rested there a moment, then clung to him with a touch of panic.

"Jack," she whispered, pulling his head down so she could kiss him. They kissed for a long time.

"It's only for a few days," he teased. "When I get back you should be ready for some proper lovemaking."

"How can you think about that now?" she muttered, her heart beating wildly. This was her chance, and she knew it. He was riding out, and she could be gone before he ever came back to camp. She felt panicky, sick, guilty, and terrified. She couldn't let go of him.

"Let me say good-bye to Christina," he said gently, tearing her hands away. With something that sounded suspiciously like a choked-off sob, Candice turned her back so Jack could smile at her daughter, stroking her tiny face with one forefinger. She didn't even wake up.

"I'll see you soon, Candie," he said, wondering why she looked so stricken. "Don't worry, I'll be fine."

"Good-bye, Jack," she whispered, fighting tears. She watched him swing gracefully into the saddle, flash her a warm, devastating smile, and lope away. Oh, God!

This was it. She had to think of Christina. Because if it was just her, she would stay. She would never be able to leave Jack, as long as he kept good his promise to marry off Datiye. Now he wouldn't even have to do that. She felt a terrible jealousy at the thought of leaving the two of them together. She strode to Datiye with grim resolution.

"Datiye, I need your help." It was the first time she had spoken to her since she had had her child.

Datiye stared, startled.

"You owe me," Candice said. "I'm running away. I want to leave at dawn. I need a pony, a rifle, supplies. And I need a guide out of the stronghold. From the entrance I can find my way home." Home. The High C. She was too sick at heart to dwell on what her family's reactions to her arrival with Christina would be, but at least she knew she could count on Luke to help her go East.

"I do not understand," Datiye said, standing. "You love him. He loves you. Why do you leave?"

"Because of my daughter. Christina is not an Indian, and I won't have her turned into a squaw."

"He will come after you."

"By the time he does, I will be safe at the ranch. He won't be able to talk his way in. And, Datiye, Cochise must not know. No one must know. I want you to cover for me while I'm gone. If someone asks for me, which is unlikely, say I am bathing or something."

Datiye nodded, smiling. "No one will notice your absence."

"Don't look so pleased," Candice snapped.

"Why should I not be pleased? Our husband is Apache, more than white. He needs a woman who understands him. And I have given him a boy—a son. In time he will forget you. I will comfort him so that he does."

"He will never love you," Candice cried. She had an untimely vision of Datiye naked in Jack's arms, and it made her sick. "Never. He loves me. He may take your body, but he will never give you his heart." They stood and glared at each other.

"I would like to leave before dawn, so no one sees. I want to be outside the stronghold as the sun rises."

"I will arrange everything."

Candice watched Datiye walk away. She went and found a piece of charcoal and began to compose a note, one that she hoped would be cruel enough to deter him from coming after her.

She would no longer think about the man she was leaving.

CHAPTER EIGHTY-THREE

He leaned against the wall, straining to hear. Above, on the parapet, he could hear the sentry snoring. There was no sound from within the fort, which was a small area enclosed by ten-foot stone walls, ridiculously easy to scale. He could make out the forms of the few buildings within the walls. There were two long, low log buildings, which were the soldiers' and noncommissioned officers' quarters. Infantry and cavalry. Behind that was the mess hall; across the courtyard the adjutant's office; and near that the larger residence of the commanding officer. To the right were five small, separate buildings housing the officers, including Lieutenant Morris. He had watched all day and had not only identified Morris, but his quarters as well

Knife in hand, he ran in a creeping position, keeping low to the ground and in the shadows. He slipped past the adjutant's office, then two of the buildings for the commissioned officers. He didn't pause at the third. He slipped through an open window to stand inside, adjusting to the even dimmer light within. Perspiration beaded his face. It was no cooler this far north than it was in the stronghold.

Without even a backward glance, for his ears were attuned to every sound around him, Jack stepped across the small chamber to the bed and leaned over the sleeping man, pressing the long blade of his knife against the lieutenant's throat. Morris stirred, then suddenly his eyes flew open. He started to rise, his hands flinching prior to coming up to grasp for the knife. One word from Jack stopped him, that and the increasing pressure of the blade. "Don't."

Morris's eyes bulged, but he lay so still, staring up at Jack, that he didn't seem to be breathing. A long, hushed silence was finally broken. "Who are you?" Morris whispered.

"Niño Salvaje."

"What do you want?" It was a croak.

Jack smiled grimly. "Your life."

Morris gasped, and the movement of his throat made the knife cut skin. A dark, black stream appeared by the cutting edge of the blade. "Please," Morris whispered desperately. Sweat gleaned on his forehead; his eyes teared. He was panting.

"For my brother," Jack said. "For the hangings of six Apaches." With one swift movement, he slit Morris's throat from ear to ear. Blood gushed with a faint gurgling sound. He moved quickly, then, to the window and back out. Shortly after, he was on his stallion and riding back the way he had come.

This time he felt no sickness, no guilt. Retribution had been just in the Apache way. It had to be done. He could not have lived without avenging his brother's death. His brother would have done the same for him.

His brother. His family was gone—Machu, Nalee, Shozkay, Luz. But now he had Candice and Christina. He felt a flooding relief. They were his family, his priority, and all he wanted was to provide for them in peace. Was that too much to ask?

There had been enough killing. He knew it wouldn't stop, that it would go on and on, and only Usen might foresee how many years of bloodshed and warfare there would be. He should have known that he couldn't participate in this war. He had exiled himself once before for the very same weakness—his inability to kill whites. In truth, it was not his fault. He was half white. But not completely. And there was a part of his heart and soul that was Apache, and it would always be that way.

He felt uplifted. Eager. To see his wife, take her and his daughter away. To start over. He knew he and Candice would be happy away from all this. Although things hadn't been so bad, despite the war and Datiye. Candice had changed, he realized. Motherhood agreed with her. She had matured. They would go away, maybe to Texas, where there were few Apaches, or to California, and they would build a fine ranch, raise many children. His desire to see her and share his plans with her was overwhelming. He rode faster. In a day or two he would be back at the stronghold.

He tried not to think of his son. He loved him, there was no doubt, but the boy belonged with his mother. He would leave him behind because he had to, in fairness to Datiye. The decision was made, and he would not think about it.

He would think only about Candice and their future.

CHAPTER EIGHTY-FOUR

Christina started to cry.

Candice was awake, unable to sleep, staring up at the glittering stars, listening to every rustle of sage and mesquite, feeling every whisper of air. She shifted Christina, opening her blouse and bringing her to her breast. She wondered what time it was. After midnight, she guessed. She hadn't dared to make a fire. She was afraid of Indians, other Apaches, whites, Jack. It would be the height of irony if he stumbled across them.

Close by, an owl hooted. Candice had been among the Apaches long enough to know that they would think it was some spirit haunting the earth. Despite herself, she shivered. It was cool out. Compared to the heat of the day, the night air seemed colder than it was. Christina finished and Candice tucked her into the crook of her arm, nestling back down. She wished she could fall asleep.

This was only their first night on the trail. There would probably be three more. Candice had kept the pony to a steady trot all day, stopping only to feed Christina and change her. Christina was a wonderful traveler. But, Candice supposed, it might be because she was still so young, not even a month old.

She finally fell asleep, until the brightness of the early-morning sun awoke her—that, and Christina gurgling against her side. Candice fed her, ate some jerky, nuts, and berries, then placed Christina in her cradleboard and slipped it onto her back. She had devised a buckskin flap over the headpiece when Christina was first born, to shade her from the sun. Her baby had a tawny complexion, shades darker than her own but lighter than Jack's, and Jack's sable hair. Candice was very relieved that she didn't have a dark complexion to mark her Indian blood, so she would be spared the bigotry of society when she was old enough to understand.

Images of Jack tugged at her heart.

Don't think about him, she told herself sternly, and mounted and set off.

They approached Dragoon Springs later that morning.

They were actually following the Butterfield Overland Trail, although that stage, she knew, was no longer in service here. The Apache wars had made it too dangerous.

She watered the pony thoroughly, fed Christina again, and bathed her and her own face and chest with a wet cloth. She set Jack's Stetson back on her head, and was about to put the cradleboard with her daughter on her back when her pony snorted, then neighed, making her look up.

Approaching from the direction she had come were riders—three of them.

Candice quickly reached for her rifle and drew it out of its scabbard. She laid it at her feet and put Christina on her back. She retrieved and cocked the rifle, holding it loosely but with a hint of menace in the crook of her arm.

Then she saw that the riders were soldiers and relief flooded her. And with it, hope. Her first thought was that maybe they would escort her back to the High C.

The men pulled up, staring at her with surprise and interest. "Ma'am," drawled a bulky, middle-age man with a sergeant's stripes. "Are you okay?"

"Yes, Sergeant, thank you," Candice said, holding her rifle casually. She became aware of her appearance—of her faded white blouse stretched too tautly over her swollen breasts, of the griminess of her brown skirt, her reddened hands, her sunburned nose.

"What are you doing out here alone, ma'am?"

"I'm on my way to the High C," she began.

"Damn," exclaimed a young soldier. "I thought that was her! Sarge! That's Candice Carter!"

The sergeant's gray eyes widened. "The one who eloped with Kincaid but returned with the breed that rides with Cochise?"

"The very one," the young man exclaimed.

Candice tensed. She felt the change in the atmosphere immediately, as slightly perceptible as it was. The soldiers' manner went from polite concern to tense, perhaps even hostile and lascivious interest.

"Sarge," the young man said hastily. "I heard that the breed killed Kincaid in El Paso—over her."

They stared.

Candice felt sweat dripping down her temple.

"I dunno about Kincaid," the sergeant finally said. "But Jack Savage is wanted for the murder of two men in El Paso in April."

Candice remembered how the mob had come after them when Jack had returned to her in the spring. Oh, God. It wouldn't matter to these soldiers that Jack had been protecting her and himself—that it had been self-defense.

"And she's got a kid," the same man said, nudging his horse forward. "A *papoose.*" He grinned. "Looks like a half-breed."

Candice raised her rifle, whirling on the man, who was not much older than she was, but whose intent was questionable while his lust was not. "Stay back!"

He chuckled. "Little Injun whore's got some spunk, Sarge! What do you say?"

"Relax, Ladd. Where are you coming from?" the sergeant asked harshly, eyes hard.

Candice thought quickly. But not quickly enough.

"Bet you she was with that breed. Look at the kid—in a cradleboard and buckskins. She must be coming from Cochise's camp," Ladd said shrewdly.

Then Ladd, the sergeant, and the third soldier exchanged worried glances. "Where's Savage?" the sergeant asked abruptly.

She made her decision. "He's out scouting, miles from here. I've run away from him. I need your help—please. He abducted me against my will—kept me prisoner. I waited until the child was old enough to travel. Won't you please help me?" Her tone was feminine and desperate, helpless and seductive.

The sergeant stared with doubtful and piercing eyes. "I heard all about you, Miss Carter. Or is it Mrs. Kincaid? I ain't sure whether to believe a word you say, especially not as you got that little breed on your back."

"Christina's white," Candice cried furiously.

"Let's make her talk," Ladd said eagerly. "A woman like that, hell, she's already a whore. What'll one or two more times matter?" He chuckled.

"If you touch me—a white woman, abducted by a man against her will, kept prisoner in an Apache rancheria—you'll all be court-martialed," Candice said as firmly as she could. She was frightened.

"She's got the best tits I ever seen," Ladd said huskily.

"She's right," the sergeant said. "We'll take her back to the fort and let the major decide what to do with her."

"Let's have some of what she's got first," Ladd growled.

"No."

The man hadn't spoken before, but it was so vicious that everyone, including Candice, swung to look at him. He was very young, no older than Candice, badly sunburned, red-haired and blue-eyed. "She's a white woman, you can see that," he said, staring at her. "No white woman deserves to be raped."

"You jerk, McDowell," Ladd said. "She's no different from any whore in any saloon. She'd like it, believe me!"

"Enough. We're taking her back to the fort. Hand over that rifle, ma'am," the sergeant ordered.

Candice gripped her rifle harder. She hesitated. There were three of them. What was she going to do? Kill one or two? Then she'd hang for murder, woman or not. And she had Christina to think about, to protect. Frowning, thinking, she lowered the rifle. The sergeant looked at Ladd, who rode over and took it away.

"Maybe she's got a knife on her," Ladd suggested, almost smiling.

"Search her," the sergeant said.

Ladd jumped down, eager to comply. He stared at Candice's clenched face, then eyed her bosom.

"I'm not carrying a knife," Candice lied. She was, but it wasn't on her person, it was in her saddlebags. "You can see," she said, holding out her arms so he could see there was no weapon stuck in the waistband of her skirt.

He reached out and placed both hands on her waist, ostensibly feeling for a knife. Candice shrugged away angrily. He grinned. "Lift up your skirts," he said.

She stared.

"Either you do it or I do it," he said, grinning.

"You carrying a knife under there?" the sergeant asked.

"No," Candice said firmly. Her heart was hammering too rapidly.

"Then lift 'em. You want Ladd to lift 'em?"

She didn't. She lifted her skirts, to just above her knees.

"She's not wearing pantalets," Ladd breathed, staring at her bare calves and knees. The other men were staring too. Ladd bent and checked each boot, then stood. He eyed her calves again. "Higher," he said.

"You bastard," she hissed. "What do you think, it's glued to my thigh?"

"Maybe stuck in a piece of rawhide." Ladd grinned. He reached up and grabbed her skirt and raised it. "Mother of God." He gasped, staring at her shapely thighs and the patch of gold hair curling between them.

Candice spun away. "Satisfied?" She tried not to tremble. There was a large bulge in his trousers, one impossible to miss. She was afraid.

"Mount up," the sergeant said grimly.

Candice obeyed, daring to look at the men. They were all excited, she could see the animal hunger in their eyes. Even the redhead who had tried to defend her, but at least he wasn't looking at her; he seemed embarrassed at his own reaction.

It will be at least another day and a half until we reach the fort, Candice thought desperately. Good God. How was she going to protect herself and Christina during that time?

And what would she do when she got there? Somehow, she would have to protect Jack too.

CHAPTER EIGHTY-FIVE

"Won't you sit down, Mrs. Kincaid?"

Candice stood with Christina in her arms, watching Major Bradley warily. She had waited outside his office for thirty minutes while he was closeted with Sergeant Holden. True to his word, they had ridden hard all day and had arrived at Fort Buchanan while it was still light. She sat, letting her Stetson drop onto her back.

"It is Mrs. Kincaid?"

What did it matter? Candice nodded.

They gazed at each other with equal intent. Candice was very much aware of the major's regard, from the top of her head to the tip of her boots. There was, possibly, the faintest glimmer of male interest, but she wasn't sure. He was lean, of medium height, about forty, quite attractive in a formal, military way. He smiled at her and sat behind his desk. "I hope the past few days haven't been too trying on you, Mrs. Kincaid."

"I was very lucky to have run across your men," Candice said demurely.

"Indeed you were. Tell me what you were doing alone in the desert, Mrs. Kincaid."

Candice was prepared to do whatever she had to to protect her child, herself, and Jack. She knew that if the major even suspected her feelings for Jack, or knew that Jack was Christina's father, he would try and use her against Jack and the Apaches. The fact that word had already drifted this far about Jack's killing Kincaid made it impossible for her to deny that she had been with him. And now she had to worry about the murders of the two men in El Paso. Any lies she told would have to be told very well.

"I was running away," she cried passionately, a quaver in her voice. "He abducted me. He killed Virgil and kidnapped me. I fought him, but he tied me up. He knew I was with child. He kept me prisoner in the Apache camp. I finally pretended I was no longer interested in running away, and after Christina was born, I took the first chance I could get, and I escaped." She willed tears to fill her eyes, and they did.

She looked at him pleadingly. A vulnerable, helpless female. He did not seem moved.

He was studying her with great attention, but she could see the cold doubt in his eyes. "Who is this child's father?"

She hated telling this lie more than the others. "Virgil was."

He stared at her unblinkingly, and Candice blessed the fact that Kincaid had the physical attributes that could make him Christina's father.

"I find it difficult to believe you could escape after being held prisoner all that time."

She lifted her chin. "He had another woman, a squaw. And child. She hated me. She was happy to help me escape." She began to cry. "I just want to go home. Back to my family." She blinked at him. "Please help me." She gazed at him with all the pitifulness she could muster.

He studied her, then poured himself a glass of whiskey, studying it before drinking it. "You were in Cochise's stronghold?"

"Yes." Careful, she warned herself.

"So you know where it is?"

"It's in the Chiricahua Mountains," she said honestly, but that was a commonly known fact.

"Perhaps you can prove your story by helping us locate the stronghold."

"But I would never be able to find it!" She gasped. And it was true. "Jack brought me there almost seven months ago, and I never left it once." A complete lie. "Until this time. Datiye—his wife—arranged for a guide. I don't know how she did it. But we left before dawn, at dark, the morning after Jack went out scouting. When the sun came up I was in the Sulphur Springs Valley, and the guide left me there. I would love to help you, more than anything I'd love to see that bastard caught and hanged, but how could I ever find it again? The entrance, from what I've heard, is narrow and secret, impossible to find unless you know where it is."

Her heart was pounding. He had to believe she hated Jack and the Apaches but knew nothing. If not, he could keep her as a prisoner indefinitely. Worse, release her and let her fend off the soldiers who considered her a breed's whore. He was a soldier fighting against the Apaches, so the safest bet for her and Christina, she had realized since she had first been taken prisoner by Sergeant Holden, was to pretend she was on their side. But—wasn't she?

Before, she had thought she was, and thought it was clear cut. Now she didn't know what she thought. She only knew she would never want anything to happen to Jack, or Shoshi, or Cochise and his family. It was very fortunate that she probably never could find the stronghold, and that she knew nothing of their war plans.

"You must be tired," the major said suddenly. "I will give you my quarters and have hot water brought for you. I would be honored if you would agree to dine with me afterward."

So he does find me attractive, she thought, smiling brightly. Or is this another game? What is he thinking? "I would love your company for dinner," she breathed. "After living with nothing but savages, and then your men . . . a real gentleman would be such a pleasure." She fluttered her lashes delicately.

"Good. I'll have my aide escort you to my quarters." He stood.

"Major?"

"Yes?"

"Will I be given an escort home tomorrow?" While she smiled easily, inside she was tensed in knots.

"In a few days," he said. "Certainly you don't mind sharing what you can of your experiences in Cochise's rancheria? It might prove to be of vast importance to the army in their campaign against him."

She lowered her lashes docilely. "No, of course not. Perhaps—you could send word to my family that I'll be on my way home soon?"

"As soon as I have a man available," he said, and ushered her out.

Major Bradley paced to the window, waiting. He watched as she appeared and crossed the yard, her baby in her arms, wearing the cowboy hat, the aide at her side, his face flushed. Incredible, he thought, that a woman dressed as she was could still be so desirable. And he knew he had been in this godforsaken land too long.

He turned as Sergeant Holden entered. "How can we make it known she's here?" he asked. Holden was a veteran of many Indian wars. Bradley didn't mind asking his advice; in fact, he relied on it quite often.

"Who do you want to know?"

"Jack Savage," he said, smiling. "The man went to a lot of trouble to kidnap her, and if Ladd is right, he killed Kincaid to do it, then kept her prisoner—against her will or not —for a long time. I do believe she ran away from him, because there's no other explanation for her being alone in the middle of the desert. I also believe he'll come after her. Especially if the child is his—and I think it is." He stared back out the window. "Although she is a commendable little liar."

"I see," Holden said, not smiling, but with professional interest. "I'll have sentries and pickets on double watch. Do you want him alive?"

"Absolutely," Bradley snapped. "He's our key to Cochise." *And to my future, preferably behind a desk in Washington.* "But we still have to let him know we have her."

"That's easy," Holden said. "Don't even worry about it. Cochise knows everything that goes on from Fort Yuma to El Paso. He's got scouts everywhere. They talk with their smoke signs. I'll bet the news that we got Savage's woman is already drifting back to him."

"But I want to be sure."

Holden frowned. "Well, we don't want to make it too obvious, like we're sending out an invitation. The best we can do is send a few boys into town to spread the word. But I know Cochise will hear of it through his own sources before ours."

"Do it anyway," Bradley said. "Thank you, Sergeant."

CHAPTER EIGHTY-SIX

He rode into the stronghold at twilight, with a searching gaze. Of course she didn't know he was returning tonight. It was not like the arrival of a war party, the news of which flew through the camp, although certainly the sentries at the stronghold's entrance would be relaying news of his return privately to Cochise. He urged the black into a lope. His heart was thudding in excitement. He couldn't wait to see her face when he told her it was over—that they were leaving and would be building a new life together in Texas. He was sure Candice would love Texas.

He dismounted at the *gohwah* to find Datiye coming up to him, smiling, taking his horse from him. As she led the black away, giving him a warm look, he got a glimpse of his son. Shoshi was awake, his eyes bright, at a new stage where he was starting to absorb all the stimuli around him. He seemed to smile at his father. Savage a felt a pang of regret to be leaving him behind.

"Candie," Jack called, stepping into their *gohwah*. He stepped back out, then walked over to Datiye. "How's my boy?" he said crooningly, lifting him out of the cradleboard. Shoshi squirmed, fists flying against his father's face. "He's bigger already," Jack said, startled.

"He will be big and brave, like his father," Datiye said, her eyes intent on his face. "You must be hungry."

"Starved. Where's Candice?"

"I do not know," Datiye said. "I have not seen her for days."

Savage straightened, a sudden sense of warning shooting through him. "What the hell does that mean?"

"Sometimes we go days without seeing each other," Datiye replied evenly. "You know that."

His jaw clenched. That was impossible, not unless Candice was furious over something and was going out of her way to avoid Datiye. "I'm going to go find her," he said. "I'll eat when we get back."

"I found this yesterday," Datiye said, her face impassive,

holding out a piece of buckskin, a square scrap. "It has white man's writing on it, I think."

He took it and saw that it did indeed have writing on it, scrawled in charcoal. He went to the fire and squatted down by the light. His heart stopped.

"Jack, I've taken Christina and left you. By the time you get this I will be en route East. Don't bother coming after me. It's over. You can't give Christina and me what we need . . . C."

He sat there staring at the crude, cruel note, feeling as if his heart had been ripped out of his body. She had left him—run away. Taken Christina. He couldn't believe it.

He stood. "When the hell did you find this?"

Datiye flinched. "Yesterday."

"When was the last time you saw her?"

Datiye thought. "Not today, maybe not yesterday. But definitely the night before."

He stared at her, suddenly alert to some nuance in her tone. "What are you hiding from me? Did you know she was leaving me?"

She hesitated. "No."

"You knew!" He was sure of it then, saw the lie in her eyes. He grabbed her, raising his hand, about to backhand her with all the pain and rage he was feeling. She didn't flinch. He caught himself just in time and dropped his hand, clenching his fist tightly. "Tell me everything, Datiye, now. If you don't—I will beat it out of you."

"She wanted to go," Datiye suddenly cried. "After she saved Shoshi, I could not refuse her help when she asked me for it—especially when she asked in the Apache way. How could I refuse?"

"Damn you," Jack snarled. He paced rigidly. "When? When did she leave?"

"Before dawn, the morning after you left," Datiye said.

"Four days," he gritted. "She's had four days headstart!" He wanted to kill her. "If anything's happened to her . . ."

"It is her right to divorce you," Datiye said defensively.

"Just like it's my right to divorce you!" Jack said harshly. He was too angry to care. She had betrayed him, and helped Candice to leave, possibly jeopardizing her and Christina's

life. He would never forgive her; even now he could barely
look at her.

"Please," she said softly. "I could not refuse her."

"You owed me more than you owed her," Jack said
coldly. "I am going to find her, Datiye, and when I do, Candice and I will be leaving—forever."

"No," she said.

"Be glad I leave our son with you. Because it's almost in
my heart to deny you even him."

Datiye blinked back tears. "She is not worth your love."

"Maybe not, and you're probably right—but she has it
anyway." He went and resaddled the black. He had to leave
that night. Had she really gone East? With what money? No!
By now she would be at the High C. He hoped. And if she
wasn't at the High C, she was in trouble—maybe dead.

Don't think of that!

He remembered with utter clarity how he had found her
almost a year ago, lying more dead than alive in the desert.
And then she hadn't had an infant with her. He tried to shut
out the horrible image. The fool! If he found her he'd beat
the hell out of her!

You can't give us what we need.

He inhaled sharply. God, she had left him. She had
made a choice and left him. How could she have done it?
Couldn't she have trusted him? Loved him enough to trust
him? *She didn't love him.*

It didn't matter. She was a fool to think he'd let her go,
no matter what her feelings were. Not now. He was too selfish to live without her, even if she hated him. He would get
her back. And this time he would win her heart if it took the
rest of his life.

"Are you coming back?" Datiye asked fearfully.

"I will come back, to say good-bye to Shoshi," Jack told
her grimly.

"My brother leaves again so soon?" Cochise asked, stepping out of the shadows.

He stared harshly. "It is done. Morris is dead. Now I
must go after my wife." He almost spat out the last word.

"I know," Cochise said seriously.

Jack stared. "You know she is gone?"

"I found out a short time ago that she is at Fort Buchanan."

"What?" He was stunned.

"A scout returned with the news he read in a sign. My scouts at the fort recognized Sun Daughter immediately. How could they not?"

"Yes, how could they not?" Jack gritted under his breath. Why was she at the fort? She couldn't . . . she wouldn't. . . . "What happened?"

"The soldiers found her riding west. They do not let her go."

"She is a prisoner?"

"I don't know," Cochise replied.

If they knew who she was, if they knew of her relationship to him . . . Jack's heart was thundering.

"She has betrayed you, her husband," Cochise said. "Will she betray me, and my people?"

"She knows nothing," Jack said tersely.

Would she betray them? She had already betrayed him. Pain seared him. He should have known. How could he have trusted her? How could he have been fooled into thinking she could adapt to her abduction, especially with Datiye here? Had the entire past seven months been a masquerade, leading up to this—her betrayal?

No!

But he was sick with uncertainty. He swung into the saddle.

"You should let her go," Cochise said. "No woman is worth betrayal."

"I can't," he said.

PART FIVE

Love and Resolution

CHAPTER EIGHTY-SEVEN

Candice knew he was lying.

She stared out of the window of the major's quarters. The day had dragged endlessly. It was sometime past noon, and there was nothing for her to do in the fort except to take care of Christina and read the major's books. He had joined her again for lunch, and as he had been the night before at supper, he was a perfect gentlemen, except when his eyes drifted downward to her bosom. Not once had he brought up Cochise, Jack, or the wars. In fact, they had talked of everything but those three topics, and Candice had the distinct impression he was luring her into a feeling of complacency before springing the jaws of a deadly trap. But why? Exactly what did he want? Did he really think she had information? Did he see through her façade? Did he know she loved Jack, not hated him?

She was sure he had lied when he told her there were no men available for a proper escort home. It was true that there did not seem to be very many men within the fort, but there were at least a dozen. Where were the others? Out on patrol? Maybe he meant that there were no trustworthy ones, or no officers available. She didn't think so. She had a bad feeling, a feeling of dread. He was toying with her the way a cat does with a mouse. She wished he would ask her what he wanted to know and get it over with.

Had Jack returned to the Apache camp yet and found her gone?

Unconsciously she clapped a hand over her bosom as if to ease the ache there. A knock sounded on her door, and Candice went to open it. Corporal Tarnower smiled at her. "Missus Kincaid. The major has requested your presence, if you're not too busy."

She almost laughed, but instead smiled sweetly. "Certainly." She picked up Christina, who had just been fed and put down. The baby whimpered in her sleep and then was still. Candice followed the corporal across the dry, dusty parade ground and to the adjutant's office. She was glad the waiting was over.

The major smiled warmly, too warmly. "Please, Candice, do sit down."

Candice sat, her daughter in her arms.

"Why don't you let Corporal Tarnower look after the baby for a few moments? She seems quite soundly asleep."

Reluctantly Candice agreed, handing Christina to a surprisingly eager Tarnower, who exited. She turned her full attention on Major Bradley.

"Tell me about your captivity, Candice," the major said, sitting casually on the edge of his desk.

"What would you like to know?"

"How did you spend your days?"

Making love with Jack, she thought wickedly, but refrained from saying so. "I helped with the preparing of food. We were always drying all sorts of roots and stems and berries for storage. I would say preparing, cooking, and storing food takes up eighty percent of an Apache woman's time."

He started asking her specific questions about the items she had prepared, and Candice was sure he was not interested in Apache culture. However, she answered as best she could.

"An abundant land for those who know what to look for," he said later, casually. "Gathering must have been tiring work."

"Yes . . . I mean, I suppose so, I wouldn't know, though," Candice said, wondering if he'd caught her mistake. She had almost agreed that gathering was hard work—which was an admission that she'd been out of the stronghold.

He studied her, then smiled.

"Tell me about Cochise."

"I saw him only from a distance, a few times."

Again he tried to trap her. This time Candice refused to be lulled into confidence, and successfully avoided a comment designed to lead her into an admission of having conversed with the Chiricahua chief. Bradley swiftly moved on, without a pause. He asked questions about the morale of the Apaches, and Candice was relieved to be able to answer honestly that it seemed fine.

"Will Jack Savage come after you again?"

She started, then a glimmer of comprehension dawned. He was using her as bait! Jack would come after her, she knew it, deep inside, and maybe she had expected that all along.

Maybe she had hoped her leaving would jolt him to his senses and he would choose her over the Apaches. Yes, she had known he would follow her, just as Bradley somehow knew, and that's why he was keeping her there—it was a trap! "I doubt it," she said unevenly, beginning to perspire.

"Sometimes you lie very well, and sometimes not so well, as now."

She sucked in her breath. "A rude remark."

"A dozen expressions crossed your face, including comprehension and fear. For whom are you afraid, Candice? I doubt it's for yourself or your child—or are you afraid of him? Savage?"

"Yes," she cried, jumping at that explanation.

"Or are you afraid *for* him?"

"I hate him," she cried. "I live for the day that bastard is hanged!"

He smiled. "Then you have no objection to remaining as my guest a few more days?"

She swallowed. "None." Could she sneak away at night? And how would Jack even know she was there?

This time Bradley did not change the topic. He wanted to know how many war parties she had seen ride out, how many were in the parties, how many braves were in the tribe. Candice lied constantly. She refused to give an accurate picture of the Chiricahua strength. She found herself underestimating their numbers when pressed beyond an initial "I don't know." She could barely believe what she was doing: lying to the United States Army. They were in a war. She was, with her lies, aiding the enemy. But she couldn't tell him the truth! And thank God she didn't know where the stronghold was.

Of course they came back to that topic. Almost an hour and a half must have passed. Candice was too tense to worry about Christina, although the child was always in the back of her mind. In a little while she would be hungry. How long was this going to go on?

"You rode into the stronghold in the light of day after Savage abducted you."

"Yes."

"Surely you can estimate how far south from the pass the entrance was."

"No. I can't."

"Did you go through Apache Pass to reach the entrance or down Sulphur Springs Valley?"

"I—I can't remember."

"Surely you remember where the guide left you just a few days ago. Where was that?"

"On the Butterfield Overland Trail," she lied. It had been in Sulphur Springs Valley.

"How long did it take to reach there from the time you left the camp?"

She tried to breathe more easily. "About forty minutes." A total fabrication. In any case, now he would think the entrance was much farther north than it was.

"Where on the Butterfield Trail?"

She swallowed. "Close to Apache Pass. East of the summit." She was thinking desperately. It was a middle-ground answer. They could or could not have gone through the pass after leaving the entrance to the stronghold.

"Surely you'd recollect the descent if you had gone through the pass?"

Trapped. Even at dark, there was no way a person would not be aware of the descent from the summit. "Yes, you're right. We did go through. We must have." At least, she thought, he would think the entrance to the stronghold was on the west side of the Chiricahua Mountains, when it was on the east side. But she had slipped. He was wearing her down.

"All lies," he stated flatly.

"What?" Her heart sank.

He smiled. "Yesterday you told me that after the guide had left you, you found yourself in Sulphur Springs Valley."

How could she have said something so stupid!

"Who are you protecting? Are you—"

There was a knock on the door.

Bradley paced forward with controlled anger. "I asked not to be disturbed," he said stiffly.

"Sir, we got him. Savage."

Candice gasped, standing. Bradley noted her reaction, and the way she moved to the left to see past Sergeant Holden's form in the hallway. But there was no one there.

"Good work," Bradley said. "Is he harmed?"

"He's got a bullet in his shoulder, but it's just a flesh wound. He gut-stabbed Myers, though, and nicked Lewis. Lewis is okay. Myers is dying. Savage is outside."

"Heavily guarded, I hope."

"Yes."

"Take him to the stockade. Have the surgeon fix him up. Under no condition shall he die. Do you understand? This prisoner is invaluable."

"Yes, sir." Holden gave a lazy salute and left.

Candice couldn't move. She was frozen, and Bradley was looking at her. Too late, she tried desperately to relax her face, but she couldn't.

"You love him," he said with interest. "But you obviously ran away. Why?"

She walked to the window, giving him her back. She saw him then, clad only in buckskin pants, his torso bare, wrists shackled behind his back. They were leading him away. He walked proudly erect, the sinewy muscles of his back rippling in the harsh summer sunlight, his sable hair shimmering with rich highlights. There was a soldier on each arm, and a few paces behind, Holden held a rifle pointed at his back.

"Because of Christina," Candice said unevenly. She could hear her heart beating, it was pounding so loudly. "I could not let her become a squaw, hating her own people."

She turned to him. "What will you do with him?"

"Interrogate him."

"And then?"

"He'll hang."

CHAPTER EIGHTY-EIGHT

Jack knew she was still there, he could feel it. His shoulder throbbed. Despite his wound, his wrists were still shackled behind his back, and because he could lie only on his back, it made the pain in his shoulder worse.

Why was she there?

Had she betrayed him again by betraying his people?

He heard a baby crying. Startled, he sat upright, knowing beyond a doubt that it was his daughter. An ache swept through him that had nothing to do with his wound, and he stood, shakily, almost falling, but managed to stagger to the wall where there was a narrow, barred window. He gazed out, across the parade ground, toward where the baby's crying had come from. She was quiet. Candice was probably nursing her.

By now they had to know who she was. Had she already been questioned, interrogated? Had she told them what they wanted to hear? She was his wife, but she was also his enemy. . . .He was sick with doubt, with fear.

He had been so furious and hurt that she'd left him, he had been careless, and he now knew he had fallen into a trap. Had she stayed to be a willing part of that trap? Had she known all along that he would come after her? Had she led him there, right into the hands of the army, in revenge? Did she want to see him hang? Hadn't she stopped loving him a long time ago?

He cursed.

"That won't help," Major Bradley said as the door to his cell was unlocked.

Jack moved weakly toward the cot, almost falling onto it.

"You should be conserving your strength," Bradley remarked, entering the cell with two soldiers, one big and brawny, the other carrying a revolver, which he had trained on him. "You'll need it."

Jack looked at him without expression.

"We can do this the easy way," Bradley said, "or the hard way." When there was no response, he said, "I want information. If you give it to me, you will be released. If not, you will die."

Jack smiled slightly.

"Where is the stronghold?"

There was no reply.

Bradley made a barely perceptible gesture. The brawny soldier moved forward implacably. Jack tensed. The man reached down, grabbed him, and then a fist came smashing into his face. There was a simultaneous explosion of pain and sparking lights, then a black fog tried to descend. Jack sought it, did not try to resist. But cold water dumped on his head brought him back to consciousness, sputtering and coughing.

He tasted blood. His own. With cold eyes, he met Bradley's impassive gaze.

"Shall we try again? Where is the stronghold?"

Jack smiled. The next blow cracked his jaw and brought another brief respite of black oblivion. He tried to hang on to it, but his mind surged out of the gray mists with a kind of determination, and with one overwhelming coherent thought. He was facing death.

For he would have to be beaten to death before he would tell them anything that might betray Cochise.

CHAPTER EIGHTY-NINE

Candice paced. She had been served dinner alone. She was afraid. Bradley had not bothered with her because he had Jack to attend to. Hours ago she had seen Bradley cross the yard and enter the small stone building that was the stockade. He had been with two other soldiers, and they had not yet come out. Was Jack dying?

She had to see him!

She stared out the window. The night was starless, moonless, heavily black. She could barely see the shadowy shapes of the buildings. She listened for the sound of footsteps. Was Bradley still with Jack? If so, he had been interrogating a wounded man for hours and hours. Candice knew Jack would not bend. Ever. They would kill him before he said anything. Dear God—this was all her fault! She had led him right into a trap, and now he would be hanged because of what she had done! It was up to her to get him out, but how?

She was so absorbed in her desperate thoughts that she almost missed Bradley and the soldiers striding across the parade ground. She cried out, then flew to the door and threw it open. "Major! Major, wait!"

He stopped, an almost formless shape in the thick darkness until she was upon him. "It's late. What a pleasant surprise."

"Is Jack all right?"

"As well as can be expected."

"I want to see him," she pleaded, aghast at how her own voice sounded.

"Impossible. Perhaps tomorrow—before you leave."

"Leave?"

"Surely you want to return home?"

Candice couldn't speak.

"Let me escort you inside, Candice," Bradley said politely, and she let him take her arm and lead her back to her quarters. She was barely aware of him, didn't even respond when he said good night. She leaned her back against the door, fists clenched. How could she save Jack?

And why had she been such a fool as to run away?

First she had to see him, talk to him. Jack was no fool. She was sure he had been furious when he'd found her gone, even more so when he'd read her note. And surely hurt as well. He had to know by now that this had been a trap. Did he think her a part of it—after she had run away, after that horrid note, how could he not?

He'll understand when I explain, she thought frantically.

She would seduce Bradley for Jack's release, if she thought for a minute that would work. But she didn't think so. On the other hand, once Bradley realized Jack would never speak, he might accept her charms for his release. And if that didn't work, she could always seduce the guard at the stockade and break Jack out!

Both plans frightened her.

One thing was certain, she could not, would not, leave tomorrow.

She couldn't sleep. Christina, sensing her mother's distress, was also restless, crying intermittently. Candice sought comfort in her child even as she comforted her. The night was endless, but she did finally fall asleep when the sky was turning from black to a husky gray.

When she awoke to Christina's insistent crying, the sun was already high. Candice quickly fed and changed her, then washed up at the basin, wanting to look her best for her interview with the major. She would begin her seduction now if she had to. She left Christina in the cradleboard on the bed, stepped outside, and started across the parade ground to the adjutant's office. She instantly froze in her tracks.

"Jack!"

He was staked out in the middle of the yard, Indian style, naked. She understood. It was torture. The temperature could reach 110 in the desert in the middle of the summer. She was running to him. His face was unrecognizable. Swollen, bloody. One eye was swollen shut. His nose was broken, his lips split. She cried out, dropping to her knees beside him. The bandage on his shoulder was bloodstained, seeping. His torso was marred with bruises.

"Oh, Jack, what have they done?" she cried.

He looked at her out of one eye. It was hard, and cold. "You left me," he said, his words slurred because his lips were split and swollen. "You traitorous bitch." He made a great effort to make sure she understood what he said.

"I won't let them hurt you anymore," she promised. "Jack, I didn't mean for this to happen! You have to believe me!"

"Did you . . . lead me here?" Anger blazed in his eyes —and desperation.

"No, I swear it, no! Jack, you have to believe me!"

"Get up, Missus Kincaid, you can't talk to him," a man said pityingly behind her.

"No!" she screamed, looking up at Corporal Tarnower. "Get me some water. And rags. Untie him, instantly!"

"Please, ma'am, please get up. You shouldn't have to see this." He dragged her to her feet.

She wrenched away. "You'll kill him! You can't be so cruel! You can't!"

"We have orders," Tarnower said, leading her away.

She looked back, crying. He wasn't looking at her. He was staring out of one eye straight ahead. "Jack," she moaned. "Jack, I'm sorry."

He didn't turn his head or even give a sign he heard her —or believed her.

Candice ran to the major's office, shrugging free of the young corporal. She burst in without knocking. He was startled, bent over paperwork, but not surprised. He raised two brows. "I take it you wish a word with me?"

"Do you intend to kill him?"

"I intend to hang him—after he tells us everything."

"He will die before he tells you anything," Candice screamed. "Don't you understand?"

"He will break," Bradley said confidently.

"No, he is Apache!"

"He is half white."

"But he was raised by the Apaches! Raised to tolerate pain, endure pain! You will hurt him, yes, maim him, but he will die before ever crying out, much less speaking! Please! Don't do this!"

"Perhaps there is another way to convince him," Bradley said thoughtfully. Gazing at her.

"What—what do you mean?"

"A man might be able to stand a lot of pain when it is

inflicted upon himself, but not upon those he loves. His wife —his child."

"You wouldn't." She wasn't afraid for herself. She would gladly suffer if it would relieve Jack. But Christina . . .

"You're right," Bradley said. "I'm human, and I would never harm you or your baby. But still . . . I do have you both in my possession."

She could see him thinking.

"There must be a way I could use you both to weaken him," Bradley muttered. "Without jeopardizing my career."

Her heart was pounding.

"Tarnower," he snapped, and the door flew open. "See Missus Kincaid to her room. Bring her lunch. Post a guard. I don't want her going near the prisoner."

"Yessir," the corporal said. And led her away.

CHAPTER NINETY

Candice couldn't eat. She was too sick. It was finally blessedly, dusk. Jack was still staked out, passed out. His calves, genitals, and hips were an angry red, his thighs a lesser shade of red, even his torso and arms and face, normally dark from the sun, were burned, but less badly. She had tried to get past the guard at her door with water in midafternoon. She had fought and screamed and cursed, kicking wildly, and it had taken another soldier to help restrain her, and then she had been locked in her quarters. She picked up her plate and threw it at the wall. It gave her no satisfaction.

She heard footsteps outside. She froze, having no idea what to expect. The door was unlocked, and she saw Major Bradley first, then Jack. Slumped, being dragged by two men, barely conscious. She couldn't believe it. They helped him into her room and dropped him across the bed. With a strangled cry she flew to him.

"Oh, Jack." She sobbed, touching his hair, clutching strands of it, wrapping them around her fingers.

His one eye opened, vague, unfocused. Then he saw her and confusion mounted. But he recognized her. "Candice." A ragged whisper.

She needed salve, grease, anything. She grabbed the pitcher of water and ripped her petticoat. Then she realized Bradley was standing there, watching with great interest. "Please," she said, "get me some grease. Please."

She turned to Jack, but was very much aware that Bradley had not moved. Why had he brought Jack there? She helped him to drink. She knew that throughout the day the soldiers had given him small sips of water, under orders, enough so he wouldn't die. He knew better than to drink too quickly. He was so stoic.

She wet the cloth and carefully, very carefully, began to clean his face. She wiped off the blood and was relieved to see that he didn't need stitches. She was as gentle as she could be. He watched her, without expression. But not warily.

His nose was crooked. Candice set aside the rag, giving him a falsely assuring smile. Then, in one motion, she snapped it back into place. He grunted, but when he looked at her she thought there was a faint glint of humor in his gaze. It was hard to tell.

"Don't worry," she whispered, stroking his thick, dust-coated hair. She wanted to know why they had been given this respite and had the awful, instinctive feeling that Bradley was about to close the steel jaws of another trap. She wondered if this was all for nothing, to keep him well enough to be able to talk, so that he could be hanged properly later. The feeling of sick fear increased.

"I will try not to hurt you," she said, moving aside the edge of the bandage and wishing she had lard to soothe his burned body.

He said nothing.

So far there was no sign of infection, the one blessed part of this whole ordeal. Jack was looking at her, and she realized finally that she saw trust and relief in his eyes. It overwhelmed her with the desire to weep.

He knew. He knew she would never betray him.

She touched his hair. She wanted to tell him she loved him, that she always had and always would, but Bradley was behind her, so interested in everything she was doing.

"Come here, Candice," he said. "I didn't bring him here for your ministrations."

She started, standing slowly. She looked into his eyes for a clue. Coldly gleaming. She looked at Jack, lying prostrate, but attentive on the bed. "What now? Can't you please bring me some lard?"

Bradley gave her a small smile, went to Jack, and in the blink of an eye cuffed one red wrist to the bedpost. He straightened. "Never underestimate your enemy," he said conversationally. "Take off your clothes, Candice."

"What?"

"Perhaps your husband enjoys voyeurism? Perhaps not. We shall see. In any case, undress."

She stared, unsure. Jack was rigid, expressionless, unmoving. "If I sleep with you, will you release Jack?"

"Your charms are not that great. I expect him to speak up before I actually have to rape you. Of course, we can avoid much unpleasantness if he speaks up now. Where is the stronghold?"

Jack stared impassively.

"Undress," the major said, removing his own jacket casually. "And after I'm through I'll let my soldiers at you—every woman-starved one."

Candice sucked in her breath. "Jack will never tell you what you want. Even if you do rape me."

"I think you're wrong," the major said. "I think even a man reared by the Apaches would eventually break down. Especially as my men will more likely than not tear you apart —literally."

Candice looked at Jack. "It's all right," she told him, unbuttoning her blouse. "It doesn't mean anything. It doesn't matter. Don't say anything." Their gazes met. She saw that his mouth was clamped hard together. She tried to reassure him silently. She pulled off her shirt, letting it drop to the floor. She let her skirt drop to her ankles. Her petticoat followed. She was wearing nothing underneath—she had no pantalets. She shrugged out of her chemise.

"Incredibly beautiful," Bradley said, a touch of huskiness creeping into his tone. He smiled, stepped closer, and reached out to cup her breasts. "Incredibly beautiful."

Candice looked briefly at Jack, and saw that he was trying to control his breathing and his anger. She tried to ignore the major's caressing hand. "I won't give you the satisfaction of raping me. I won't fight you."

"Has he tasted your mother's milk?" Bradley murmured, and he bent his head, taking her nipple in his mouth.

Jack lunged upward against the cuff. If he hadn't been so weak and hurt, he would have gotten to his feet and dragged the bed with him. Candice looked wildly around the room for a weapon. Her eyes lit on Bradley's gun, but it was in a buttoned-down holster. He doesn't really know me, she thought with sudden hope. She was his enemy too.

She looked frantically at Jack. He was gesturing at the tray where her dinner plate had been, on the table by the bed. What did he think? There was no knife there, they hadn't given her one. Then she saw the lead paperweight, in the shape of a bear.

"Good God." Bradley gasped, coming up for air. "Your milk is so sweet." He was shaking.

Candice pulled him a step toward the bed, sinking onto

the floor, the table with the paperweight not far from her head. She smiled, lips parted, as if she were highly aroused, and beckoned for him, legs and arms spread.

He came, unbuttoning his pants and freeing his member. He knelt, moving on top of her. Candice felt a stab, both of fear and a tentative thrust that could not penetrate past her dry skin. Jack! Could he reach the damn paperweight? Normally that would be easy. But he was so weak. And Bradley was battering her, trying to enter, with all the clumsiness of a schoolboy.

And then she saw Jack's hand, heard his grunt of pain, and she averted her own head as the paperweight came crashing onto Bradley's skull, not a perfect shot by any means, skimming the side and his temple. He stared wildly at her for an instant, his movements stopping, stunned and not comprehending.

Like a snake, Candice had her hand on his holster, was unsnapping it and releasing the gun. She sent it crashing against the same temple, and he slumped on top of her with a breath of exhaled air.

She lay very still, her heart pounding. Then she shoved him up and rose, to collapse on the bed at Jack's side. He was panting, eyes closed. "We have to get you out of here," she said.

He opened his eye. "Get the key," he said hoarsely.

She scrambled to obey. She found it in one of Bradley's pockets, then unlocked the handcuffs. Jack sat, staring at her. On the floor, the major stirred.

Jack stood, picking up the gun, moving to the window. There were two soldiers at the front door. He went to the other window. It was just around the corner from the major's quarters, but it was the only way out. He paused, then, to regard her steadily. Grimly.

"You're leaving me!" She gasped. "You're leaving me and Christina?"

"You'll be all right," he said. "I hit the major, not you." It was a warning.

"Jack! But—" She stopped, unable to believe it as he cuffed her wrist to the bedpost. Then he climbed through the window, naked, gun in hand, and dropped silently and stiffly to the other side. She clapped her free hand over her mouth. *He was leaving without her.* The major groaned.

Jack paused for the barest of seconds, and his gaze locked with hers. His was filled with resolution. Candice watched helplessly, feeling as if her heart were breaking, again. "Please don't." She gasped.

And then he was gone. She sat shaking, naked, her right wrist handcuffed to the bedpost. He was free, but she felt only an agonizing pain in her heart.

He had left without her.

CHAPTER NINETY-ONE

He wasn't coming.

Candice stared out of her bedroom window, not even seeing the dusty yard, the corrals, the barns, the walls surrounding the High C. Instead, she saw Jack, squatting by the fire in front of the *gohwah*, Datiye and Shoshi by his side. Tears came into her eyes. But this was what she had wanted, wasn't it?

No! All along, maybe not even consciously, she had wanted him to follow her, declare his undying love for her, and join her in making a new life, even if it meant leaving the Territory. But that wasn't going to happen. She didn't understand why he had come after her at Fort Buchanan almost a month ago if he wasn't coming after her now.

The major had still been groggy when the two soldiers had burst in, after she had been inspired to call out for help. They'd gaped at her sitting naked, cuffed to the bed, their major on the floor, pants unbuttoned, the prisoner gone. Because the situation was so embarrassing, Corporal Tarnower had immediately been sent for and had taken charge. Both guards were threatened with court-martial if a word of what they'd seen got around. And, of course, because no one could think otherwise when she had been found naked and cuffed to the bed, Tarnower believed that Jack had knocked Bradley out with the paperweight, stolen his gun, forced Candice to free him, then cuffed her to the bed in malicious spite. Even Bradley believed it. The major, who had a serious concussion, had sent her home with his apologies two days later with a small military escort.

Candice knew she had been a sight in her worn, ragged clothes with her peeling nose. And the cradleboard with Christina on her back. There had been a long moment of absolute silence while her father, Luke, Mark, and John-John had stared in shocked speculation. Candice had lifted her chin high. She had calmly removed the cradleboard and picked up Christina, smiling at her baby—then she'd looked at Luke. "Don't you want to say hello to your niece?"

He'd come out of his trance with a quick stride and a

sudden smile to knuckle Christina's cheek. Then he looked at
Candice. "Hello, Sis. You look awful."

"Thank you, Luke, I love you too."

He kissed her cheek, smiling.

Her father reacted next, wanting to know where Kincaid
was and if she was all right. She met his eye, then everyone
else's, as calmly as she could. "Kincaid is dead, honest-to-
goodness dead."

"Where the hell have you been?" Mark exclaimed, while
her father and John-John came over to hug her and inspect
the baby.

"Jack Savage killed Kincaid," Candice stated. "For what
he did to me. And this is our daughter."

No one moved.

"Kincaid's daughter?" Luke asked levelly.

"No, Jack's daughter. He's my husband."

A shocked, incredulous silence ensued. Mark went
white, then red. Her father stared. Luke began rolling a ciga-
rette casually. John-John broke the silence. "I don't believe
it!"

"Jack is my husband and I love him, and if you love me,
you'll try to understand."

"I'll never understand," Mark rasped. "You'd lie with
that breed willingly?" He turned and stalked to the door.

"Mark," Candice cried, "please try to understand. Jack
didn't kill Linda!"

He slammed the door behind him.

Candice looked up, starting to tremble. Christina started
to whimper and move restlessly. Candice held her tighter.
She looked at her father. She could see the shock in his eyes.
He still hadn't moved. "I'm very tired," Candice said. "Pop?
Do you want me to leave?"

John sat down heavily. "Candice, my God, do you know
what you've done?"

"I love him," she said simply. "He's brave and strong and
he's got integrity of steel. Even if I never see him again, I'll
always love him. There'll never be anyone else for me."

John rubbed his face with his hands.

Luke came to her, taking her arm, a smile crinkling the
corners of his eyes as his gaze went to his niece. "Why don't

you lie down upstairs," he said softly. "I think everyone needs some time to adjust."

"Will Mark ever adjust?" she heard herself ask bitterly.

He still hadn't. Mark would give her long, condemning looks, but he wouldn't talk to her. He never looked at Christina; he ignored his niece as if she didn't exist. Her father seemed ten years older from the impact of the truth. Funny enough, John-John had eased back into their old relationship in the past few weeks, being too young to seriously hold a grudge. Once Candice even caught him lying on the floor and playing with Christina.

God bless Luke. If it wasn't for him she might have gone insane from the condemnation of her father and Mark, the cowboys and their neighbors. She'd finally confided the entire story to him and ended up weeping in his arms while he held her close and stroked her hair. The only thing she didn't tell him was that the preacher who had married them had not been real.

And every day she listened for the sentry's shout, "Rider approaching," waiting for Jack.

Troops had been sent out the night of his escape to find him. For the two days she had remained at the fort, she had been breathless with fear for his safety. But she had hoped, and even thought, that he had holed up somewhere in a cave full of cached supplies until he was stronger. Even then, once he set out for the stronghold, he would probably travel only by night, to protect himself both from further burning and from the patrols. But what if an infection had set in? What if he'd had an accident in his condition—or died?

She could not give up hoping that he would come for her.

She had told him not to come, had told him he couldn't give her and their child what they needed. Had he come to believe that ridiculous note with the passage of time? Or did he now understand, finally, how important it was to her to raise Christina as a white woman? As a lady? And had he chosen, irrevocably, the Apache over her and their child?

She tried to tell herself that it was for the best, but the words rang hopelessly hollow and false in her mind.

CHAPTER NINETY-TWO

"So, the time has come," Cochise remarked, his gaze unwavering.

"Yes, it has," Jack returned. He felt that he should say something, explain why he was leaving, why he would never come back. He groped for words Cochise would understand. "It's been too difficult for my heart," he finally said, feeling that the words were totally inept.

"I understand," Cochise said. It was that simple.

Jack turned, then, and walked away, feeling sad. It wasn't the kind of sadness that the thought of never seeing Candice again induced—that was gut-wrenching. Soon, he thought—his heart leaping at the thought of seeing her again.

But the sight of Datiye and Shoshi made him very, very grim. This sadness was more like a pain. He loved his son. He knew Shoshi belonged with his mother, but he did not want to leave him behind. There was no other way.

Datiye looked at him with great control. Her eyes were red. Last night she had obviously been crying. It was yesterday that he'd told her he was leaving, for good. But now her chin was thrust forward, her mouth set in a tight line. She forced a smile. "Wherever you ride, I know my prayers will follow. The *gans* love you, will still protect you."

"Thank you," he said. "Datiye, remarry. It is for the best."

She didn't respond.

"May I hold him?" His voice was suspiciously shaky.

Shoshi was in Datiye's arms. He was smiling, eyes silvery and bright, and one hand reached for his father, whom he recognized. He babbled something happy and indistinguishable.

"You must take him," she said, handing him over.

Jack thought she meant hold him, of course, and hugged his son tightly, feeling like crying. That was ridiculous. Shoshi would grow up to be a brave Apache. It was a part of his heritage. Then he looked at Datiye, who was placing saddlebags on the black. He had stolen his horse back the night after he'd escaped. "What are you doing?"

"These are his things," she said, and her voice caught.

He understood, shocked. "You—want me to take him with me? No, Datiye, I could not do that to you."

"You must."

"But a child belongs with his mother."

Tears welled up in her eyes. "No, Niño Salvaje, for I saw the dream."

He was very still. "What dream?"

"A terrible dream," she said, choking. A tear trickled down her face.

"Tell me," he demanded hoarsely.

"You know I shouldn't," she whispered.

"Tell me, Datiye."

She took a breath. "A day when our son was a grown man. A day of caged earth. Not even this earth. A land far away, to the east, on an endless body of water."

"Don't talk in riddles," he said harshly.

"That is what I saw! Many Apaches, including our son, caged like animals in a strange, faraway land! If you leave him, he will not be free—you must take him."

He felt both sick and elated. Everyone knew dreams were omens. He could not leave his child there to be caged up on a reservation in some faraway land.

"You must take him," she said, crying. She made a great effort to stop. "I will remarry soon. Tahzay has shown interest in me. He will ask for me once you are gone, I know it."

Tahzay was Cochise's first son, a man grown already, a brave, strong warrior. One day he would be chief if he lived—if the Apache stayed free.

But how could they? Hadn't he and Cochise known all along this war would be their last? They were so few, the whites so many. . . .

"I will take him, Datiye, and I will never forget you for giving me back my son."

She smiled through shimmering tears. "Go, now," she said. She turned and walked away, toward the woods, holding her back straight and rigid, then started running and kept running until she was gone.

He set Shoshi down and looked in the saddlebags. A teat

and milk. Enough to last him until he got to the High C. He wondered if Candice would accept Shoshi. She would have to. If not, he'd find a wet nurse and take her with them.

He saw that Datiye had enlarged the straps of the cradleboard to accommodate his shoulders. He slipped Shoshi in, then set the board on his back. He mounted, still overwhelmed by what she had done. Then he urged the black forward, every nerve in his body quivering, a riot of emotions.

CHAPTER NINETY-THREE

She heard the commotion downstairs.

And instantly recognized *his* voice. *Jack.*

She flew down the stairs, skirts in one hand, her feet barely touching the ground. She pulled up short at the sight of him, and for a moment just drank in his magnificent, bronzed presence.

He stiffened, turned his head away from her father and Luke, and their gazes met.

It was then that Candice became aware of Mark, crimson-faced, standing behind her father and Luke, one hand on his gun and looking lethally dangerous. "Let's hang him up right now!" he shouted.

Jack faced the three men, his profile to her, and didn't move a muscle. "I've come for my wife and daughter," he said quietly.

"We know damn well who you've come for," Mark shouted. "You've ruined my sister, and now I'm going to kill you!"

"Cool down," Luke snapped warningly, as Candice flew to her husband to stand pressed to his side.

"Mark, stop it," she said desperately. "Please stop this insane hating. I'm leaving with Jack, and I don't want to lose you as my brother."

"You should have killed yourself before submitting to him," Mark spat. "Much less liking it and bearing his breed brat. To me, you are dead!"

Candice cried out.

Mark whirled and strode away, ignoring their father, who called after him. A heavy silence fell. Tears at her brother's ultimate rejection filled Candice's eyes. She became aware of Jack holding her hand. Then he brushed a tear from her cheek with a callused thumb. She looked into his eyes and felt her heart take wing and soar.

Luke broke the moment, stepping forward, hand extended. "Welcome to the High C," he said. He wasn't smiling, but his gaze was level and sincere.

Stunned, Jack stared at the offered hand, and then with a

delayed reaction, he took it—awkwardly. Candice looked at the two clasped hands and felt as if her heart would expand right out of her rib cage. She gazed at Luke with tearing eyes and he smiled slightly at her, understanding her silent thanks.

Her father shoved his hands into his pockets and the gesture stood out as if a bell had sounded. She saw the indecision on his face and wanted to weep. She thought that he was trying, but knew he would never forgive her husband for ruining, in his eyes, his little girl. There was a long silence, but her father didn't speak.

Jack turned to her. "Let's get Christina and go," he said softly.

She heard, from outside, a familiar infant's howling. Her eyes widened in surprise and delight. "Jack? Did you bring Shoshi?"

A faint smile crossed his face and lingered in his eyes as they swept over her features. "Yes."

And then she felt the uncertainty, and with it sick fear. "Datiye?"

"No."

Candice turned to her father and saw his steady, pain-filled gaze. "Oh, Pop," she said, and hugged him hard before flying up the stairs to get Christina and a few things. She didn't even wonder where they were going. It didn't matter. All that mattered was the man downstairs, the man she loved more than life itself.

When she came downstairs with a small bag and Christina in her arms Jack leapt forward, and she let him take the baby from her arms. He smiled at his daughter, love lighting up his features. Candice's heart expanded to impossible dimensions.

"Candice," her father said hoarsely.

She froze and met his gaze.

He came hesitantly to her, then embraced her in a bear hug. When he pulled back he smoothed tendrils of hair away from her face. "It's not safe for you to stay here," he said, the silent words *with him* as clear as if he'd spoken them.

In that instant Candice forgave her father for being who and what he was. He was trying, and maybe one day he would accept Jack as her husband. "I know."

"Write to me, to us," he said.

"I will," she said, as John-John burst in the door at a run.

"You're leaving," he cried, and swept her into his arms. She clung to him and started to cry. She hugged Luke again, and Maria, who had appeared, weeping. When they finally rode through the ranch gates, Candice on her palomino filly with Christina, Jack on the black with Shoshi, she was in a teary daze. It wasn't until he pulled her to the ground and into his arms that she realized the ranch was out of sight and that they had stopped. His gray eyes were searing her face poignantly.

Joy brought forth more tears. "You're all healed," she said foolishly.

"My nose is still a little crooked," he said, gazing at her steadily, his eyes silver, intent, too bright.

"You were too handsome before," she said breathlessly as a liquid warmth stole over her.

"Did he hurt you?"

She knew he was referring to Bradley. She shook her head. "No."

"Did you . . . did you have to sleep with him? After I left?"

She bit her lip. "He had a concussion. I told everyone you'd forced me to unlock you after you hit him. Because you locked me up, no one doubted it, not for a minute."

"I'm sorry I had to leave you." His eyes searched her face.

"It was better that way."

A small smile touched his mouth. "They were probably too excited to listen to what you said."

"I was so afraid."

"I had to leave you."

"I was afraid for you, not me . . . Jack."

"It's okay," he said, pulling her closer against his long, hard frame. "It's over, Candice, *shijii,* it's over."

She leaned against him and almost wept. "I thought you weren't coming back," she cried.

"You fool," he said tenderly. "Did you really think you could run away from me?"

She looked up. Her eyes were wet, and she saw, startled,

that his were moist too. "I didn't mean anything in that letter, Jack, I never stopped loving you, not ever."

"I realized that at Fort Buchanan."

"But you doubted it before?"

"You left me."

"I had to. Christina deserves better than what you wanted to give her." She felt tears trickling out of her eyes and down her face.

He wiped them away with the pad of a callused finger. "Did you ask me what I planned to give her? Why didn't you ask me?"

"I don't understand."

"We're starting over, Candice, you, me, Christina, and Shoshi. We'll go to California. What do—will you come with me?" His voice was husky. Pleading.

"You're leaving Cochise?"

"If you had just waited, I would have told you after I came back from scouting. I never went scouting. I went to Fort Breckenridge." He held her gaze. "To end it. I killed the lieutenant who ordered the hangings. I avenged Shozkay." He stared at her, waiting, heart pounding, for horror, disgust, withdrawal. It never came.

"Is it really finished?" she cried, clinging to him.

"Yes, I swear, it's finished. It took me a while to realize, Candice, what's really important, but you and our children are the most important things in my life. Will you come? Let me take you away, make you happy?" He heard the anxious, pleading note in his voice, but didn't care. He cupped her face and held it. "I will make you happy, that I promise."

"If I said no," she said with a smile, through her tears, "would you listen?"

"No."

"I would come," she said, "even if you wanted to go back to Cochise. I can't live without you, Jack."

He crushed her to him. "I love you, *shijii*. And this time we'll make sure the preacher is real, I promise."

"I love you, *bilnadeshi shijii*," she murmured. "Husband of my heart."

He began kissing her. "I love you," he whispered. His mouth moved over her hair, her ears, her face. "I love you, Candice, desperately." His lips played softly on hers, his hands stroked down her back. "How could you have ever thought I'd let you go, *shijii*? Never." He caught her mouth with his. "If I had to follow you across the seven seas to China, I would. There is no desert wide enough, no mountain high enough, no forest thick enough, to keep me away from you.

There's nowhere you could go that could be far enough away to stop me from finding you—don't you know that by now, *shijii*?"

Her response was to hold his face, twining his hair in her fingers as he kissed her again and again.

AUTHOR'S NOTE

. . . every Apache man, wherever found, should be killed on sight and the women and children sold into slavery.

—COLONEL BAYLOR, Confederate Governor of the Arizona Territory of President Jefferson Davis

The men [Apaches and Navajos] are to be slain where found. The women and children are to be taken prisoner, but, of course, they are not to be killed.

—Standing orders of General Carleton to all men under his command during the "Slaughtering Sixties"

When I was young, I walked all over this country and saw no people other than Apaches. After many summers I walked again and found another race of people who had come to take it. How is it?

Why is it the Apaches want to die—that they carry their lives in their fingernails? They roam over the hills and plains and want the heavens to fall on them. The Apaches were once a great nation; they are now but a few . . . many have died in battle . . . Tell me, if the Virgin Mary has walked throughout all the land, why has she never entered the lodge of the Apache?

—*COCHISE*, September 1871, shortly before his final surrender to President Grant's personal representative

Cochise surrendered in October 1871. He died three years later.

The events of February 1861 as I have recounted them are accurate within the bounds of historical controversy. The army denied, up until the turn of the century—when the issue became irrelevant—that Lieutenant Bascom flew a white flag and betrayed Cochise purposefully. Those fate-filled days of February, referred to by some historians as Bascom's Folly and considered by those same historians to have directly triggered Cochise's war with the white man, did begin with the kidnapping of the son of a Sonoita rancher's common-law wife. Possibly the boy was fathered by a Coyotero, possibly by a man from a previous marraige. The rancher accused Cochise of the kidnapping, and later it was found that the Coyoteros did indeed kidnap the boy, who later gained fame as the Apache scout Mickey Free.

The cast of characters who are real personages are as follows: Pete Kitchen, William S. Oury, William Buckley, Wallace, Culver, and Welsh, Lieutenant Bascom, Geronimo, Nahilzay, Cochise's family, and Cochise.

The fate of the rancher whom I called Warden was pure fiction, as was the fate of Lieutenant Morris, who was based on the actual Lieutenant Moore. Moore brought reinforcements from Fort Breckenridge and finally ordered the hangings of the six Apaches. All the events of those days in February are as accurate as possible, based on the problem of deciding between conflicting versions of historians. It is possible Bascom did not fly a white flag. However, Cochise was at peace with the whites using Apache Pass—in fact, the Chiricahua supplied the Butterfield Station with wood. Some historians have written that Cochise was at peace only with the Butterfield Overland Mail and warred on other whites. I found more evidence to show him as I have.

A few minor points might be inaccurate. Some accounts states that Cochise and five braves greeted Bascom, not Cochise and his relatives, wife, and son. One account held that Cochise had six prisoners, not three, and the reason six Apaches were hanged was in direct retaliation for finding the six (not three) mutilated corpses.

For ten years Cochise and his warriors brought devastation upon the settlers and troops of the New Mexico Territory. Other tribes, led by other chiefs, fought for their freedom as well. But it was a losing battle. The Apaches were being exterminated slowly but surely, and in the process of hit-and-run warfare, they were also starving. After Cochise crushingly defeated the army's best column of Indian fighters, led by Lieutenant Howard Cushing, who was also killed in the attack, the army decided upon a policy of conciliation. President Grant's personal representative was sent to negotiate a peace with Cochise, who met with him and accepted the terms. The Chiricahua were promised that they could stay in their own land, but several months after the peace they were removed to Tularosa, New Mexico. They later fled back into their own mountains.

While General George Crook began his vicious, unrelenting, and eventually successful campaign against the Tonto Apaches, General O. O. Howard and the famous frontiersman and ex-scout, Captain Tom Jeffords (who was also Cochise's blood brother) negotiated another surrender from him. This time the Chiricahua got most of the land that was theirs as their reservation, and Jeffords was their agent.

But all the government's promises did not materialize. The schools, hospitals, trading posts, supplies, and food never appeared. What food did come was the wrong kind, such as wheat, with which the Apaches were unfamiliar and did not know how to cook. Game was scarce, the Apaches were starving. Young braves resorted more and more to whiskey, and under its influence even continued to raid south. When two American whiskey peddlers were killed on the reservation, Congress took action, Jeffords was removed as the Indian agent, and the government prepared to remove the Chiricahuas to the swampland of the San Carlos reservation.

Cochise was dead. His son, Tahzay, and several other headmen were in favor of submission. Geronimo, Juh, and Nolgee fled with their followers south to the Sierra Madres. About 325 remaining Chiricahuas were moved to San Carlos.

Geronimo and other renegades fought viciously and brutally for another ten years. In April 1886, the last renegades, including Geronimo, were captured and surrendered at Fort Bowie in Apache Pass. They were shipped to Fort Marion, Florida.

There they were forgotten for years. Eventually they were moved to Alabama, then Oklahoma, and finally some 250 survivors were allowed to return to the Mescalero reservation in New Mexico. They were all that remained of what was originally a population of close to fifteen hundred. The government's policy of extermination had almost been fulfilled.

I would like to add a final note. After I had written the first draft of this novel and was doing further research on the Apaches, I stumbled across an article at the Arizona Historical Society, written by Professor R. A. Mulligan of the University of Arizona. He states that just prior to the events of February 1861, there were three Chiricahua chiefs: Cochise, Esconolea, and a man named Jack. . . .

Outstanding historical romances by bestselling author

HEATHER GRAHAM

The American Woman Series

☐ **SWEET SAVAGE EDEN**   20235-3 $3.95

☐ **PIRATE'S PLEASURE**   20236-1 $3.95

☐ **LOVE NOT A REBEL**   20237-X $3.95

Other Titles You Will Enjoy

☐ **DEVIL'S MISTRESS**   11740-2 $3.95

☐ **EVERY TIME I LOVE YOU**   20087-3 $3.95

☐ **GOLDEN SURRENDER**   12973-7 $3.95

Reckless abandon. Intrigue. And spirited love. A magnificent array of tempestuous, passionate historical romances to capture your heart.

☐ **THE RAVEN AND THE ROSE**
   by Virginia Henley   17161-X $3.95

☐ **TO LOVE AN EAGLE**
   by Joanne Redd   18982-9 $3.95

☐ **DESIRE'S MASQUERADE**
   by Kathryn Kramer   11876-X $3.95

☐ **SWEET TALKIN' STRANGER**
   by Lori Copeland   20325-2 $3.95

☐ **IF MY LOVE COULD HOLD YOU**
   by Elaine Coffman   20262-0 $3.95

At your local bookstore or use this handy page for ordering:

DELL READERS SERVICE, DEPT. DHR
P.O. Box 5057, Des Plaines, IL . 60017-5057

Please send me the above title(s). I am enclosing $_____.
(Please add $2.00 per order to cover shipping and handling.) Send
check or money order—no cash or C.O.D.s please.

Ms./Mrs./Mr._____

Address _____

City/State _____ Zip _____

DHR-12/89

Prices and availability subject to change without notice. Please allow four to six
weeks for delivery.